THE SUN VALLEY SERIES

unexpected

EJ Blaise

For Hannah
I cannot imagine my life without you in it or this book without your influence.
Thank you

CONTENT NOTE

This story contains explicit sexual content, profanity, loss of a loved one, and mild violence.

A substantial portion of the female main character's journey revolves around the after effects of leaving an emotionally and physically abusive relationship. If this is a sensitive topic for you, please take that into consideration. If it isn't, please exercise compassion.

PLAYLIST

She Will Be Loved - Maroon 5
I'm A Mess - Ed Sheeran
Cupid's Chokehold / Breakfast in America - Gym Class Heroes
Habit - Still Woozy
Karma - Taylor Swift
Skin - Dijon
Take It Easy - Surfaces
Low - Surfaces
Tiny Dancer - Elton John
Shake It Out - Florence + The Machine
Bitter - Fletcher, Kito
Streets - Doja Cat
Sparks Fly - Taylor Swift
Kiss Me - Ed Sheeran
Nonsense - Sabrina Carpenter
Honeymoon Avenue - Ariana Grande
Cherry Wine - Hozier
man - quinnie
Anti-Hero - Taylor Swift
Matilda - Harry Styles
Unfold - Alina Baraz, Galimatias

And in the middle of my chaos,
There was you.

1

AMELIA

GOD, I am so *fucked*.

An unseasonably cold wind whips at the stray pieces of paper peeking out from my chemistry textbook, mocking me mercilessly as it sends the pages fluttering to the ground. With a frustrated groan, I drop to my knees and grab at them frantically, barely resisting the urge to stick out my tongue at the invisible, elemental prankster trying to make me more fucked than I already am.

The one time I needed it not to, class ran later than usual. Some fool decided today was the day for him to attempt to juggle test tubes. Test tubes that happened to contain some not-so-fun chemicals.

Needless to say, it did not end well.

A pile of broken glass, some mild chemical burns, and a rather impressive ass-chewing from my chemistry professor later, we were finally released—a mere twenty minutes late. Which is how I've ended up sprinting across campus, cursing at the wind, and praying my boss won't fire me. Punctuality is one of his 'lines,' as he likes to call them. Cross one and you're done, and I've crossed more than a couple lately.

Stuffing the hopefully not important runaway loose sheets into my coat pocket, I haul ass across the courtyard, ignoring my legs as they scream in protest and hoping my grossly heavy backpack doesn't do permanent damage.

Taking a shift that gives me barely thirty minutes of breathing room after my last class is my own fault but I couldn't resist. The lucrative Friday night shift is too good to pass up, with students practically teleporting from class to the bar, ready to blow their meager budgets on copious amounts of alcohol to drown out an undoubtedly shitty week. It's what I would be doing, if not for work.

By some grace of God, I slip in the back door of The Green Dragon with a whole three minutes to spare, only slightly breathless but so red in the face, I practically blend in with my hair. Flopping down on the lumpy couch decorating the minuscule staff room, I waste a precious minute regaining my breath, eyes shut and pants heavy as my head hits the wall.

"You're late."

I groan as I crack open an eye and lift my head, pouting at the pretty blonde suddenly looming in the doorway. "My class ran late."

Luna Evans pouts right back as she crosses the room to flop down beside me, blowing out a heavy breath of her own. "I've had to deal with the masses on my own."

Patting her thigh in apology, I assure her, "I'll be out in two minutes."

Pale blue eyes flick downwards to survey my outfit, a brow crooking. "You're not dressed."

"In two minutes, I will be."

With a roll of her eyes, Luna reluctantly clambers to her feet, making sure to tap the watch adorning her wrist pointedly before leaving the room, leaving me chuckling in her wake. Anyone who knows my best friend knows damn well 'dealing with the masses' is something she could do in her sleep. Especially if the masses are men, considering her uncanny ability to bend them to her will. It's the being alone thing she's not so great at. Or, more specifically, the being without a gossip buddy for any length of time longer than twenty minutes.

I'll admit it; it takes me marginally longer than two minutes to shuck off my outfit and slip into my uniform, but barely. Like a fraction of a second. Not long enough for my needy friend to come looking for me again, so I call that a win.

As I try to tame my curls—the wind combined with the rush has left the neat braid I fashioned this morning in a state of disarray—I sigh deeply at my reflection in the shitty mirror hanging on the staff room wall. *Little lion,* I can practically hear my dad quipping at the sight of the red mane framing my face wildly.

"Mils, come on. Your section is overflowing." A head peeks around the door, and I sigh again at Luna's sleek ponytail, the polar opposite of my disastrous one, not a hair out of place. Even in our work uniform—jeans and a tank top adorned with Greenies' logo—the girl looks like a runway model. Honestly, she could wear a trash bag and still look photo-shoot ready.

If I didn't love her so much, I would hate her.

Catching the apron and notepad she tosses my way, I follow Luna out the door, internally cringing at the wave of noise and heat that immediately hits me. As I suspected and as Luna complained, the bar is packed. Not that it takes much for it to get full, with it being roughly the size of a matchbox, but we're truly at full capacity tonight. I have to shove my way past a horde of already drunk students to get to the back, where the bar suddenly becomes a restaurant. Of sorts. A diner, really, but God forbid anyone calls it what it is. "Diners are tacky," Tim, my boss, says a million times a day. Looking around the small space, I swallow a laugh.

Yeah. Because nothing says 'classy' like underage college students doing sneaky shots under the table.

"Is Tim here?" I ask Luna as she leads me through the throng

"He left already." She casts me a pointed look over her shoulder. "I told him you had a doctor's appointment."

Earlier statement amended; I am no longer fucked. "You're an angel."

Perfectly manicured fingers pinch my bare arm. "Do some work, suck up."

"Yes, ma'am." I blow my friend a dramatic kiss before parting ways, heading towards my section of the definitely-not-a-diner.

Luna wasn't lying; my section is overflowing. It's only four tables and a small outdoor area but, jeez, do they manage to squeeze them-selves in. One of the booths has eight people crammed into it; granted, two of them are girls perched on the laps of the guys they're with, but still. Quite the feat.

Spotting the myriad of empty glasses decorating their table, I walk, no, *slide* over to them, courtesy of the alcohol-slick floors. With my customer-friendly smile slapped in place, I poise my pen and notepad to take what I can guess is an order consisting of beer, beer, and more beer. "What can I get you?"

Eight pairs of glassy eyes slide towards me, and I shift under the sudden onslaught of attention. Specifically, the male attention. Two of them are smiling politely, clearly the poster-children nice guys of the group. Another few are finding the v-shaped dip in my tank a hell of a lot more interesting than my face, and I'm resisting the urge to snap my fingers and pull a 'my eyes are up here, buddy' move. And one is... unnerving.

No expression graces his face as he stares at me, eyes cutting through to my freaking soul with their intensity. Pretty eyes, a golden color, almost glittering in the shitty diner lighting. Those eyes bore into me like he knows me, which is weird because he definitely doesn't. God knows I'd remember if I befriended this man because, Jesus Christ, is he hot. Really fucking hot.

Most notably, someone in my life would probably have an issue with me being friends with someone I instantly label as *really fucking hot,* and that person would not quietly endorse said friendship.

I'm still—completely objectively and not at all lustfully—marveling at the stranger's hotness when he plants his elbows on the table. Dark, curly hair falling over his forehead as he leans towards me, eyes the color of honey scanning me slowly, the smirking tilt to full lips screaming trouble. When he speaks in a low, raspy voice, his words are slightly slurred, a tell-tale sign he's been here way longer than I have. "Are you even old enough to be here?"

And just like that, his hotness is forgotten.

God dammit. It's always the hot ones.

"Are you?" I retort, cocking my head. "I'm afraid I'll need to see some ID."

That smirk vanishes quicker than free alcohol at a kegger. The chuckles that had begun to ring out around the table die down too, quickly replaced by the sounds of protesting grumbles and the rummaging through pockets and purses. I'm rocking a Cheshire Cat grin as almost all of them hand over slivers of plastic for me to inspect, including Mr. Smart Ass, who does so with less scowling than expected. More of an intrigued sneer.

I barely look at the coughed-up IDs—likely fake—before handing them back. I'm more focused on the three unlucky, empty-handed souls. "Sorry guys."

The girls glare at me with narrowed eyes, presumably plotting my death since I've effectively ruined their chances with their *delightful* companions. Smiling innocently, I shrug my shoulders in a 'hey, what can you do?' kind of manner. My third victim, a baby-faced kid who barely looks old enough to drive, pleads with wide eyes, "Come on, I swear I'm twenty-one. Aren't you in one of my classes?"

I bite my lip to stop a burgeoning smile. "Nice try, kid."

Blame your big-mouthed buddy. Maybe now he'll learn not to be rude to waiters.

Impatiently tapping my pen against my notepad, I wait for the trio to reluctantly slide from the booth. As they slope off, tossing daggers over their shoulders, I wave them off and my smile up a notch until I'm practically glowing.

When I turn back to the remnants of the group, I don't even care that I might've robbed myself of a tip because *ha ha*. "Now, what can I get you?"

~

The upside of a disgustingly busy night shift; time flies.

In the blink of an eye, the clock strikes midnight, and most of the students clear out in favor of whatever frat party is wreaking havoc. Only a few stragglers remain—unfortunately, those stragglers include Mr. Smart Ass and his very drunk, obnoxiously loud posse.

As I sit with my back to them, tiredly marrying ketchup bottles and wishing I had headphones to block out their grating voices, I swear I feel a gaze burning a hole in the back of my head.

"I am never working on a Friday again," Luna swears as she slips onto the stool beside me, her forehead hitting the sticky counter for a split second before she remedies that mistake. Straightening up with a grimace, she soothes herself by stroking the thick wad of tips clutched in her hand. I grunt in agreement even though I know damn well I'll be back here next week; the cash she holds is incentive enough.

We groan in unison when the bell hanging above the front door chimes, signaling an unwanted, late arrival. Opening her mouth to curse out whoever dares enter at this time of night, Luna trails off with a disappointed sigh when she recognizes the newest arrival.

A tall figure strides towards us, his hands fixing wind-blown, dirty blond hair, his cheeks bright from the nippy October air. "Hello, gorgeous," he all but yells as he stops in front of me, pressing a harsh kiss to my lips without warning. Despite my face being numb from hours of smiling at strangers, I fix one in place once more.

Dylan Wells caught my eye the very first day of freshman year when he accidentally almost knocked me out with a heavy lecture hall door. A very convincing apology and a 'please forgive me' cappuccino later, we were dating. Two weeks after that, he was all mine. And now, a year on, he still is.

Not quite the same, but still mine.

"Hey, Lu," he murmurs a half-hearted greeting at the girl perched beside me as he winds his arms around my waist, nuzzling his face against my hair in a way I hate because it always smushes the curls.

Luna grunts a greeting without looking his way. She's never liked Dylan. Not at the beginning and even less so when, a couple of weeks ago, I stumbled into our apartment with tear-streaked cheeks and unexplainable bruises.

"You ready to go, babe?" Dylan's nuzzling shifts from my hair to my neck, and I shy from the affection.

Pushing him away gently, I nod towards the lone table of customers very pointedly not watching us. "I've still got a table."

My boyfriend huffs his disapproval. Lips pepper kisses too wet, sloppy and suggestive for public along my jaw. "Lu can take it."

The woman in question snorts. Angling my head towards her, I cast my friend an apologetic glance before nodding in the direction of the staff room, a silent plea and permission for her to escape what is quickly becoming a very awkward situation. Luna hesitates for a moment before sighing, hopping off the stool, and disappearing into the back.

"I'll be done soon," I attempt to placate the impatient man pawing at me, my smile strained as I try to push him away using more force than I'd prefer yet still, he doesn't budge.

"You're coming to the Halloween thing next week, right?"

My nose crinkles at his question. Spending my night in a sweaty house filled with even sweatier strangers is not exactly my ideal night. "I don't know," I answer carefully. "I've got an early class the next day."

6

Instantly, Dylan goes from loving to tense. Slowly, he pulls back, a frown creasing his face, his voice a decibel louder than it was before as he asks, "Are you serious?"

I chew on my lip as I glance over his shoulder nervously at the table of guys who are all very invested in studying the dregs of their drinks. All but one of them. Slightly narrowed honey eyes watch me carefully, a dark brow raised in question or concern, I can't tell, a hard set to that annoyingly handsome face. Only for a split second do I let my gaze linger on him before returning my attention to my more-irritated-by-the-second boyfriend. "Dylan-"

"Come on, Mils. I feel like I never see you anymore."

Not true. He saw me last night, the night before, and the night before that. What he means is he never sees me in public where he can show me off to his friends like a living trophy. "I'll try, I promise," I blatantly lie, praying he believes me.

He doesn't.

The arms holding me tightly drop, a muttered 'whatever' lingering in the air as he backs up and moves towards the door.

My brow furrows in confusion. "You're not taking me home?"

The son of a bitch ignores me, actually ignores me, his only response is the slamming of Greenies' front door as he storms outside.

God, I wish I could say it's the first time he's done that.

I'm gaping after him in a state of shock when a throat clears behind me, and I whip around to find my favorite customer leaning against the bar.

Ordinarily, I'd be embarrassed because I'm assuming he heard every last word of my boyfriend's temper tantrum. However, I'm distracted right now, momentarily arrested by how goddamn good-looking this man is. The epitome of tall, dark, and handsome, with dark hair and bronzed skin and those pretty freaking eyes and a lilt to his voice suggesting a hidden accent. An internal sigh echoes in my brain because, seriously, what a shame. Damn whatever cosmic force decided the prettiest men must always be the biggest assholes.

Collecting myself, I quirk a brow. "You need something?"

"You need a ride?" The words flow off his tongue easily, everything in his cocky stance and his sure tone indicating he genuinely thinks I'll say to hell with the rest of my shift, with the boyfriend who was here mere moments prior, and run off with him. He has the ease of a man who's not told 'no' very often, and I'm so damn sick of cocksure men, so I do the very opposite.

Scoffing a laugh, I turn on my heel and saunter away from him, glancing over my shoulder before I dart into the staff room. "I'd rather walk."

2

AMELIA

THE SUN SET AN HOUR AGO, the night is young, yet the unfamiliar two-story house before me is already swarming with people. Empty beer cans and drunk students are scattered across the lawn, the smell of sweat and alcohol permeating the night air. I grimace as a guy stumbles past me and the stench becomes overwhelming, making my head spin a little.

I already hate this.

Girlfriend guilt got the better of me, as it so often does, which is how I've ended up standing in front of a random house wearing crappy devil horns and a red dress, an angel and a cat flanking me.

"This was a terrible idea," the cat laments, her disgust for our current situation mercifully matching mine. I glance over my shoulder at the costume-clad girl dithering beside me, a matching grimace on her pretty face. Like me and my horns, she's made the minimum effort tonight. Slapping on a pair of equally cheap cat ears and digging a black two-piece out of her closet, she called it a day, dodging Luna like she had the plague when she tried to paint whiskers on her. White-blonde braids spill down her back, a stark contrast against her dark skin, a similar shade to her deep brown eyes.They turn sympathetic when they meet mine, and we share a tired sigh.

Kate Butcher was the first person I met when I moved to California. She took one look at me, wide-eyed and terrified on my first day in a brand new high school in a brand new town, and took me under her wing. Or more like she shoved me under her wing. Not that I was complaining; I needed a friend and I guess she sensed that because a friend, I got. A best friend. We graduated together, got into the University of California, Sun Valley together, and, by some stroke of luck, got put into the same dorm our freshman year where we met Luna, the missing piece to our puzzle.

A year later, our little trio snagged a decent apartment near campus. Granted, it's small and Kate's bedroom is little more than a renovated office and we're almost certain our neighbors are drug dealers—although, their dodgy possible profession is counteracted by one of them being the spitting image of Pitbull—but it's ours. It's home.

And I would much rather be snuggled up on our tiny sofa right now than about to enter the depths of what I strongly consider hell.

Of my two beloved best friends, Kate was the one who at least tried to take my anti-party side. She knows I hate these kinds of things, especially when a certain undoubtedly drunk boyfriend is concerned. Drunk Dylan is a walking advert for PDA. Drunk Amelia, and sober Amelia, are not. It's not that I'm against it. It's more that I can't stomach the way Dylan totes me around like a prize he's won, kissing me without even looking at me.

This isn't Kate's idea of a perfect night either but, alas, we were overruled. All it took was Luna hearing the word 'party' and any arguments became null and void and her one-track mind took over.

And, let me tell you, Luna Evans is not an easy person to say 'no' to.

"Suck it up." A sharp elbow catches both Kate and me in the side, a sharper gaze shooting us a warning glare. "Complain again and you don't get McDonald's on the way home."

Oh, *and*, Kate and I are extremely susceptible to bribery.

Miming zipping out mouths shut, Kate and I fake smiles for our friend who, on the complete opposite end of the spectrum, takes Halloween very seriously. Luna is always gorgeous but right now, wearing a tight, white ensemble she spent hours painstakingly picking out with glitter sprinkled on her tan skin, flimsy white wings strapped to her back, and a halo nestled in her perfectly curled hair, she's downright ethereal.

Angel is not quite the name I'd attach to her costume. *Goddess* is more accurate.

A third grimace in a matter of minutes creases my face as I glance down at my outfit, the cute red dress I'd thought looked cute before we left the apartment suddenly seeming way too plain. I complained my ass off earlier when Luna cornered me, armed with an arsenal of makeup and a pair of heels that made my feet hurt just looking at them, but now, I'm grateful she made me up so I don't look quite as... *frumpy* next to her and Kate. In an odd turn of events, I'm especially grateful for the heels because for once, I'm somewhere within the realm of being an average height.

"It'll be fun, okay?" Luna slips an arm through the crook of mine, doing the same thing to Kate, and tugging us both towards the house. "We'll drink, we'll dance, we'll find me a *delectable* baseball player to rub up against," Kate and I snort in unison, "and if you still hate your life in an hour, we'll re-assess." Her slender body sways from side to side, bumping each of our hips. "Deal?"

Leaning forward to sneak a look at Kate, both of us adopt reluctant grins. "Deal."

A wave of obliterating heat hits us the second we step in the front door, knocking the air out of me and instantly making me sweatier than I was a moment ago. Music pulses around us, so loud I feel like I'm vibrating, and it's practically impossible to move without brushing up against an equally sweaty, writhing body.

Unlinking herself from the trio, Luna steps in front of us, intending to use herself as a battering ram since she's the tallest. She needn't have bothered; the crowd parts for her like they're a curtain and she's freaking daylight. I resist the urge to laugh at the many, many, *many* male gazes swinging her way as she struts past with us in her wake.

May the odds be ever in your favor, I silently tell them all.

We shuffle our way into the kitchen, making it there in half the time it would've taken without Luna's magic powers. She barely steps a heeled foot on the tiled kitchen floor before we're surrounded, every flavor of boy begging for her attention. Shaking my head with a laugh, I elbow my way out of the panting throng, leaving Luna in the capable hands of herself and making my way to the kitchen island. It's laden with drinks, everything from wine to soda to tequila available for my drinking pleasure. I retch internally at the sight of the latter; Amelia and tequila are not friends.

Before I can make my decision, Kate appears at my side and pushes a cup full of dark liquid into my hand. "Your favorite," she sings in my ear, clinking her own full cup against mine.

A pleased hum escapes me at the first mouthful, warmth spreading under my skin as the sweet taste of rum and cola fills my mouth. My favorite, indeed. I lift my cup in a silent thank you, about to verbalize the statement when a thick arm winds its way around my thought, cutting me off as it yanks me roughly against a hard chest. "You came, baby."

Tilting my head back, I smile cautiously up at a red-faced, clearly intoxicated Dylan. "I did."

He drops a kiss on my forehead, the smell of whiskey and smoke invading my senses, and I will my nose not to wrinkle in disgust. I hate smoking, detest it wholeheartedly, but I know better than to nag. Nagging annoys him. I think it spurs him on to do it more, honestly. So, I keep my mouth shut. Especially since it seems like Dylan is in a good mood. Happy Drunk Dylan rarely makes an appearance; most of the time, whiskey has the opposite effect on him. So, I'm going to savor it.

I'm savoring it as I let Dylan cradle me tightly to his chest, let him press soft kisses to my neck as we dance and mingle and drink. Heavy on the latter. I'm savoring it when he whispers in my ear that we should go somewhere quieter, as he corrals me upstairs into an empty bathroom, hoists me onto a counter, and kisses me hard. I'm savoring it when he unzips his jeans and I press him closer to me because fuck it. We're drunk and we're happy and he rarely wants to touch me lately, in private, at least. Why not have a little fun?

I'm clinging onto that little thread of happy hope so tightly, I don't even mind when it's an... unsatisfying encounter, nor when he abandons me pretty much the second he disposes of the condom, leaving me with my dress around my thighs and my panties around my ankles. I keep clinging as I clean myself up, head back downstairs alone, and mingle and dance and drink again except this time, I do it all sans my boyfriend. I distract myself with all the mingling and the dancing and the drinking until an hour passes and I can't distract myself anymore. Until my overthinking gene regains control and I notice, hey, I haven't seen that clingy boyfriend of mine in a while.

Half-listening to whatever the group around me is chatting about, I rise on my tiptoes, craning my neck to peer over the crowd as best as I can to try to find him. A couple of minutes of fruitless searching pass before I hit the jackpot; a familiar tuft of dirty blond hair and a broad back clad with a t-shirt I bought him sneaking upstairs. Excusing myself from the group, I make a beeline for the stairs, my calls of his name drowned out by the oppressive music.

It takes a solid ten minutes to wrestle my way through the crowd, another five before I can even make it up the stairs, due to the congregation of people who've chosen the bottom step as their designated conversation zone. I'm out of breath by the time I make it upstairs, huffing a little as I frown at the long stretch of empty hallway before me. Weird. Maybe he's looking for a bathroom or something.

Stumbling slightly because heels and rum are a dangerous combination, I reach the first door, lifting a hand to wrap my knuckles against the wood. My fingers freeze mid-air when, all of a sudden, the unmistakable sound of moans fills the hallway.

"Dylan."

～

The moan is as bloodcurdling as a scream.

My chest constricts at the sound of it, my heart dropping to my feet, the weight of that single word hitting me like a truck. Tears already burn my eyes as, against my better judgment, I shove the door open, praying to every and any god I'm not going to find what I know I'm going to find.

Pure and utter rage dries up those tears as I take in the scene before me.

Dylan on his back on a bed that isn't his. Red-flushed cheeks. Jeans around his ankles. Shirt unbuttoned.

A very naked girl straddling him.

Riding him.

His eyes, dark with lust, move from his bouncing chest and land on me, frozen with a mixture of shock, disbelief, and fury.

He sits up so quickly he almost knocks his little mistress right off his lap. "Amelia..."

My name barely leaves his lips before I turn on my heel and stalk away. He says it again but the way he utters my name doesn't sound sweet like it used to. It doesn't make my heart flutter and speed up. Instead, it makes my heart crack in half.

"Baby, please, it was a mistake."

A furious laugh escapes me as I spin back around, almost colliding with him as he chases after me. He's managed to yank his jeans into place, unzipped but covering his fucking still-hard dick, but his shirtless chest still mocks me, my fists balling at the sight of fresh claw marks decorating his skin, of the hickies on his neck. "Fuck you."

"I swear-"

"A mistake?" I seethe, shoving him away because he's too damn close. "No, fucking you in the bathroom an hour ago was a mistake. A very *unsatisfying* mistake."

The words burn as they leave my tongue, a pleasurable pain. I want to hurt him, and I know exactly where to strike. It feels *good* to hurt him. And it feels even better knowing it's the truth.

Satisfied with myself, I try to turn away, but strong fingers gripping my wrist inhibit my movements. "You little *bitch*."

Pain lances up my arm as I'm yanked backward, my wrist emitting an odd popping sound echoed by a thump as I'm slammed against the wall. Blue eyes I thought I loved turn into pools of black tar as they glare at me, pure vicious. I wriggle, attempting to free myself from his grip, but it's futile. "You're hurting me."

"Shut up," are the spat words my whimpered pleas are met with. Moving until his body is flush with me, pushing me harder against the wall, Dylan plants a hand on my hip, fingers digging into my skin. Hard. Leaning down so his mouth is level with my ear, he whispers, "You don't get to talk to me like that."

I recoil at his words. No, not at his words. At his voice. The usually smooth tone descends into something else, something terrifying. A voice I've heard before, only once.

Fear rushes through me like a wild rapid.

"Please, Dylan," I try again. "You're hurting me."

My pathetic cries only make him laugh, a harsh chuckle that chills me to the bone, as much as this awful transformation is. Gone is the charming smile, replaced by a repulsive smirk that makes me sick to my stomach. Eyes that once soothed me now suddenly make every hair on my body stand up. It's the look in those eyes that has the most profound effect, though. The pure predator look causes bile to rush up my throat because, honestly, it looks like he's enjoying this.

A cruel curve to his lips, he opens his mouth to say something, but another voice interrupts him.

"Is there a problem here?"

An audible cry of relief escapes me when Dylan's hands suddenly drop and I'm freed. In a panic, I look towards the staircase where a man leans against the banister, watching us. Dylan's narrowed gaze burns into the side of my face, daring me to say something, and that bravado I was feeling earlier? Dead and gone.

Instead, I drop my gaze, staring intently at the floor as I try not to cradle my sore wrist, shaking my head ever so slightly. When a minute passes and no one speaks, no one moves, I take the opportunity to dart away from Dylan.

A deep voice stops me before I can descend the stairs. "You okay?"

My savior watches me carefully, intently, and for a moment, I watch him right back. Obscenely tall, dressed in all black, dark hair slicked back and his face painted to resemble a skeleton. Golden eyes blaze with barely contained rage, and I recoil a little at the sight. His expression softens all of a sudden, his brow furrowing, and mine copies. They're oddly familiar, those eyes and the intensity, but my fuzzy, drunk brain can't quite place him, and I don't care enough to try. Shaking my head to clear the fog, I shoot him what I'm sure is a weak, pathetic smile. "I'm fine."

A throat clears behind us and I rip my gaze from the maybe-not-so-stranger, glancing behind me. Burning hot anger flushes my skin at the sight of Dylan standing there, still shirtless, still covered in another woman's lipstick, still staring at me like I'm the shit on his shoe. "If you ever touch me again," I start, my voice mercifully stronger and less shaky than I feel. "You'll regret it."

I don't wait for a response before I dart downstairs and into the safety of the kitchen, allowing myself to become just another body in the crowd.

3

NICK

"DUDE, the hot chick from Greenies is here."

I glance up from the floor with lightning speed, immediately searching for the redheaded waitress who left me wanting the other day. Instead, I find the one Jackson's been drooling over for the past year. Like he is right now, looking like a pathetic, love-struck puppy, eyes glazed and tongue lolling. Raising my hand, I cuff him on the back of the head. "Grow a pair and talk to the girl, dumbass."

Lost in his lusting, I don't think he even hears me. Gaze drifting back over to where the waitress stands, swarmed by seemingly every man at this party, I survey the object of Jackson's affection. She's hot, that much is undeniable. Leggy, busty, blonde. The trifecta. She's more my usual type than Jackson's but I'm not going to fuck with the whole horny teenager thing he's got going on.

"Not the waitress you were thinking of, is it, Nicky boy?"

With a huffed sigh, I glance at the kid leaning on the counter across from me with a knowing smirk on his hairless face. At first glance, you'd never guess this Halloween party was my newest, youngest, roommate's idea; his costume is jack shit. I spent an hour being tortured with face paints but somehow, the little shit gets away with throwing on his base-ball uniform and calling it a fucking costume. Even Jackson is more creative, and all he did was stick a cowboy hat on his messy head.

"Shut up," I grunt, shooting him a scowl before taking another slug of my drink. The tang of rum is undeniable, stronger than I usually have, a tell-tale sign Ben mixed my drink. Kid has the tolerance of a toddler so he makes the rest of our drinks stronger to balance the scales. Infallible logic, I have to admit.

"Oh, come on, Nicky," Ben ignores my instructions in favor of busting my balls harder. "You've been perving at the girl every time we're in Greenies for months now. I thought you were gonna cry when you finally spoke the other day."

Ben's smirk is a full-blown grin now and Jackson, finally having torn his attention away from his favorite waitress, hides his own smile behind his beer. "I thought he was gonna cry when she rejected him."

I ignore my housemates. *Perving.* Dramatic assholes. So what if I stare at the girl every now and then? View's pretty good. Jackson barely takes his eyes off the blonde and no one gives him shit. No, they reserve all their shit-giving for me.

"Nicky's got a crush and he doesn't even know her name," Ben sings, bouncing on the balls of his feet like the excitable child he is. For the hundredth time since this semester started, I wonder why the fuck I agreed to let a freshman move in. Fuck, Cass and Jackson seriously screwed me with their blindsiding.

"I don't have a fucking crush."

My 'friends' exchange glances before rolling their eyes. "Yeah, yeah, we know. The big, bad Nicolas Silva doesn't get measly crushes. He sleeps with women and doesn't call them, eats girl's hearts for breakfast, hooks up with their mothers, blah blah blah, feelings are for the weak. We know, big guy."

If looks could kill, I'm confident Ben would be six feet under. Ever since he moved in, the kid's had a gripe with my lifestyle. Just because he fucks to settle down doesn't mean I should. Because I think it's easier for everyone if feelings don't get involved—something I make very fucking clear from the get-go—I'm the bad guy. For God's sake, he's only seventeen. What the hell does he know?

Besides, it's all a moot point. I don't have a crush on Red. She's just… interesting. Intriguing. Captivating, with those pretty green eyes, all those messy curls framing her face like flames. My lips turn up at the memory of her rejecting me and looking so damn proud of herself as she did.

I wonder if she'd look that proud if she knew how much I love a challenge.

I wonder if she's nearby, considering her friend's proximity. She must be at the party, at least.

Gaze wandering back in Blondie's direction, my head cocks in curiosity when I find another girl at her side. The newcomer, not quite as tall as her friend but just as hot, rises on her toes to whisper something in Blondie's ear. Matching concerned frowns mar their faces as they scan the room simultaneously. I watch as Not-Blondie rubs one of those white-blonde braids of hers between her fingers, an obvious display of stress, and there's my opening. I give Jackson a nudge of warning a split second before I stride in their direction.

"Can I help you ladies with something?" I ask the moment I'm within earshot, my mouth turned up in a lazy smile. Not-Blondie, dressed as a poor interpretation of a cat, regards me first, brown eyes narrowing when they meet mine. As if they know me. As if she doesn't like me.

Interesting.

"No," is her curt response, uttered at the same time her much friend-lier buddy replies, "We're looking for our friend."

My posture straightens ever so slightly. A certain redhead, maybe?

"Want us to help?" I find myself offering before I can think my words through, jerking my head towards Jackson who's finally managed to unstick his cowardly ass from the kitchen counter and creep towards us. Looking Blondie in the eye is still too tall of a task for him, apparently, so I take the initiative to introduce both of us, slapping my friend on the back in an attempt to snap him out of his silent stupor. "I'm Nick, this is Jackson."

Eye contact is clearly not a problem for Blondie; she's staring at Jackson with a dangerous glint in her eye, like a cat surveying a mouse. She extends a hand towards him, full lips curling into a smooth smile, a smile that looks an awful lot like the one I gave Red the other day.

I like this girl.

"Luna," she introduces herself, voice low and sultry, and fuck yeah, I like this girl. Her slender fingers wrap around Jackson's and I swear to God, the man almost collapses from one simple touch. Truly pathetic.

Glancing aside, I find Luna's friends watching the pair with raised brows, seemingly as amused as me. When she catches me looking, however, her face smoothes into a disinterested expression.

Pasting on my most winning smile, I wink. "I'll check upstairs, you check outside?"

Eyes still narrowed, she huffs a sigh before disappearing, calling a brief description of her lost friend over her shoulder as she goes. Red hair, green eyes, dressed as a devil.

Sounds like the girl I'm looking for.

~

As I shove through the crowd of people littering my living room, I find another reason for Ben to own spot number one on my shit list; he said this was going to be a small thing. Lying little bastard.

The sheer number of people stuffed in here is hindering my ability to find Red, so there's another thing for me to be pissed about. My fucking elbows hurt by the time my feet hit the stairs, and I maybe shove the last remaining people in my way a little harder than necessary, just for the fun of it. I cast a glare back at the surely hundreds of drunk students stumbling around, strongly considering kicking everyone out because the heat and the thumping music are starting to get to me when the sound of voices distracts me.

Very loud, very angry voices, a guy and a girl arguing.

Intrigued, I pause to listen, wincing when the girl hisses pure poison, "No, fucking you in the bathroom an hour ago was a mistake. A very un*satisfying* mistake."

Ai. Hitting him right where it hurts. Guy must have fucked up bad.

I'm considering leaving them to it—fuck if I want to get in the middle of that—when the guy swears loudly, his curse echoed by a thud and a quiet whimper, and suddenly, I'm taking the stairs two at a time.

I make it to the top in time to see some vaguely familiar blond guy slam the very redhead I've been searching for against the wall. He—the handsy dipshit from the diner, if I'm not mistaken—leans in close, speaking low and quiet, uttering something I can't hear but whatever it is has Red's face crumpling in fear, another whimper escaping her lips.

It takes every ounce of self-control I possess to freeze my feet to the floor and not flatten the fucker the way my body and brain are begging me to.

"Is there a problem here?" I will my voice to come out flat and even, not threatening and booming like it wants to. Red's shaking hard enough to shatter; I don't want to scare her any more than *he* already has.

The second he notices my presence, the guy drops Red's arm before taking a step back, and my temper flares when I notice the way Red cradles her wrist with a wince. Immediately, she steps away from him, closer to me. No, closer to the stairs.

Good girl. Get the hell out of here.

It's no kind of comfort when Red shakes her head slightly, a quiet lie to my question. Neither of them says a word yet the palpable, uneasy silence speaks volumes, the glare Jackass fixes Red with saying it all.

When she makes her move, darting towards the stairs, it hurts, resisting the urge to reach out and stop her. Instead, I use my voice. "You okay?"

Green eyes dart to mine, wide and glassy and terrified and, God, I want to punch that asshole. Frowning slightly, she takes me in, head tilted, brow furrowed. Trying to figure out where she knows me from, I realize. Either I didn't make a lasting impression or she's too drunk to remember because no recognition flashes in those pretty eyes. Shooting me the least convincing smile I've ever seen, she mumbles an even less convincing *'I'm fine'* before bolting down the stairs.

Not before she threatens the giant lump of shit still glaring at her.

A weird feeling of pride bursts in my chest at the sound of her spat words.

In a flurry of red curls, she disappears downstairs, and when Jackass tries to follow her, I block the way. A hand on his chest, I shove him backward. "You think hurting your girlfriend makes you a big man, huh?"

Eyes rolling, he barks a laugh. "Mind your business, Silva."

I frown at his use of my last name. Fuck, do I know this asshole? Squinting a little, I examine the little twerp. Shitty blond hair, shitty blue eyes, a shitty garish bird tattooed on his shitty bare chest....I suppress a groan.

Dylan fucking Wells.

My freshman year roommate. God, how did I forget him? I had to deal with his bitching and whining for an entire academic year. Dylan was a massive pain in the ass. He makes Ben seem completely tolerable. Apparently, he still is a massive pain in the ass.

A massive *abusive* pain in the ass.

"Get out of my house, Wells." I step to the side, jerking my head towards the stairs. "I see you back here again or touching another girl like that, I'll make sure your girlfriend's little promise comes true."

I'm a little disappointed when Dylan takes the first warning issued, scowling before storming down the stairs. Thirty seconds later, I hear the front door slam. Damn. I was kind of hoping he'd argue so I'd have an excuse to physically throw his ass out.

Sucking in a steadying breath, I follow him down, peeking out the front door to check he's not lurking like the cockroach he is, before fixing my attention on more important matters.

It doesn't take me long to find her again. A red-headed devil downing tequila like it's water isn't exactly hard to track down. Head tipped back, she holds the bottle to her parted mouth, her skin glowing a pretty pink color as the alcohol works its way into her bloodstream and, fuck. She's gorgeous. I have to physically shake my head to clear it of images of full, pouty lips before approaching her.

"You sure you're okay?" She jumps at the sound of my voice, whirling around to face me, and I try very hard not to imagine licking away the droplets of liquor dripping down the side of her mouth.

Dragging the back of her hand across her mouth, she smiles tightly, her second silent lie to me.

"You here alone?" I already know the answer before she nods, obviously. Her friends are wandering around here somewhere, completely oblivious to whatever the hell happened upstairs. I should find them for her but a small, selfish part of me is reluctant to share. Even if I don't have her full attention.

She keeps looking past me, scanning what she can see of the living room, and from the guarded edge in her gaze, I have a solid bet who she's cautiously searching for.

"I kicked him out," I reassure her softly, relief glimmering in those emerald eyes. She cocks her head at me, opening her mouth to speak, but the sudden arrival of two shrieking women interrupts whatever she was about to say.

"There you are," a high-pitched voice squeals, a delighted Luna damn near suffocating her friend with the force of her hug. "We've been looking everywhere for you."

Not-Blondie snorts as she tugs on a strand of her friend's hair. "I'm sorry, did you think she was lost in Oscar Jackson's eyes?"

Braids fly as Not-Blondie gets shoved. "Shut up."

My presence barely gets an acknowledgment; a disdainful nod from Not-Blondie and a flutter of lashes from Luna before they ignore my existence in favor of dragging each other towards the dance floor.

I'm ready to follow, I'm so fucking ready to follow, especially when Red glances over her shoulder, seeking me out a last time. I've already taken a step in her direction and I'm taking another but a hand clutching my bicep holds me in place. Glancing down, I take one look at the blood-red talons, I get a single whiff of suffocating perfume, and I groan. Before I even hear a saccharine voice purr, "hi, handsome," I'm already regretting all of my past choices. Specifically, the ones that led to me repeatedly fucking the woman attaching herself to my side, smirking up at me, caressing my arm like it's a fucking puppy.

She was fun the first time. She was convenient the second time. The third time, I was drunk off my fucking ass and honestly have very little recollection of it. Her name is a mystery to me and I truly don't think I could pick her out of a line-up but judging by the way she's pressing up on me right now, she doesn't mind. "Wanna dance?"

With her? No.

Does that stop me from slinging an arm around her shoulders and letting her lead me onto the dance floor, towards the person I actually want to dance with?

No.

4

NICK

THE GIRL IS A LIVING FLAME.

Fiery curls fly around her as she dances, so wild yet fluid in her movements, so eye-catching. And that dress, that fucking red dress. So tight around her chest but loose around her hips, flaring every time she spins to the music, riding higher and higher on her thighs with every twirl, the sight of creamy, freckled flesh sending a jolt of heat to my groin. She tips her head towards the ceiling, lips parted, cheeks flushed, chest heaving as she breathes heavily. When she buries her hands in her hair, pulling the thick curls into a ponytail, I groan in frustration, my jeans suddenly impossibly tight.

I can't take my fucking eyes off of her.

My dance partner—Janine, maybe?—simpers up at me, clearly thinking my excitement is for her, a result of her gyrating against my hips. She couldn't be more wrong.

It's embarrassing, how fucking hard I am from watching a girl dance. From watching her tip tequila down her throat and laugh with her friends. Embarrassing and inconvenient and I need to do something about it.

It hurts to tear my eyes away from Red but I manage. Before the invisible force begging for my gaze can kick in again, I grab Janine or Jean or whatever the fuck her name is and drag her to the bathroom, kissing her hard the moment the door closes behind us. She's more than a willing participant, giving herself to me eagerly, hands roaming until I can't take it anymore. It takes a second to roll on one of the condoms stashed in the bathroom cabinet, another to turn her around and bend her over the sink, one more to sink inside of her, and then I'm fucking her, thrusting again and again in an attempt to rid my mind of piercing green eyes.

Instead, I come to them.

Fuck.

∼

I'm lurking in the kitchen, regretting my life choices and hiding from the hook-up I left behind in the bathroom when I spot a familiar face shoving her way through the mob of dancing students. It's not the face I'm looking for but it catches my attention all the same.

Not-Blondie—I need to learn her name—sighs as she comes to a stop in front of me, an expression of concern twisting her face.

"Lost her again?" I ask, slightly amused that Red keeps giving everyone the slip. Wild little thing.

My new unnamed friend sighs again and nods.

"And the other one?"

"Ask your roommate."

Alright. Good for you, cowboy.

"I'll take upstairs again," I call over my shoulder as I head for the staircase again with a parting salute, hoping I don't find anything close to resembling earlier's scene. Thankfully, the hallway is empty, all doors firmly shut bar one. My bedroom door, I realize.

If someone's fucking in my bed, I'll lose it.

Relief hits me like a goddamn truck when I find my room as empty as the hallway, exactly how I left it except for the pair of heels dropped outside the ensuite door.

Red heels.

Crossing the room in record time, I gently push the ajar door open, rapping my knuckles against the wood before peering around the edge. Lo and behold, as I expected, there she is. Sitting on the tiles with her back against the tiled wall, knees tucked up to her chest and causing her dress to pool in her lap, flashing a glimpse of matching panties.

Fucking hell.

"Hey, trouble."

Red starts at the sound of my voice, her head snapping up fast enough to give herself whiplash. She frowns at me for a moment, rubbing at her eyes and smearing black stuff everywhere. "I'm looking for my friends," is all she says in a voice so soft and soothing, I could probably fall asleep to it.

Bracing a shoulder against the door jamb, I cock a brow. "One of your friends happen to be a cat?"

Her frowning increases tenfold, head tilting to the side in an assessing way. Slowly, her head dips in a nod, a leisurely smile curving her lips, and damn if the room doesn't get a little brighter.

Taking a careful step forward, I reach out a hand towards her, a silent offer to help her up that she accepts. And good fucking thing too because the girl wobbles like a newborn deer taking its first steps as she clambers to her feet. She grips my hand with both of hers, an action that draws my attention to the growing bruise on her wrist. Various shades of purple and yellow, it wraps around her wrist like a nauseating bracelet, and I have to look away before the urge to murder Dylan fucking Wells becomes too strong not to give into.

Dropping my hands as soon as she's steady enough, I take a step back, creating a space for her to slip through. She does just that, wobbling out the door, leaning down as she goes to clumsily scoop up her heels and flashing me again in the process. I stifle a groan as I become particularly familiar with the birthmark marring her left ass cheek and wonder what exactly I did in a past life to deserve this torture.

"Do you want me to find your-" I don't manage to get my question out because, as though summoned by her prospective mention, Not-Blondie miraculously appears in the doorway, her worried expression melting away when she catches sight of her wily friend.

"Kitty Kate!" Red squeals and throws herself into her friend's arms. Not-Blondie, Kate, stumbles as she catches her, her quiet laugh filling the air. For the first time in my presence, Kate smiles.

"I've been looking everywhere for you, Amelia."

Amelia. Finally. A pretty name for a pretty girl.

A cough grabs my attention, drawing it to Ben lurking nearby too, a shit-eating grin on his face. "*Amelia,*" he mouths, and I can just hear his would-be teasing tone.

I oh-so-discreetly use my middle finger to scratch my cheek, not-discreetly-at-all scowling at the little shit. Ben only laughs, the noise alerting the subject of his mockery to his presence. Head tilting again, Amelia rocks on the balls of her feet as she scans Ben thoroughly.

I scowl harder.

Slowly, she leans into Kate until they're practically nose-to-nose. "Your friend is very pretty," she states in an overly loud whisper, and Ben's expression erupts with amusement.

"Sorry to disappoint, beautiful, but I'm afraid we have one too many things in common."

Amelia blinks at him cluelessly, too drunk to get the joke. Rolling her eyes, Kate pokes her friend playfully in the ribs. "He's gay, Mils."

Mouth opening in a perfect 'o,' she makes an accompanying sound before breaking out in a smile and poking her friend back. "Like you."

"Sure, sweetie."

"Such a shame," Amelia sighs and clicks her tongue. "I'm on the hunt for a rebound."

Well, if that little line doesn't steal my attention.

"I'm sorry, what?" Kate questions, grabbing her friend by the shoulders in a useless quest for her fleeting attention. "You and Dylan broke up?"

A hum is the only response she receives, Amelia's drunken mind already wandering to what she deems more interesting topics—namely Ben. She's back to assessing him, her lips pursed, a finger tapping against the slightly fuller bottom one.

It's like a light bulb flickers to life above her head as she has a eureka moment, recognition flashing in her gaze, a grin brightening her features, "Baby face!"

Ben's amusement mingles with bewilderment as slender fingers probe his face, poking and pinching his cheeks playfully. "Excuse me?"

"I kicked you out of Greenies the other day," she slurs in explanation through bouts of giggled laughter. "You were lying about your age, right? I knew you were lying."

"Because I have a baby face?"

She snaps her fingers. "Exactly."

"That's because he is a baby," I mumble beneath my breath. Remembering my presence, at last, Amelia spins towards me. After a moment of assessment, an accusing finger jabs my way. "You!"

A lazy grin pulls at my lips. "Me?"

"You were rude to me."

She remembers me, is all my twisted brain gets out of that exclamation. "You got my friends kicked out."

"No, *you* got your friends kicked out by *being rude to me*."

She's yelling but she might as well be whispering sweet nothings with the way I'm gazing at her. Drinking in the sight of her. She looks exactly like she did that day. Hands on her hips, hair unruly, those fucking eyes pinning me in place. Intoxicating, dark green eyes, the color of an evergreen forest seconds before the sun goes down. My hands itch for my camera, longing to snap a picture of her but I highly doubt she'd be okay with that.

One day, maybe.

For now, I'll settle for committing that glower to memory

I'm almost disappointed when the glowering ceases and she turns back to Kate with a tired sigh, that fire of hers extinguished in the blink of an eye. "Where's Luna?" she asks through a yawn.

Kate chuckles as she jerks her head towards the room across the hall. Jackson's room. If that didn't tell me everything I needed to know, the look of pride on Ben's face does. God, the guy's going to be insufferable tomorrow.

"Go, Luna." Tiredly, she pumps a fist in the air, jaw stretching in another yawn as she stumbles into the hall, managing a grand total of three steps before tripping over her own feet, prompting me to swoop in and stop her pretty face from meeting the hard floor. "I wanna dance."

"Maybe you should sit down for a minute." My kind suggestion earns me not one but two glares, a glower from the girl I'm holding upright and a scowl from her friend. The latter nudges me aside and takes my place, guiding Amelia's pale arms around her neck, and it's a good thing Amelia is so small she all but flops in Kate's grip.

Despite her obvious distrust for me and that ever-present scowl, Kate takes my advice and leads her friend to my bed. "Can you get her some water?"

The gentlemanly thing to do would be to leave the room in search of the requested beverage.

I don't move except to shoot a pointed look in Ben's direction.

Hey, I never claimed to be a gentleman.

~

"You know, I see you around the diner a lot."

I jump at the unexpected voice interrupting the rummaging I'm doing through Cass' bathroom cabinets in search of a spare toothbrush because I know the guy keeps a stash in here. Turns out, I'm more of a gentleman than previously anticipated. They must've been buried deep down, those gentlemanly instincts, inspired to arise at the sight of a drunk girl sprawled on my bed and her friend cursing and swearing as she tried to get an Uber.

"You can stay here," I found myself saying before I knew it. "If you want. I'll take the couch."

Kate seemed as surprised at my offer as I was, and I swear I almost earn a smile.

Any chance of pleasantries dissipate, though, when I mention a third —absent tonight—roommate's stash of spare toiletries in his bathroom. What Kate gets from that, noting with a poignant huff and a meaningful look, is that my roommate is kinder to his overnight guests than I am.

"I know you," she remarks suddenly, surveying me from the doorway of Cass' ensuite as I crouch on my haunches and dig around in his cabinet.

An unopened toothbrush clasped in my fist, I get to my feet. "What?"

"The diner." Long fingers tap against crossed arms. "You're there a lot."

"So?"

"No one loves diner food that much."

"Maybe I do."

Dark brows shoot up, an all-too-knowing glimmer in her darker eyes. "Really?"

"The booze is cheap."

"Uh-huh."

"It's close to college."

"And the view is great, hm?"

My eyes narrow, my quips momentarily drying up. If I didn't know any better, I would think *Kitty Kate* has been conspiring with my friends. "Jackson thinks so."

She hums, assessing me for a moment longer before turning on her heel and crossing the hall back towards my bedroom, towards the drunk, sleepy girl curled up amongst my pillows.

I huff out a breath, raking a hand over my face before following. "You want some clothes?"

Although she looks less than inclined to spend a night in my clothes, Kate nods stiffly. I keep my gaze averted from Amelia as I head for my closet; that outfit of hers leaves little to the imagination when she's upright but horizontal, it's nothing but trouble. I utter a silent thank you to my past self for doing laundry yesterday as I fish out a couple of clean t-shirts and accompanying sweats. "Gonna be big but-"

"What the fuck is this?"

Whirling around at the shouted, panicked question, I'm met with fiery rage and accusing eyes, and the cause isn't hard to find. In her quest for a comfortable position, Amelia wriggled around so much her dress has ridden up. But, remarkably, it's not the red panties holding my attention.

It's the ugly bruise spanning her hip, identical to the one on her wrist in color and rage-inducing tendencies.

My hands fly up in a display of innocence but it only takes one real look at Kate to note her fury isn't directed at me. No, something about the look on her face tells me she knows exactly who's responsible. And if it didn't, the next words out of her mouth do. "I'm gonna fucking kill him."

Join the queue, sweetheart.

"I found them up here a couple hours ago," I explain carefully, quietly, with the finesse of a man defusing a bomb. "I think she walked in on him with someone else or something. They were yelling at each other and he..." Lacking words, I gesture at the bruises, seeing the exact moment where Kate notices the second one marring her friend's wrist. "I kicked him out and stayed with her until you found her."

Kate's face softens with something akin to gratefulness. She's silent as she carefully fixes Amelia's skirt, stroking her palms over her hair and murmuring something I don't catch. Without a word, I set the to-be-borrowed clothes on the nightstand beside them, next to the glass of water and the aspirin Ben must have brought up here at some point. Those gentlemanly instincts of mine flare again as I head for the door, intending on making myself scarce. My hand's on the door knob when a soft mumble stops me in my tracks.

"He hurt me again."

It's so quiet, I wonder momentarily if I imagined it. I hope I did. But as the words ring in my ears like a damn siren, I know I didn't.

Kate doesn't reply. When I glance over my shoulder, I find her perched on the edge of the bed with clenched fists and a ramrod straight back. I can't see her face but I'm willing to bet it's painted with murderous intentions.

Oblivious to the reaction her words have caused, Amelia sighs sleepily. Eyes closed, she reaches blindly for Kate's hand, tangling their fingers together. "Love you, Kate."

Kate's expression cracks, tight lips melting into a soft smile. Leaning down, she kisses her friend on the forehead and suddenly, I feel like I'm intruding. "And I love you."

The floorboards creak as I move to leave and glossy eyes flit my way, Kate's thoughtful yet heartbroken expression affecting me way more than it should. "She's never said it out loud before."

Again. Before. It's becoming more and more obvious what happened tonight wasn't an accident nor a one-time thing, and my chest tightens inexplicably at the thought.

A long moment passes of us staring at each other silently, something tangible passing between us, before Kate tears her gaze away, breaking the odd connection. I take my cue, ducking out of the room and closing the door quietly behind me. I shake my head as I trudge downstairs, trying very, very hard not to think about the complicated woman curled up in my sheets.

5

AMELIA

My head is pounding and I have no idea where I am.

Those are the first things that become clear when I wake up with the hangover from hell in a bed that's definitely not mine; it's too big, the comforter isn't as comfortable, and the pillows aren't as plump. Not to mention the distinct scent of something unequivocally masculine permeating the air.

With a hearty groan, I force my eyes open, unwelcome light immediately assaulting me until I'm tearing up. I slap a hand over my eyes quickly in an attempt to block out some of the offensive sun, another groan echoing around the room.

A sound that's met with chuckling.

I almost fall out of the damn bed, almost tripping over my feet in my scramble to get up. Whipping around, my eyes widen at the sight of a man lingering on the other side of the room, lurking in the doorway of what looks like an ensuite bathroom.

A very wet, very half-naked, *very* hot guy.

It takes all of my willpower not to let my gaze drop to the tattooed chest on full display. Or the gray sweatpants slung low on his hips. No, my eyes remain firmly trained on his face. His beautiful, smirking face.

Fuck my life.

"I think this is the part where you say good morning, *querida*."

God. A hot voice to go with a hot body. A very familiar hot voice.

A flick of a memory comes back to me at the sound of it, at the sight of that freaking smirk. A memory of him smirking at me the way he is now on more than one occasion, one of those occasions being whilst I was crumpled on a bathroom floor. His bathroom floor, I'm guessing, the one he's exiting now. I search my brain for the not-so-stranger's name but come up blank. The nickname I gave springs to mind but I'm not sure calling him Smart Ass would be wise right now considering I just rolled out of his bed.

"I'm sorry," I choke on the words. "Who are you?"

Lips that have no business being so full and belonging to a man curl into a playful grin, a mocking arch to his brows. "You don't remember? I'm hurt." He takes a step forward, and my head tilts back with the closer proximity because Jesus, the guy is tall. He's got at least a foot on my diminutive five-foot-two stature. More, probably. "You often spend a night with a man without getting their name?"

He's got an accent. A hint of something lilting peeks its head out as his low voice teases me. I'm so distracted by the foreign cadence it takes me a second for his words to sink in. When they do, however, they land with a bang. "What?" I splutter, stumbling back a step. "I didn't... we didn't... I have-"

Laughter cuts me off, genuinely evil laughter. "I'm fucking with you." He shakes his head at me, holding out a hand. "Nicolas Silva. Friends call me Nick."

"Nicolas," I repeat, not feeling particularly friendly towards the man right now. God, if there was an award for worst first impressions, I think this guy would win. It seems he's got a penchant for pissing me off.

Nevertheless, I take his hand, trying to ignore the warmth seeping from his to mine and runs all the way up my arm. "Amelia Hanlon."

Nicolas, Nick, whatever, hums, taking his time shaking my hand in an odd display of formality that contradicts the entirely non-formal way his honey-colored eyes burn into me with an intensity that's beginning to feel familiar.

When he releases me after a lingering moment, an odd chill tickles my palm. I shove my suddenly icy hand in my pocket, and then I frown; I remember a distinct lack of pockets in the dress I wore last night. Glancing down, my frown deepens.

Gone is my red dress, replaced with a black hoodie that's not mine. My heels have been replaced with thick, warm socks that my subconscious is already planning to steal. God knows where my bra is but I find solace in the uncomfortable itch of my thong because at least something on my body actually belongs to me. "What the hell am I wearing?"

Nick chuckles again, a soft sound that seems to soothe my aching head, and adopts a shit-eating grin as he folds his arms over his chest. His sculpted, intricately tattooed chest. Such pretty designs sprawl from his chest to his shoulders, down his arms, ending at his wrists like permanent sleeves. An odd urge to step closer and get a better look hits me but luckily, Nick's voice stops me before I can. "Well, *someone* decided their dress wasn't comfortable anymore so *someone* decided to strip off and run around my house half-naked at the crack of dawn."

Once fooled, twice shy, I narrow my eyes. "Please tell me you're kidding."

"It took three of us to pin you down and force you into that."

Terrific.

My hands fly up to shield my scarlet face, the pads of my fingers digging into my eye sockets as though if I press hard enough, the memories of last night might suddenly erase. "I'm so fucking sorry."

"Don't worry about it." I peek through my fingers and catch the amusement glittering in his gaze, fixed on my wrist, fade. "You had a rough night."

My embarrassment is replaced by confusion. It's a short-lasting emotion, however, dissipating the moment I lay eyes on what's captivating Nick's attention; the ugly, purple bruise snaking its way up my arm. The blood drains from my face as a dam bursts in my mind, memories hitting me like a flood.

Dylan cheating on me. Yelling at me. Grabbing me and hurting me.

Nick swooping in before it got too ugly and kicking Dylan out, I remember him telling me that now.

I also remember drowning my sorrows in a bottle of my best friend, tequila, apparently so effectively, I forgot the whole thing.

Right.

That.

"Are you, uh," Nick shifts, body tense and awkward, things I don't think he feels very often if the uncomfortable hunch of his body is anything to go by, "okay?"

"I'm fine." I force a smile that's probably as weak and meek as my voice. I hate the sound of it. I hate that Dylan makes me sound like that. Tears sting my eyes but I force them away.

Wait, I tell them. *Later.*

I clench my fists to stop them from swiping at my slightly damp eyes. "Thank you," I fumble awkwardly over the words, "for last night."

"Don't worry about it," Nick repeats his earlier sentiment. He shifts again before clearing his throat, jerking a thumb towards the bedroom door. "Your friend's downstairs. Kate."

I'm both relieved at the knowledge I wasn't abandoned and dreading an encounter with my perceptive friend. With a stiff nod and an awkward smile, I skid out of the room as fast as my socked feet will take me, hopefully never to return.

~

"There she is!"

I grimace as I descend the staircase and am immediately met with a teasing exclamation and an ear-to-ear grin courtesy of my best friend. Perched on one of the three sofas scattered around the living room—haphazardly positioned in a way that screams 'men live here'—in clothes that aren't hers, Kate nurses a cup of what I can only pray is freshly brewed coffee, alternating between sipping and smirking. Beside her sits a vaguely familiar blond guy. There's no point in hoping he's not one of the ones who had a part in wrangling my drunk ass last night; the wry look on his face says it all.

"Not a word," I warn as I throw myself on an unoccupied sofa, looking everywhere but directly at the smug duo across from me as I tuck my knees up to my chest, huddling beneath the tent of a hoodie. I'm not in the mood for an interrogation or even conversation. I want to curl up in a ball, close my eyes, and drift into a sleep I don't wake up from for a couple of years, preferably.

"What, no good morning for Kate's very pretty friend?"

Wishful thinking, of course.

My cheeks flush with embarrassment as I smile sheepishly at Ben, I remember his name now. I mutter an apology that he waves off. "Having a beautiful girl call me pretty is not something I expect an apology for. Kicking me out of Greenies, however…"

"I've been told that was my fault, kid."

I don't know why I expected Nick to stay upstairs. I hoped he would, if only for the sake of my sanity. And my poor fire-truck-red cheeks. No, he does the very opposite of what I prayed. He saunters downstairs, taking a brief detour to the kitchen before returning with two mugs of steaming coffee, the smell permeating the air and damn near making me drool. When he hands one to me with an off-balancing wink, I almost forgive his morning, and diner, antics. When he flops down beside me—close since that's all the two-person sofa will allow—my hackles rise again.

It's pretty pathetic that my first instinct is to shift away. Not because my bare thigh is crushed against a man I don't know outside of a couple less than ideal encounters—even if the coffee and the whole hero act last night are redeeming him slightly—but because I'm worried about my boyfriend's reaction.

Ex-boyfriend.

I'm faintly aware that an official break-up was never proclaimed but I reckon it was implied with the whole 'touch me again and you'll regret it' thing.

Anyway. *Ex.*

The thought of my *ex* has me plastering myself against the arm of the sofa lest I hurt, or incur the wrath of, my *ex.* God, I should freaking climb right on top of Nick in an act of payback. *He* deserves a little payback, and Nicolas Silva is an excellent candidate.

But no. I cower like a fool for the sake of a man who's done nothing but hurt me recently.

Freaking conscience.

"Is Lu still here?" I ask in an effort to direct my thoughts to safe territory, sipping my coffee. Black and sweet, the way I like it. In the back of my mind, a small part of me wonders how this relative stranger knows my exact coffee order but I don't dwell.

Kate jerks her head skywards, brows wiggling suggestively. "Bagged a baseball player."

As much as that statement piques my interest, something in my chest pangs at the mention of the sport. A whole lot of childhood memories I've gone to painstaking efforts to bury revolved around baseball. Nevertheless, I ask, "A baseball player, huh? Which one?"

It's Ben who answers. "Oscar Jackson. Poor guy's been pining for your friend for months. Last night was probably the best night of his life."

Interesting.

Grinning at Kate, I say, "You know what they say about baseball players."

She grins back. "Good with their hands."

"Amen."

"I play too," Ben chimes in, gaze trained on me. "So does our other roommate. Might be a suitable candidate for that rebound you mentioned."

My nose wrinkles as I groan, my companions chuckling, and I scramble to keep the subject off me and my embarrassment. "So, Lu stayed the night too?"

I'm surprised, honestly. Lu's never been one for relationships. Or any minor display of commitment. Or sharing a bed for longer than it takes to secure an orgasm. The girl was downright furious when I got cuffed twenty minutes into freshman year, as she so eloquently put it. When Kate met her girlfriend, she basically threw a tantrum.

'Relationships in college are as pointless as a fucking circle' is what she preached to both of us for weeks.

I'm starting to see her point.

"Well, well, well." As though summoned by the conversation, Luna materializes, wearing nothing but a shirt that grazes the tops of her long legs as she breezes down the stairs. The extremely sated smile on her face shifts to downright devious as she struts towards me. "I heard our Amelia had a very interesting night."

I extend a leg to boot her in the thigh as she passes, heading for the third sofa. "Could say the same to you, Blondie."

Luna grins like a Cheshire cat, languishly sprawling on the couch cushions. Last night's conquest—the infamous Oscar Jackson—isn't far behind her, shuffling into the room and looking every bit as pleased as Luna, and oh, look at that. It's another one of the diner boys. The nice one, I note approvingly. A regular, I realize, which makes sense if Ben's pining theory is to be believed.

He's not her typical type. He's a lot leaner than she usually likes them, and I didn't think long hair was her thing. Full of surprises, our Luna.

Neither Kate nor I can hide our shock when he—Jackson, the boys greet him as—scoops Luna up, takes her seat, and sets her down in his lap, and our friend doesn't utter a word of protest. She settles into him, shooting us both a glare that screams *'shut the fuck up or I'll throw a tantrum again.'* Wisely, we listen.

When she's satisfied with our silence, she hums with a smile, and I smell trouble before her mouth even opens. "So," she directs her glittering gaze in my direction, "how's the single life treating you?"

"Luna..." Kate warns, reaching over to pinch our friend on the thigh.

"I'm proud of you, you know." Batting Kate's hand away, she ignores her warning, instead playing with fire by stealing her coffee. Through a lengthy, smug sip, she continues, "That jackass needed to be dumped a long time ago."

Nick grumbles something beside me, the specifics of it drowned out by Luna as she continues her rambling, her long, long list of everything wrong with Dylan, and why I should've kicked him to the curb sooner.

I'm almost grateful when the front door opens, an interruption to her rant. That is until a voice rings out and the urge to sink into the ground that's been plaguing me all morning ramps up a notch. "Hey, what's this I hear about some girl running around naked at 4AM?"

Kill me. Kill me now.

Against my better judgment, I peek over my shoulder at the latest man responsible for my glowing cheeks as he hangs his keys off the hook next to the door—the last roommate, presumably. He's tall, as every occupant of this house seems to be, with light brown skin and black curls cut close to his scalp. My brain itches at the sight, his side profile maddeningly familiar.

When he turns to face me, warm brown eyes locking with mine and mimicking their widening, I almost fall off the sofa. "Oh my God, Cassie?"

6

AMELIA

WHEN I WAS six years old, my mother left.

The day she walked out of my life is one of the only memories I have of her. I remember watching her pack up the dresses I sneakily tried on, the makeup I begged her to teach me to use, the heels I got in trouble for prancing around in. I remember following her into the driveway as she silently packed up the car. I remember asking where she was going only to be ignored. And I remember sitting there and watching as she got in her car and drove off without so much as a goodbye.

What I don't remember is how long I sat there before Cass Morgan appeared at my side.

I just know that at some point, I jumped as an arm brushed mine, a skinny body plopped on the pavement beside me, a curious voice asked, "What're you doing?"

"Waiting for my mom," I'd replied.

"Where'd she go?" he'd asked.

"I don't know."

"Where's your dad?"

"Work."

It continued that way for a while. Him asking questions, me replying with nondescript, monosyllabic answers. I was never a very social kid, straddling the border between quiet and shy, but God knows that didn't deter Cass. He wrenched every drop of information out of me he could. And when he ran out of questions, when night fell and my driveway

38

grew dark and I started shivering, he took me by the hand, yanked me to my feet, and dragged me inside his house where his mother called my dad.

I also don't remember how long I sat quietly in the Morgans' kitchen waiting for the only parent I had set to return to the house that was no longer a home.

The next day, when I naively set up shop on the driveway again, it took all of ten minutes for Cass to join me. And the next day and the next day and the next day. For two weeks, he sat with me, chattering away, only leaving my side to get food he forced me to eat until finally, I accepted that my mother wasn't coming home. When I burst into tears, it was Cass who consoled me, dragged me into his house and force-fed me ice cream, and taught me how to play his video games until I wasn't as sad anymore.

Cass Morgan and his family were my family for ten years until my dad and I moved.

It's been three years since I've had any contact with him and now, all of a sudden, there he stands, my childhood best friend, the boy I considered a brother, open-mouthed in the doorway of the random house that happened to host the party I was forced to attend.

I barely get the chance to blink before I'm airborne, lifted off the couch and into Cass' arms, my legs dangling in the air as I'm hugged within an inch of my life. "Holy fucking shit, *Amelia*."

With every bit of force he's exerting into hugging me, I'm returning the favor tenfold. My arms wind tightly around his neck, clinging to him like he might disappear, as I bury my face in the crook, tears threatening to spill over as I blubber his name. "Cass, what the fuck?"

Way too soon for my liking, my feet hit the floor again as I'm gently set down. My head is removed from where it's attempting to burrow, soft skin grazing mine as Cass leans down to lightly press our foreheads together. "What the hell are you doing here?" he asks softly, expression laced with so much affection, it makes me want to cry.

Pulling away, I gesture at the carnage littering the room. "Rumor has it this place throws a kickass party."

"Wait a minute, you're the Amelia who was running around naked?"

"I wasn't naked." I cringe, smacking his arm. "I had underwear on."

"Oh, well, that's okay then," he quips sarcastically.

"Sorry to interrupt-" We tear our gazes off each other, only now remembering the five other people in the room staring at us with looks of utter confusion. Brow crumpled in question, Ben gestures between the two of us. "But what the fuck is going on here?"

Tugging me close, Cass wraps his arms around my shoulders, resting his chin atop my head and reminding me of how much taller than me he is. I've always hated that; as a young girl, it was very inconvenient. He won every race and game and tree-climbing competition we ever had with those damn long limbs. "Well-"

"Wait," Ben interrupts before we can give him the explanation he asked for, and I watch as some sort of realization seems to dawn on him. "*She's* Tiny?"

It's almost comical how two little words have the seated men in the room shooting upright so rapidly, the three of them exchanging wide-eyed looks I can't decipher.

"Well," Ben muses, leaning back in his seat, hands laced behind his head, the smile on his face inexplicably mischievous. "Isn't this an interesting turn of events?" His gaze flickers to Nick. "Amelia is Tiny."

If I wasn't so busy grimacing at the childhood nickname, I might've noticed the tense set to Nick's jaw, might've questioned how intensely he glares at Ben for his comment, might've wondered why Ben is teasing him in the first place. Instead, I'm caught up on hearing that damn nickname for the first time in years.

To a seven-year-old Cass and his older brother, it was the pinnacle of creative humor. To a six-year-old Amelia, it was the pinnacle of annoyance. Yet for some reason, I can't fight the nostalgic smile that fights my grimace for first place. It's been a long time since I've heard it, and it's oddly comforting. Even if it does inspire the mocking grins my friend's are wearing.

"Tiny?" My nosy blonde friends repeat, face the picture of mischief. "How *cute*."

"And fitting," Kate adds, bottom lip jutting out in a teasing pout.

"And definitely deserving of an explanation," Luna finishes. Fair brows raise expectantly, impatiently, because if there's anything she hates more than relationships, it's being left out of the loop.

"This-" I jerk an elbow back into Cass' ribs. "-is Cass. We grew up next door to each other." A gross under-exaggeration of the extent of our relationship but the watered-down version is all they need.

The girls adopt that same 'dawn of realization' expression the guys have. "This is Cassie?"

Luna barks out a laugh. "Cassie is a man?"

Fingers tug on my hair, a scoff brushing the top of my head. "Cass is definitely a man." Lowering his mouth to my ear, he mutters, "And Cassie is a little offended your best friends have no idea who I am."

Cass' comment is teasing, and when I glance upwards with an apologetic grimace, I'm only met with sympathy and understanding. Yet still, my gut twists with guilt.

My life before I moved to California isn't something I talk about. Hell, it's not even something I think about. So much happened, so much shit and chaos, and everything that led to the move was... too much. So much that I fled my home town, and abandoned my family, without so much as a goodbye, hence the radio silence over the years. I never told my friends much about Cass; I vaguely alluded to a neighbor I was close to, a gross under-exaggeration of the depth of our relationship, because that was all I could handle.

Cass, the person who knows me best in the world, or at least did at one point, knows my reasoning without me having to voice it. I know he knows it. Yet still, I find myself whispering an apology.

An arm hooks around my neck and squeezes. "Shut up. I'm just glad you're here." With one last squeeze and a kiss dropped to my temple, Cass releases me. "I can't believe you're here."

I'm not quite ready to let him go yet—I'm still not entirely sure he's really here—so I wrap my arms around his middle, hugging him tightly, relishing in the knowledge that Cass' uncanny ability to always be there when I need it seems not to have waned over the years. "Took the words right out my mouth."

～

"So you go here? To Sun Valley?"

I hum a yes, gratefully accepting my second cup of coffee of the day as Cass hands it to me. "Just started sophomore year." A year below Cass' status as a junior.

"What are the fucking odds?" Cass whistles with a shake of his head, sipping at his own coffee as he leans against the counter. Much to the chagrin of our audience, we relocated our reunion to the kitchen; it's hard to properly catch up with your long-lost kind of brother when there are five nosy pairs of ears eagerly listening in. There's only an archway separating us from the others but at least we can pretend we have privacy, with the others being out of sight and all. "How the hell have we gone a whole year living in the same town without bumping into each other?"

That, I have no answer for. It's wild to think about. And God, I can't wrap my head around the fact we both ended up here. It's not like this place is huge or particularly renowned, the university or the town. I don't buy into the whole fate thing, not really, but shit. Might make a believer of me yet. "I guess we don't run in the same circles."

"Baseball players aren't your thing anymore?"

A flashing memory of a boy, a teenager clad in a baseball uniform waving at me from a field, assaults me, and my smile abruptly drops. Cass' soon follows. "Fuck, Amelia, I'm sorry. That was a shitty joke."

"It's okay." I force my smile back into place. "You still play?"

Cass flashes a hesitant yet supremely cocky grin. "You think I would waste God-given talent?"

"Still humble too, I see." Humble but honest. For a decade, I attended every baseball game Cass ever played in and still, I never failed to be amazed at how fucking good he was at the sport. How good he *is*, I guess. I sat through countless hours of games, I even went to some of his practices. Partly because yeah, once upon a time, baseball players were my thing. Hot boys in very tight pants? Can't complain. But mostly, I endured them because I loved watching him play. I loved how good he was, *is*. I loved that he was mine to be proud of.

God, I didn't realize how much I missed that until now. "I'm gonna have to come see you play."

One of those long legs of his reaches out to tap me on the shin. "You better."

There's a pause while he sips his coffee, assessing me over the lip of his mug.

I fidget under the scrutiny. "What?"

"You look good, Mils."

"Now, imagine how good I look when I've showered."

Cass' laugh echoes off the walls. "I do have a question though."

"Yeah?"

"I don't know if I want the answer."

Intriguing. "Go on."

"Why the fuck are you wearing Nick's clothes?"

For some reason, I freeze like a guilty party caught in the act. "How do you know they're Nick's?"

Cass reaches out to flick the logo stitched on my borrowed hoodie. "That's the gym he works at."

Huh. weird. The same one I go to—once in a blue moon. "Nothing happened if that's what you're asking."

"Thank God." Cass huffs a breath of relief. "I love the guy, I do, but he is the last guy you want your little sister hooking up with."

Why? I want to ask. "There was no hooking up," is what I clarify instead.

"And there never will be."

"Okay, *Dad*." I roll my eyes. "How do you guys know each other, anyway?"

An awkward pause follows my question. "He, uh, moved in next door. After you left, his family bought the place."

"Oh." God, that's weird. Imagining him living in my house. His house, evidently, but my house, once upon a time.

"He turned your studio into a gym."

A lump settles in my throat. "Really?"

"Uh-huh." Cass hesitates again. "Do you still dance?"

That lump attempts to choke me, my knee panging with phantom pains as his simple question sinks into my bones. "Nope."

"Liar," a voice sings a second before Ben breezes into the kitchen. "I saw you shaking your ass last night."

I'm grateful for the distraction but I act annoyed, elbowing him indignantly as he props himself against the counter beside me.

Cass watches us with faint amusement laced with a touch of confusion, a little bit of awe and disbelief thrown in there for good measure, as if he can't fathom the sight. "Remind me again how you guys know each other?"

Lips curling upwards, Ben sneaks an arm around my shoulders and gives me a playful shake. "Tiny here is our favorite waitress."

"We met at Greenies," I add. Well, technically, we officially met last night but since I can't entirely remember that encounter, I'm using Greenies as a jumping off point for our relationship.

"Amelia works there." I don't know why Ben says such a simple explanation in such a loaded way, and I'm even more clueless as to why Cass' expression darkens slightly.

"She does?"

"Uh-huh. Isn't that right, Nicky?" Ben addresses the man as he strolls into the room with his empty mug in hand, an instant look of regret twisting his handsome features. "We know Amelia from Greenies, don't we?"

I'm unable to help feeling like I'm missing something as Nick's shifty gaze darts to Cass, the two of them engaging in some kind of silent, brooding conversation as the former shrugs a vague response. "Yup."

"How come I've never seen you there?" I butt in, eager to ease some of the odd tension thickening the air. I am genuinely interested in the answer; The Green Dragon is kind of an institution around here. It's a regular haunt for baseball players, hence Ben and Jackson's frequent visits. So, it doesn't quite make sense that I've never bumped into Cass there.

That is, until Ben explains with an all-too-pleased grin, "Cass isn't allowed in Greenies."

"Seriously?" I cock my head at Cass. "Why?"

He pauses his glaring long enough to adopt a sheepish expression. "I got banned freshman year."

"For doing what?"

It doesn't matter that Cass suddenly becomes tight-lipped; Ben is more than eager to share his friend's exploits. "Because your boss frowns upon public nudity."

"Especially when combined with dancing on bars."

Nick's teasing addition draws Cass' attention back to him, and the tense set of my brother's jaw returns, hostile energy emanating from him in waves. And just like that, my attempt at changing the subject, at lightening the mood, fails. "You invited her here last night?"

Nick shakes his head at the same time I clarify, "I came with my boyfriend."

"You have a boyfriend?"

"Ex-boyfriend," Nick and I correct simultaneously. I add, "We broke up last night."

"Aw, shit," Cass frowns. "Do I need to kick some ass?"

I shake my head, positive I'm the only one who hears Nick mumble a quiet, 'yes.'

A cooing 'aw' sound falling from his lips, Cass closes the short distance between us, patting the top of my head. "C'mon. Let's go for breakfast. I'll buy you pancakes."

"Pity pancakes?"

"With extra maple syrup."

"And coffee?"

"Yes." He pinches my chin between his thumb and forefinger, shaking my head gently. "You can have some coffee with your sugar."

"Ha." I poke his stomach. "As appealing as that sounds," I pause, gesturing to my outfit. "I don't think I'm fit for being in public right now."

"Look fine to me."

The words are barely out of Nick's mouth before he goes flying sideways. "Nope," Cass shakes his head rapidly from side to side. "Absolutely not."

"What?" Nick protests, staring at Cass with a look of wide-eyed, completely fake innocence, stumbling when he gets shoved again, his large body smacking into the wall. "I didn't do anything!"

"*You-*" Cass jabs an accusing finger in his roommate's direction. "-do not flirt with *her*."

"I wasn't flirting." Golden eyes roll, mischief curling the corner of his mouth upwards. "You wanna see flirting, *Cassie*, I'll show you flirting."

"I'd rather die, Nicolas," Cass deadpans, brandishing a middle finger at his chuckling friend. "I'd literally rather die."

7

AMELIA

"So you guys never..."

I groan at Ben's suggestive tone, cringing at the rude hand gestures he makes. An hour spent painstakingly laying out every detail of mine and Cass' relationship, and that is the burning question at the forefront of Ben's mind. Of everyone's minds, if the curious expressions on everyone's faces are anything to go by. Typical.

Exchanging a disgusted grimace with Cass, we simultaneously screech a very firm, "No."

"Jeez," Ben scoffs, dragging a piece of waffle through a puddle of maple syrup. "It was just a question."

"You're awfully defensive," the instigator supreme pipes up, blue eyes simpering as Luna flutters her lashes innocently.

"Trust me." The hand draped loosely over my shoulder lifts to tug on my hair. "You see this face one too many times first thing in the morning, the appeal dies pretty quick."

Scowling playfully, I elbow Cass in the ribs. "Funny."

Of all the ways I imagined today turning out, not a single rendition involved me squished in a diner booth, a mountain of greasy food spread out before me, with Cass on one side of me, the man whose bed I stole last night on the other.

Word got out quickly and within seconds, Cass and I's breakfast outing became a group affair. There was no point arguing with the clamoring insistence to join; I know better than to get between my hungover friends and food and, apparently, Cass knows the same. Apparently, his friends are as needy and clingy as mine. And apparently, as I've learned over the course of this impromptu outing, our friends get along ridiculously well. As well as Cass and I do. Another thing to add to the list of weird coincidences aligning with the whole fate thing.

It took some rallying but we managed to get everyone out of the house in somewhat of a timely manner, relocating to one of the many diners scattered around campus. It wasn't exactly a unique idea; I think every attendee of last night's party occupy the booths around us, the students of UCSV unanimous in their decision to skip class today. The place is filled to the brim with slouching, blurry-eyed, groaning young adults, all sporting the remnants of Halloween costumes in the form of glitter and fake blood and cotton cobwebs.

As odd as this whole thing is, it's kind of nice. I need a shower, and I need a nap even more, but still, it's nice. And it's better than the alternative; being holed up alone in my room, forced to process last night.

It's a shame the universe decides to deliver a big 'fuck you' and force me anyway.

I'm eating the promised pancakes Cass delivered, laughing at some joke one of the guys cracked, when a shadow falls over our table, both literally and figuratively.

My previously delicious, sugar-coated mouthful turns to cardboard when a familiar voice barks my name, as palms hit the edge of our table and the last person I want to see today appears. "We need to talk."

No hello. No apology. Not even a smile. All Dylan greets me with is an angry, accusing stare and a barked command.

I bristle at his unexpected appearance, and I'm not the only one. Silence settles around the table, everyone jolting upright, an immediate tense edge thickening the air. The only one yet to meet the infamous Dylan, Cass frowns. "Who are you?"

Dylan scoffs as though the question is preposterous. "Her boyfriend."

"Ex-boyfriend," more than one person corrects. Most notably, the snarling men on either side of me, and the seething women across from me. I don't know what Cass is snarling about; the full extent of last night's events is something he's not privy to yet, nor does he know anything about Dylan and our relationship. He hates him on principle, and I kind of love him for it. Luna and Kate, I understand; they weren't his biggest fans to begin with. And Nick… it's got to be a principle thing too. See a girl get hurt, snarl at the hurter. Relatively speaking, it seems to be a universal dislike, something in the air, because even Ben and Jackson are shooting him evil eyes and they don't even know the guy.

Dylan blinks disbelievingly at each of us in turn before his gaze lingers on Cass. Specifically, on his arm slung around the back of the booth, grazing my shoulders. "And who the fuck are you?"

Cass kisses his teeth. "I'm her brother."

"She doesn't have a brother."

"*She* is right here," I butt in, setting a placating hand on Cass' tense shoulders and willing myself not to cower as I address Dylan, "And you need to leave."

"Not until you talk to me."

"Dylan-"

"Five minutes," he interrupts, a whining quality to his voice. "Amelia, c'mon."

"I-"

"*Please.*"

"She told you to leave."

Dylan's narrowed eyes bounce to my other side. "Fuck off, Silva."

I'm jostled as Nick starts to get up, hindered by the table trapping his big body and by Jackson half-standing across from him, attempting to shove his friend back down with a warning look and a muttered 'behave.' Nick ignores him, hands fisted on the table as he death-stares Dylan, looking liable to leap over the table and tackle him at any moment. Dylan's not helping the matter, goading him with a smug sneer, just daring him to do it. But that's not even the worst of my worries; Cass, with a curious frown, glances between Dylan, Nick, and me, searching for whatever he's missing, looking close to finding it.

My head hurts at all the commotion, my wrist throbbing as Dylan pleads, "Talk to me, baby, please."

"Take a hint, Wells. Fuck off."

"Luna, for once in your life, shut your mouth."

"Hey!" Luna's voice is echoed by Jackson's, the latter abandoning his peacekeeping tendencies as he copies Nick, rising to a half-hovering stance. "Watch it."

It's sweet, his show of chivalry, but unnecessary. Unneeded. Luna's liable to attack when unprovoked. When provoked, when her murder face comes out to play… run for your damn life.

It's the appearance of said murder-face that has me interrupting the chaos, raising my voice a couple of decibels to be heard over the bickering. "That's enough."

I'm surprised when the yammering actually stops, and I shrink a little when all eyes turn to me. Resisting the urge to massage my temples, I blow out a relenting breath and look at Dylan. "Five minutes."

Five minutes in exchange for some peace. For the sake of my blood pressure. So Luna can maintain a squeaky-clean record. To keep my dirty laundry from being aired to a diner full of my peers.

A round of protesting calls of my name breaks out but I silence my friends with a look and a promise. "I'll be right back."

Across from me, Luna harrumphs loudly, side-eyeing Dylan menacingly. "You better be."

Before anyone can stop me, I nudge Cass out of the booth and shimmy to my feet. I ignore the hand Dylan offers me in favor of walking straight past him, not sparing him or anyone else at the table another glance.

Heavy footsteps follow me through the diner and out the front door. They come to a stop when I do, as I lean against a wall just around the corner, far away enough from prying eyes and ears, close enough to yell for rescue if needed. Arms crossed protectively over my chest, I hold my head up high. "What do you want?"

For someone so intent on talking a moment ago, Dylan is silent for a long minute, his narrowed gaze fixed on my clothes. "What are you wearing?"

I hug myself a little tighter. "Clothes."

Dylan's jaw clenches. "Who's?"

Nick's hoodie, Ben's sweats, but he doesn't need to know that. "Is this seriously what you wanted to talk about?"

"It's a fucking question, Amelia," he snaps, and I force myself not to flinch, to remain steady. "I'm allowed to ask questions when my girlfriend's wearing another man's clothes."

As I rake my hands over my face in frustration, a chorus of my friend's voice rings in my ears. "*Ex*-girlfriend."

"C'mon, Amelia." He reaches out to take my hands but I jerk away, keeping them steadfastly fisted at my side. "You don't mean that."

"Yes, Dylan, I really do."

"Amelia," Dylan groans my name like I'm annoying him, like I'm the problem here. "You're gonna throw a year away over one little mistake?"

I can't help but laugh. One little mistake. God, we have different definitions of 'little.' "You fucked another girl, Dylan."

"It was one time."

Because that makes it so much better. "We're done," I state firmly, finally. " Leave me alone."

"Amelia!"

I try to leave but I'm halted by a hand around my bicep, a hand I never want to touch me again. Ripping my arm from his grasp, I whirl around, palms meeting a hard chest as I shove him away with all of my might. "Don't fucking touch me."

"You're being dramatic."

"Dramatic?" Shaking my head, I roll up my sleeve, thrusting my bruised wrist, the dark purple imprint of his fingers on my pale skin, in his face. "You fucking hurt me, Dylan. You *bruised* me."

He swats my hand away without looking, dismissing me with a wave and a handful of words. "That was an accident."

An accident. It's always an accident. "Stay away from me."

Dylan's nostrils flare in unison with his temper as he steps forward, red creeping up his neck and encroaching on his jaw. "You're a fucking hypocrite. Giving me shit while you're strutting around in another man's clothes? Cozying up to him at breakfast?"

"I wasn't-"

"*Brother*," he scoffs, distrust written all over his tense features. "Do I look stupid?"

"Yeah," a deep, accented voice drawls. "You do."

I glance aside as Nick rounds the corner, casual in tone and stance, entirely un-casual in expression. That strong jaw of his looks fit to shatter at any moment, he's clenching it so hard. His smirk is tight, forced, not the easy going one I've become familiar with. And his eyes...

they're burning. Like golden flames. Furious, golden flames firmly fixed on Dylan.

Dylan snickers sarcastically. "Good one, Silva."

It didn't click before, Dylan using Nick's last name, but it does this time. The familiarity in the way he uses it, the venom behind his tone, it registers with me this time. "You two know each other?"

Neither man answers; they're too busy glowering at each other. I'm beginning to feel a little ignored, honestly, when Nick finally tears his eyes off my ex just long enough to check me over quickly. "You okay?"

"She's fine," Dylan answers for me.

"I wasn't talking to you."

"Mind your own fucking business."

Jesus Christ.

Before they have a chance to whip their dicks out and start measuring, I clear my throat. "I'm going back inside." Dylan opens his mouth to argue but I cut him off like he so often does to me. "Don't follow me. Don't call me. Don't talk to me ever again. Stay away from me," I repeat. "I'm done."

Dylan scoffs and splutters, no actual words coming from his mouth as he gapes at me. I can practically see his tiny brain whirring, searching for a viable argument, but I walk away before he can find one.

I half expect him to follow me as I head back inside but he doesn't; of his own volition or because a certain inexplicably angry man is holding him off, I'm not sure, but either way, I'm grateful. I'm grateful for the crowded diner too because the sea of people means no one notices my re-entry so I'm free to take a detour. Cutting across the room, I make for the hallway housing the bathrooms, seeking a second of privacy before I'm bombarded with questions.

The second I'm out of anyone's line of sight, I sag against the wall, the fire that fuelled me when giving Dylan the boot abruptly fizzling out. It's the first moment I've had to myself all day, the first semblance of quiet, the first second to think, and it's like everything catches up with me all at once.

My boyfriend cheated on me.

My boyfriend hurt me.

I no longer have a boyfriend.

I hate him, I genuinely hate him, and I have no rational explanation for the sudden burning behind my eyes because I shouldn't be crying. I can't cry over him. I'm not allowed to cry over him, according to the rule I made about thirty seconds ago, yet still, wet eyes become wet cheeks as salty tears escape and track paths down my cheeks. My wrist aches as I dig the heels of my hand into my leaking eyes, an attempt to stem the stream but it only makes it worse. Within seconds, it's a full-on sob fest, embarrassing sounds escaping me, my body shaking as I cry over someone who doesn't deserve it.

I jump when fingers graze my arm suddenly, recoiling from the mystery touch. A croaked, incomprehensible but undeniably panicked noise leaves me.

"Shit." Nick snatches his hand away, my visceral reaction making him back up a step. "Fuck, sorry. I didn't mean to scare you. I said your name but…"

"It's fine." Sniffling, I dry my face as best I can with the sleeve of my hoodie. Crap, no. Not my hoodie. His hoodie. I got my tears and snot all over Nick's damn hoodie. Fuck. "Sorry."

"It's fine," he parrots my assurance. Ensuring a safe distance between us, he leans against the wall opposite me, so careful as he regards me. He doesn't say anything else, not a word, but I see the silent question on his face.

With a sigh, I swipe at my eyes again, sucking in a steadying breath before employing what seems to be my new favorite phrase. "I'm fine," I insist. "Really. I don't even know why I'm crying."

Nick's silence continues, seemingly content with surveying me, and I shift under the attention. I've never been one for silence, particularly those of the awkward variety, which is probably why I break it by blurting out, "Thanks for the save. Again."

"My pleasure," he says like he means it. I'm tempted to ask why he came after me, why he swooped in once again. But that has its down-falls. Potential embarrassment when he reveals it to be accidental—he happened to stumble upon us. Definite pity because poor little Amelia. And more embarrassment, again because of poor little Amelia, so back-boneless being pushed around by a man, so weak being constantly saved by another. So, yeah. *No.* I keep quiet, and silence settles between us, only permeated by my occasional sniffling and the odd post-sob hiccup.

"So about that rebound you mentioned last night," Nick suddenly says, and I jerk in a mixture of surprise and disgust for my past, drunken self. "Anyone in mind?"

"*What?*"

"Because I'd be more than willing,"

"Nick!"

"*What?*" He mimics my tone and the wide-eyed look I'm giving him. "I'm hot. I'm good in bed. I come with no strings attached. I'm perfect."

"And modest."

"Honest," he corrects.

Choking on a disbelieving breath, I'm incapable of doing anything but blinking at him in confusion for a long moment before my tongue untangles itself. "Are you seriously hitting on me right now?"

"Is it making you feel better?"

Is a hot man propositioning me making me feel better? "A little."

"Then, yeah." Perfect white teeth glint in the shitty diner lighting as full lips stretch in a self-satisfied smile. "I am."

"You are unbelievable." Practically able to see the dirty joke forming on his lips, I cut him off before he can say it. "*No.* Thank you," *yeah, Amelia, thank the man for offering to pity-fuck you,* "but no."

Nick is unphased by the rejection. He simply shrugs his broad shoulders, his smile never faltering as he makes his exit. "If you change your mind, you know where to find me."

"I won't," I call after his retreating form, a smile on my face that definitely wasn't there a couple of minutes ago, and I wonder if that was his intention all along.

8

AMELIA

THE SECOND I walk into my apartment, a storm hits.

A tall, slender, blonde storm with a penchant for gossip and drama.

"How-" Luna shrieks, slamming the front door shut behind her and tossing the heels in her hand aside. "-the actual fuck did I not know that your old neighbor Cassie is *the* Cass Morgan?"

With a tired sigh, I collapse on our sofa, letting my own heels drop to the floor. "Lu, I didn't even know my Cass was *the* Cass Morgan. I didn't even know there was a *the* Cass Morgan."

Apparently, I've been living under a rock for the past year. A rock impermeable to any baseball-related news. Because my Cass, Cass Morgan, *the* Cass Morgan, is something of a legend around here. He's the star of UCSV's baseball team, unsurprisingly. Sun Valley's very own household name. Lu knew who he was, Kate knew who he was, and I'm a little embarrassed that I didn't.

Oblivious, I say.

Isolated, Luna claims, from all things non-Dylan related.

Either way, the information skipped right over me.

"Did you guys really never hook up? Because there were major touchy-feely vibes going on there and I've never seen you willingly partake in PDA with, like, anyone. Ever."

I almost give myself whiplash shaking my head so hard. "Definitely not. I told you, he's like my brother."

"Brother-brother or step-brother because the latter..."

Luna's joke ends in a grunt as my foot hits her stomach. "You're sick."

"Forget Cass." Kate plops down on the sofa beside me, legs crossed beneath her, expression insistent. "What happened with Dylan?"

"Oh yeah! Tell us about that," Lu screeches, her lithe body completing our trio as she snuggles in between us, her head hitting my lap at the same time her feet land on Kate's. "God, you've had an eventful twenty-four hours, hm?"

"Hey." I poke the narrow strip of belly exposed above the waistband of her borrowed sweats—Jackson's, undoubtedly. "Pot, kettle, black."

In a typical show of Luna-style avoidance, she pretends to be overly intrigued by a chip in her manicure. "I have no idea what you're talking about."

Kate snorts, making Luna jolt when she tickles the soles of her feet. "Okay, Mrs Oscar Jackson."

One of the decorative pillows littering our sofa smacks Kate in the face, and I get a wallop too as punishment for my giggle. "You two are so dramatic," the queen of drama chastises us.

"And you," Kate snickers, "are officially dicked down."

Luna's head flies upright. "Take that back."

My fingers yank on a lock of her hair. "You did sleep over."

Her head falls back into my lap again, an accusing look directed upwards at me. "So did you!"

"I passed out," I correct her. "Next to Kate, not a hook-up."

"And you were all over him this morning," Kate adds, earning herself another pillow-slap.

"I was *not*."

A scoffed laugh escapes me. "Tell that to the imprint of your ass on his lap."

"You!" A white-tipped finger stabs into my chest. "Stop tryna change the subject! Dylan. Break-up. Go."

Despite the gut feeling insisting that I'm not going to get out of this without providing details, I still aim for nonchalance. "We just broke up."

Slowly, with a sigh, Luna sits up. "You just broke up," she repeats, blinking at me. "Seriously?"

Avoiding her gaze, I shrug.

"Nope." Blonde hair flies as Luna's head shakes from side to side. "Bulllshit. Cough it up."

My relenting sigh echoes off the walls. I could keep playing dumb, could try to keep the full extent of last night under wraps, but honestly, I'm too tired.

So, I cough it up. I give as thorough a play-by-play of last night as I can tolerate, skillfully glossing over the more… aggressive aspects. I've already had one breakdown today; I'm not shooting for a second.

And I would've gotten away with it, too, if it weren't for that damn perceptive Kate.

Lips pursed, she reaches across Luna's lap. Gentle fingers seek out my arm, holding me below the elbow and lifting until my sleeve slips down, revealing the evidence of my half-truths. "And this?"

Wriggling my arm out of her grip, I shrug. "Oh, uh, I think I got that on my half-naked jaunt this morning."

"I saw it last night." Kate debunks my lie easily. "I saw your hip too."

Lu's ears prick up like a freaking dog's. "What happened to your hip?"

"Nothing." I slap away the hands making a beeline for the waistband of my sweats. Nick's sweats, I remind myself. God, I dread having to give them back, and not only because they're comfy as hell. "I don't remember, okay?" I lie through my teeth. "I must've fallen or something."

"Amelia," Kate murmurs my name gently. "You don't have to lie to us."

"I'm not lying."

"You're protecting him." Luna stands with a huff, hands braced on her hips as she pins me in place with a no-nonsense stare. "Like you did last-"

Me abruptly shooting to my feet cuts Luna off. "I need to shower."

I need to not have this conversation.

I need to not think about him or my wrist or anything.

My friends call after me as I flee the room but I ignore them, shutting out their voices with the soft click of my bedroom door locking. My sigh of relief mingles with the thud of my forehead hitting the closed door, resting there for a moment as I relish the silence I've been trying to avoid all day. Because that's the theme of today, it seems. Avoidance. And I intend to continue with it as long as possible.

My tiny bedroom has never looked as good as it does right now, but it's nothing compared to my microscopic ensuite. The shower calls to me as I stride towards it, peeling off my clothes and letting them fall to the floor as I go. It's as I reach to flick on the shower, practically purring as warm water begins to stream, that I get a glimpse of myself in the mirror hanging above the sink.

Jesus, I look like shit.

A face so pale it's almost transparent stares back at me. Half-lidded, red-rimmed eyes look a little less green than usual. My hair really takes the cake though; at some point last night, someone piled it into a sorry excuse for a bun and there it remains, like a bird's nest atop my head, limp curls making drastic attempts for escape. It's a miracle Cass even recognised me, to be honest.

It's a miracle Nick hit on me, even if it was a flirtation born of pity.

Any semblance of a smile that might've been summoned when thinking of the odd moment we shared suddenly dies when my gaze lands on the ugly purple bruises—the perfect shape and size of finger-tips—peppering my hip. They're so small, only noticeable due to the stark contrast between their color and my alabaster skin, yet the disgust swirling in my gut is anything but small. The disappointment, in the person who did it to me as well as in myself for letting it happen. The embarrassment, the anger, none of them are small and they all meld together in a cesspool of overwhelming emotion I can't stem because I can't take my eyes off the source.

Only when steam obscures my view do I step away from the mirror, the immense need to scrub last night from my body overtaking my morbid fascination. Scalding water burns my skin as I step into the shower, a burn I'm grateful for because, shit, I'd rather feel that than the ache in my chest. I'd rather feel the tingling uncomfortableness of over-sensitized skin as I scrub and scrub and scrub, wishing the discolored contusions would wash down the drain with the rest of the dirt and grime.

No such luck.

~

It's the middle of the night when my bedroom door creaks open, light spilling in the crack along with two shadows. Ordinarily, a girl would be worried at the sudden intrusion. And I probably would be.

If one of the shadows wasn't wearing a pink satin nightgown and bunny slippers, the other clad in the t-shirt I've been looking for for a month.

Pausing the movie I was half-watching, I set my laptop on the night-stand as they creep towards me, jostling each other and shushing each other, trying to be quiet and failing miserably. Without a word but with a heavy sigh, I shove down my duvet so they can crawl beneath, a body curling up on either side of me.

"I'm sorry." A lithe arm wraps around my middle, a bunny slipper poking my foot. "I didn't mean to push."

"I know." Luna never does. I learned very soon in our relationship that in Lu's mind, boundaries are made to be pushed. And push, she does.

Frequently.

With the best of intentions, of course, a fact that's proven when she whispers, "I'm worried about you."

That, I know too.

I set a hand on her arm, my palm coasting up and down the smooth skin. "I wanna forget about it, okay? I don't wanna talk about him."

The satin hair wrap Kate wears to bed at night is soft against my skin as she tucks her head into the crook of my neck, a third arm joining our pile as she wraps her fingers around mine and squeezes gently. "It might help."

It's not often that I disagree with Kate, mostly because the girl is always right, but this is one of those rare occasions. I don't feel like it'll help. I feel like talking about him, about it, will only make it worse. Make me worse. "Can we talk about something else please?"

Two sighs sound, one more of a disapproving huff, the other disappointed. "Fine." Luna relents, and I almost wish she hadn't because the playful grin lighting up her face as she props herself up on her elbow and peers down at me is undoubtedly worse than discussing my past relationship would've been. "How about you tell us what's going on with you and Nicolas Silva?"

I choke on a laugh of disbelief. "Excuse me?"

"There was a vibe," my delusional friend sings, fair brows waggling suggestively.

"There was no vibe!"

Husky laughter harmonizes with Luna's evil cackle. "Oh, there absolutely was."

"Kate!" God, do I hate when they gang up on me like this.

Shrugging, her lips curl up at the corners. "Just saying."

Like I said, delusional. Both of them. The only vibe between Nick and I was discomfort. Awkwardness. Intense, consuming embarrassment. A hint of kindness I wasn't expecting but I was grateful for all the same. Unless the girls happened to witness our bathroom encounter—which I still maintain was born out of pity—nothing akin to the vibe they're hinting at existed between Nick and I.

Luna makes a humming noise as she stretches out beside me, still grinning. "He's a total player, you know."

I didn't know that. I suspected it, definitely; the guy looks like heartbreak wrapped up in a perfectly sculpted package. He looks like the kind of guy to ruin a girl's life, honestly, with one wink of those pretty golden eyes.

"But he seems nice."

Kate elbows me, lips pursed in a sorry attempt to hide her smile. "He does."

"And he's hot."

I grunt a non-answer, careful not to give Luna what she's not-so-discreetly poking around for. Unsurprisingly, my silence does nothing to deter her. "Excellent in bed, too."

Side-eying her, I quirk a brow. "You know that from experience?" I know the answer before Luna provides it; if she'd brought Nick home before, I definitely would've noticed. And if she'd been in that house before last night, we would've known about it; Luna is a lot of things, and shy is not one of them. Her exploits are a regular breakfast topic between the three of us and a guy like Nick undoubtedly would've been breaking news.

Knowing all this, I still feel oddly relieved at the shake of her head. For the sake of Jackson, obviously. Nice guys never like sharing."

"People talk," Luna explains with a nonchalant wave. "Particularly drunk girls lamenting over the boy who ghosted them. They talk *a lot*."

My nose wrinkles. Sure, Kate, Luna, and I share the intimate details of our hookups on a regular basis. Or at least, Kate and Luna do; I've never had much to share. But that's done privately. Quietly. Whispered or giggled over a cup of coffee while hunched over a table tucked away in the corner of whatever cafe we stumble in.

Yelling that information for everyone around to hear? I'm not a fan. I value my privacy. I couldn't imagine having my sex life broadcasted around campus for all to comment on.

"Is there a point to your rambling?"

"Is there ever?" Kate quips, earning her a pink bunny slipper to the face.

Luna glares at Kate momentarily before returning her attention to me. "You know what they say." At my blank stare, Luna continues, "The best way to get over someone is to get under someone new."

"That is terrible advice." Kate groans, the slapping sound of her face-palming ringing in my ears. "Please, do not take relationship advice from her."

"Hey, I'm very wise." Playing offended, Luna scoffs, mouth gaping as she flattens a hand against her chest. The charade only lasts a moment before she breaks, a smile splitting her face once again as she nudges me. "He asked for your number."

Suspicion, and something else I can't put a name to, tickles my spine. "When?"

"Like, an hour ago. Nick asked Jackson to ask me for it. Cass slapped him."

I snort. Sounds about right. "Did you give it to him?"

My friend feigns offense once again. "Excuse me, *no*. Girl code." Like before, it takes no time for her grin to slip out again. "Do you want me to?"

Dark fingers flick her on the forehead. "Hey, how about we let her be single for longer than ten seconds before tryna shuck her off on another man?"

Luna flops onto her back with a huff. "You're so boring."

"It's called being sensible," Kate retorts. "You should try it some time."

"Like I said. *Boring*."

9

NICK

I was eighteen the first time I stepped foot in a boxing ring.

It's kind of a lost year, my eighteenth year. A hazy sea of vague, nondescript memories clouded by too many emotions. But the first time I slipped on a pair of gloves and got the shit beaten out of me, I remember as clearly as if it had happened yesterday, not five years ago.

It's a hard thing to forget.

In the blink of an eye—or, more accurately, in the time it took a fist to smash into my cheekbone—I fell in love with the sport. With the raw, vicious power behind it. With the way it made my brain turn off, made me forget all the shit going on during that time of my life. With the way it gave me an outlet for all the anger I had back then. I needed it.

Just like I need it now.

The tires of my truck screech as I tear into the gym parking lot, more eager to throw myself into a good sparring session than I have been in weeks. I crave the mental shut-off, the mindlessness, when you can't think about anything other than keeping your breathing steady and your movements sharp.

My brain's been too busy for my liking lately, and I like the object of its attention, its affection, even less.

Fucking Amelia.

Tiny.

My waitress crush, as Ben has coined her.

Sister, as Cass describes her.

"What are the odds?" Cass has been muttering on repeat over the course of the last week, and I'm inclined to agree. What *are* the fucking odds that the girl I've been eyeing for the last couple of weeks, or months, maybe, is my best friend's sister? Huh? What are the actual chances of that happening, and who the hell did I piss off in a past life to make it happen to me?

If I were a better person, the big reveal would've firmly sequestered Amelia to the off-limits portion of my psyche. I don't need it, the drama she would unwittingly, most definitely bring. And I tried, I really did. Maybe not when I cornered her in the diner and offered myself up on a silver platter. Or when I asked Jackson for her number and got clattered upside the head as a consequence.

But after that, in the week since it all went down, I did. I've kept my distance. She comes around the house, I make myself scarce. She comes up in conversation, which she so often does, I keep my mouth shut. This is the longest I've gone without visiting Greenies in two years, since I first started at UCSV, but I've stayed away. Physically, I've got this no-Amelia thing down.

Mentally... that's another story.

No matter how hard I try, I can't stop thinking about the girl. Even without her physical presence, she's always there, lurking in the back of my mind, and it's sickening. Off-balancing. Fucking weird because I've met the girl, what, twice? She shouldn't occupy me so wholly. No matter how... poignant our encounters have been. The incessant thoughts of her are like a fucking plague and it's messing with me, throwing me off my game.

Twice this week, I've gone out with the guys, fully intending to find a warm body to occupy my evening. And twice, I've ended my night at home alone with cold sheets and a limp dick because apparently, my dick has decided he's partial to green-eyed red-heads who are not-technically-but-definitely-in-spirit related to my best friend.

So, yeah. I need to blow off some steam and I have every intention of taking my frustrations out on a punching bag. And it's safe to say those frustrations bubble up a little when my ringing phone interrupts my rushed retrieval of my gym bag from the truck's back seat.

With a sigh, and no choice because I know a relentless woman when she raises me, I accept the call. "*Mamãe? Tudo jóia?*"

A wince twists my features when my mother's heavily accented voice screams down the line. *"Nicolas? Você tá me ouvindo?"*

"Sim, mamãe." I'm pretty sure everyone in the parking lot can hear her. Sometimes, when I go a while without seeing her, I forget my mom only has one fucking volume. *I'm from a big family* is always her excuse. *I have to be loud to be heard.* "You don't have to yell."

"Desculpa," she chuckles at a much more tolerable decibel before continuing in stilted English. "You sound tired, Nico."

"Obrigado," I drawl sarcastically as I shoulder open the double doors leading to the gym's reception, nodding hello to the guy at reception as I head for the locker room. "I'm fine, *mamãe.* Everything okay?"

It's my mom's turn to draw on sarcasm. "Something has to be wrong for me to call you, hm?"

Ai, meu Deus. *"Não."*

"E?" she presses, impatience leaking into her tone as she fires a round of questions at me in one long breath, the volume increasing with each one. *"Me diga.* How are you? How's school? How're the boys?"

"I'm good. School is good. The boys are good."

She makes an annoyed noise and I can picture the golden eyes I inherited rolling. "Don't give me too many details, Nico."

"I don't have any details to give."

"Hm." It's amazing, really, how one little noise has my hackles raising. "That's not what Lynn said."

My steps stutter slightly at the mention of Cass' mom. "Lynn, *hein?"* Fuck, it's always a recipe for disaster when our moms get to talking. I used to be grateful for Lynn's presence, for the support she gave my mom when she needed it most.

And then, my common sense kicked in and I realized a higher power shoved them together to make my life hell.

"Tell me about Amelia," she says, and I find myself wishing I'd never answered the damn phone. At the mention of the very person I'm trying to forget, I groan and, *foda,* doesn't Ma pounce on that. "What? What's wrong? You don't like her? Lynn said she's a lovely girl. Cried when Cass called her, *sabe. Você a conheceu, Nico, não é?"*

I am never answering my phone again. *"Mamãe, basta.* I met her, like, twice. I don't know the girl."

You want to, though, a tiny evil voice in my head snickers.

"Oh." Ma huffs a noise of disappointment.

"Is that the only reason you called me? For gossip?"

"No," she scoffs indignantly. "I was going to ask if you're coming home for Thanksgiving."

I snort. As excuses go, that's a pretty shit one. "You know I am."

"*Ótimo.*" A pause. "So you really have nothing to tell me?"

Jesus Christic.

∼

I'm two hours deep into destroying a punching bag when music drifts towards me.

No. Not drifts. *Stampedes.*

My eardrums are assaulted by heavy, brooding, really fucking loud music. Too loud for a weekday evening, especially with the slight hangover I'm nursing from last night's failed hook-up attempt. So loud it fucks with my concentration, my glove skimming the sack of leather suspended before me completely.

"*Merda,*" I curse as I shuck off my glove, leaving my hands wrapped because hopefully, it won't take too long to rip the head off whatever *filho da puta* is ignoring gym etiquette. Irritation prickling the back of my neck, I stride towards the source of the music; one of the studios plastered wall-to-wall with mirrors. My fist raises to pound on the ajar door, intending on grabbing the attention of whoever's disturbing the peace. However, my hand rapidly falls when the first knock pushes the door more open, revealing the culprit.

I expected to walk in on a vigorous workout. I thought there'd be some chick in here smashing out a pilates routine because that's what this room is usually used for. I didn't expect to intrude on a girl spread-eagled on the floor.

But there she is. Lying on her back in the center of the room, limbs akimbo and eyes closed, is Amelia. Concern grips me for a split second, my mind instantly conjuring up the worst, until I note the prominent rise and fall of her chest and her fingers tapping the beat of the music against the wooden floor.

She's not injured, then. Taking a break. Or experiencing some kind of a breakdown. Maybe carrying out a personal therapy session. Whatever's happening here, I should back away quietly. Pretend I was never there and didn't see a thing and keep up my perfect record of avoidance.

Instead, I stand there watching her like every bit the stalker Ben claims I am.

Goddamn, she really is beautiful.

Despite the godawful thumping music, she looks peaceful lying there. Serene. Her expression is as carefree as I've ever seen it, completely placid. Nothing but tight black shorts and a matching sports bra cover that trim body, baring so much creamy, pale skin for my viewing pleasure, showcasing the constellations of freckles dotted all over her.

I'm so fucking entraced, it takes a solid couple of seconds for me to realize the music has stopped, only a voice filling the unexpected silence jerking me from my reverie. "You gonna stand there all day or would you prefer to take a picture?"

God, you have no idea.

My gaze flits upwards to meet the green one laser-focused on me. A minute ago, despite the godawful thumping music, she looked peaceful lying there. Serene. Her expression was as carefree as I've ever seen it, void of a crumpled brow or narrowed eyes, or worried lips. Now, it's contorted in a combination of all three aimed directly at me and my creeping self.

Shit.

Clearing my throat, I aim for nonchalance as I lean against the doorway, crossing my arms over my chest. "Heard the noise. Came to investigate," I explain, copying the arched brow she's sporting. "Needed a nap?"

"I was warming down," Amelia snaps as she clambers upright. Fuck, is that nickname of hers apt. She really is tiny, and not just height-wise. She's short, yeah, but she's slight too. Frail. Like she must snap under too much pressure. Not quite the frame of the strong, exceptional dancer Cass' described more than once.

An irritated noise has my gaze rising again, settling on the pink lips pouting indignantly at me. "Did you need something? Other than to stare at my boobs?"

"I wasn't staring at your tits." My own lips curl upwards in a lazy grin. "I can if you want me to."

Amelia huffs in annoyance as she flounces away from me, stomping her way to the other side of the room where a green tote bag sits next to a pair of battered sneakers. When she bends at the waist to pull on a pair of socks and hoist up her bag, I choke on a groan. She didn't want me staring at her tits so I'm sure the ass is off-limits too but fuck. I couldn't look away if I tried. It's a perfect view, and I have the sudden urge to weep when I'm deprived of it as she straightens, shoves her feet into her shoes, and whirls to face me again. "Seriously, Nick," she sighs, fiddling with the strap of her tote as she slings it over her shoulder. "What do you want?"

I cock my head at her, mimicking the way she's staring at me. "Someone's in a mood."

"Maybe I'm just not in the mood for you."

Someone woke up on the snarky side of the bed. A good look on her but a concerning one. "Hey." I move to block her way when she tries to slip past me, hating how she flinches at the small movement. "Did something happen?"

Did that little shit do something again? is what I want to ask but I'm shooting for subtlety.

Amelia sighs again, an unsteady noise, before shaking her head. "No."

The tension holding my shoulders taut eases. "Are you okay?"

A tired attempt at a smile lights up her pretty face. "Getting kinda sick of you asking me that."

"Getting kinda sick of asking it."

"I'm fine." Her favorite response. "Bad mood."

The delusional section of my brain is disappointed she doesn't offer up more. It whines at me to dig deeper but I slap it away, holding off on the urge. Instead, I let her slip out of the room, following close behind and gently, non-threateningly looping my fingers around the crook of her elbow when she makes for the exit. "Wanna blow off some steam?" When she scoffs and shoots me a look of disbelief, I laugh. "That wasn't a line." My free hand gestures toward the row of punching bags lined up neatly in the corner. "I meant that."

"Boxing?" The freckles on her nose clump together as she wrinkles it, gaze flitting between me and the suspended leather sacks. "You box?"

I hum a yes, something in my belly pulsing when I see a flash of interest in those alluring eyes. "Do you fight competitively?" she asks, head tilted in that curious, assessing way I find entirely too endearing. In a way that exposes the slope of her neck and makes me want to trace the curve with my fingers to see how silky the skin there is, to test for soft spots.

I'm so absorbed in, obsessed with, her fucking neck, I almost forget to answer her question. "Nah," I force out the word. It's always been a hobby for me. My version of therapy. Beating the shit out of other people —and getting the shit beat of me—for a living never appealed to me. Nor did it appeal to my mother; I came home after a sparring session once with a black eye and she cried for two days. "You wanna try it?"

I see it on the tip of her tongue. The 'yes' she wants to say if only to curb her curiosity. I see it die too, get swallowed down as she shakes her head. "No, thanks."

I shrug to hide my disappointment. "If you change your mind, you know where I live. Knowing a little self-defense can't hurt."

Amelia's spine straightens, the physical embodiment of her guard flying up, and I instantly know I've said the wrong thing. "If you want," I add quickly. "Or, like I said, if you wanna blow off some steam."

Drop the defenses, querida. I'm not tryna take care of you. Tryna help you take care of yourself.

Dainty fingers fiddle with the strap of her bag, straight white teeth chewing on her bottom lip thoughtfully. "Maybe," she muses slowly, quietly. "Some other time."

A grin tugs at my mouth. Better than an out-and-out no. "I'll hold you to that."

Green eyes roll. "Bye, Nicolas."

This time, when she tries to leave, I let her. I keep my hands to myself as she strides away but when she glances over her shoulder, the smallest upward tilt to her lips, and waggles her finger in a wave, I just can't fucking help myself. "Need a ride?"

Laughter, real, genuine, laughter, floats towards me, and fuck if I don't smile a little harder. "I'd rather walk."

10

AMELIA

Two weeks have passed since the Great Halloween Incident when Cass struts into Greenies, causing me to pause the tedious task of marrying ketchup bottles. Suspicion narrows my eyes at the sight of him.

Not because he's at Greenies; his presence here has become a regular thing during my shifts since I got his ban expunged. All it cost me was spending every weekend for probably the rest of my life in this shithole.

No, it's the smirk on his face, screaming of trouble, and the way he's swaggering towards the counter that has a groan bubbling up in my throat. He's got his phone pressed to his ear, humming into the receiver as he slides onto a stool across from me. "I'm with her right now."

"Who's that?" I mouth, leaning over the counter to try to get a peek at the caller ID, yelping when I'm unceremoniously shoved away by a palm to the forehead. "Hey!"

Ignoring me, Cass holds up a single finger in the universal, condescending as fuck symbol for 'just a minute.' I pout as he *uhms* and *ahs* into the phone, giving me one-sided dribs and drabs of a conversation, clearly taking sick pleasure in my obvious impatience. "Okay, I'm putting you on speaker." Stabbing a thumb at the screen, Cass finally holds the phone out between us and sings, "Say hello to your second favorite child, Patrick."

Patrick? "Dad?"

The voice that replies sparks a lonely pang in my chest. "Hey, sweetie."

"Hi," I reply slowly, eyeballing Cass with no small amount of confusion and suspicion. "How did you get his number?"

"He called me!" Cass' free hand rises, his fingers forming the scout's salute. Funny, because he was never a scout and his honor is questionable. The quirk of his lip proves it. "This time."

There's no time to question why my dad rang Cass instead of me; I'm too busy internally groaning at the renewed friendship that, God, drove me freaking mad over the years. It's only fair, I suppose. It's not like I haven't been sharing almost-daily phone calls with Cass' mom. Hell, I talk to the woman more than I talk to Dad.

Our first conversation in almost four years was little more than sobs and unintelligible wept words. For so many years, Lynn Morgan was my parent. The only mother I ever really knew. And I was her daughter, her only daughter. I missed her, I always missed her, but the weight of it didn't truly hit me until that first call connected and a hesitant but oh-so-comforting voice murmured my name, and the tears just erupted.

Like Cass' visit to my workplace, his mother's calls quickly became the norm. Brief check-ins that always leave me feeling a little guilty because I wonder if she's calling only to check I haven't disappeared again.

That disheartening thought doesn't have long to linger; it's elbowed aside by the playful groan echoing through the phone. "I can't tell if I'm happy or terrified that you two found each other again."

Cass and I share a grin. Lynn shared a similar sentiment earlier this week; she'd added our time apart was the universe's way of balancing out the chaos we caused over the decade we spent joined at the hip. Admittedly, we were menaces in our younger years. Always trolling for trouble, always causing our parents all kinds of grief, and always proud of it. Sometimes, I wonder if, buried deep, they were a little glad for the break.

"You two burn anything down yet?" Dad continues in a droll tone.

"Not yet." Cass' waggling brows are audible in his teasing tone. "But the night is young."

The two men share a laugh, and my face can't decide whether to grin or grimace. "Did you call just to make fun of us?"

With a clearing of his throat, Dad sombers, and my gut tells me exactly what he's going to say. "I've got some bad news, sweetie."

I have to work for Thanksgiving.

I say the words in my head in unison with Dad as he utters them aloud.

My eyes flutter closed momentarily, puffing out a disappointed but unsurprised sigh. I should've expected it. I spent the last two alone— why would this year be any different?

I've never resented my dad for his hectic work schedule when I was younger. After the Morgans entered my life—or, rather, after I crashed into theirs—the many, many hours without him were wholly occupied by them. I barely noticed if I'm being brutally honest. But after the move, when it was just me and him, that's when his absence became glaringly obvious. That's when the resentment began to creep in, an emotion I'm capable of keeping at bay because, hey, such is the life of a surgeon's daughter. I always lose my grip a little around the holidays, though.

"It's fine." God, I've said that word more over the past couple of weeks than I have in my entire life.

"I'm sorry. I know I promised."

A soft touch caresses the back of my hand. Opening my eyes, I return Cass' sad, sympathetic smile. "Seriously, Dad. Don't worry about it."

"Silver lining," Cass chimes in, squeezing my hand tightly. "You can spend Thanksgiving with us."

A weird tingle of excitement swirls in my belly as nerves stutter my speech. "Really?"

Cass hums an enthusiastic yes. "It was Mom's idea. I'm under strict instructions to kidnap you if you say no."

A snort leaves me even as apprehension settles in my gut. It's a tempting offer. So damn tempting. I want to—I don't know if I can. I'm not sure I can do it, physically or mentally. In the three years since I left, I've never once had the urge to go back. My chest tightens at the mere thought. My palms get clammy. A phantom, metallic taste fills my mouth. A dull, non-existent ache emanates from my long-since healed kneecap. I... "I don't know."

"I think it's a good idea, Mils," Dad says gently. "It'd make me feel better, knowing you're not alone."

"Mom said the same."

Bastards. Guilt-tripping bastards.

The fingers not being held hostage by Cass drum rapidly against the counter in an off-beat rhythm as I contemplate my choices. Granted, being alone on Thanksgiving fucking sucks. And while it might've been a while, Lynn's Thanksgiving dinners are ingrained in my memory; my mouth waters at the prospect of them. And, beneath the unease and the guilt, I want to see the Morgans again. But I'm worried about what seeing them will lead to, worried the things I've worked hard to bury deep will arise. Plain and simple; I'm scared.

"Hey," Cass' voice pulls me from the worry wormhole I'm dangerously close to falling into. Phone nowhere to be seen—he must've said goodbye without me noticing—he wraps both my hands in his and leans in close, uncaring that I'm at work and we're surrounded by a fuck ton of people. It's only him and I as he murmurs, "We don't have to leave the house. We don't have to see anyone. We can just chill."

We can just chill. Him and I and the family.

Slowly, hesitantly, half-regretting it as soon as I do, I nod. "Yeah. Okay."

I'm soothed more than a little by the great, whopping beam threatening to split Cass's face in two. "Great," he says, eyes the richest brown as they twinkle at me. "Cuz I already made you a road trip playlist."

"You are such a little shit."

"You love me."

I do. Ordinarily, I do. However, I love him a little less when, still grinning, he props his chin in his hand and blinks innocently at me. "So, you know the Silvas spend Thanksgiving with us, right?"

Oh, fuck my life.

Eyes drooping, my jaw aches with a yawn as I follow Cass through a crowded pub; the last place I want to be tonight.

"We're going out," my beloved brother declared the moment my shift ended, the groan I'd replied going ignored.

With exhaustion weakening my freaking bones, I'd tried to argue but he didn't leave much room for it. Before I knew it, I was being steered a couple of hundred feet down the street from my workplace and shoved through the doors of another one of Sun Valley's favorite student haunts.

"I'm not impressed," I warn Luna, yelling over the clamoring din of the pub when she springs to her feet at the sight of me, palms smacking together excitedly. It took exactly one brain cell to figure out who acted as Cass' little helper; he shoved a tote bag containing a change of clothes into my reluctant arms and the outfit reeks of Luna. Meaning there's not a lot to it; a silky, green slip skirt that leaves no aspect of my lower body to the imagination and a white tank with a similar effect. Thank God she shoved my boots in there. Otherwise, the urge to kick her in the shin might've overwhelmed me.

"I did it for your own good," my friend yells back. "You gotta get out more."

"I go out!"

"You go to work and class," she retorts, poking the pale sliver of my stomach revealed by the outfit she chose. "You've been hiding lately. You're withering away."

"I am not *withering*." I'm not hiding either. I'm... self-preserving. Limiting the chances of an encounter with *him*, at least until the physical reminder of his existence branded on my wrist fades. Plus, I do go out. I go to Cass'. I go to the gym.

I have witnesses for both.

Ignoring my thunderous expression, Luna grins, tugging on the disheveled plaits I did this morning. "You look hot."

"I'm fucking freezing."

Manicured fingers, painted her signature baby pink, pat my cheek mockingly. "Beauty is pain, baby. Suck it up."

I shove her away with an eye roll before turning my attention to the booth Luna leapt out of, raising my brows at the only person who looks as unhappy to be here as I am. "How'd they get you out?"

Kate raises a pint glass filled to the brim with murky brown liquid. "Bribery."

God dammit. I should've held out until Cass turned to bribery as a resort. I'm trying to find him and demand compensation for my presence when waggling fingers and pale green eyes sparkling with mischief catch my attention. "Hi, Tiny."

My face tightens in a glower—my body's natural reaction to that freaking nickname–but it's half-hearted, lightened by the grin begging to break through. It's very, very hard not to grin when in the kid's presence. "Hi, Ben."

I learned very quickly it wasn't only Cass I had to make room for in my life; I had to carve out space for his little prodigy sidekick too. Not that I mind; I kind of fucking adore the kid. He's a big ball of infectious energy that, admittedly, makes my brain feel like it's rattling sometimes but I like him all the same.

Movement in my peripheral catches my attention, and I resist the urge to gape as Luna plops herself in the lap of the long-haired baseball player she picked up a couple of weeks ago because, yeah, that's still a thing. I'm surprised as hell but I'm keeping my reactions to a minimum, treating this budding relationship with kid gloves lest I spook Luna like a feral cat. So, I purse my lips and stay silent, even if a teasing comment is begging to rip free.

"You want my jacket?" Jackson offers, completely genuine, and okay. I see it. The nice guy appeal. A girl could get used to all the kindness in those narrow, hooded eyes. I wonder how Luna survives under the weight of it.

I decline his offer with a shake of my head before gesturing to the bar. "I'm gonna get a drink."

Cass, who's made himself comfy in the booth squished among our friends already, raises a brow, a silent *want me to come?*

I wave him off and start to elbow my way through the crowd. The Sunshine Tavern is like the fun younger sibling of Greenies; a little bit wilder, a lot less regulated. It's the only place in town that doesn't give a shit about ID'ing, probably because the owner is filthy rich and pays the cops off. It's a lot cheaper here too which is why I'm considering splurging on a fancy cocktail instead of the cheap cider I usually relegate to nights out like this. If I can even get a drink; if the bartender ever makes his way through the mass of people also seeking a beverage.

I'm studying the bodies crowding around me, mentally calculating how long this is going to take, when my gaze lands on a familiar face and suddenly, inexplicably, I get the urge to hide.

Nick, stationed at the opposite end of the bar, hasn't seen me yet. Lounging on a stool, he's got his back to the bar, legs spread to make room for the girl pressed to his front. She's pretty. A redhead like me but not quite as vibrant. More strawberry blonde, less Anne with an E. A slightly starstruck expression paints her face like she can't believe she's worthy of having her ass manhandled by Nicolas freaking Silva, and honestly, I get it. I've only got access to his side profile and I'm gazing a little.

There's something about him. A quality I can't quite put my finger on. He's hard to look away from but beyond being ridiculously handsome. Yeah, it's the strong jaw, the distinct cheekbones, the panty-dropping smile, and, fuck me, eyes the exact shade of burnt honey that grab your attention but something else keeps it. Something... magnetic. Addictive. I've experienced it more than once. Hell, I'm experiencing it right now.

I feel like a creep as I rake my gaze over him, noting every detail almost against my will. The deep dimple peeking out every so often, the dark hair falling in thick curls, the thin gray jumper clinging to every inch of his well-honed physique.

A half-groan, half-snicker gets caught in my throat when I reach the black Dr. Martens on his feet, exactly mine but much bigger. Similarly battered and well-worn, though. For God's sake, I didn't think he could get any hotter.

Whatever choked noise I'm making abruptly dries up, my body stiffening, when the distinct sensation of someone watching me tickles the back of my neck. Slowly, stifling what's definitely a groan this time, I drag my gaze upwards, already anticipating the golden one I know I'm going to meet because isn't that just my luck?

The sneaking suspicion I've been caught red-handed in the middle of my perusal is quickly confirmed; Nick's staring right at me, those damn hypnotic eyes burning my skin. Or maybe that's the blush creeping up my neck, fanning across my cheeks. Acting like he didn't catch me blatantly checking him out, I act casual, adopting an easy smile, lifting my hand in a friendly wave.

A wave that stutters and dies when it's met with nothing.

Absolutely nothing.

The son of a bitch ignores me.

He graces me with a second of eye contact before breaking our gazes like they never met at all. The only proof he saw me—which he did, he looked right fucking at me—is the unnatural clench of his jaw as his expression becomes pissier than it was a moment ago.

Well, fuck you too then.

With a scoffed laugh, I shake my head and turn back to the bar. Planting my elbows on the slightly sticky wood, arms stacked, I impatiently rock back and forth as I try to catch the bartender's attention, needing that drink even more now. But there must be something in the air because I swear to God, he's ignoring me too.

"Fucking men," I mutter aloud.

Fucking men, I repeat in my head when an unwanted hand lands on my lower back.

I jolt forward in surprise, my face contorting in a wince when my ribs smash against the lip of the bar. Glancing over my shoulder at the offender, my expression falls flat.

Oh, fuck me.

"What do you want?" My tone comes out uninterested, unamused, unimpressed, all things I feel towards the man towering over me. I never was a fan of any of Dylan's friends. They were rude assholes, honestly, who never made an effort with me, unless that effort was a misogynistic comment or leering. But one of them always topped my shit list with his obnoxious personality, and he's staring at me like I'm the shit on his shoe.

Will ignores my obvious disdain in favor of scoffing, his hot breath slapping me in the face. "Didn't take you long."

I half-turn so I can glare up at him properly, hating how close his face looms. "Excuse me?"

"Heard you've shacked up with some other guy," he sneers, making no effort to hide his contempt for me, just as I make no effort to hide mine from him. "You didn't embarrass Dylan enough, huh? You needa run around campus like a slut too?"

"Are you kidding me?" I can only laugh. Dylan cheated on me but yeah, I'm the slut. Makes sense. With a roll of my eyes, I turn away. "Fuck off, Will."

He doesn't.

"You always thought you were too good for him." I cringe as beer-stinking breath invades my senses. He's too close, his fingers still digging into me, purposely lingering on my bare skin. "You deserve everything he did to you."

My whole body freezes. My lungs cease to function. I think my heart even stops for a minute. The only part of me working is my brain, conjuring up unwelcome images of a night not too long ago when, just for a moment, I thought I wasn't going to make it home.

I'm so out of it, I almost don't notice the abrupt disappearance of Will's clammy hand, his unsolicited presence. It's not until it's replaced by a different one, higher up, the warmth of a new palm seeping through my thin tank, that I restart.

I jerk away and the hand immediately falls but the owner remains near. Nick, I realize, when I pivot and find him playing the ignoring game again. Or at least that's what I assume at first. It takes a minute for it to sink in that he's not looking at me because he's wholly occupied trying to eviscerate Will with the sheer force of his glare.

I wouldn't be surprised if he could.

"Fuck off," the man demands, the deep timbre of his voice making me shiver.

"You fuck off," Will so creatively retorts and I almost laugh.

Fucking *boys*.

Willing the ugly knot in my chest to disappear, I muster up all my energy, directing it into a glare aimed at Will. "Stay away from me," I repeat the same sentiment I offered his friend. "Leave. Me. Alone."

Anger flushes Will's skin, his nostrils flaring in an unattractive display of indignance. His whiny mouth opens, probably to hiss more hate, but he doesn't get the chance.

"Don't make her tell you again."

Nick's low warning, uttered in a more distinctly accented voice than usual, isn't aimed at me yet I feel it in my freaking bones. It makes my breath catch, my knees wobble, a coil in my belly tightens.

I try very hard to disregard that last one.

Will's contemplation is an almost visible thing. He assesses Nick, sizing him up, wondering if he can take him in the fight he so clearly desperately wants to start.

He can't.

I know it, the smug quirk of Nick's lips says he knows it, and, apparently, so does Will.

"Whatever," he spits. "She's not worth it anyway."

With those charming parting words, Will stomps into the crowd, not a single breath inflating my lungs until he disappears completely and the bravado I've been forcing disappears with him. It's like my body deflates, my shoulders hunching as I curl in on myself, my arms wrapping around my torso and squeezing, my vision blurring as my head spins, my chest aches.

One night. I just wanted one night.

11

AMELIA

OUT OF MY PERIPHERAL, I watch as Nick raises a hand. It floats towards me, hovering near my arm like it might settle there but at the last moment, he thinks better of it. Instead, he shoves his hands in his pockets.

"I'm fine," I answer his question before he can voice it.

"Wasn't gonna ask," he drawls in reply, his presence becoming even harder to ignore as he shuffles a step closer. "Didn't know you were coming out tonight."

"Didn't know I needed your permission."

A beat of silence, of stillness, follows my snapped words.

Nick peers at me, his expression hovering somewhere between amused and concerned like he can't decide which to be. His inquisitive gaze pins me in place, intense and searching and making me feel remarkably akin to prey being eyed up by a predator. When he steps toward me, I resist the urge to back up. Not out of fear but because the man is overwhelming from a distance; close proximity could kill a girl. As could the dimple that makes an appearance as his lips quirk upwards. "You mad at me, *querida*?"

It's hard to be when he calls me whatever that word is. I had a firm disdain for the terms of endearment Dylan used to address me but something about that word, whether it be something sweet or whether he's blatantly insulting me to my oblivious face, inspires goosebumps across my skin. I have a hunch it has little to do with the word itself and

77

everything to do with the man saying it. With the way he says it; rich and smooth like the honey I associate with his irises.

Steeling myself, I mentally don armor that protects my silly little emotions from pretty men and their pretty words. "You ignoring me, Silva?"

That dimple becomes a little less pronounced as Nick's smirk slips ever so slightly. "I was busy."

Ha. So he did see me. "Better get back to it, then."

Go bang the beautiful girl so I can melt down in private, please.

My fingers tap impatiently against my bare arms as I wait for him to hop to it; I have grand plans of slipping out of here and catching an Uber home the second he turns his back.

Except he doesn't.

Nick goes nowhere except closer.

His tall form folds as he bends down, his perfect features crystal clear as he wholly invades my personal space. Not threateningly; he's never threatening, towards me at least. Just... close. Close enough for me to note he has freckles, a brown smattering bridging his nose and fanning out to his cheeks that practically blend into his bronzed skin but this close, I can see them. Close enough I'm enveloped with the scent of citrus and spice. Close enough we're practically sharing breath. If I leaned forward even a little, we'd bump noses.

God, why am I tempted to do that?

"Who was that?"

Jolting at Nick's voice, I blink away the freckle-induced haze trying to convince me to freaking rub noses with Nicolas Silva. It's a testament to how much his proximity is rattling me because I don't even try to evade his question. "One of Dylan's friends."

The muscles in his jaw clench as he kisses his teeth. "He always treat you like that?"

"Like what?" I ask even though I know exactly what he means.

The look he gives me says he knows I know yet he indulges me anyway. "Talking to you like that. Looking at you like that. Manhandling you."

I shift from one foot to the other as I shrug.

"That's a yes, then," Nick drawls, no humor in his words, all fire in his gaze as it scans the room behind me.

"I can handle it."

An indistinct hum rumbles in his throat. I can't tell if it's in agreement or protest and I don't get the chance to ask because the universe once again reminds me why I shouldn't leave the house; one second, I'm all but flush with Nick. The next, I'm stumbling to the side as a body collides with mine.

"Nick?" A high-pitched, screeching voice threatens to bust my eardrums at the same time an aggressively sweet perfume assaults my nostrils. "Oh my God, baby, hi!"

I right myself as a pretty brunette attaches herself to Nick's side, hands roaming like they have every right to. Although, what do I know? Maybe they do. However, I'd hazard a guess based on Nick's grimace, they don't.

"Do I know you?" he asks in a tone so harsh I'd feel bad for the girl if the little bitch hadn't just bodychecked me with the force of a fucking rugby player. I think she bruised a damn rib.

The freakishly strong mystery woman pouts at Nick, one hand twirling a lock of her highlight-streaked, ashy brown hair while the other wraps around his bicep like a perfectly manicured boa constrictor. "You're so funny, babe," she preens, damn near creating a wind with the fluttering of her lashes. "It's Janine."

She states her name like he's supposed to know it and, God, is it hard not to laugh when Nick's perfectly blank expression remains unchanging.

"Janine," the not-as-memorable-as-she-thinks woman repeats, rolling her eyes playfully with a tittering laugh like this is all one big joke. She shoots me a dramatic 'can you believe this guy?' look which I return with nothing more than a closed-mouthed, wide-eyed brow raise. There's a hint of something nasty in the upward tilt of her lips as she stares right at me while addressing Nick with a confident flip of her hair, "Like you could forget me after Halloween." Her suggestive tone leaves no guessing as to what kind of unforgettable activity they engaged in that night. Withholding the grimace begging to make an appearance, I silently pray whatever happened didn't occur in the bed I slept in.

"Oh." Realization finally dawns on Nick's face. "Janice? From the bathroom?"

I have to press my lips together so, so tightly to keep from laughing while simultaneously huffing an internal sigh of relief. Bathroom, not his bed. Damn, busy night for that location.

Janine's face lights up for a split second before falling into a frown. *"Janine,"* she repeats for a third time and *dear God, Amelia, do not laugh.*

Nick blinks. "Does it matter?"

Subtly, I extend a leg, my foot colliding with Nick's shin. *Don't be cruel,* I mouth with a pointed look.

Help me, he mouths back with a pointed look of his own.

I roll my eyes but I'm already plotting; I do owe him. Wide-eyed, I shimmy my shoulders discreetly. Jerking his head in acknowledgment, he obeys what I silently command, carefully shaking off his oddly violent groupie, that easy, placating smile of his occupying her attention so she barely notices. The minute she's off him, I'm replacing her, slipping in front of Nick like a human barrier. Instantly, without encouragement, a hand cups my hip and tugs me backwards into a hard chest. The muscles in my stomach contract as a warm palm splays across my skin, and I will my smile not to falter as something somersaults in my belly. "Hi. I'm Amelia."

Oh, if looks could kill. Janine grits her teeth like they're liable to tear into me if given the chance, forming the sorriest excuse for a smile I've ever seen as she spits a pitiful greeting of her own. "Hi."

I hope no one notices the tremor of my hand as I set it over the one making my insides wobble, my fingers slotting into place atop Nick's. "Can we help you with something?"

To her credit, Janine adapts quickly. Within seconds, her furious scowl melting into a saccharine grin aimed at Nick, and Nick alone. Like I'm not plastered to the front of him, like an extension of himself. Like his thumb isn't dangerously close to brushing the underside of my boob.

To be fair, I'm pretending that's not happening too.

"I was gonna ask if you wanted to buy me a drink."

"I'm busy."

I snort, the noise morphing into a sharp inhale when the pads of Nick's warm fingers press harder into my skin. My breathing remains stagnant as his other hand travels upwards, relocating from my hip, trailing up my bare arm. His pinky grazes my collarbone as he brushes a red plait aside, thick fingers curling around my shoulder and squeezing gently.

Janine tracks the movement, practically glowing green. "Well, maybe we could-"

"Listen, Jean," Nick cuts her off and my chest actually hurts from stifling laughter yet again. "I'm tryna talk to my girl so if you could leave us alone, that'd be great."

My girl, my silly little brain sings.

Jesus, I need to get out of here.

Embarrassment flushes Janine's cheeks. I'd feel sorry for the girl, I really would, if not for the bruises I'm sure are blooming. "Yeah," she clears her throat, tossing her hair again. "Okay. I'll see you later."

"No, you won't," Nick mutters and this time, there's no force in the world that could keep my laughter in, even if it does earn me a parting scowl as Janine flounces off, her hips swaying in a way I guess is supposed to be alluring.

I tilt my head back, seeking out Nick's gaze but it's already on me. I'm momentarily ensnared by his smile because God knows it's a good one. It takes more time than I'm willing to admit to snap myself out of it but I manage, narrowing my eyes at his grin. "Wipe that smile off your face, Silva. I'm pretty sure I'm going to wake up with a stiletto in my back tomorrow."

His laugh catches me off guard. The rich, husky chuckle that bursts from him, vibrating from his body through mine and almost making my knees buckle. He's freaking luminous as he smirks down at me, eyes teasing. "Could always sleep in my bed. I'll protect you."

"Dream on."

"Believe me, *querida*, I will."

Mustering an unimpressed look, I reluctantly duck out of his grasp, immediately feeling cold without his warmth surrounding me. It was distracting, him touching me, us messing with his groupie, but now, the moment's passed. The exhaustion is seeping back in. So, with a nod towards the exit, I say, "Think I've had enough fun for one night. Tell Cass I said bye?"

"Wait." A hand catches me by my shoulder before I can disappear like I'm desperate too. With a bone-rattling sigh, I glance at Nick expectantly, an odd mixture of foreboding and exhilaration settling in my gut when I find him brandishing car keys. "I have an idea."

Four words scream trouble. A bright red warning sign flashes in my mind. My common sense chastises me for even considering taking the hand he offers me.

Yet I accept his offer anyway.

~

Heavy panting breaths tickle my cheek as hands hold my hips firmly, a hard front presses flush against my sweat-soaked back. "Another one," a husky voice commands and I shiver despite my elevated temperature.

"I can't," I groan, every inch of my body aching.

"Come on, *querida*," my torturer coos. "You can do one more."

"You're trying to kill me."

Even without looking, I know he's adopted that infuriating smirk. "You asked for it."

Of all the scenarios I imagined as Nick led me out of the pub—carefully avoiding our friends because we knew they'd kick up a fuss no matter what we told them—this wasn't one of them. I didn't expect to be breathless and sweaty and plastered against an equally breathless and sweaty Nick with the clock steadily ticking towards midnight. I didn't think his big idea would involve whisking me away to Sun Valley Fitness Centre and introducing me to the punishing world of boxing.

I can't feel my arms. Genuinely, if I couldn't see them poised in front of me, weighted down by the gloves protecting my hands, I'd think they'd fallen off. My whole body feels numb, ready to buckle, yet somehow, I have enough energy to tense when Nick's hand moves from my hip to my stomach.

"You're holding too much tension here," he murmurs, tapping the bare strip of stomach between my tank and the shorts I borrowed from him. Unsurprisingly, they don't fit. I secured them at the back with a hair tie but I've long since stopped worrying about them potentially falling down; I'm more worried about me falling down, period.

"You've gotta loosen up," Nick continues, and if my breath was capable of catching right, it would. I should be used to him handling me by now; it's been hours of him using gentle touches to guide me. Yet every time, he elicits a physical reaction from me. "Use your whole body, not just your arms."

"I'm not tense," I protest. "I'm exhausted."

His chuckle has the hair on the back of my neck standing to attention. "One more. Then we can stop."

I groan. I grumble. I consider expelling my last shreds of energy by socking Nick in the gut but I don't. Instead, when he backs up and calls out a combination I'm beginning to feel familiar with, I do it.

And despite my complaining, despite the aching burning emanating from my freaking bones, I like it. I really, really like it. A stiff wind might be able to flatten me right now but regardless, I feel strong. Powerful. Simultaneously shattered beyond belief and brimming with adrenaline.

I was hesitant when we first got here. Hesitance nagged at me, even as Nick's intentions became clear when he tossed me a change of pants and started wrapping some kind of soft material around his hands. He did the same to me, thumbs brushing my racing pulse as he secured fabric around my wrists, thumbs, and palms. To ensure I don't sprain anything, he explained. Then, without giving me a second to question it, he slipped a pair of boxing gloves over my hands, laced them up, and gently nudged me towards one of the heavy leather bags suspended from the ceiling.

"Just punch," he murmured. "Don't think, just punch."

So, I did.

And I kept punching.

For hours, we've alternated between him demonstrating and me copying. He's put me through my paces, teaching me a billion combinations and yelling me through a series of his favorite workouts, and while I really want to punch him, I kind of want to kiss him too.

Platonically, of course.

Because I didn't realize how much I needed an outlet like this until the sweat started flowing.

I want to burst into grateful, relieved tears as I finish my final combination and all but collapse on the floor, landing on my ass with a thump. Bracing my forearms against my knees, my head flops forward, my fore-head sticking to my gloves as I try and fail to breathe. "I think I'm dying."

"You're fine." The little shit who did this to me snickers. I hear him plop down in front of me, another groan ripping from my throat when strong hands wrap around my ankles and yank me a couple of inches closer until I'm nestled between his legs.

I'm literally trapped between his thighs, my feet basically tucked beneath his ass, but I can't find it in me to give a crap when I have bigger things to worry about. "I'm never gonna be able to breathe again."

More deep laughter contradicts my excessive groans as he pries my arms away from me, extending them so he can unlace my gloves and yank them off. He takes his time unwrapping my hands, his attention lingering on one wrist in particular. The pad of his thumb smooths over the purple imperfection doing its best to last. "Does it hurt?"

"Nope." It pangs every so often but I'm so hopped up on endorphins, I've barely noticed. Tomorrow, it'll probably ache a little. I don't particularly care.

With a jerky nod, Nick drops my hands, leaning back on his palms and honestly, fuck him for looking so attractive right now. He's as sweaty and flushed and disheveled as I am yet he pulls it off. I look like I've been dragged backward through a hedge. He looks like he's about to pose for Men's Health. I'm fighting for my life. He's grinning like he could go another couple of rounds.

"I think I hate you."

"You mean *'thank you so much, Nicolas'*?"

Knocking my knees against the inner thighs cocooning me, I fix him with a glare. It only lasts a second, though, before softening. "Thank you, Nicolas."

"Anytime, *querida*."

12

NICK

"CAN YOU, like, not touch her so much?"

For what feels like the millionth time, I groan, a sound Amelia echoes. Dropping her gloved hands, her shoulder brushing the bare skin of my abs as she pivots to scowl at the whiny asshole scrutinizing us from the corner. "Can you, like, shut up?"

"He's groping you!" Cass falsely accuses, eyeing my hands where they rest on Amelia's waist as if I'm cupping her fucking tits.

Amelia's head drops back, her eyes screwing shut as she makes a whining noise. "He's helping me! We're working out, Cass. It's not like he's feeling me up in a dark hallway."

I wish, I mutter internally at the same time Cass barks, "I fucking hope not."

The first workout Amelia and I shared—the one that's inspired many a cold shower since its occurrence—was the beginning of a routine, a routine born without any discussion. Every evening around the same time Amelia will appear, always hovering with an initial hesitance that melts away the second I toss her the spare, smaller gloves I've taken to storing in my gym bag. And for an hour, sometimes two, we'll steadily work through the regime I may or may not have conjured up with her in mind.

Are there many, many other ways I could get her worked up and breathless that have nothing to do with boxing, that I'd much prefer?

Fuck yes. Does working out with her mean my training is suffering? Yeah, a little. Do I give a shit? Absolutely not.

Despite the fact my skin constantly feels a size too tight for my body, despite the fact my dick hasn't stopped aching for almost a week, despite the fact she's trying to kill me with her little matching athletic sets—today, it's emerald green shorts and a matching crop top with an open back that makes me clench my jaw so hard, I'm a step away from grinding my teeth to dust—I fucking love our sessions. There's something about watching her get stronger and more confident and looking so fucking proud of herself when she nails a combination... *fuck*.

I need an extra long cold shower after each and every one of them, but it's worth it.

It's our fifth session in a row and the first time we've had an audience. Unsurprisingly, I prefer when it's just me and her. Although, aggravating Cass is one of my favorite hobbies.

And aggravated he most definitely is.

His dark eyes are narrowed as they flit between my hands, my smirk, my bare chest. "Put on a fucking shirt."

He literally harrumphed when I took it off in the first place, acting like I was doing it as some kind of mating ritual and not because it was more sweat than material. Usually, I'd swap it out for one of the spares I always keep handy but that disgruntled reaction had me staying shirtless purely out of wry spite.

And maybe it had something to do with the way Amelia's eyes went wide as they scanned me quickly before shyly darting away, a pretty blush staining her cheeks.

"Am I distracting you, Morgan?" I tease, simpering at my friend as I make a show of raising both arms, curling them so my biceps bulge while I tense my stomach. Beside me, Amelia makes a choking noise and I shoot her an admittedly asshole-ish wink, finding all too much satisfaction in how that lovely blush deepens.

Cass' expression remains deadpan. "Stop preening. It's annoying."

"Both of you are annoying." I expel a surprised puff of air when soft leather grazes my abs in a weak punch, an exasperated noise leaving Amelia. "Why do you only have these dick-measuring contests around me?"

I scoff, eyeballing Cass. "There's no *contest*."

"Drop 'em, pretty boy."

"Oh my *God*." Amelia socks me again—perfect form, I note proudly —before holding her hands out towards me, hidden palms up, a silent plea to unlace her gloves that I oblige.

Tossing the discarded gloves in my bag, I quirk a brow. "Done?"

Amelia nods. "I'm starving."

I can't help letting my gaze drop, eyeing her flat stomach as the Brazilian in me screams *feed her, feed her, feed her.*

"Me too," Cass chimes in, abandoning the dumbbells he's been pretending to use for the last hour. Looping an arm around Amelia's shoulders, he drags her away, tossing me a scowl over his shoulder. "Let's go."

Snickering, I bend over to grab a spare t-shirt from my bag, pulling it over my head before calling after him, "Don't you have class?"

Cass' footsteps falter. Glancing at the clock on the wall, he swears. "Raincheck?"

Amelia shoots him a dry look. "I didn't invite you in the first place."

Curling his arm around her neck, Cass grips her in a headlock, ignoring her shrieks of protest as he digs his knuckles into her skull, brutally ruffling her hair. Only when Amelia lands an elbow danger- ously close to his groin does he let her go, dropping a kiss on her mussed crown as he does. "Love you. See you tomorrow."

"Love you," Amelia returns the sentiment with a grumble, shoving her brother away with one hand, smoothing down her hair with the other.

"Love you," I can't resist mimicking.

Cass spins around, walking backward so he can flick his middle finger at me. "Keep your hands to yourself, Nicolas," he yells as he rounds the corner and disappears from view.

"No promises," I sing in reply. When I glance aside and find Amelia evil-eyeing me, the grin I'm sporting drops, replaced with a perfectly innocent expression. "I mean I promise."

"Uh-huh." My newest workout buddy shakes her head, hiding her grin by tugging a sweatshirt over her head. When she dips to grab her bag, I snatch it before she can, slinging the tote over my shoulder.

"So, where're we eating?"

Amelia blinks at me, pink lips pursing when the corners of her mouth twitch. "I don't remember inviting you either."

Ignoring her and with her bag as my hostage, I head in the direction of the tiny cafe tucked in the furthest corner of the gym. It's a glorified smoothie stall, strictly healthy superfoods, but it's not half bad. Glancing my shoulder, I crack a smile at Amelia who hasn't moved an inch. "My treat."

She blinks at me again, a hint of confusion in her vibrant gaze, and I get why. This isn't a part of our usual routine; we don't shoot the shit over shared meals. Today, though, I'm feeling reluctant to part ways. More reluctant than usual. And if the price for some extra facetime is a Green Goddess smoothie, that's no hardship.

"I never asked you how you have a key to this place."

I pause demolishing my salad—a mix of roasted cauliflower, mixed greens, chicken, poblano peppers, and chickpeas—and spare Amelia an upwards glance. "The owner gave me one."

"Why?"

Shoving a forkful of spinach into my mouth, I take my time chewing before shrugging nonchalantly. "I fucked her."

The peach ice tea Amelia just took a sip of almost comes out her nose as she chokes on it. "*Seriously?*"

I only manage to leave her in suspense for a handful of seconds before letting my grip rip free. "No, and I'm a little offended you believed that so quickly." Dodging the sweet potato fry she launches at my head, I explain, "Her kid was having problems with bullies. I gave him a couple of lessons," I didn't show him how to beat the crap out of other kids or anything—I taught him how to defend himself if it got to that point, "she was grateful, I got a key."

The dainty hand holding another fry, poised ready to fly my way, hovers mid-air as Amelia cocks her head at me. "Really?"

I nod.

"That's really nice."

"You sound surprised, *querida.*"

Popping the makeshift starchy weapon in her mouth, she asks, "What language is that?"

My eyes narrow at the subject change, but I allow it. "Portuguese."

"You're Portuguese?"

"Brazilian."

Amelia makes a thoughtful noise as she chews. "How'd you end in Sun Valley? Or in Carlton," she adds, naming her hometown.

I keep my eyes on my food as I skim over my past; born in Salvador, moved to New York when I was a kid because that's where my dad was from, where my parents originally met, and moved to Carlton when I was twenty—a year or so after Dad died—because Ma couldn't take being there when he wasn't anymore. I speed through that last bit. It's not something I like discussing and it's not anyone's business but my own, as far as I'm concerned. I'm not sure I really intended to tell Amelia; it slips out, and my body tenses as it does.

That tension rushes out of me, though, when a small, warm hand covers my fisted one, a thumb sweeping over my wrist. She doesn't say anything, doesn't mutter an apology like most people do and I'm grateful for it; I always hate the empty comfort. She simply holds my hand and when I risk a glance upwards, her eyes are as soft as her touch, lined with sympathy.

I like how that look makes me feel almost as much as I hate it.

"Anyway," clearing my throat, I smoothly retract my hand and snatch up her iced tea, stealing a sip because I'm severely regretting my green juice decision, "that's how we got invited to the Morgans' Thanksgiving. Lynn found out we don't really celebrate since it was my dad's thing and the next thing I know, I'm sitting in her kitchen with a plate of food in front of me."

Retrieving her drink with a playful sneer, Amelia snorts. "Sounds like Lynn."

I'm sauntering out of the gym, freshly showered and riding the adrenaline-induced high of winning a fight, when my phone buzzes in my pocket. I'm half-tempted to ignore; I've got a gut feeling that what-ever it is will mess with my carefully curated plan of heading straight to the nearest bar and finding a pretty girl to celebrate my win with. But it might be Ma—she always texts me after a fight—and if I don't reply, her mind will conjure up the worst possible scenario.

With a resigned sigh, I fish out my phone. Sure enough, *'mamãe'* lights up my screen, her text a blunt question; *você ganhou?* Snickering, I type an equally blunt *sim* before scrolling through the rest of my unread messages, all from Cass. One asking where I am, another detailing an address I don't recognize, a request for wine coolers—that coaxes a snort out of me—and about a dozen variations of misspelled please's and hurry up's.

Why? I tap out quickly. The reply dings as I'm slipping behind the steering wheel of my truck. Clicking on it, a picture floods my screen, a handful of people visible but my brain only seems to focus on one. My attention goes right to the beautiful redhead hiding in the right rear corner; curls a wild mess, eyes squinted shut, mouth cracked in a mid-laugh beam that I subconsciously copy. I'm so busy gawking at her like a fool, it takes a moment to notice the half-empty pint bottle of cider clutched in her grasp, a metal straw sticking out the top. Quickly scanning the rest of them and noting an array of droopy eyes and flushed cheeks, I chuckle; they look drunk off their asses.

And they sound even drunker when, twenty minutes later, I rap my knuckles against what I'm assuming is the girls' front door and a cacophony of loud voices and off-key singing seeps through the wood.

It takes four tries until the banging of my fist is heard over the noise, a round of husking and quiet giggles breaking out. Another minute passes before the door swings open to reveal the smile I broke several speed limits to see up close.

It's a shame it disappears as soon as Amelia realizes it's me darkening her doorway, balancing a case of wine coolers, a six-pack of cola, and a bottle of rum in my arms. "What're you doing here?"

Not exactly the warm reception I was hoping for. "Ouch."

"Sorry." Hazy eyes blink rapidly. "I just wasn't expecting you."

"Cass told me to come." Suddenly feeling awkward, I shift from one foot to the other, my brow knitted in a frown. "Is that not... okay?"

Shit, maybe it wasn't. We parted ways on an awkward note yesterday but I didn't think it would carry over. "Same time tomorrow?" she'd asked me, the physical embodiment of a ray of sunshine as she graced me with an effervescent beam.

"I can't." Something in my chest had ached when her face dropped. "I have plans."

Granted, I could've been more specific. I could've clarified that I'd had a fight scheduled for weeks. But I didn't and it created this weird moment of... I don't know, friction? Distance? Whatever it was, I didn't like it, and I was relieved when it dissipated almost as quickly as it formed.

"No!" Amelia all but yells. "I mean yes. Yeah, it's okay. Sorry." Pretty pink lips curl upwards in a sheepish smile. "I'm kinda drunk."

I tamp down on the sarcastic '*noooo*' perched on the tip of my tongue. Adjusting the alcohol in my arms getting heavier by the second, I quirk a brow. "Can I come in, then? Because it's fucking freezing out here."

Amelia's gaze pinballs, darting from my wet hair to my full arms to my lack of a jacket, and she seems to snap out of whatever funk she's in. "God, sorry." She steps aside and ushers me inside. "Come in."

I do as she says, only making it two steps in the door before a shriek makes me cringe, warm fingertips suddenly grazing my throbbing cheekbone. Oh, right; I almost forgot my opponent managed to get a single hit in. "What the fuck? Did you get beat up?"

I snort. "Barely."

Face crumpled with concern, Amelia leans in, her voice a comically loud whisper. "Did your date do that?"

"My what?"

"Your date," she repeats louder. "Cass said you had a hot date."

"He did, huh?" Jaw clenched, my head swivels towards the shithead lounging on a sofa three sizes too small for his lanky body and looking way too proud of himself.

The innocent way he holds up his hands is completely contradicted by his roguish snicker. "Hey, you and another man fondling each other for an hour sounds like a hot date to me."

Not even sparing him the energy it would take me to flip him off, I glance at a still-frowning Amelia. "I had a fight. Like a boxing fight," I clarify when her confusion lingers.

A long, drawn out 'ohhhh' sounds before a tiny fist whacks my bicep. "Why didn't you tell me?" she demands. "I would've gone."

She would've? "Really?"

The indignant, slightly lopsided 'duh' look she shoots me says it all.

"Okay." Fuck me, I'm smiling like a loser. "Next time."

"C'mon." Fingers loop around my wrist and shake. "I've got Arnica in the kitchen."

Before letting her drag me to the kitchen, I make a pit stop to drop off Cass' fucking wine coolers, slapping him upside the head for his meddling and doing the same to Ben, just because. Jackson, I steer clear of; the guy's too busy mooning over the blonde in his lap to notice my arrival anyway.

"What was that about?" I murmur once we reach the relative privacy of the kitchen.

Amelia glances over her shoulder fleetingly as she attempts to scale the kitchen counter, a precarious wobble to her movements. "Hm?"

I nod towards the front door as I nudge her aside, following her grumbled directions and snagging the first aid kit from the top cabinet, nestled in a basket right at the back of the first shelf. When she gestures for me to sit at one of the stools lining the counter, I oblige, leaning down so my face is within her range. "The cold front."

"Oh." She keeps her gaze downcast, focusing on unscrewing the half-empty tube and depositing a dollop of the thick, white cream on the pad of her index finger. "I told you, I wasn't expecting you."

"Amelia," I coo her name, my tone making her glance up warily. "You can tell me the truth."

Emerald eyes narrow in suspicion. "I am."

I wait until she's smoothed Arnica evenly across my bruised cheek-bone before smirking. "You were jealous of my imaginary hot date, weren't you?"

"*No.*" Slender fingers flick my forehead. "Jesus Christ. I'm surprised your head fits through doorways, you know."

"It's okay," I croon, her hair silky soft beneath my palms as I pat her head. "It's only natural. I know I'm hard to share."

She's wondering if she can chuck the Arnica tube at my head and get away with it, I can tell, but she can't hide the upwards twitch of her lips. "I really don't like you."

Yeah. I really don't like her either.

13

NICK

"No."

The young face peering at me from the doorway pouts. *"Please?"*

"Absolutely not."

A remarkably dog-like whining noise escapes Ben as he stomps into my room like a disgruntled child. One thing I learned very quickly about the kid; 'no' is not in his vocabulary. "But it's your birthday."

"Exactly." With a grunt, I tear my gaze from the book I'm attempting to read for class so I can glare at the youngest and most annoying of my roommates. "It's *my* birthday. And I don't wanna do anything."

"But that's *boring.*"

"Yeah, well." If not filling my house with a fuck ton of messy, drunk students—half of whom I probably won't even know, some of whom are still teenagers, and most of whom consider twenty-four to be ancient in their worlds—makes me boring, then so be it. I learned my lesson after Halloween; the house was a fucking disaster and inexplicably, I was delegated most of the clean-up. And as much as I was raised in an environment that uses birthdays as an excuse for elaborate family affairs, when you don't have a myriad of friends and cousins and cousins of cousins of cousins to help clean up, it's not worth it.

Ben, unsurprisingly, wholeheartedly disagrees. "But it'll be fun."

I huff a noise of disagreement that's no deterrent to Ben. With a dramatic sigh, he flops on the foot of my bed. I resist the urge to boot him off as he stretches out sideways, propping his head up on his fist and sighing again. "The girls are gonna be so disappointed."

Paper crinkles as I pause mid-page turn. "What?"

"Cass already invited them." Fuck me, the kid might be some kind of baseball prodigy but he's godawful at acting; his attempt at nonchalance is almost laughable. "They sounded so excited. Oh well."

Slowly, and regretting it before I even do it, I lower my book and offer Ben my full attention, knowing precisely what he's fishing for yet still asking, "What girls?"

"Oh, you know. Kate, Luna," he smirks, "Amelia."

Another thing he's shit at; subtlety.

"Whatever you're thinking," I drawl slowly, my foot itching with the urge to kick. "Stop it."

"I'm just saying." His innocent blink is anything but. "Now they have no reason to come here."

Manipulation. I'm being manipulated by a fucking seventeen-year-old.

And the worst part; it's fucking working. The mention of Amelia's name has my ears pricking up like a fucking dog and it's fucking pathetic. An errant thought floats through my head, convincing me maybe a party wouldn't be too bad if Amelia was there. Sure, we'd see each other anyway at the gym. But maybe a house full of relative strangers would be better than the fucking soft porn our workouts have quickly turned into. And maybe, *finally*, an opportunity to get laid would arise, as much as that thought makes an inexplicable, uncomfortable knot settle in my gut.

"If you wanna throw a party," I word carefully, casually, my eyes firmly focused on the book I long since stopped reading. "Throw a party, I don't give a shit. Don't do it on my account."

If I paid attention for a second longer, I would've caught the slightly rabid, wholly chaotic, catastrophically mischievous expression contorting Ben's face the moment those words left my mouth.

Alas, hindsight.

∼

I'm going to kill him.

Ben Smith is about to get murdered. As a birthday present, I'm going to make Cass and Jackson help me hide his body. Although, I might off them because I'm almost positive they were in on this bullshit.

Fucking hell, where did they get all this shit? Our house is a little boy's birthday dream. I can't take a step without kicking a balloon or copping a streamer to the face or, fucking hell, grimacing at one of the many, many, many blown-up photos of me at various ages littering the walls—add matricide to my to-do list because there's only one person my asshole friends could've gotten my fucking baby pictures from. Someone's already drawn a dick on the forehead of at least four of them and it's only been an hour since we opened the doors. And the *pièce de résistance*; a banner strung up on the longest wall with *Happy 40th Birthday Nicolas* scrawled on the blue plastic fabric.

Fucking assholes.

I'm sulking in the kitchen, contemplating how I'm going to exact revenge on my so-called friends when fingers graze my forearm. "You know," a sweet voice coos as the scent of coconut overwhelms me, a scent that's been plaguing me for weeks. "You're gonna have to give me your skincare routine. You don't look a day over thirty-five."

I want her so bad.

That's the only thought in my head when I glance down at Amelia and it was my only thought when I watched her strut in about half an hour ago. I barely noticed Luna by her side, towering over her shorter friend since one had donned heels and the other forewent them in place of, fuck me, scuffed black Dr. Martens. I was too busy ogling her, greedily soaking up every inch.

Fuck, I thought. *I need to burn that dress.*

The Halloween one too. They're too much for me. Too short, too tight, too demanding of my attention. Before I could stop myself, I found myself wondering if the fabric clinging to her was as soft as her skin. I wondered if the angelic white would look as good crumpled on my bedroom floor as the devilish red did. I wondered how nicely I'd have to ask for her to let me be the one to take it off this time.

I'd downed my drink—blessedly extra strong since Ben made it—to soothe the groan caught in my throat and turned my back on her. For the longest thirty minutes of my life, I tried to ignore her presence. I tried to pay attention to the array of other girls here but my brain worked against me.

That girl's pretty, I would think. *Amelia is so fucking beautiful it makes your chest hurt,* it would remind me.

Nice smile, I notice. *But it doesn't compare to hers.*

Could take someone upstairs and no one would notice—but you don't fucking want to.

If she was anyone else, the ignoring thing would work. If only the thought of tearing my gaze away from her didn't sound as painful, as difficult, as prying out my eyeballs.

The distance didn't do her justice.

She's.... light. She's literal sunshine. And it makes a burst of anger shoot through me because I know that for so long, she was with someone who did nothing but dim her.

Amelia gazes up at me, her brows drawn together slightly, and I clear my throat when I realize I've been staring too long without saying anything. Forcing my lips into a smirk, I knock my shoulder against her playfully. "Couldn't stay away from me for a day, could you, *querida?*"

Amelia rolls her eyes like she always does when I flirt with her, always automatically assuming I'm messing with her. Which I am.

Sometimes.

When she gestures towards the living room, I follow her gaze to where Luna and Jackson are grinding on the makeshift dance floor, matching looks of euphoria lighting up their faces. Fuck, it blows my mind that they've yet to put a label on what is so obviously a relationship. I've got to give Luna props for making him work for it.

"Kate's with her girlfriend so I'm on wingwoman duties," Amelia explains as she turns to the kitchen island laden with alcohol, every bottle and can and glass courtesy of Jackson as usual. The quietest of my roommates doesn't talk about his family often—with the exception of his beloved sisters—but I know his grandparents are filthy rich and willing to share. I also know the only time Jackson ever extravagantly blows that money is when it's for other people.

Note to self; add Jackson to hit-list. He probably paid for all this *merda.*

"So you didn't come to wish me a happy birthday?" Propping my hip against the counter, I watch as she reaches for the nearest bottle of rum with one hand, the other grabbing a couple of the red cups scattered around. She tips a healthy amount into each, topping them both up with cola. "I'm hurt."

The laugh I own washes over me like a warm, refreshing wave. Internally, I drop my head back, eyes drifting closed as I sigh contentedly. Externally, I calmly, cooly, collectedly take the full cup she offers me. Tipping her own forward, she clinks them together in a cheers. "*Feliz aniversarió*, Nicolas," she murmurs, her smile hesitant. "Did I say that right?"

Wrong. So, so wrong. Not her pronunciation but the thoughts popping into my head at the sound of her crooning my mother tongue.

I hum a response because I don't trust myself to speak, and she seems to accept that with a pleased hum of her own. Sipping on her drink, she copies my stance, leaning sideways against the counter and peering up at me. "I'm guessing you're not actually forty."

"I'm twenty-four." When her brows raise in question, I continue. "I took a couple of years off after high school." Considering my prospective college was the one my dead dad used to work at, the appeal wasn't exactly there. Plus, I had more important things to do, people to take care of. Without hesitation, I shoved the idea of furthering my studies to the back of my mind and it didn't arise again until Cass was researching Sun Valley and the well-reviewed English department caught my eye.

Another one of those damned laughs make me grit my teeth like a man in pain. "I was wondering why Ben kept calling you old man."

My eye twitches at the mention of the little shit. "I'm barely six years older than him," *less than four years older than her*, "and he acts like it's sixty."

Amelia laughs again and I contemplate asking her, begging her, to please, please stop before I lose my fucking mind. I don't know what's wrong with me tonight, why I'm particularly affected by her tonight. She always has some kind of a hold on me but tonight, it's like I have no control over myself. It's like I've willingly handed it over to her and that's not normal for me. It's not what I'm used to and I'm not sure I like it. Whatever it is threatening to drive me mad, it ups its efforts when Amelia suddenly turns towards the living room, her back against the counter as she scans the crowd searchingly. "Hey, have you seen Cass?"

I hate myself, I really fucking do, when, against my will, a little green monster thrashes in my gut. "He went upstairs a while ago." I keep my gaze on her, gauging her reaction. "With a *friend*." Amelia's cute, freckled nose scrunches up in a grimace, and I'm so distracted by the fact I called her fucking nose cute, I don't hear the question she asks me. "Sorry, what?"

"I asked why you're looking at me like I should care." Amelia doesn't wait for me to respond before groaning like she already knows what I'm going to say. "Why is it so hard to believe nothing ever happened between us?"

Because Cass might be a big dumbass but he's not that *foolish*. Three weeks with the girl and I'm addicted. Hell, a few months of knowing her only as the hot redheaded waitress and I was hooked. Ten years with her everywhere all the time? I'd be a goner.

I don't voice any of that. I only shrug and Amelia huffs her discontent. "He's like my brother, you creeps. And even if he wasn't, he's not my type, okay? Let it die."

"What is your type?"

Me. *Por favor Deus*, be me.

A pink tongue darts out and drags over a pinker bottom lip as she crooks her head thoughtfully, frowning. "I don't think I know anymore."

Lemme show you, I coo silently. *I'll make it so much fun.*

I'm losing it. I genuinely think I'm losing it, driven mad by coconut and rum, and I don't know if it's out of habit or because I'm panicking but all of a sudden, I'm slipping into my default setting and manwhore Nick comes out to play for the first time in a while. "Did I mention you look really fucking hot tonight?"

Immediately, I know I fucked up.

Amelia cringes. She actually visibly cringes, something I can't say has ever happened to me before. Nor has a girl ever sneered at me the way she does, face dark with shock and umbrage and a gut-wrenching amount of disappointment. "Don't do that."

"Do what?"

"Hit on me like I'm one of your hook-ups." She won't even look at me. "I have no interest in joining your little fan club."

"I'm not-" I'm grappling for an excuse I don't have when the worst possible thing that could happen, happens.

Before the woman suddenly clinging to my side even speaks, I know who it is. And it's perfect, Jan-Jean-whatever the fuck her name is' timing. She must have a sixth sense for shit-stirring because there is no better moment she could've chosen to cement her palm against my chest, balance on her tip-toes, and warble in my ear. "Hi, birthday boy."

Her grip has improved since last time; my attempts to shake her off are futile. "Not now, Janice."

She ignores me. "Can I steal you for a dance?"

Fuck no, I open my mouth to say but someone beats me to it. "Go ahead." Amelia laughs but it's not the sound I was fawning over minutes ago. It's... not quite bitter but something close.

"Amelia-" My tone is a step away from begging but it's too late; I blink and she's gone, swallowed up by the crowd and *porra*. How did everything go to shit so quickly? I try to go after her, cursing again when I'm pulled back by someone I honestly forgot was even there. "Get off me," I snap, wrenching my arm away with more force than I'd prefer to use. If I wasn't so pissed, I'd laugh at how confused J-whatever looks. "I'm not fucking interested." The latter is yelled over my shoulder as I exit the kitchen and power through the rabble, laser-focused on the crown of red curls I catch disappearing outside.

She's halfway down the drive when I catch up with her, calling her name a second before I grab her arm and...

She flinches.

Amelia spins around, fear flashing in eyes that have never looked at me the way they're looking at me right now, and she flinches. A gut reaction that fades the moment she realizes it's me but fuck, does it cut me deep. I practically recoil as I snatch my hand back, the most intense sense of nausea I've ever felt washing over me. And the look on her face, *honesto a Deus*, makes me want to cry.

"Sorry." I hate the hollowness in her voice as much as I hate the fact she's apologizing for something that's never going to be her fault. "I didn't know it was you."

Sucking in a breath, I tentatively—so fucking tentatively—close the distance between us in tiny, careful steps. Just as slowly, my hand rises, hovering for an agonizing moment before my palm glides over her cheek, and there goes the urge to cry again when she leans into me the tiniest bit, almost subconsciously. "I would never hurt you."

I'm waiting for her reply, desperate for the assurance that she knows, when suddenly, searing pain erupts across my temple, I'm ripped away from her, and all hell breaks loose.

14

AMELIA

"GET your fucking hands off my girlfriend."

The growling voice reverberating through the night air freezes my feet to the concrete driveway. I watch, unable to move as Nick is ripped away from me, the sucker punch he receives to the temple quickly followed by another to the gut. I watch, horrified as his eyes take on a dazed look before fluttering shut, his body crumpling to the floor in the most sickening way. And I watch, fear chilling me to the bone as Dylan turns his steely, furious gaze on me.

"What the fuck is wrong with you?" he demands which, in any other situation, would be funny because that's exactly what I was thinking. It's his hand reaching for me that snaps me out of my stupor, causes me to stumble backward, away from him, but it's pointless. He grabs me easily, rough fingers encircling my wrist the same way they did almost a month ago, yanking me forward with so much force, I swear something pops.

"Let me go." I struggle weakly, my voice little more than a whimper and I hate myself for it. I cast a look at Nick, groaning on the concrete, vulnerable in a way I've never seen him before, and I whimper again.

Dylan ignores me. If anything, his grip tightens as he drags me away from Nick, from the house full of people oblivious to what's happening. "You think I'm gonna let you run around like a little whore?" he spits, face bright red, eyes ablaze, features twisted in the most awful leer. "What were you gonna do, huh? Fuck him to get back at me?"

"Stop it."

He doesn't. He hauls me across the thin strip of grass separating the guys' drive from their neighbors, making a beeline for the car I recognize as his. For the first time, I realize Dylan didn't come alone; his friends are leaning against his car, laughing as I wrestle and try not to cry. "Get your ass in my car before I throw you in there."

Every inch of common sense I possess screams in warning. I can't get in that car, I know I can't. Using all my strength, I dig my heels into the grass and wrench my arm from him, ignoring the pain lancing up the limb. "No."

I cradle my wrist to my chest, unable to breathe as Dylan turns towards me slowly, his entire body taut with furious tension. *"No?"* He repeats incredulously.

"No." My voice shakes, my entire body shakes but I don't back down. "I'm not your girlfriend anymore, Dylan. You don't get a say in what I do."

It's a physical thing, the process of my words sinking into Dylan's consciousness. I watch it happen, as it twists his features even more until he resembles the man, the monster, I'm terrified of. "You're gonna regret talking to me like that."

It's a menacing promise followed up by the lifting of his hand. Fear chases the fight from my body as I freeze once again, powerless to do anything other than close my eyes and brace for impact as his palm arcs towards me on a perfect trajectory for my cheek.

But the impact never comes.

A loud grunt and a clapping sound have my eyes reopening just as a broad body tackles Dylan to the ground, Nick's fist rearing back to deliver a revenge blow across my ex-boyfriend's cheek. Momentarily, I'm stunned as he delivers blow after blow, unsure if it's relief or horror or something else entirely coursing through me.

It's definitely horror I feel when, in a flurry of bodies, the cowardly, sorry excuses for men watching this all happen approach and haul Nick off their coughing, spluttering friend, two of them hoisting him up by the armpits while a third socks him in the stomach.

A scream rips from my throat as fists fly and groans fill the air, Nick's groans, as he's pummelled by punch after punch. He's strong, I know he's strong, but three against one is too much for even him and he's been drinking and, *fuck*, he might have a concussion and…

Panic drives me forward. I'm rushing towards him, screaming for them to stop, when a thick arm hooks around my waist, holding me back. "Not so fast," a sickeningly amused voice coos in my ear, fueling my panic. I cringe away from Will and he laughs, he fucking laughs, holding me fast as I kick and howl and flail like a feral cat.

"*Nick.*" I scream his name and he shouts mine back, a hoarse sound that reminds me of something.

Elbow and knees, he'd said to me. *You're small but if you catch a guy in the groin with an elbow, he's going down.*

And that's what I do; I jerk an elbow back and it must connect with something sensitive because Will hisses loudly. Abruptly, he drops me, tossing me aside like a piece of trash. I hit the ground hard, the force of it reverberating up my knees and palms but I ignore the ache. I'm barely down before I'm scrambling to my feet, panicking and shrieking all over again when a new set of arms wrap around my waist and haul me upright. A soothing voice hushes me. "Amelia, it's me."

I choke on a sob of relief, my body going limp in Ben's arms. "Please help him."

It's as the words leave my mouth that two more bodies appear in my peripheral. My relief becomes overwhelming, threatening to buckle my knees, as Jackson and Cass and some of their baseball buddies rush into the fray, picking those assholes off one by one.

I can't see Nick, there's too many bulky bodies blocking my view, but I see Dylan. I see him storm towards me, steam practically pouring from his ears, spittle flying as he yells, "You fuck them too, Mils? You really are a little slu-"

He doesn't get a chance to finish; Cass' fist smashing into his cheekbone cuts him off. Dylan hits the ground like a lead sack, unmoving, and for a terrifying moment, I wonder if Cass accidentally knocked the life out of him.

For an exhilarating moment, I almost hope he has.

I'm flushed with an odd feeling when Dylan groans and struggles to his feet, blood rushing from his nose as he staggers a step toward me. "Amelia, baby." His crooning has the same effect on me as I imagine drinking battery acid would. A bloody hand stretches out in my direction, a pathetic look begging for pity contorting his fucked-up face. It makes me so mad, so unbelievably livid that I find myself stepping out of Ben's safe embrace, ignoring the protests of him and others. My anger only grows when relief floods Dylan's face.

Relief I kill with a smack of my palm, smacking him like he planned on smacking me. But it's not enough, it's not close to satisfying. So, I ball my fist, careful to keep my thumb untucked, and I punch the bastard who keeps trying to ruin my life.

"You are a pathetic excuse for a man," I seethe, ignoring the throbbing pain in my knuckles amplifying the ache of my wrist. "If you ever touch me or my friends or anyone else again, I'll fucking kill you."

I mean it. God, do I mean it and there must be something on my face that proves it because Dylan, in the smartest move of his life, backs up. One step, then another, his mouth open in a perfect 'o' of shock as he cradles the jaw I wish I was strong enough to break. He wants to argue. I can see it in his bloodshot eyes. But then they dart to something over my shoulder and his mouth snaps shut, he stumbles back another step. "Fuck you," he can't help but hiss, spitting out a mouthful of dark red blood before ambling away.

His friends—I completely forgot about his friends right now but they're all as bloody as their leader, all brimming with the same barely contained anger—follow behind him, each and every one of them throwing me despicable glares.

Only when they round the corner and disappear from sight do I let my legs give out like they're begging to.

A few things happen all at once.

Vaguely, I hear someone shouting for everyone to leave, and only then do I realize we've garnered an audience. A semi-circle of drunken students disperses under Jackson's command. I can only imagine the stories already brewing, ready to circulate campus.

A slender body plops on the ground beside me. A dainty hand slips into my uninjured one. Blonde hair tickles my shoulder as Luna huddles close, her voice urgent as it enquires whether I'm okay.

There's only a second of delay between her appearance and Cass'. He crouches in front of me, all but yelling his concerns and not at all soothed by my weak nod of assurance. He's gentle as he lifts me to my feet, cradling me under his arm as he guides me somewhere.

It's not until a wooden floor creaks beneath my feet do I register I'm inside. Cool leather sticks to my thighs as I'm set down gently and, for some reason, it's the sight of my grass-stained knees that has reality flooding in to attack me. Tears I desperately try to keep at bay suddenly escape, flowing freely down my cheeks in hot streams, gradually getting more and more intense as sobs wrack my body. A hand on the back of my head guides me towards a hard chest, and I clutch hopelessly at Cass' shirt. "I'm sorry. I'm so, so sorry."

He says something but I don't hear it. I can't focus on anything other than overwhelming emotions and my racing mind. A million thoughts fight for the spotlight but only one manages to take precedence.

"Nick." His name leaves me in a gasp as my head snaps upwards, eyes frantically searching for a man I was furious with no more than ten minutes ago, the man with an uncanny knack for saving me when I need it. It doesn't take me long to find him and when I do, when my gaze falls on him battered and bleeding and bruised, a whole new round of sobs overcome me. I push Cass away from me, suddenly despising his comfort, suddenly feeling guilty for wanting it. He's probably injured too. And Jackson and God knows who else, all because of me. Squeezing my eyes shut, I cradle my face in my hands, hiding from all the sympa-thetic stares I don't deserve. "This is all my fault."

A mere five seconds pass before someone's gently prying my hands away.

"Look at me, *querida*," a hoarse voice softly requests and even though I don't want to, I force my eyes open. A pair of honey-coloured ones lurk inches away, framed by already darkening bruises and drying blood. I try to cringe away, to hide again, but Nick doesn't let me. Crouching in front of me, as close as he can get, he laces his fingers through mine. "This isn't your fault," he tells me quietly, his deep voice almost a whisper.

When he says it, I almost believe him.

Almost.

"I dragged you all into this," is my croaked reply, sounding almost as empty as I feel.

"You did nothing wrong." Not only Nick claims but several other voices too. I know they're trying to help but it only makes me feel worse, like I'm drowning in a tidal wave of shame and embarrassment and so much fucking guilt. I drop my gaze, staring at Nick and I's clasped hands, the state of his knuckles making me feel sick to my stomach. I withdraw my hands from his, readying myself to get up and leave no matter how hard they try to stop me because I want to go home, when a sentence paralyzes me.

"You can't do this again." Across from me, Luna stands, her tone steady and serious, her blue eyes dark. "This is the third time he's hurt you. *The third time.* You have to report him."

Silence settles over all of us, so profound you could hear a pin drop. So silent I can practically hear my little white lies disintegrating. So silent I hear Cass' sharp intake of breath. "The third time?"

I wince at his confused question at the same time Luna lets out a loud, dry cackle. "You think that's bad?" She gestures to my ever-injured wrist. "Two months ago she came home with a split lip and a concussion after he-"

"*Luna.*"

Cass tenses beside me. "He hit you?"

"No!" I promise in a shaky voice.

"No, he just slammed a car door in your face."

It's like all the air rushes out of the room, leaving behind only palpable shock. Almost as soon as the words leave her mouth, Luna's sneer falls. Her eyes go wide, her mouth opening and closing as an apology forms and dies on her lips.

An apology I'm in no state to hear.

"You have no right to tell them that," I seethe, anger joining the myriad of other emotions plaguing me. My gaze ping-pongs around the room, flitting from Cass to Nick to Jackson to Ben and finding the same thing on each of their faces.

Pity.

Exactly what I didn't want, exactly why I've kept my mouth shut. I didn't want them looking at me the way they're looking at me right now. The way I catch Kate and Luna looking at me when they think I won't notice. The way that makes me want to throw up and pull out my hair and lock myself in my room, never to be seen again.

Two stares in particular are killing me the most. I choose what feels like the easier, the less daunting, of the pair, glancing aside to where Cass sits stiffly, a silent question on his face. *Why didn't you tell me?*

"I didn't want you to do anything stupid," is my answer, my pathetic excuse. I know my brother. If I had told him, he would've strangled

Dylan with his bare hands and ruined his own life in the process. "Please, don't be mad at me."

Cass blinks at me once, twice, and then he melts. An arm slinking around my shoulders, he pulls me into his side and hugs me fiercely. "You can't keep shit like that from me, Tiny," he whispers into my air, the words thick with emotion. "Don't do it again, please."

Tears tighten my throat so I simply nod, hugging him just as tightly.

Every single person in the room jumps when the front door suddenly flies open. Cass spins in his seat, a protective hand gripping my thigh while Nick—still crouching in front of me, watching the whole ordeal silently—springs to his feet, acting as a defensive barrier between me and the intruder.

A palpable wave of repose washes over the room when we find Kate standing in the doorway—I completely forgot she said she was going to try to stop by after her date. Expression furrowed with confusion, she scans the room, silently taking in the boys' bloody states and her tear-stained cheeks. With a sigh, she shuts the door behind her. Without a word, she disappears into the kitchen. Cupboards slam and a few muttered curses sound before my friend reappears, an unopened bottle of tequila in one hand, a first aid kit in the other. "Well?" she probes. "Who wants to start?"

15

AMELIA

ALCOHOL STEMS my apprehension as I shift on my feet outside Nick's bedroom door. Laughter floats towards me from downstairs where Kate and Luna are stitching up the boys; Ben escaped the brawl unscathed but Cass and Jackson both have pretty nasty-looking knuckles. Nick, in the worst state out of all of them, disappeared before anyone could get to him, grumbling something about cleaning himself up. However, he left the first aid kit on the coffee table and I doubt hand soap is going to do much to heal his wounds.

So, I'm hovering outside his room, the first aid kit and a bottle of rum cradled in my arm, trying to find the courage to knock because the least I can do is clean him up, since he's all banged up because of me, but what if he's mad? If I was him, I'd be mad. I ruined his birthday, I got him punched in the face, I snapped at him in the kitchen because I was feeling weird and jealous and insecure.

Sucking in a deep breath, I push my preoccupations aside because I owe him this much. Like I said, it's the least I can do. And maybe I want to make sure he's okay.

Not long passes after I rap my knuckles—the ones not swollen and sore—against the door do I hear a gruff permission to enter. Opening the door, I peek my head into the room. The dim, empty room, only lit by the small amount of light coming from the ensuite. The door closes behind me with a soft click as I pad towards the bathroom, nudging open the slightly ajar door with my foot.

A shirtless Nick stands in front of the sink. The tap running, he splashes water on his face and hands, a pitiful attempt to get the blood off of him, completely missing the dried red splotches staining his neck and collarbone. My eyes roam, not to admire or fawn over the perfect ridges and muscles making up Nick's torso but to note each bruise and cut. Stomach turning and resisting the urge to cry, I lean against the doorframe and clear my throat. "You should just shower."

Nick's head jerks towards me and I wince as I'm fully confronted by the sight of him. In a mere half hour, his injuries have gone from bad to worse. The bleeding has stopped but the multiple bruises scattered across his face and body have darkened considerably, an ugly rainbow of purple, yellow, and blue. Yet despite his pitiable appearance, those pretty eyes light up with a familiar cocky glint and his lips—despite the fact the top one is cut and must hurt like a bitch—slant upward. "Are you offering to join me?"

Tears tickle the back of my throat but I swallow them down. Rolling my eyes, I brandish the goods I snagged from downstairs. "Shower, please, so I can sew you up."

It should be illegal, really, how he manages to look so handsome, so charming, with a face that damaged. "If I'm a good boy, do I get a drink?"

And it should be illegal that not even a severe beating can knock the flirt out of him.

"Shower," I repeat sternly, awkwardly jostling the things in my arms so I can grasp the door knob. "Or I'm handing you over to Ben."

It's a bluff, of course. I'll help fix him up even if I have to tie him down to do it. But it has the desired effect; Nick's groan is muffled as I pull the door shut, the smallest chuckle escaping me despite the situation. Setting the supplies on the nightstand, I perch on the edge of Nick's bed, nervously wringing my hands in my lap. I smile faintly when the shower turns on, feeling a fleeting sense of accomplishment because at least I've done one thing right tonight. However, my face soon falls when I catch sight of my reflection in the mirror hanging on the back of the bathroom door.

Honestly, Nick's beat-up face has nothing on me.

He looks like he's in pain but I look straight-up dead, even worse than I did the last time I woke up here. There isn't a hint of color in my pale skin, no sign of life behind green irises, even my damn hair looks dull. With the dark circles under my eyes, I look like the one who took several punches. And my dress, my poor beautiful dress, is white no more. Splattered with blood, stained with grass stains, and inciting the overwhelming urge to rip it off and burn it.

I'm wondering if Nick would mind me stealing more of his clothes when my reflection blurs, the door abruptly swinging open to reveal a wet, half-naked Nick. A flutter of deja-vu hits me except, contrary to last time, I can't stop my eyes from drifting to his chest. Purely because that's where my eyeline is, of course.

No other reason.

Like earlier, though, I can't focus on the sculpted brawn or the deep valleys between his pronounced abs or the tempting v of muscles leading to the towel wrapped low and loose around his hips. No, all I can see is the swirling mass of bruises slightly hidden by his tattoos.

"Enjoying the view?" My gaze darts up to find his teasing but soft. Comforting. "It looks worse than it is, *querida*."

Hm. Didn't I just claim the same about my wrist and knuckles less than ten minutes ago when both are smarting something fierce? "You should see a doctor.."

Nick quirks a challenging brow, glancing pointedly at my wrist. "I will if you do."

"You might have a concussion."

"I don't."

"Is that your professional opinion?"

"It's the opinion of someone who's had a concussion before." Crossing the room to rifle in the chest of drawers tucked in the corner, Nick gives no warning before dropping his towel. A muffled squeak gets caught in my throat as I quickly avert my gaze, not quite quick enough to avoid an eyeful of bronzed, toned ass that's probably going to be stamped in my brain until the end of time. Cheeks flushed for a myriad of reasons, I only risk an upward glance when footsteps sound and stop right in front of me. A semi-clothed Nick—he forewent a top but at least he's wearing sweats—smirks down at me. "Why would I go to a doctor when I have you?"

"I'm not a doctor."

"You study medicine."

"Physiotherapy," I correct. Big freaking difference.

Nick tuts, waving a dismissive hand in the air. "Eh, same thing."

I don't get the chance to argue that no, they're not the same thing. I forget I was going to argue at all, actually, when he pulls me gently to my feet and switches our positions, sitting in the spot I vacated and guiding me to stand in front of him. My traitorous heart skips a beat when he spreads his legs and maneuvers me between them, pesky guilt suddenly fighting for dominance over something else entirely as I'm trapped between a pair of thick thighs. "Fix me up, doc."

It's a miracle I manage to soak a handful of cotton balls without getting antiseptic solution everywhere; my hands are shaking something fierce and I can only pray when my fingers skirt his jawline, tilting his head from side to side so I can assess the damage, he doesn't notice the tremors. In my defense, it's hard to keep your composure when there's a very large pair of hands dangerously close to your ass.

Resigned to my fate, I warn, "This is gonna sting a bit."

Nick crooks a dark, split brow. "I'm a big boy, *querida*."

I bite down on my bottom lip to prevent a smile when the second I press the cotton to one of the many scrapes littering his face, he winces and hisses out a curse. But once again, my cheer is short-lived; it fizzles out when he reacts the same again and again and again for every cut I dab.

"I'm sorry," I whisper as my thumb sweeps over his cheek in a way meant to be comforting but is probably weird.

"Stop apologizing," Nick murmurs, his breath washing over my hand as I swipe his bloody lip clean. I must press too hard, though, because he jolts slightly, his quiet groan echoed by my hushed gasp when his hands suddenly grip the backs of my thighs, his long fingers hot against my skin. It only lasts a split second—like it was a gut reaction or a reflex or something—but the impression feels branding. The aftermath too, a lingering, tangible thing making it difficult for me to breathe properly.

It's Nick's turn to apologize, his gaze squarely fixed on my collarbone as his jaw clenches. If I didn't know any better, I'd think there was blush creeping up his neck, discoloring his bronze skin.

"It's okay." I toss the newest bloodied cotton ball into the growing pile on the nightstand before stepping back an inch, making enough room between us for me to pick up his hands and inspect his knuckles. Like the rest of him, they're pretty banged up, bruised and swollen from repeatedly pummelling Dylan but they're not split.

Nodding my satisfaction, I drop his hands and step away to retrieve the trusty Arnica, wondering if a single tube is even enough.

My patient, however, has other plans.

"Can I just…" Nick starts and doesn't finish. His hands flex and clench repeatedly where they rest on his thighs as he momentarily grapples for words. Sighing, he peers up at me so softly, so gently, it makes me want to cry all over again. "C'mere for a second."

I'm not sure I have a choice but I'm also not sure I'd object. Not when strong hands wrap pull me between his thighs again. I'm silent and pliant as he guides me to sit sideways on one of his broad thighs. One hand glides to rest on the small of my back while the other coasts upwards. His palms glide over my neck, his thumb tracing my jawbone, and he holds me like that. He stares at me, something undecipherable flooding his golden irises as they inspect me carefully.

"What're you doing?" I ask in a whisper, for some reason. Probably because it feels like we're doing something… not wrong, exactly. Illicit isn't the right word either. Dangerous, maybe.

Dangerous because when he cups the back of my head, coaxes it to rest in the crook where his neck meets his shoulder, and nestles his face in my hair, it feels like the most natural thing in the world.

And when he murmurs, "I just gotta hold you for a sec," in a quiet, calm, honest voice, that feels pretty freaking perilous too.

Nick gets his chance to play nurse.

After holding me for what simultaneously feels like too long and not long enough, he shoos me into the bathroom with a change of clothes bundled in my arms. "Trying to get me out of my dress, Silva?" I'd quipped and almost immediately, I'd regretted it.

Not a single beat passed before he was flashing me that killer—if currently a little distorted smile—and those freaking wonderful dimples made an appearance. They winked at me in all their glory and suddenly, the long line of women begging for Nick's attention made even more sense; I'd probably beg a little too if it got me personal access to that smile, those dimples, on a regular basis.

"Can't blame a guy for trying," was his quick response and while externally, I'd simply rolled my eyes and disappeared into the ensuite, internally, I was fawning like a damsel.

And when I try to leave the bathroom—my ruined dress swapped for another pair of too-big sweats and another form-swallowing t-shirt and the softest, most luxurious socks I've ever worn in my freaking life —and Nick stops me with a firm hand on my shoulder, I fawn all over again.

"My turn to take care of you," he informs me, leaving no room for arguments; before I can even begin to formulate one, he's hoisting me up and setting me on the bathroom counter. With a tenderness contradicting his hulking form, he cradles my hands, a contradicting glare on his face as he inspects them thoroughly. His chest—still bare because he's obviously trying to punish me—heave as he sucks in a deep breath, releasing it in an angry puff. "You know, I don't know whether I should be furious at you for almost breaking your hand or weirdly proud for giving him what he deserves."

"Personally, I'm leaning towards the latter."

Nick huffs again, an odd cross between a snarl and a laugh. When he determines my wounds aren't fatal, he sets my hands gently on my thighs. I expect him to back away but, as usual, he surprises me. Pressing closer until my knees dig into his lower stomach, his palms come down on either side of me, caging me in. He doesn't say anything, seemingly content with staring at my hands, and I fidget under the intensity. Silence morphs into tension, thick between us, and when I can't take it anymore, I dig my knee into him harder. "Does your scowl have healing powers or something?"

His gaze darts to mine and I reel back at the emotions swarming it, none of them distinguishable but all of them so potent. "It's my fault you're hurt."

"No, it's not." It's no one's fault but my own.

"You were outside because of me," he says through gritted teeth. "Because I made you uncomfortable."

"You didn't. I got... spooked."

God, he's going to break his own damn jaw with all that clenching. "I scared you."

"Spooked," I repeat with emphasis because there's a definite difference. "It caught me off guard."

It upset me if I'm being honest. My silly little head took what he said
—*did I mention you look really fucking hot tonight?*—and ran with it
because of course he was hitting on me. Of course, that's what this has
all been about. Why else would he go through all that effort—the
boxing, the heroics, all the little moments I ridiculously thought were
special—if not for it to all be a ploy to get into my pants?

To quote Luna quoting some drunk, scorned woman; Nicolas Silva
doesn't fuck with feelings.

Nicolas Silva just fucks.

Sure, he flirts and he teases and he charms on a regular basis. I don't
think he can turn it off. But this was different; he got that look on his face
I've seen him use on other women, he complimented me with empty
words, and I had never felt more disappointed in myself or in someone
else as I did in that moment.

And then he got his freaking ass beat on my behalf and I realized I'm
an overreacting fool.

But that's not something you divulge. It makes me sound petty and
pitiful and jealous over something, someone, I have no right to be
jealous over. So, in lieu of all that, I say, "It was weird. You hitting on me
was weird.

"Weird," Nick repeats slowly, rolling the word like it tastes bad on
his tongue.

"Yeah." I shift. "Because we're friends."

Again, he parrots, "Friends."

I nod, gaining enough courage to add, "You've helped me a lot these
past few weeks. I freaked and thought maybe it was all some ulterior
motive and I didn't like that."

"It wasn't." He's so quick to reassure me I have no choice but to
believe him.

"Okay." Taking the hand he offers me, I hop down off the counter.

He keeps a hold of me, his thumb swiping over my pulse. "Are we
good?"

I squeeze his hand. "We're good."

What the hell else am I going to say? No? Screw you and your poor,
beaten body, you heroic little shit?

"Wanna go back downstairs?"

My nose wrinkles at the suggestion. "Not really."

Part of the reason I came up here in the first place was to escape Cass' suffocating gaze. I love him so much and I understand why he's so concerned but the constant attention only serves to remind me of what I'd rather forget. Right now, what I need is a distraction.

And staying up here with Nick seems like a pretty good one.

16

NICK

"CASS DEFINITELY THINKS I'm corrupting you right now," I think aloud between greedy sips of rum.

Amelia scoffs, stealing the bottle from my grip and sucking down its content just as eagerly. "Cass suffers from a hefty dose of Big Brother Syndrome."

Fucking cheers to that. The second we opted out of rejoining the others in favor of getting shitfaced by ourselves in my room, I knew I was going to cop shit from Cass in the morning. I couldn't find it in me to care, though, not when the opportunity of having Amelia all to myself was dangling in front of me. Not when I'm unhinged with the need to have her close so I know she's safe, so I can keep her safe, so it's a little easier to resist the urge to find Dylan and finish what he foolishly started. Sitting side by side on my bed, our backs against the headboard with only an almost-empty bottle of liquor between us is worth any kind of big brother intimidation.

It's struck me more than once that while, no, this isn't the first time I've had a girl in this bed, it is the first time I've had one without the intention of fucking her. These sheets have seen a lot of things; conversation isn't one of them.

Intentions, no. Bone-deep desperation, fuck yes.

But I'm not thinking about that right now; one big, rage-inducing revelation Amelia refuses to discuss knocked any amorous notions right out of my head.

EJ BLAISE

"We should play a game," she declares out of nowhere—something she's been doing a lot, blurting out random things, I think in the hopes I won't ask what she knows I'm dying to ask.

I know what she's doing yet still a smirk twists my lips before I can stop it. "Is it a naked game?" God, I should've learned my lesson earlier but I can't help myself. Any opportunity to tease her—whether I'm drunk or sober—I take it. And as long as I don't go too far like earlier, I'm either rewarded with a mischievous grin and a retorting quip or a cute pout and a thwap on the arm.

It's not fair to pick favorites, I know, but the latter option? Sign me up any time.

It must be my lucky day because the latter is what I get. The slap is a little more timid than usual, wary of my sorry state, but the pout is just as furious. I have to clasp my hands together to stop myself from reaching out and rubbing a thumb against her plump bottom lip.

"Get your mind out of the gutter," she chastises but that pout is trembling, struggling to hide a smile.

Little does she know my mind has been in the gutter since she crept into my room and performed that whole sexy nurse bit. I think I'd take a million beatings if it meant having her standing between my legs looking at me with all that concern again.

"Fact for a fact," she slurs, her face adorably flushed as the copious amounts of liquor flooding her tiny body kicks in. "I tell you something, you tell me something."

Interesting. An opportunity to learn more about someone who keeps so much so close to her chest. And who the fuck am I to say no to a pretty girl wanting to learn more about me?

She squeals in delight when I nod my agreement. Tilting her head—fuck, I love when she does that—she gestures for me to go first, chewing on her lip, and fuck, I love when she does that too.

I think for a moment, slugging another drink before choosing the path of least resistance, the easy subject of personal interests. "I was the photographer for my high school yearbook."

A choked laugh comes from the other side of the bed. "I don't know if I'm more surprised you're a photographer or that you participated in high school."

"Excuse me, I was a model student." I flatten my palm against my chest in a display of mock offense that only lasts a moment before I drop

116

it because yeah, that's a lie. The only thing I did right in school was graduate with decent enough grades and leave. "They were offering extra credit for participation, I had a camera, it made sense. And I'm not a photographer, I just like photography."

"You still like it?"

As a response, I gesture towards my desk where one of my cameras is strewn, the wall behind it littered with photos. Cooing an intrigued noise, Amelia scrambles to her feet and scampers to the other side of the room. "Hey," I call after her. "You owe me a fact."

She waves a dismissive hand in my direction, her attention occupied by the various pictures I've snapped over the years. "These are really good, Nick."

"You're a cheat, Amelia."

Scowling, Amelia spins to face me again, propping her ass on the desk, and oh, doesn't that bring my mind to places they have no business being. "I used to be a dancer."

"Nope," I tut, shaking my head. "Doesn't count. I already knew that."

"How?"

"I moved into your house, remember?" A fact that still blows my mind because what are the fucking chances? "I saw the studio. Plus, there are at least a dozen pictures of a red-headed little girl prancing around in leotards and tutus in the Morgans' living room."

"There are?"

I frown at her meek question. I never paid much attention to the Morgans' house decor but Lynn's love of family photos is unavoidable. They're everywhere, framed and hung on walls or propped on the mantelpiece or arranged in collages. Amelia's in almost all of them, as many pictures of her as there are of Cass and his older brother—so many that I'm a real dumbass for not recognizing her sooner. "Why wouldn't there be?"

"I thought they'd take them down."

"Why?" The question barely leaves my lips and I already know I'm not going to get an answer. I anticipate the responding shrug of her delicate shoulders. And as much as I want to know, I think I've tested enough boundaries for tonight. But she still owes me a fact, so. "Tell me why you stopped dancing."

Apparently, that's not the safe territory I assumed it would be.

Amelia tenses as she wraps her arms around herself, hugging herself tightly. "I hurt my knee."

Instinctively, my gaze drops to the aforementioned joints. Even hidden by her—*my*—sweats, I know the only obvious injuries are the ones from tonight, from when that dickhead tossed her to the ground. Concern balls in my chest. She landed pretty hard; if she already had an injury, that could make it worse, right? Fuck, what if I made it worse? With all the training? God, if she was in pain, she wouldn't even tell me, I know she wouldn't.

As if reading my panicked thoughts, Amelia adds, "It rarely hurts anymore."

Rarely. Not never. "What happened?"

Green eyes narrow to slits. "Now who's the cheat?"

"Jackson and I have matching tattoos." I throw out the first random fact that pops into my head, not allowing her any time to dwell before asking, "Is that why you left Carlton?"

Amelia doesn't reply but something tells me I hit the nail on the head.

My ribs protest as I scoot to the edge of the bed, planting my bare feet on the floor and waiting expectantly. Amelia dithers momentarily before joining, sinking onto the mattress with her thigh flush against mine. "I don't like talking about it."

"You don't have to."

Amelia shifts, pulling her knees up to her chest and resting her cheek on top of them. For a minute, she stares at me silently, eyes searching for something I'm not privy to before she sighs. "I was in a car accident. That's how I got hurt. I-" She averts her gaze as she swallows hard. "It was my fault and I kinda went off the rails a little after it happened."

"You were driving?" A shake of her head is the only response I get. "Then how-"

"Dad decided we needed a fresh start," Amelia cuts me off, dragging her knuckles across her eyes, "so we packed up and we left. No note, no goodbye, no nothing. We left in the middle of the night like criminals. The Morgans helped raise me and I just left them. They should hate me for it."

The sheer amount of guilt in her voice hits me as hard as her ex-boyfriend did, and it's twice as painful and disconcerting. It sends an inane urge to soothe ricocheting through me, and my arm sneaks its way around her shoulder without any conscious thought. "They don't." I know that with the utmost certainty. "They talk about you all the time."

Curious, disbelieving eyes slide to mine. "Really?"

"Non-stop, Amelia. I was sick of you before I even knew you."

A choked, watery laugh escapes her. "Oh yeah?"

"Uh-huh." *No.*

With the slightest tug, Amelia is falling into me, her head dropping to my shoulder—where it belongs, a weird little voice in my head whispers—and her knees slanting sideways over my thighs. "Whatever happened," I have a feeling the specifics are not something I'll ever be privy to, "they don't blame you for it."

Her response is so quiet, so clearly unintended for my ears, I pretend I didn't hear it. "They should."

Never in my life have I found it as hard to get out of bed as I did this morning. Honest to God I wanted to weep when I opened my eyes after a pitiful amount of rest and a peaceful sleep—probably the best I've ever had—faded into a reality that involved every inch of my body screaming in agony. However, all that pain seemed to dissipate when my vision focused and I clocked the mane of red hair my face was buried in.

We were holding hands. We were cuddling in bed, close as can be, with our fingers intertwined and clasped to her chest and the first thought that popped into my head was *damn. I wouldn't mind waking up like this every morning.*

The second thought? *Fuck me, am I in trouble.*

I'm no stranger to fleeing a bed after spending the night with a girl to avoid the awkward morning-after conversation but this morning was the first time I fled in a state of borderline panic. Honestly, I've been in that state since last night. It's hard to pinpoint the source; it might be the residual effects of watching her get berated and belittled and manhandled and being able to do jack-shit about it; or maybe it's because Luna's words are still ringing in my ears and it's killing me not knowing the specifics, knowing it's not my place to ask. I have a sneaky feeling, though, that it has everything to do with the steadily creeping realization that I'm way more than just intrigued by Amelia and I have no idea how to handle that.

I thought getting out of the house, forcing some distance between us, before anyone else woke up and ruining this collegiate year's almost imperfect attendance record would give me some respite but no. Now, I'm stuck in a lecture hall not paying a single iota of attention to anything my professor is saying, my mind wholly occupied wondering whether or not Amelia is still in my bed.

More than one gaze swung my way when I strolled in later, a wave of hushed murmurs breaking out. I ignored the nosy motherfuckers as I slumped into a seat near the back, yanking my baseball cap further down to cover more of my busted face and hoping my glare would properly convey my lower tolerance for conversation and bullshit gossip.

Alas, the dark cloud hovering above my head isn't formidable enough.

"Some party last night, Nick."

Before I even glance at the unwelcome speaker, I'm stifling a groan. His name is a mystery to me—John something, maybe—and the irony isn't lost on me, considering he was allegedly one of the people celebrating my birthday last night. But I do know him. Or more like I know his mouth; we have more than a couple of classes in common this semester and I've already heard enough of his shit-talk.

I grunt a non-response and face forward again, pretending to be engrossed in the lecturer's presentation on Mark Twain's 'A Connecticut Yankee in King Arthur's Court' as if I don't have my dad's old, detailed notes burning a hole in my copy of the novel; he started practicing his lectures on me when I was six and Twain was a frequent favorite.

Either Maybe-John doesn't clock my disinterest or he isn't phased by it. "Looks like you got your birthday beatings," he snickers. "Rumor has it Wells beat the shit out of you because you fucked his girlfriend."

I snort. The only punch Dylan landed was a cheap shot. It was his three little shit friends who ambushed me. "Rumor has it I beat the shit out of him first."

"Right. Fuck, you know he looks worse than you?"

And if that doesn't perk up my morning; I almost get the urge to smile.

Maybe-John kills that urge pretty quickly by opening his mouth.

"And that little Amelia helped." I tense at the mention of her name, his tone as he says it. My hands ball into fists when he lets out a long, low whistle. "Fuck, man, she was hot before but watching her sock him one? Permanent place in my spank bank."

Do not start a fight in class, my common sense chastises.

But I want to, my sketchy impulse control whines.

To my dismay, common sense wins out. As much as I want to—and fuck, I want to—knocking this guy's lights out would only earn fleeting satisfaction and possibly an expulsion, Plus, one more punch and I think my knuckles might give out.

So, itching with the urge to do more, I kiss my teeth and slowly turn to face whoever the fuck this guy is, hoping the full extent of my scowl can pierce the asshole's thick skull. "You don't talk about her," I warn, my voice low and threatening and so deadly fucking serious. "You don't look at her. You don't even think about her. If you do, fucking trust me, I will make what I did to Dylan last night look like a fucking spa treatment. Okay?"

It must be obvious that I mean every word I say because John's smug expression falls flat. "I was kidding."

"Don't," I spit. "Stay the fuck away from her."

Laughing nervously, John shifts in his seat, expression a lame attempt at unbothered. "She your girlfriend or something, Silva?"

I don't take my eyes off him, don't relax, as I reply. "Or something."

17

AMELIA

He's drunk.

Belligerently drunk, more whiskey running through his veins than blood.

The smell of it overwhelms me as I haul my boyfriend into the car, almost crushing myself in the process, sighing in relief when I get him situated and shut the passenger door behind him. I hate driving but tonight, I'm glad I took on the role of designated driver; Dylan has a habit of not recognizing his own intoxication and he doesn't like to be told no.

Muttering a few choice words about brainless, childish boyfriends who can't hold their liquor, I dash to the driver's side and slip into the car, my hands shaking as I fumble to fit the keys into the ignition. It's colder than it usually is this time of year, a chill in the air that my minuscule outfit doesn't agree with; the short dress with very little material Dylan begged me to wear does nothing to ward off the cold.

A suit jacket tucked around my shoulders would've made all the difference but alas, add thoughtless to my long list of grievances with my boyfriend tonight. I should know by now that chivalry is off the cards when he's wasted.

I should know by now that chivalry is off the cards when he's sober most of the time.

The drunk oaf occupying the seat beside me slaps my hand away when I try to turn the radio on so the drive to his place passes in relative silence, a weird tension in the air. We were supposed to stay in mine tonight, and I prefer that a million times more than spending the night surrounded by Dylan's stand-offish roommates, but there's no way I'm subjecting Luna and Kate to his drunken-ness—bad roommate etiquette.

"You need help getting inside, babe?" I ask softly as I pull into his drive, reaching over to rest a hand on one of his hunched shoulders. The minute I make contact, he's shucking me off. Hazy, unfocused blue eyes snap to mine, an anger in them that matches the scowl contorting his features, and I recoil at the feroc-ity. "What's wrong?"

"I saw how you were looking at him," he snaps, the words slurred and senseless.

"What?"

"Don't act stupid." In one jerky movement, he undoes his seatbelt and turns awkwardly to face me, leaning in too close. "You were flirting with him all night and you know it."

My head snaps back in shock, the crown smacking against the window behind me. Dylan wastes no time filling the space I created between us, his large frame suffocating my smaller one even in a car with not much room for intimi-dation. "Dylan, I wasn't flirting with anyone."

"Bullshit." He's seething, face red for reasons beyond alcohol levels. "I take you somewhere nice, treat you well, and this is how you repay me?"

Somewhere nice.

The circumstances don't call for it yet still, I resist the urge to laugh.

Dylan's definition of 'somewhere nice' greatly differs from mine. His version involves a function organized by one of his lecturers as a way to meet potential employers. His 'somewhere nice' was a stuffy room filled with stuffier people, none of whom I knew, not the romantic date night his accusations make it sound.

"Babe," I keep my voice calm and steady, knowing how he gets when he's drunk. "I have no idea what you're talking about. The only person I talked to tonight was you."

Even that's a stretch; I neglect to mention that most of my night was spent lurking on the sidelines watching him schmooze and charm. Any talking I did wasn't talking at all. It was smiling and looking pretty and letting myself be toted around like a trophy wife. The closest thing to stimulating conversation I had was with the waiter who dropped off our flavorless food.

His disbelief as evident as his anger, Dylan scoffs and draws away, clumsily opening the passenger door before slamming it shut behind him. "Dyl, come on." With a sigh, I elbow open my door and start to get out too. He's in a mood, I tell myself. He'll get over it in the morning.

I'm halfway out of the car, hovering in an awkward half-standing position when my vision suddenly goes black. Searing pain ricochets through the side of my face, confusion clouding my senses as I totter unsteadily on too-high heels. It feels like forever passes before I realize that the sharp sting, the hot stickiness dripping from what I assume is a gash on my temple, is a result of the car door slamming into me, catching me at a weird angle and biting into my skin. I've barely come to that conclusion before it happens again, harder this time, hard enough to knock me off-balance and cause the bank of my head to rebound off the roof of the car. Stars float behind my eyes, robbing me of my sight and the ability to think.

Blinking rapidly, the dark spots in my vision recede enough so I can make out Dylan standing in front of me, one large hand gripping the car door so tightly his knuckles turning white, his face hard and uncaring. With a shaky hand, I touch the throbbing spot on the crown of my head, staring in disbelief at my fingertips when they come away bloody. "Did you..." I start and finish, my throat tight. "Was that an accident?"

Dylan doesn't respond. All he does is stare, not a single regretful thought or emotion behind clear blue eyes, before spinning on his feet and storming into his apartment complex without another word.

I'm numb, working on autopilot as I shakily climb back into my car. I'm not sure how I make it back to my apartment in one piece, eyes blurring and the sickeningly familiar metallic taste of blood filling my mouth, but I do. It's not until I stumble inside my apartment, until I'm greeted by the worried shrieks of my roommates, that it starts to sink in what the fuck just happened.

Silence follows the clumsy recollection of one of the worst nights of my life.

I fiddle with the corner of Cass' duvet in an attempt to keep my nerves at bay, my gaze firmly fixed on my fingers as they trace the linear pattern of the navy material. I don't realize I've been holding my breath, anticipation seizing my lungs until Cass murmurs my name, one of his hands covers mine, and all the air leaves me in one big whoosh.

"I'm fine, okay?" I force myself to look at him, to smile. "It really wasn't that big of a deal."

"I-" He stops and starts the same sentence several times, never quite managing to finish it. I get it; I couldn't form a coherent sentence for two days after the whole ordeal. That might've been because of the concussion, though. "When was this?"

"Uh, sometime in September." September fourth, just shy of midnight, not that I'm keeping track of specifics.

September eighth, he came to my apartment. Days to ruminate on an apology he never made, not really. He cried his eyes out and begged for forgiveness but all the while, he was blaming me, the alcohol, that fucking dress with so much conviction, I started blaming myself too.

And how could I break up with him for something we both eventually deemed my fault?

"I know I shouldn't have taken him back, okay?" I preemptively assure Cass, anticipating the lecture prepped on the tip of his tongue. "I know I made the wrong choice but I didn't know what else to do."

"You could've told someone. Reported him."

"Really, Cass? You really think that would've worked?" I can't help but laugh. "What would my story have been? 'Hey, officer, my model student boyfriend with a spotless record slammed a car door in my face. Evidence? Witnesses? No, I have none of that.' All it would've taken was one denial on Dylan's part and boom, case closed, I know it."

"You had medical records," Cass protests. "You went to the hospital."

"Medical records that state I tripped and fell." Because that's what I told them. I said I'd have too much to drink and that combined with my heels led to my balance failing me. If it had been up to me I wouldn't have even gone to the hospital; Kate and Luna dragged me there.

"Amelia-"

"No," I cut Cass off firmly. I know I did the wrong thing in taking Dylan back, that I can admit to, but reporting him wasn't an option, not then and not now. I was, *I am*, protecting myself. Nothing good would ever come from it; it would only make things worse. I want him to leave me alone and if I accuse him of something he'll never be convicted of doing, he never will. "Please, stop."

I can tell it physically hurts Cass to keep his mouth shut, to strangle the big brother urges begging him to intervene, to fix. Full lips press together in a grim, straight line, worry lines etched into his light brown skin. "I don't like it, Mils."

"You don't have to like it." I scoot closer, slipping my hand into his. "You have to trust me to deal with it on my own."

With a heavy sigh, Cass slumps forward, resignation evident in his gaze as he angles his head towards me. "Fine."

I wonder if he would relent so easily if he remembered my own personal brand of dealing is avoidance.

～

There's a man outside my apartment.

I spot him through the windshield of my car when I park outside my building but it's not until I reach the exterior walkway on my floor that I recognize who's crouched beside my front door. "Nick?"

The man in question clambers to his feet as I approach, the jingle of my keys obnoxiously loud as I nervously toss them from one hand to the other. "Hey."

"Hi." My steps falter a few feet before I reach him. "What're you doing here?"

"I was in the neighborhood," he lies with a wonky smile. "Thought I'd swing by."

Squinting at him through suspicious eyes, I sigh. "You're checking on me." Nick scoffs indignantly but he doesn't deny it. I sigh again—more of a groan, really—and edge past him to unlock the front door. "What, is it your shift? You were assigned the afternoon and Cass is gonna tag you out before dinner?"

"I'm pulling double duty, actually." Nick's teasing tone follows me into the apartment, his breath tickling the top of my head as he leans down to murmur, "And I volunteered."

I don't get a chance to retort; I'm too busy trying not to fall on my ass when I'm suddenly bombarded by a flurry of blonde hair and enveloped by a pair of tan, slender arms. I stumble back a step, knocking against a hard chest, and Nick rights me as Luna cries in my ear, "I'm sorry. I'm so, so sorry, Amelia."

It takes a moment to remember what my roommate has to apologize for. Even when I do, I don't feel the same rush of anger that I did last night. Honestly, my emotions are spent—I don't have it in me to be furious even though I have every right to be—and it's my lack of energy that has me melting in Luna's embrace.

"I'm so sorry," my impulsive friend repeats, squeezing me tight enough to steal air. "I was angry and worried about you but that's no excuse. I should've kept my mouth shut."

"Agreed," I murmur into the tresses trying to suffocate me. "It's not okay but I forgive you."

God, even if I had been angry, it wouldn't have lasted long. It would've been wiped away by the laughter inspired when Luna peppers dramatic, smacking kisses all over my face. Over her shoulder, I spot Kate lounging on the sofa silently observing, lips pressed together like she's trying not to laugh.

"Now that's fixed," she calls out as Luna releases me from her death grip, a smile that promises trouble lighting up both of their pretty faces. "What is Nick doing here?"

It briefly slipped my mind that Nick was even here but his presence becomes unignorable when he lays a hand on my shoulder, fingers grazing my collarbone while his thumb digs into my nape, inspiring warmth to emanate throughout my entire body. "I was craving the warm welcome you ladies always greet me with."

White teeth glint as Kate adopts a remarkably shark-like, entirely fake grin. "If I'm less welcoming, will you go away?"

Unphased, Nick grins right back. "Treat 'em mean, keep 'em keen."

"Your love life's motto?"

"Claws in, Katie." Flouncing towards the sofa, Luna drops down beside our friend, manicured fingers flicking her temple. "You're gonna scare the nice man away."

Kate hums thoughtfully. "Do you scare easily, Nicolas?"

Before he can answer—and God knows what kind of answer that would be—I nudge Nick in the direction of my bedroom, hot on his tail as he takes the hint. "Ignore them." My eyes shoot daggers at my supposed friends. "I do."

"Leave that door open, young lady!" Luna sings as we disappear down the hall, the command half yell, half cackle.

I slam it shut extra loud.

Leaving Nick and I alone in my bedroom.

God, does he look out of place here.

Everything about my room, about our apartment in general, is small and Nick looks almost comical as he noses around, making all my belongings seem even tinier. For God's sake, the plant pots lining my windowsill and desk look like Legos as he studies the array of greenery I've somehow managed to keep alive. He lingers on the patch of my wall covered with photos and posters and other trinkets collected over the years—I've got a thing for vintage postcards and movie ticket stubs—and he huffs a laugh when he gets to the pitiful stack of books tucked in the corner.

"I had a bookshelf." My nose wrinkles as red flushes my cheek. "It broke." *Because Luna, Kate, and I built it dastardly incorrectly,* I decline to add.

My bed—a small double that even I find puny at times—creaks under Nick's bulking weight as he sits on the edge, smoothing his colossal hands over my bedsheets before really making himself comfortable. Kicking off his shoes, he scoots until his back hits the wall, crooking one leg and resting his forearm on his knee, the epitome of casual and comfortable. "Wanna watch a movie?"

Am I sweating? I think I might be sweating. Shifting awkwardly from one foot to the other, I clear my throat. "I don't need a babysitter."

"That's great." He blinks at me. "Do you wanna watch a movie?"

"Whatever you're doing, you don't have to."

"Amelia." Nick sighs my name, looking one step away from pinching the bridge of his nose. "Is it so hard to believe that I like spending time with you?"

Yeah. It kind of is. "You do?"

"No," he deadpans. "I always spend three hours at the gym every single night. And I love the food at Greenies."

Yeah, I'm definitely sweating. Blushing too. And a little shaky as I cross the room and clamber onto the bed, settling with as healthy a distance between us as I can maintain on the compact piece of furniture. As I set up my laptop—movie it is, I guess—I feel him watching me with that ever-present smirk I once found infuriating yet is starting to grow on me. I itch under the weight of his stare, my throat tight with the need to fill the loaded silence before it suffocates me. "I'm sorry I ruined your birthday, by the way."

"You didn't."

It's my turn to deadpan him. "My ex-boyfriend beat the crap out of you for talking to me."

"And the night ended with a pretty girl in my bed, fawning over me," Nick retorts smoothly. "I'd call that a win."

18

NICK

"Your mom is gonna flip the fuck out."

I take my eyes off the road just long enough to glare at the snickering man in my passenger seat. "Shut up."

"You look like you fell off a cliff."

T's too fucking early for this shit. "Shut up, Cass."

He does no such thing. "Seriously, how are you gonna explain that to Ana?"

My hands clench around the steering wheel. I have no idea. Not one. I've spent the last three days praying the bruises highlighting my left cheekbone and the contours of both eyes would magically disappear and I wouldn't have to conjure up an explanation. Instead, they've reached their absolute worst; dark and blatant and liable to give my mother an aneurysm. "I'll figure it out."

Another mocking snicker echoes around the interior of my car. "Good luck."

"Hey, you're not exactly spotless either." I side-eye my friend, gaze lingering on his busted knuckles.

"I bet you twenty bucks my mom doesn't even notice I'm there. She's about to have her favorite child back."

Instinctively, I tense at the mention of Amelia. I've been pushing it to the back of my mind, the fact that we're on the way to get her right now, a hard thing to do considering we're less than ten minutes away from her apartment. I don't want to think about the fact I'm about to be stuck in a car with her and Cass for the next five hours. Or that we're up at the crack of dawn because we're driving home for Thanksgiving where I'm going to spend five *days* trapped in a house with her, Cass, and our entire families.

Mentally calculating the odds of my survival, it's not looking good.

Surprisingly, I faced no repercussions for mine and Amelia's impromptu sleepover; Cass didn't say a word about it, not even sparing me a threatening glance or a disapproving grunt. More for Amelia's sake than mine, I guess, and I was grateful for it at first. However, very quickly, I started wishing I'd received a verbal lashing because my foolish, horny brain read too much into his lack of a reaction. Gave me notions. Strived to convince me that Cass wouldn't mind me—fuck it, I'm going to admit it—having a big, fat, pathetic crush on his sister.

It's surface-deep; I'm not trying to marry the girl or anything close to that. It's purely a carnal thing. I want to fuck her. Regularly. Exclusively. I'm not built for anything more—many people will attest to that—but I want her.

And I can't.

Because Cass would care. It's an unforgivable thing, fucking around with your best friend's sister, even I know that. Even if nothing came from it—which is highly likely because Amelia's already made it clear that she doesn't want me—the very existence of the crush would ruin everything.

So, in short, until I work this, *her*, out of my system, until I wait out this damn crush, I'm fucked.

And I get a little more fucked when we pull up outside Amelia's building and she comes sloping outside in a pair of shorter-than-short pajama bottoms and my goddamn hoodie. She looks as unhappy to be up with the sun as I am, a grumpy tilt to her lips as she tosses a duffel bag and a pillow in the back seat, throwing herself in after them.

"Still not a morning person, I see." The teasing comment doesn't fully leave Cass' mouth before a slim middle finger is brandished in his direction. Clicking her seatbelt into place, Amelia tucks the pillow between her and the door, slouching lazily against it without a single word.

"Morning."

Weary eyes meet mine in the rearview mirror. Yawning, Amelia returns the sentiment. "Good morning."

I let my gaze flit over her, lingering on her hoodie. "Nice outfit," I can't resist quipping.

Glancing downward, Amelia sucks in a breath, the wrinkle of her nose telling me her outfit choice was unintentional; in a tired daze, she simply grabbed the closest thing and threw it on.

My brain has a fucking field day theorizing why that happened to be my clothes.

"Don't worry," I drawl. "Looks better on you anyways."

The pretty blush encroaching on pale, freckled cheeks is worth Cass' knuckles connecting with my shoulder.

Amelia huffs, slumping further into her seat, arms crossed over her chest. "Does that line really work for you?"

"Wouldn't know." I wrench my gaze from hers as I set the car in motion, steering us in the direction of the California-Nevada border. "I don't make a habit of giving out my clothes."

"Yeah," Amelia muses, humor lightening her tone. "It would probably throw off your game if your groupies had matching uniforms."

"Amelia!" A choked laugh escapes Cass.

"What?" She grins, wide and unabashed, her exhaustion suddenly moot. "A little teasing is good for him. Keeps his ego in check. Stops his big head from getting stuck in doorways."

Yeah. I'm fucked.

"Can I help you with anything?"

I start at the sudden question. Dragging my eyes away from the spot outside they've been fixated on for the last ten minutes, I spare the gas station attendant hovering by my side a gritted smile. "No, thanks."

The girl dithers, abnormally thick lashes fluttering. "You sure?"

I rein in a snort. And a grimace. Yeah, I'm sure; the girl might be plastered in a deceiving amount of makeup but her age is still apparent—she can't be older than Ben. Nodding briskly, I avert my gaze and it instinctively wanders to the window, to outside, again. A tiny huff is followed by footsteps as the girl slopes off and no less than ten seconds later, I hear her pipe up again. The same question, the same attempted sultry tone, but directed at Cass this time. I don't have to hear my friend's response to know the young girl strikes out again;

Cass had his eye on the guy behind the counter the moment we walked in here.

It's our second—and hopefully final—break before we reach Carlton and while Cass and I stock up on snacks, Amelia opted to stay with my truck. Not in the truck, though. No, she's popped the tailgate and hopped onto the bed, flopped on her back to soak up the mild November Arizonan sun. I can't see much more than her legs dangling off the edge—bare because she's still wearing those fucking shorts—but I know she stripped off the hoodie a while ago, leaving a skimpy tank in its place.

And while I can't see her, the creeps parked behind me have a clear fucking view. Even from a distance, I can tell they're lapping it up.

Everything gathered in my arms hits the counter with a thump as I pin the latest object of Cass' ever-fleeting attention with an impatient stare. It's a miracle he manages to drag his attention away from my friend long enough to scan my items, and he even has the gall to look irritated by my presence, ungracefully shoving my purchases into a plastic bag.

"What's up your ass?"

I counter Cass' question with one of my own. "Can you hurry up?"

"Since you asked so nicely," white teeth glint as Cass grins wide, "no."

Flipping him off, I snatch my stuff and stalk outside without another word. Unsurprisingly, Cass doesn't follow me and I'm glad for it. His absence means I don't have to explain why my shitty mood only gets shittier when I round my truck and find Amelia stretched out with her eyes closed, earphones in, oblivious to the world as she taps a rhythm against a sliver of bare stomach.

When I roughly drop the stuff beside her, she jolts into an upright position, her palm flush against her chest as she sucks in a sharp breath. "Jesus Christ." As she tugs out her earphones, her foot jabs my knee gently. "You scared the crap out of me."

With a grunt, I glance over my shoulder, stiffening when I find those guys still leering—three of them in some shitty little topless sports car, preppy looking motherfuckers who aren't being even a little bit subtle about their gawking. Briefly, I'm torn between shifting to stand in front of Amelia, blocking her from their view, or hopping up beside her, facing them so I can keep an eye out for trouble. I settle on the latter, propping my ass against the metal as close as I can get to Amelia without fucking sitting on her. "What're you doing?"

"Nothing." I keep watching the guys as I reach an arm behind me to grab the plastic bag, plopping it on Amelia's lap. "Did those guys bother you?"

Squinting, Amelia peers in the direction I nod my head, nose wrinkling as she shakes her head. "I didn't even notice them."

I huff. Like I said; oblivious.

As the sound of crinkling plastic fills the air around us, a pleased noise vibrates in Amelia's chest. Glancing aside, my lips downturned in a grimace. Red Vines and coffee, that's a reasonable request I can get behind. But those godawful gas station nachos covered in that fake plastic cheese? A fucking crime. "How can you eat those?"

Scoffing, Amelia brandishes a bright yellow tortilla chip in my direction. "You do not get to judge me. You drink wheatgrass shots for fun."

I bark out a laugh, unable to keep from grinning at her like a damn fool. She grins back, a pretty pink tongue briefly peeking out at me playfully before she chucks the sorry excuse for a nacho in her mouth, washing it down with a hearty glug of coffee.

If that doesn't turn me off her, I doubt anything ever will.

"You gonna eat?" Amelia asks, plucking out the lone granola bar I got for myself—not turning up at Ma's house starving would be a grave mistake—waving it in front of me. "Or are you too busy staking your claim?"

Snatching my bar, I narrow my eyes at her wry grin. "What?"

"Don't worry." With a patronizing pat on my thigh, Amelia pointedly glances ahead of us at the creeps who are annoyingly undeterred by my presence. "I think it's sweet. Very leading man in a romance movie of you."

Scrubbing a hand down my face, I shift under the warm weight of Amelia's palm still heavy on my thigh. "I wasn't *staking my claim.*"

"Don't be embarrassed," Amelia coos. "I told you, I think it's sweet. A little overboard, though, because contrary to popular belief, I'm not entirely helpless. I don't need protection at all times."

I bite back the urge to remind her that her track record over the last few weeks proves otherwise. Instead, I scoff, my palms hitting warm metal as I lean back, my head lolling towards Amelia. "I'm not sweet, *querida*." I'm sure as fuck not being sweet right now; I'm being a jealous, possessive shit. She doesn't know that though.

She wouldn't be looking at me all soft and sweet if she did. Head cocked, something akin to a question swirls in emerald irises that have progressed from only haunting my dreams; they're encroaching on my waking moments too. "You're sweet to me."

"Because I like you," I reply too quickly, too easily. Clearing my throat, I wipe my softening expression clean and force my gaze forward; it's easier to focus on the bubbling irritation our leery audience provokes instead of the itching warmth staring at Amelia for too long incites. "We're friends."

"Hm." My fists clench at the feeling of Amelia's stare sweeping over me. "And friends don't let friends get eye-fucked by strangers right?"

"Right."

She hums again and fuck if the inflection of the noise doesn't scream trouble. "Guess you're not as intimidating as you thought. Since they're still looking and all."

I can't help it; my head rolls to the side again, heart thumping as green overwhelms me, voice raspy as I drawl, "Maybe I'm not making myself clear enough."

I see her breath catch in her throat. The fine tendons in her slender neck become taut. Pretty pink lips part, perfect white teeth sinking into the bottom one. "Maybe not."

I'm about to. I'm contemplating all the ways I can make it so fucking clear, mind spinning trying to decide where to start, when the human equivalent of a bucket of ice-cold water being poured over my head comes barreling out of the gas station.

"Let's go, losers." It's almost violent, the way I jerk away from Amelia at the sound of Cass' holler, practically falling off the bed of my truck in my haste to put distance between us, to clear the suspicious tension lingering in the air around them. "I need to shit and this ass is not touching a public toilet seat."

The second I pull up to the curb outside my mother's house, the front door swings open. Long, dark curls fly messily around Ma's head as she sprints down the driveway with the energy of a woman half her age, impatience oozing from her as she waits for me to turn off the car and exit the vehicle before throwing herself at me. *"Meu Nico,"* she murmurs against my chest, patting my back affectionately. *"Eu estava com saudades!"*

"I miss-" My attempt at returning the sentiment falters when Ma pulls back to assess me in that motherly way only for her affectionate smile to fade, replaced by shock and irritation. When a weak backhand strikes my bicep, I exclaim, *"Que diabos?"*

"Nicolas Cauã Silva, o que aconteceu com seu rosto?" The woman shrieks at a decibel only audible to canines. Utter horror lines her features as she delicately pokes at the scabs and bruises marring my face.

"Mamãe, I'm fine."

"Fine!" Throwing her hands in the air, she murmurs a few choice expletives beneath her breath. "Is this from one of your fights?" I barely manage to rein in a wince when she pokes the bruise spanning most of my left rib cage; if my face warrants this level of freakout, I can only imagine what reaction the rest of me would garner. "Nico, I told you I don't like all the fighting."

"It wasn't from a fight." I shut the car door behind me, noting Cass and Amelia haven't moved, the former openly watching with a shit-eating grin on his face while the latter looks exceptionally uncomfortable. "Well, not that kind of fight."

Beady golden eyes burn a hole in my face "What kind of fight was it?"

"One I didn't start."

Ma's huff proves she doesn't like my answer. "At least tell me you won."

With a snort, I nod; like I told Amelia a couple of days ago, I'm the one who spent the night with her in my bed. I win, hands down.

Only slightly mollified, Ma splutters and fusses, oblivious for now to our audience as she works herself into a state, a red hue tinting her bronze skin. Skin the same shade as mine, if not a touch darker. I've always been told I'm the spitting image of my mother, the differences between us few and far between. It's a long-running family joke that our baby pictures are impossible to tell apart. The Harrison genes—my dad's side of the family—were no match for the Silva ones. The only things I inherited from my dad are his love of literature and his height. And his smile, Ma likes to say.

I fix that smile into place as I tuck my apoplectic mother beneath my arm, my free hand gesturing for our spectators to join us. Cass is the first to reach us, 'I told you so' written all over his face. "Don't look at me like that," Ma warns, smacking away his attempts at a hug. "I know you had something to do with this."

"Me?" Cass mocks indignation, expression the picture of scandalized. "*I* am innocent. I know nothing. Your son is a menace to society all on his own."

"*You* are a dipshit."

A barrage of spat Portuguese chastising me for my language comes to an abrupt end when a car door opens and closes for the third time, drawing my mother's attention. The scowl slips off her face and I swear to God, her ears prick up like a dog who's spotted their new favorite toy.

In a millisecond, Cass and I are forgotten, literally shoved aside as Ma makes a beeline for the redhead shyly approaching us. Amelia changed before we left our last stop, swapping her pajamas out for a pair of denim overalls that shouldn't be hot but on her, they are, over a white sweater, the collar of which she tugs on nervously. I should've reassured her that any nerves would be unfounded; Ma's never met a person she didn't like and she quickly proves Amelia is no exception.

"You must be Amelia!" Ma gushes, wrapping Amelia up in a tight hug faster than the girl can blink. "I've heard so much about you."

I'm not going to dwell on how Ma looks right at me when she says that, a glint in her eyes that promises trouble.

Amelia is wide-eyed, clearly surprised by Ma's display of affection but she returns it and the sight sparks a bone-deep level of satisfaction within me. "It's nice to meet you too, Mrs Silva."

"Please." Ma pulls away, regarding Amelia warmly as her palms cup her shoulders. "Call me Ana."

The hesitance in Amelia's smile fades as she nods, returning my mother's amiability. Ma accepts it greedily, practically glowing as she hugs her again—we're a hugging family, I should've warned her—before releasing her. Internally, I groan when she sets her sights on me next, grabbing me and dragging me the short distance towards the Morgans' place. "Sofia's next door. She's been helping Lynn cook for two days," she tells me, purposely and suspiciously loud. Casting a glance over her shoulder, she yanks me down to her level, voice hushed even though she speaks in a language only her and I understand, *"Amelia é muito linda."*

I keep my mouth shut; I know a trap when I hear one.

Undeterred, Ma persists. "Is that your hoodie?" She peeks over her shoulder again and I don't have to see it to know she's smirking. "You two must be close."

I side-eye my meddling mother. "We're friends."

Ma hums, grinning as though I've cracked the funniest of jokes. I don't like how she's ogling me, examining me like she knows something I don't know, inciting alarm bells to go off in my head. With a quiet groan, I check that Amelia and Cass are out of earshot—they're still grabbing their shit from the car—before narrowing my eyes at Ma. "Did someone tell you something?"

"Is there something to tell?" she counters.

"No."

Ma snorts. *"Mentiroso.* You're blushing, Nico."

"Não estou!"

"Don't lie to your mother, Nicolas," she chastises, patting my cheek playfully before sneaking a peek over her shoulder again. "I like her."

Shit, why does that make me *itch*? "You just met her."

"I have very good intuition," Ma claims. "You like her too."

"Your intuition tell you that?"

"No." The back of her hand wallops me in the chest as she grins up at me, dark brows wiggling. "You and your googly eyes did."

19

AMELIA

I'M SHITTING MYSELF.

There's no point sugar-coating it or putting on a brave face; I am dreading the interaction I know is going to happen within the next few minutes and I have been since we passed the sign welcoming us to Carlton. I kept my gaze downcast after that, watching my fingers as they fiddled with the rips in the legs of my overalls—I figured seeing my old neighborhood was going to be triggering enough for today, I didn't need a tour of the whole town.

They look the exact same, mine and Cass' houses, two Tudor-style houses tucked side-by-side at the end of a cul-de-sac. I don't know why I expected anything different—it's not like it's been a lifetime since I left, even if it feels like it has been. Maybe it's because I'm so different compared to who I was when I left here.

I'm stalling at the end of Cass' driveway, staring at my old house when someone bumps my shoulder gently. "You can go in, if you want."

I grimace up at Nick, shaking my head—I have no interest in reliving any of the memories lurking in there. All the good ones live in the Morgans' house, and one of them greets me as I force myself a few steps up the drive, Nick silently following close behind. Despite the apprehension bubbling in my gut, I can't help but smile at the inscription permanently indented in the cement; C.M + A.H = BFF.

We'd gotten one hell of a lecture for that little antic. I think we were nine or ten and Lynn had gotten the driveway repaved after Cass and I destroyed the thing during a particularly vigorous paint fight. One look at the wet cement and we couldn't resist the urge to immortalize our friendship.

I raise my gaze and I'm hit with another; from here, I can see the towering oak tree in Cass' backyard, the cause of more than one child-hood injury. One competitive sister versus two wild older brothers meant many bruises bravely suffered so that little girl felt equal. The more I stare at the three, the more I swear I can see three fearless kids scaling the thing with reckless abandon, and the more the lump in my throat grows.

Calloused fingers gently brush the back of my hand. "Nervous?"

"Is it that obvious?"

"If it makes you feel any better, my mom likes you."

Weirdly, it does. "Sorry." I sigh, knuckling my eyes until the stinging behind them recedes. "I know I'm being silly." A soft huff is Nick's only reply. "What?"

"I'm just wondering how many times a day you apologize for shit that isn't your fault."

All the blood rushes to my cheeks until I swear I'm radiating heat. I mumble some nondescript answer that does nothing to ward off Nick. His pinky brushes mine a second before he hooks the digits together, tugging until I deign to look at him. He's silent as he lets his gaze flit over my face intently, making me more and more flustered by the second, before he says with so much sincerity and softness, it buckles my knees a little, "You're allowed to feel whatever you wanna feel, *querida*. If you wanna stay out here a little longer, that's fine. If you wanna go in and rip the bandaid off, that's fine too. If you wanna blow off some steam, there's a punching bag in my shed. And if it's all too much and you wanna leave, take my keys."

Stop being so nice to me, I command silently. *Stop it before I freaking fall in love with you.*

It's bad enough that I already have our earlier interaction on reply in my hopelessly romantic brain. I don't need anything else to fuel the fantasies created against my will.

I'm not sweet.

You're sweet to me.

Because I like you.

There was a moment, one reckless, idealistic flicker in time, when I thought he was going to kiss me. Touch me. Do something that would've erased the solid boundaries outlining our friendship. Honey eyes went molten as they dropped to my lips, and my insides followed suit. I was mere seconds away from becoming nothing more than a puddle at his feet.

Then the moment ended and I solidified.

I force myself to laugh, to joke, to act like my heart isn't threatening to beat right out of my chest. "That mouth of yours is dangerous, you know?"

So slow is the positively filthy smile that twists his lips upward. "I've been told."

I walked right into that one.

It's a struggle to formulate a response that doesn't involve me panting like a dog, and I'm an odd mixture of disappointed and relieved when it turns out I don't have to. Nick drops my hand like it's on fire when a holler rings out, a single word and voice that makes me simultaneously groan and smile.

"Tiny!" A man the spitting image of Cass materializes on the front porch, face split in a grin as he squints at me. "What, are you waiting for an invitation?"

My laugh becomes a squeal when James Morgan closes the distance between us in a handful of long strides and greets me the exact same way his younger brother did almost a month ago; by sweeping me up in his arms and squeezing the life out of me as he twirls us in a circle.

My relationship with the eldest Morgan sibling has always been different to my one with Cass, nowhere near as tightly-knit, the line between friend and sibling a lot less blurred. Vaguely, I remember having a teeny adolescent crush on him—he's the kind of guy everyone has a crush on—but that died quickly, murdered by his obsession with calling me 'kiddo.' Regardless, he's always, *always*, been part of my family, and I cling to him as tightly as I did Cass, sniffling a quiet greeting.

"Shit, kid, I've missed you." James keeps me tucked beneath his arm as he sets me down, steering me towards the front door. "You were right, Nick. She grew up good."

My head whips around, catching Nick as he raises his hands in a display of innocence that's oddly unbecoming on him. "He's shit-stirring. I never said anything."

"Oh," James hums, "so you don't think she's pretty?"

Golden eyes narrow. "Stop it."

"Still breaking girls' hearts I see." James tuts playfully, shooting me a sly wink. "It's okay, kiddo. You're too good for him anyway."

An hour ago, I didn't think I'd be laughing as I crossed the threshold into the Morgans' home for the first time in almost four years but I am, James' joking doing a world of good in helping me forget my apprehension. I'm glad—it means when James is abruptly bowled aside and a different, curvier body collides with mine, there's no guilt holding me back from reciprocating.

"Here's my girl," Lynn sobs in my ear as, for the second time in as many minutes, I'm robbed of breath. Not entirely because of the restricting hug. "Oh, sweetie, I missed you."

I try to return the sentiment but I fear it'll come out as nothing more than a mangled blubber so I stay silent, hoping my bone-crushing grip speaks for me. Suddenly, I can't believe there was ever a moment when I doubted Lynn. When I considered that she wouldn't greet me with the same affection and love and ferocity as she always did. I should've known better.

Hovering beside us, Cass scoffs and whines, "Why didn't I get a greeting like that?"

Lynn pulls back just enough to whack Cass upside the head. "I see you all the time. Let me have a moment with my only daughter." It's half a joke, half serious, and entirely tear-inducing.

I might've lost a biological mother all those years ago but I definitely never went without a mom. I found one in the form of Lynn, and no one could ever make me feel as loved as she does.

Like this house, Lynn looks exactly how I remember her. Smooth skin a couple of shades darker than her sons', the same inky hair and eyes, and a smile that has always signified home to me.

The only mother I've ever really known smoothes her hands over my hair before cupping my cheeks, the two of us sniffling in unison. "Look at you," she coos. "You look so beautiful, Amelia."

"See, Nick." Over Lynn's shoulder, I watch James nail Nick in the ribs. "That's how you compliment a woman."

The rest of the day passes in a whirlwind of barely restrained emotions and words left unsaid.

I'm a mess as Lynn steers me towards the living room, a stiff wind away from crumpling when what Nick told me the night of his birthday rings true—the pictures of me scattered around the Morgans' house have gone nowhere. With a breakdown imminent, I'm grateful when Cass' dad, Tom, swoops in and snatches my attention, hugging me in that way only a dad can and whispering more sweet sentiments.

We don't talk about it. The elephant in the room. The big *why*. It's like we all make an unconscious, unanimous decision to ignore it. We don't talk about the missing years either, treating it like a gateway drug. Like if we reminisce on the time we lost, the reason we lost it will inevitably come up. I don't know about anyone else but I'm content with that decision, despite the palpable weight of it.

One weekend, one normal weekend with my family, is all I want and I'm going to do everything in my power to get it.

Well, with my family and Nick's. Not that that's a hardship; I freaking love Ana. She's the type of person who instantly makes you feel welcome and comfortable and wanted—my favorite type of person. And Sofia, his little sister, is adorable. A mini version of her mother, pint-sized yet larger than life, zipping around and filling the whole house with tangible positive energy.

She attached herself to me pretty promptly, sitting next to me at dinner and snuggling beside me during the movie we all watched together and dragging me upstairs after, insisting she had to see my bedroom before they left. The spare room, technically, but it was always treated as mine, and it seems it still is. The same lilac comforter adorns the bed, the same ridiculously extravagant vanity that Tom built me for Christmas one year is still tucked in the corner, the same slightly wonky flowers Lynn and I spent an afternoon painting decorate the pastel walls. Perched on the edge of the bed, I trace them absently as the inquisitive eight-year-old pokes around at her leisure.

"Is Cass your boyfriend?" she asks at one point in that random way kids do.

I can't help but snicker. "No. More like my brother."

"I have a brother," she states like I don't already know, like I don't spend a healthy chunk of my waking hours with the man. Not that she knows that. It's cute, how she proudly puffs her chest out as she mentions Nick, her face aglow with unmistakable admiration. The same admiration he clearly has for her.

Honest to God, it could do a girl in, watching Nicolas Silva interact with children.

Sofia abandons the stack of books holding her attention—I was a Meg Cabot girl back in the day—and joins me on the bed, butt bouncing excitedly on the mattress. With eyes the same shade as her brother's, she blinks up at me, so deceivingly innocent. "Is my brother your boyfriend?"

I choke on my next breath, spluttering a squeaky, "No!"

"Why not?"

Out of a hundred reasons, I lamely settle on, "We're friends."

Sofia hits me with a look way too pointed, too wise and all-knowing, for a child. "My mom says my dad was her best friend."

"That's…" God, how do I respond to that? "Nice?"

"And they were in love. So-"

Before Sofia can spout whatever childlike logic that makes perfect sense to her, an overly loud cough interrupts us. I straighten up at the sight of Nick lazily leaning against the doorway, hands shoved in his pockets, simmering with amusement. "*Minha anjinha*," he drawls and Sofia perks up. "Time to go."

The little girl pins her brother with a wide-eyed, pouty-lipped expression I recognize as one I used to use on my brothers when trying to get my way. "Can't I stay here?"

"Not tonight." In anticipation of the protests brewing, he adds, "Tomorrow."

I was pre-warned that the Silva's tend to spend the night on Thanksgiving—I've yet to consider the reality of that.

Huffing, Sofia reluctantly stands, and I jolt in surprise when she throws her arms around my neck. The Silvas are a hugging family, I've learned. "Night, Tiny," she sings in my ear before skipping out the door, Nick ruffling her hair as she passes.

"You coming?" she yells from the hallway when her brother fails to immediately follow her.

"Right behind you," is his rumbled reply.

Her little footsteps thunder downstairs, punctuated by the sound of everyone issuing drawn-out goodbyes, and still, Nick doesn't move. Well, he does—in the wrong direction. He enters my room, bringing with him the thick tension that seems to permanently exist between us, always out to make my heart thump a beat faster, my stomach tight, my hands clammy. I can't put a name to it, or at least not one I want to admit it. It's just *there*. Always. Alive and pulsating.

My eyelids feel heavy as I track his wandering, making like his sister and studying every inch of my old room. His lips quirk at the pile of teddies nestled among my old, frilly pillows, the shrine to the heart-throbs of my youth decorating a wall, the cactus sitting on the vanity that someone must've kept thriving over the years. All the obvious indications that I inhabited this room for a decade. "Makes sense," he mutters beneath his breath, and I frown.

"What?"

"Your room at my house," he starts to explain, jerking his head towards the place that oddly served as a home for both of us. "I remember thinking it didn't look lived in. Because you lived here?"

The house next door was only my home by a technicality; I spent more days, more nights, here by a mile. But it feels like a betrayal to admit that. Like I'm doing my dad dirty, implying he was negligent when he wasn't, he was busy.

Nick accepts my silence as an answer, fingers drumming against the solid white wood of the vanity. When they lift, aiming for the array of faded polaroids tucked in the frame of the mirror, I tense. And when he reaches for one in particular—I know what it is by placement alone, that's how long I once spent starting at it, at the face immortalized in film yet painfully mortal in reality—I'm on my feet before I know it, across the room and gripping his wrist to halt his movements. "Don't."

Nick's hand stills but his eyes don't. They flick to the tiny bordered photo that causes bile to rise in my throat from thought alone. I can't bear to look but I know what he sees; a red-haired teenager clinging to a boy with dirty blond hair, both of them smiling wide, so young and innocent and unaware. "Who is it?"

My grip tightens, his pulse fluttering beneath my fingertips. "Someone I'd rather not talk about."

And that's all I have to say. The only reason I need to give for him to drop it, to avert his gaze and move on. That's one of the things I like most about Nick, I think; when it matters most, he doesn't push.

As smoothly as he does most things in life, Nick changes the subject. He shakes me off so he can toy with the drawstrings of the hoodie I've long since claimed as my own. Even if no matter how many times I wash it, something distinctly Nick still lingers. "You sleep in this or something?"

My poor cheeks can't catch a damn break. "Or something."

A huffed laugh is hot as it wafts over my skin. Nick tugs on the string tangled around his index finger and the action draws me closer, just an inch but an inch is everything considering how close we already are. Always so close, like personal space becomes a distant memory the moment I'm in his vicinity.

At this proximity, his six-foot-four frame—I don't know how Luna garnered that specific information, and I didn't ask—challenges me, forcing me to crank my neck back to peer up at him, the opposite of how he dips his chin downward. "Thanks for letting Sofia hang out."

"I didn't mind," I assure him, my pulse bordering on rapturous when his smile grows. "She's a sweet kid."

Nick hums his agreement. "You have a good day?"

Again, I answer. "I did."

"Good." With a satisfied nod that does weird things to my lower belly, Nick tugs one last time before releasing me, leaving me oddly bereft as he moves toward the door. "See you tomorrow, *querida*."

I pray to every higher power in existence that when I issue my own goodbye, it isn't actually as breathy as it sounds to my own ears, "Night, Nick."

20

AMELIA

It's funny how you forget what home feels like until you're surrounded by it.

And it's even funnier how that feeling hits not when we're gathered around the dining room table, ready to eat the elaborate Thanksgiving meal Lynn and Ana cooked—a freaking delectable combination of American and Brazilian food. Or when we crowd into the living room to snuggle beneath the threadbare blankets Lynn made during her crocheting phase and watch a cheesy Hallmark movie.

Apparently, I feel most at home when perched on the kitchen counter with James whipping up yet another jug of one of his infamous college-era cocktails. I have no clue what's in it, nor do I want to know. The only important thing is it's doing what's intended; getting me shit-faced drunk.

Hysterical laughter bounces around the kitchen as James regales story after story of his beloved time in college. He graduated a couple of years ago but the way he's telling them, you'd swear he was an old man reminiscing on his youth.

"You did not do that," I shriek amidst bouts of giggles, my blood alcohol levels ensuring I find everything and anything he says the epitome of hilarious.

"Swear on my life. Stark naked except for a horse mask, running across campus with a very angry security guard on my tail."

An easy enough picture to conjure up, especially if you know James, but I don't even try. Mostly because I have no interest, and a slight sense of disgust towards anything involving him naked.

James doesn't linger on any particular story, shooting them at me rapid-fire until I'm on the verge of passing out, too much laughter inhibiting my breathing capabilities.

By the time our duo becomes a party of four, I'm on the verge of tears. "We could hear you from outside," Cass quips as he strolls into the kitchen, Nick not far behind. Whilst James and I got a head start, they drove their parents to a friend of theirs' place for a Friendsgiving sort of a thing. Meaning we have the house to ourselves for the night, hence the alcohol.

I flip Cass off a little too vigorously, the sudden movement costing me my balance and causing me to almost pitch off the counter. Lucky for me, strong hands catch me before I can, steadying me by the hips and lingering for a moment longer than necessary. Blinking away the blurriness in my gaze, I'm dizzy for reasons beyond alcohol as I pat Nick on the shoulder. "Always saving me, hm?"

His laughter is as warming as any liquor. "Stop needing to be saved."

I aim a knee at his thigh but it never makes contact. His grip shifts, palm encasing the entire joint, his hand so large his fingers stretch up my thigh. They tap against the limb, coincidentally mimicking the exact *thump thump thump* of the erratic organ in my chest. "Nice try." He smirks. "Too slow."

"Blame my coach. He's kinda old. A little sluggish."

"You're talking a lot of shit for a girl who can't even sit up straight."

It's like a steel rod slams into my spine, that's how phenomenal my posture suddenly becomes. Narrowing my eyes, I scoff a telepathic *'ha.'*

"Well," an amused drawl sounds from beside us, "this is very interesting."

Like every other time we've been interrupted, Nick's affection dissipates abruptly, indifference overcoming his expression as he scuttles away until his back hits the counter opposite me. "What?"

"Whatever is going on here," James gestures between Nick and I, "I like it. Cass won't like it but I do."

Trepidation overrides my drunkenness as I twist to locate Cass and determine whether or not he's within earshot. Luckily, he's not; on the other side of the kitchen, he's got his head in the fridge, his full attention devoted to scarfing leftovers. Scowling at James, I hiss, "There's nothing going on."

Which is the truth. There is nothing going on. The occasional playful flirt or errant touch or the odd little moment when kissing seems an entirely possible concept don't count as anything. Thinking Nick is hot doesn't count as anything. Seeing him at least once a day and not getting sick of him doesn't count as anything. Being almost completely positive that if the opportunity presented itself, I would hop into bed with him doesn't count as anything. Not at all.

The *uh-huh* James snorts reeks of disbelief. "Brother's best friend." He pokes me in the thigh. "Very cliché, Tiny."

"Shut up." Clearly, I didn't learn my minimize-movements-when-drunk lesson; when I reach out to cuff James, I once again tempt a face-first encounter with the floor.

I shouldn't be surprised when someone rights me quickly, huffed foreign words brushing the top of my head as I'm steadied, not by the hips but by the safer territory of my shoulders. There's no lingering this time either. As soon as a face plant is no longer imminent, Nick lets me go, mumbling something about needing water and practically fleeing our little corner of the kitchen.

He's barely turned his back before there's a death grip on my thigh and I'm yanked down the counter, sandwiched between the marble and James. "Cough it up. You two are banging, right?"

Would you look at that; I'm suddenly completely sober. "No!"

"Why the fuck not?"

"Because we're not!"

"But you want to."

"I did not say that."

"You didn't say you don't."

With a moan, my head topples forward. "You're hurting my brain."

"What's hurting your brain?"

A shriek lodges itself in my throat at the sudden intrusion of Cass' voice, and I jump about a foot in the air when I turn to find him right beside us, frowning. "Alcohol," I answer quickly before James can cause any shit like I know he wants to, shooting the eldest of my brothers a glare that only makes him smile wider. Desperate to redirect the attention away from me, I flick the collar of Cass' neatly ironed shirt. "Why're you all dressed up?"

"I told you, I'm going out with the guys."

Right. I remember now, he did tell me that. Or asked for my permission, more like; he was very clear that if I wasn't okay with it, he'd flake on the guys and keep me company.

"You coming?" Cass clamps his hands over James' shoulders, giving our brother a shake whilst casting a look of irritated disappointment in Nick's direction. "I need a wingman. Nick was supposed to but-"

"I'll come." Nick's gruff interruption is punctuated by the clinking sound of him setting a glass of water on the counter, sliding it my way. I try to thank him but the words dry up, a frown creasing my forehead when I notice he's making a very pointed effort not to look at me. Weird.

Suspicion laces Cass' tone as he says, "You just said you wanted to stay here."

Jaw ticking with irritation, Nick grits his teeth. "I changed my mind."

In two seconds flat, Cass morphs from pissed to pleased, whooping and hollering as he claps his friend on the back. "Fuck, yeah. Coming out of retirement?"

Retirement?

"Fuck off."

"I'll give you twenty bucks if you break your dry spell."

Dry spell. Retirement.

Ah.

I feel ill as a slow smirk—one I haven't seen in a while, one I didn't react to all that well the last time I saw it—twists Nick's lips. "Make it thirty and we have a deal."

Why does the idea of Nick breaking his apparent dry spell make me feel so fucking *sick*?

Either I hide the sudden wave of nausea washing over me better than I think or everyone simply attributes it to my overt alcohol consumption because no one bats an eye when I crumple like a pathetic, trampled flower. Or maybe Cass is too delighted over the resurgence of his wingman that everything else is small potatoes. "You wanna come?"

I don't even think before declining because *hell no*. For multiple reasons. Sitting pretty near the top of the list; I'd rather carve my eyeballs out with a dull-edged spoon than witness Nick *coming out of retirement*.

Head down, I'm committed to staring at my feet until the boys leave, pretending I don't feel James' careful gaze inspecting me. "I'm gonna stay in," he says through a blatantly faked yawn. A warm palm lands on the small of my back, patting gently. "Tiny and I have some catching up to do."

I don't insist he go. I don't want to. The last thing I want, right now or ever, is to be left alone with only my rambling thoughts to keep me company.

"Suit yourself." Cass drops a kiss atop my head, promising to be back soon, insisting if I change my mind, all I have to do is call and he'll come running. Not that I will; God knows what I'd be interrupting.

I don't look up, not once, as the freaking dream team leaves the room in a flurry of heavy steps and excited chatter from Cass, a deep chuckle that doesn't sound quite right to my ears leaving his other half.

When their voices recede completely, James gently nudges me. "C'mon. I know where Mom keeps the good shit."

I jolt awake at the sound of a slamming door, my head spinning as I jackknife into a sitting position. Disoriented from a fitful sleep, it takes a moment to place where I am; living room sofa, limbs tangled beneath a blanket. Ah, yes—I fell asleep down here after silently drowning sorrows I didn't know I possessed. Pathetic sorrows revolving around a boy who isn't mine potentially railing a girl who isn't me.

Don't think about it.

It must be the guys coming home that woke me up, the door slamming and the stomping. I know it's not our parents—they rolled in somewhere between mine and James' third round of mai tais and our first caipirinha, the latter being entirely Ana's doing.

I'm a little woozy but definitely, painfully sober as I pad into the kitchen, intending on saying a quick hello followed by a quicker goodbye summed up with the quickest escape. I rethink that plan, though, when I don't find the guys in the kitchen.

Just *a* guy.

Hovering awkwardly in the doorway, I mumble a hello that Nick barely reciprocates—he offers nothing more than a grunt. No eye contact, no movement, no real acknowledgement of my presence. He stays where he is, hunched over the counter with his hands palm-down on the marble, his head hanging.

Swallowing over the lump in my throat, I glance at the clock on the wall. "You're home early."

Another grunt.

"Is Cass back?"

An almost imperceptible shake of his head.

Foolishly, I listen to the inner voice urging me to crack a joke, assuring me that's the best way to break this awful tension. "You strike out?"

A bitter, bitter laugh.

If I was smart, I'd leave. If I had a little more self-respect. If I knew how to listen to my head instead of my heart. But I think I've proven in the last month that none of those things are my forte.

Tentatively, I close the distance between Nick and I, coming to a jittery stop at the counter's edge closest to him. "Are you mad at me?"

He sighs, a long, drawn-out, weary noise. "No."

"You're acting like you are."

Daring eye contact, Nick's head snaps up, voice sharp and just a little angry. "I'm not mad."

"Don't snap at me. I haven't done anything wrong."

"No, you haven't," he agrees but it's not reassuring. It's irritated. Frustrated. *Exhausted.*

He's not the only one.

I drop my head with a shake, annoyed at myself for even trying. For caring. "Okay, then. Come find me when you're done being a little shit."

I don't make it even two steps before he stops me. Literally stops me in my tracks, blocking my escape route with his big body. "Don't walk away from me."

"Don't be a dick for no reason."

A deep, grumbling, growling noise rumbles in Nick's throat. Suddenly, his hands are on my hips, his forehead is dropped to mine, both working in tandem to force me back step after step until I hit the counter. "You don't fucking get it, do you?"

Looming over me, Nick is the picture of intimidation yet I don't shrink. I don't feel scared. His blatant frustration only fuels mine, and I steel myself under his heady, intense glare, and glare right back. "Get what?"

"I'm not sweet, Amelia." he spits. "I don't turn up at girls' houses to watch movies. I don't buy them lunch or bring them coffee. I don't let them sleep in my bed or steal my clothes. I don't get jealous when a guy so much as looks at them. I don't get in fights with their ex-boyfriends. I sure as fuck don't introduce them to my mother. I'm not that guy."

I swallow hard over a suddenly incredibly dry throat. "I don't understand."

"Join the fucking club." His dry chuckle coaxes out goosebumps up and down my arms, amplified when one of those treacherous hands drifts, tracing a buzzing path up my waist, skimming my collarbone, and settling on my neck. Thick fingers curl around the curve while a calloused thumb traces my jawbone, eyes following the movement.

"Sometimes, I find it hard to look at you," he murmurs, "because you're so fucking beautiful I can't think."

I know the feeling; thinking is not within the realm of my capabilities right now. Speaking neither. Breathing, barely.

"Thought that the first time I saw you," he continues, undeterred by my wide-eyed, slightly panicked silence. "Pissed me the fuck off."

"Are you drunk?" He must be. That's the only explanation. He's drunk or I'm dreaming.

"Not even a little." His hold on me tightens, his thumb digging into my cheek, not hard enough to hurt but enough that I couldn't pull away if I wanted to. "Thought I could go out and fuck you out of my head." I flinch, try to duck away, but he doesn't let me. "I couldn't. Didn't even try. Didn't want to."

Every time I think he's as close as he can get, he proves me wrong. One shift and there's nothing but stifling air between us, every inch of me flush with a hard inch of him. His nose brushes mine and I have to close my eyes, a useless attempt to ward off the gold irises swirling with so many emotions I can't decipher.

"You've fucking ruined me and I don't like it."

Only indignance and the hand wrapped around my throat keep me upright. "If you're waiting for an apology, you're not gonna get one."

"I'm not." Soft, smooth skin brushes my cheek and my whole body trembles. "I'm done waiting."

I don't get a chance to ask what he's been waiting for.

In a split second, every intelligible thought empties from my brain, chased away by the feeling of Nick's lips crashing down on mine.

21

AMELIA

THE KISS IS SO soft at first.

So completely contradictory to the man kissing me, to the rigid atmosphere suffocating us. It's hesitant and unsure, like he's braced for rejection, and it's so utterly un-Nick. It does something to me, sparks something simultaneously mushy yet unyielding, that obliterates the icky ball that settled in my gut as I watched him stride out of the house earlier and replaces it with something needy.

I don't want his hesitance. I want him to kiss me with the same clarity he uttered all those pretty, harsh words; like he means it. Like he wants me and he hates that he does. Because, God, do I know the feeling.

When I make an eager noise in my throat, my mouth opening ever so slightly as I sigh into his, I get my wish.

It's a clash of tongues and teeth as Nick deepens the kiss with a groan, stealing every breath from my lungs with the intensity of it. I open myself to him more than eagerly, relishing in the taste of him— sweet and smoky like he spent the night nursing a count of rum, and fuck if that doesn't make me kiss him a little harder. I'm so consumed by his mouth that I don't notice when I'm hoisted onto the counter, not until greedy hands palm my bare thighs, forcing them apart and making room for a warm body to slip between them.

I gasp when his pelvis grinds against the hottest, neediest part of me and Nick swallows the noise, echoing it with a groan that I relish. "Fuck,

Amelia," he rasps between lashes of his tongue, nips of his teeth. "*Sabia que seria assim.*"

I have no idea what that means but I moan anyway, the husky timbre of his voice traveling straight to the throbbing spot between my thighs. They clamp around Nick, eliminating any semblance of space between us. A whimper of protest rips from my throat when he suddenly pulls away but the lack of contact lasts all of a second before scorching lips find purchase along my jaw and drag down my neck, teeth scraping my collarbone as he lavishes my sensitive skin. I find myself squirming frantically as my head falls back to allow for better, unlimited access, feverish with the thought of the marks he's undoubtedly leaving and unable to control my hips as they rock against his, my hands twisting in his hair as I try to keep up.

And *his* hands, *God*, his hands. They're everywhere, all at once, caressing every bit of skin they can access with a burning reverence I have no capacity to dwell on, to properly appreciate, not when one cups the nape of my neck with head-scrambling authority, holding me in place while the other slips beneath the fabric of my t-shirt to palm the bare small of my back with surprising gentleness.

I can't say the same for myself; there's nothing gentle about my grip on his hair. It's got to hurt, how I'm practically ripping strands from roots, but Nick doesn't seem to care, and neither do I. There is very little I care about right now, and nowhere on that microscopic list is the fact we're making out in the middle of the kitchen for anyone to see. Or who I'm making out with. All I care about is keeping Nick's hand and lips on me for as long as possible.

I'm nothing more than tangled thoughts and panting breaths and tingling flesh by the time Nick works his way back up to my mouth. His ferocity tempers as he kisses me slow and hungry, like he's savoring the moment, like he knows I need to catch my breath but he can't stop. He tells me as much, whispering it against my swollen lips, and I whisper back, urging him not to. I fear that if he stops, my brain will kickstart with the loss and reality will sink in and I really don't want that to happen yet.

My stomach twists and flutters when Nick grips my thighs once again. Toying with the frilly hem of my pajama shorts, he coaxes them further up my legs, the pads of his fingers burning the revealed skin. When he grazes the crease of my pelvis, I stutter a breath, the next one released with a disapproving cry as Nick suddenly retreats. I try to follow, embarrassingly needy for more, but Nick evades me with a teasing smirk.

I wriggle impatiently, dangerously close to pouting and begging, doing nothing but causing Nick's smirk to widen. He encroaches on me again but he doesn't give me what I want. He hovers too many inches away, seemingly content to stare at me when I am anything but.

"Nick." His name is half a whine, half a pant.

Fingers graze my cheek as he tucks a wayward strand of hair behind my ear. "Yes?"

"Stop staring at me."

"I like staring at you." The tingling in my lips amps up a notch when he swipes the bottom one gently. "Do it a lot."

It's a statement that, in any ordinary conversation, would immediately be classed as creepy yet coming from Nick, it's a sweet nothing.

Shaking off the urge to melt, I lean until our foreheads clash again. "Nick," I repeat, injecting more urgency into my tone because the throb between my legs is feeling pretty damn urgent. "Stop *just* staring at me."

Dimples.

My demand earns me dimples, as if I needed another thing making me light-headed and boneless.

I get the inexplicable urge to call him an ass but it dies as soon as it's born, replaced by an entirely unattractive squawk of surprise when I'm yanked to the very edge of the counter. Nick's chuckle tickles my lips as he claims them again yet it's different this time. Not as frantic and ravenous. More lazy and unhurried as though we have all the time in the world which for some reason inspires the rumblings of an impending freak out deep in my chest. As though he can sense it, Nick does what he does best; he distracts me. Every inch of me tenses in rapt anticipation when he snaps the waistband of my panties harshly against my skin.

"You know how many times I've thought about this?" The welcome assault on my lips comes to an infuriating pause so Nick can grind out an unanswerable question through gritted teeth. And, I suspect, so he can relish in my slack-jawed expression as he cups the slick heat between my legs without warning. We both groan, neither of us making any move to stifle the noise. "So many fucking times, Amelia."

With my panties acting as a damp, useless barrier, Nick drags a knuckle through the crease of me, hissing at the wetness he finds—which is a lot. "Every time you wear those skimpy little dresses, I imagine how easy this would be. It's all I could think about on my birthday when I had you in my lap." His index finger teases the edge of my underwear, so close yet so far from where I desperately want him. "It would've been so fucking easy."

Whimpering helplessly, I clutch Nick's shirt tightly, my hips writhing in search of more than he's giving me. Never in my life have I been this turned on, this *dripping*. Never have I wanted, *needed*, someone so badly. I'm not above begging and I'm not far from it, ready to do whatever it takes before I lose my damn mind.

But, as I'm about to, Nick does it for me.

Something downright feral glinting in his eyes, Nick begs.

"Please, *querida*. Let me."

And what the hell else am I going to say other than a breathless, enthusiastic *fuck yes*?

A hand on my belly pushes me gently, a silent command to lean back on my palms, and that's all the warning I receive before Nick drops to his knees, face set in an expression I can only describe as *hungry*. He wastes no time removing my shorts and panties in one fell swoop, absentmindedly tossing them aside.

There's no chance to be shy about my sudden nakedness because Nick doesn't allow me any. I'm too busy trying to maintain my balance —and my composure—as he maneuvers me to his liking; yanking until my ass hangs off the edge of the counter, hooking my legs over his broad shoulders, and bundling my t-shirt near my belly button before all but burying his face between my thighs.

If I thought the seemingly simple task of filling my lungs with air was insurmountable before, it's nothing compared to now, as a speck of panic seizes the organ. It's been a long, long time since someone last went down on me—Dylan claimed he didn't like it, although he sure as fuck liked the reverse. Hell, it's been a long time since anyone but myself gave me an orgasm. And it's not that I'm shy or squeamish about it, not normally, but... this is Nick. Nicolas Silva. Playboy supreme. The king collector of campus pussy—the guys' words, not mine. Through his own admission, he's been with a lot of girls and it might be silly, it might be irrational, it might be unfair and judgemental and a million other things, but the knowledge sends a tendril of sour insecurity thrashing wild in my gut.

The first wet, hot stroke of his tongue and the appreciative groan that follows do a world of good in soothing me.

"Fuck, Amelia," he grumbles against me, and I have to clamp a hand over my mouth to muffle my loud reaction. "Fucking killing me."

I whine his name again, bucking my hips with all the energy I have.

"That's it, *querida*. Fuck my face like you mean it."

And with that cooed instruction, he fucking devours me.

Within seconds, Nick proves why his reputation is so stellar.

His talented tongue delves inside of me with reckless abandon, driving me near madness within seconds. A thumb joins, circling my clit hard and fast, the way I need it. My hands clutches his curls harder, an attempt to anchor myself that doesn't work.

It's almost laughable, really, that what had such a long build-up ends so quickly. I could blame it on his skills. I could blame it on my severe case of touch deprivation. But either way, an embarrassingly short amount of time passes before I go off like a rocket, every nerve in my body on fire as my back bows off the counter and a silent scream rattles in my throat.

Seconds, minutes, God knows how long passes before my body stops trembling, before Nick relents and *lets* me stop trembling. Another indiscernible length of time and I regain enough function in my limbs to move, propping myself up on shaky elbows just in time to catch Nick helping my limp legs back into my shorts, a shiver wracking my body at the sight of him licking his glossy lips. When he offers me a hand, I take it, letting him help me stand on unsteady feet, my cheeks red-hot as he resituates my disheveled clothing.

My gaze might be firmly fixed on his chest but there's no mistaking the smirk in his voice. "You gonna look at me?"

"Wasn't planning on it."

Chuckling quietly, Nick props up my chin to gently redirect my gaze to his. "Whatever you're thinking," he smooths down what I can only imagine is a wild mess of curls, "stop."

"I'm not thinking anything."

"You're panicking."

"I'm not." I am. I really, really am. With a capital 'P.' It's flooding in with all the oxygen I was momentarily deprived of because what did I do? What did I *let* him do? What did I let him do on *Lynn's fucking kitchen counter*? "We shouldn't have done that."

"*Querida*, relax." A frown creases his forehead when I step out of his reach, not-so-subtly scuttling towards the nearest exit. "It's not a big deal."

And there it is. The final nail in my spiraling coffin.

To him, it wasn't a big deal.

So, I guess it's going to have to not be a big deal to me either.

Steeling myself against the shame and regret threatening to drown me, I square my shoulders and get ready to flee. "This didn't happen."

"Amelia..."

I don't stick around to hear what he has to say, partly because the post-orgasm clarity is hitting me hard and a round of frustrated tears seems imminent, mostly because I have no interest in hearing the end of the speech Nick probably delivers to each of the notches on his bedpost after they succumb to his charm.

22

NICK

I AM in such deep shit.

A deep, bottomless pit of shit that I dug for myself and happily dove in. The second I kissed her, I knew I shouldn't have. Warning bells clanged in my head but not because I was kissing my best friend's little sister in his kitchen. No, they sounded because I was kissing her and I couldn't get enough. I couldn't fucking stop.

I wouldn't have stopped—I would've done it all again, somewhere private where I could've truly seen how wild and loud she gets when she's not holding back—if she hadn't ran like a bat out of hell.

It's been over a week and she's still running, and I let her. I gave her the rest of Thanksgiving weekend—a move partially born out of self-preservation because if Cass suspected anything amiss between us, he would've had my balls—and I suffered through the most stiflingly awkward car ride of my life without complaint. I allowed her the space she was clearly asking for because I know exactly why.

It's not a big deal.

It was a shitty, inane thing to say yet that's what came out of my mouth in a last-ditch attempt at avoiding the meltdown she was seconds away from having. I was trying to stop her from catastrophizing something that was good, *so fucking good*, and maybe, *maybe*, the goddamn horror contorting her pretty features pissed me off a little, made me say the wrong thing for the wrong reasons. I regretted it instantly but before

I could backtrack, she doled it right back and fled the kitchen like it was a fucking crime scene.

So, yeah. I've let her evade and avoid and pretend it didn't happen and I don't exist for eight whole fucking days and I'm reaching the end of my tether. Like, the very, very end where ambushing Amelia after class starts to become a sound idea.

Although an ambush wasn't my intention when I first came up with this plan, I'm not sure what else you call lurking outside a girl's lecture hall, adamant that she's not going anywhere until she talks to you. I tried the simpler route of calling her but she declined to answer. Twice. Showing up at her place uninvited and demanding to see her felt like a bad, slightly creepy idea, especially if two protective roommates have gotten wind of our situation and are feeling vicious.

We really need to talk and fix this hellish awkwardness because it's pissing me off and making me feel all itchy and tight and I don't fucking like it. So, drastic times call for drastic measures, and if those drastic measures include me making an ass of myself on a Friday morning with a peace offering disguised as a takeout coffee cup burning my palm, then so be it.

I'm leaning against the wall opposite Lecture Hall Four, mulling over what exactly I'm going to say when the bell shrilly signals the end of classes. The doors fling open and students trickle out, filling the previously silent hallway with chatter and footsteps. I straighten up, pathetically nervous as I scan the sea of oncoming people for the face I'm looking for.

I groan when I land on one I'd definitely rather avoid.

Kate looks about as happy to see me as I am to see her. My first thought; she knows and I'm about to get shanked with a pencil. But then I realize the disdain in her expression is nothing more than the usual one I'm greeted with, I clock the inquisitive narrowing of her dark eyes, and I come to the conclusion she has no idea.

I can't tell whether that makes me feel better or worse.

With a sigh audible from a distance, Kate elbows my way. Not until she comes to a stop right in front of me do I notice the golden-skinned, dark-haired girl flush against her side, their hands intertwined. Unlike Kate, her girlfriend—I'm assuming that's who she is, it's my first time meeting the girl—graces me with a bright smile that completely contradicts the bland tone with which Kate asks, "What're you doing here, Nicolas?"

I hold up the cardboard tray holding two now-lukewarm coffees. "Looking for Amelia."

"Thought she'd finally shaken you off."

"Kate," her girlfriend chastises gently, bumping her hip with an entirely too cheery scowl before smiling at me again. "I'm Sydney Acharya. Kate's girlfriend."

"I'm-"

"Oh, I know who you are." Sydney waves off my attempted introduction, squinting at me, tilting her head at a ninety-degree angle, and whistling too loud. "Wow, Luna described you really, really well."

Before I can process what I think is a compliment, Kate butts in, "Amelia's not here."

I frown; I'm sure I remember her schedule right. She only has one class on Fridays, it's hard to get that mixed up. "Where is she?"

"Home."

"Is she sick?"

"Nope."

"Are we gonna play twenty questions or are you gonna fill me in here?" When Kate rolls her eyes, I add, "I'm going over there whether you give me a heads-up on what to expect or not."

While tight-lipped might be a characteristic of Kate's, Sydney clearly doesn't share that affliction. Ignoring her girlfriend's warning stare, she admits, "Something happened with Dylan."

"What?" Concern hits me like a tidal wave. "When? What happened? Is she okay?"

Kate only deigns to answer one of my questions, and poorly so. "She's fine."

Fuck me, it's a good thing Sydney is way more generous with information because, without her, I'd be halfway to a jail sentence by now— my fists have been itching for round two with that jackass since before round one even ended. "She's okay," Sydney confirms, side-eying her girlfriend disapprovingly. "But she's been holed up in the apartment all week. We don't know what happened exactly because she won't talk to anyone but Cass and even they had a big bust-up yesterday so she's all on her own and I think it's a *great* idea for you to go check on her."

"Syd!"

"What?" Sydney quirks a thick brow at her protesting girlfriend. "It's not healthy for her to only see Cass all the time."

"You sound like Luna."

I'm pretty sure that was supposed to be an insult but Sydney simply laughs, sticking her tongue out at Kate. "Yeah, I do, because we are both very wise."

My head spins a little with their back and forth, and I'm not entirely clear where I stand—whether I'm going to have to kick down their apartment door to get inside or if I'm going to be welcomed with semi-open arms—until Sydney hits me with another sunny smile. "You can give us a ride back to the apartment. I'll let Luna know we're coming."

It's not an option, it's a command, and I'm more than eager to obey. Telling Sydney roughly where I parked, she strides in that direction, releasing Kate in favor of plucking out her phone and presumably calling Luna. When I start to follow her, I'm halted by a firm palm on my chest.

"Listen, Romeo," I would laugh at the nickname if I didn't think Kate would bite my head off for it, "whatever this is, I don't think today is the day for it. She's not in a great mood."

"I think I'll take my chances."

Kate kisses her teeth, distrust evident. "Don't make it worse."

"I won't." A spot in my chest aches at the accusation. "Believe it or not, Kate, I care about her. I'm not trying to make anything worse."

Just for a second, the hardness in her expression gives way to something genuine. "I know," she dares to admit, spitting the words as though they cause pain on their way out. "That's why I'm keeping an eye on you."

"Because I care about her?"

Kate crosses her arms over her chest defiantly, eyeballing me like I'm the one being confusing. "Because she obviously cares about you too, dipshit, and I don't want her to get hurt again."

"I'm not like Dylan."

"I know that too." For some reason, Kate finds that funny, a huffed laugh leaving her as she snags the coffee meant for Amelia and sips. "If you were, I would've gotten rid of you already."

⟿

When I knock on Amelia's bedroom door, I'm calm. Clear-headed.

I've got a plan. A rough, haphazardly thrown together plan that doesn't progress much past sitting her ass down and begging her to talk to me, but it's a plan all the same.

However, it all goes out the window the moment I open the door.

She's in bed, and it looks like she's been in bed for a while. And, fuck, I always think she looks beautiful but she doesn't look good. She doesn't look *alive*. Stony-faced, she stares at me blankly, clutching a bottle of tequila like it's a lifeline, and suddenly, I'm pissed.

I'm pissed that she's like this and I'm pissed that I didn't know and I'm pissed that it's like looking in a fucking mirror and seeing an angry, freshly dad-less eighteen-year-old who suffocated his feelings instead of dealing with them. The magnitude of it threatens to choke me, drowning out any of the clarity I felt moments ago.

In a few strides, I'm looming over her and snatching the booze from her grip. "Get up."

That pretty, pale face flushes with irritation. "Excuse me?"

Striding to her dresser, I set the bottle on top—making a mental note to pour that shit down the drain later—and yank open drawer after drawer until I find what I'm looking for. I chuck a pair of leggings and a sports bra over my shoulder, an indignant screech sounding in return. "Get up, get dressed, and let's go."

Amelia gets up alright, but only so she can storm towards me, small palms shoving me away from her things. "Who the fuck do you think you are?"

"I think I'm your friend," I snap, an acrid laugh scorching my throat. "Jury's out on that, though, unless you often ignore your friends for a week."

She echoes my laugh with one of her own, tangled curls falling around her face as she shakes her head. "Leave me alone, Nick. I'm not in the mood for you."

Ignoring the painful stabbing sensation her words cause, I foil her attempt at snatching up the tequila again, body-blocking her from taking a swig. She's not drunk—the bottle's almost completely full, she's tipsy at best—and I'm going to make sure it stays that way. "Whatever you're angry about, getting drunk is not gonna fix it." I stab a finger towards the athletic wear sprawled on her unmade bed. "Get dressed and try taking it out on a punching bag instead of alcohol."

Amelia snorts angrily. "I let you in my pants one time and you think you're the boss of me? Fuck off, Nick."

I don't like this. I don't like this at all. This isn't the Amelia I know, *my Amelia*, the downright shy girl who blushes the most brilliant shade of red and can barely look me in the eye when I flirt with her. This is an angry, contorted version and I want to know what caused her so I can make her go away. "What the hell is wrong with you?"

"Nothing is wrong with me," she lies. "It's *not a big deal*."

"You wanna act like that's what this is about?" I can't help but scoff. "Really? You're Boo Radley'ing it up in here because of something that, according to you, didn't happen?"

"Oh, don't act like I hurt your feelings, *Nicolas Silva*." I hate how she says my name, scoffs it like it has a whole other nefarious meaning. "You're just annoyed I left before you could kick me out."

Temper flaring, something nasty claws its way up and out of my throat before I can stop it, "I was more annoyed the favor wasn't returned."

It's almost imperceptible, Amelia's flinch. The tiniest dent in her furious bravado, a blink-and-it's-gone reaction. "I'm sure you have plenty of girls on speed dial willing to drop their panties."

The self-satisfied smirk I paint on hurts, makes my stomach twist and heave. "Damn right."

"Good for you."

"*Yup*," I all but yell.

"*Great*," she all but yells back.

Our words linger in the air long after they're said, rigid and implacable, punctuated by our heavy, angry breaths. I'm glaring at her and she's glaring right back until suddenly, she's not.

It's like she takes a breath and on the exhale, all the fight leaves her. Frail shoulders slump as her bottom lip trembles, and in a split second, she goes from furious to sobbing.

Merda.

"Shit, Amelia." The onslaught of anger that hit me so suddenly fades just as fast as that first tear falls, tracking a path down a quivering cheek and damn near cracking my chest in half. I half-reach for her, my hands hovering awkwardly between us. "I'm sorry."

Furious tremors wrack her body, making her look so terrifyingly small. She tries to say something but it's unintelligible and her inability to speak only seems to make her cry harder and I swear to God, she's breaking my fucking heart.

I can't take it. Cursing quietly, I tug her towards me, and all my tension seeps away when she comes easily, burying her face in my chest and clinging to me without protest. "I'm sorry." Dipping my chin, I press my lips to the top of her head, murmuring in her hair, "I didn't mean any of that, I promise."

"Neither did I." I can barely make out the bawled words, her hot breath seeping through my now-damp t-shirt. "I'm so sorry, I don't know what's wrong with me."

Shushing her gently, my hands coast the length of her back in a way meant to be soothing but it doesn't seem to be helping because it's not getting any better, she won't stop crying, and I'm fucking panicking. In a move of desperation, I gather her up and carry her to the bed, settling amongst the rumpled duvet with my back against the wall and her curled in my lap, all the while silently chanting *fuck, fuck, fuck, what the fuck am I doing* because I don't know how to comfort people, not like this.

"Please stop crying." I'm begging like an asshole and I'm well aware of it but I don't know what else to do and it doesn't matter anyway because it doesn't fucking work. "Tell me what to do, *querida*."

She doesn't. She doesn't do anything other than burrow closer to me, her wet face brushing my neck and her fingers tangling in my t-shirt. I'm incapable of doing anything but letting her, guilt eating me alive as I stroke her hair and rub her back and whisper apologies because I promised I wouldn't make it worse.

23

AMELIA

I have never been so comfortable in my entire life.

I'm pretty sure my eyes are swollen shut and I can barely swallow due to an incredibly raw throat and there's a weird crick bothering my neck yet I'm oddly cozy. A pleasant veil of warmth keeps me in a lulled state of almost-asleep that I don't want to leave. With a yawn, I arch closer to the freaking radiator I must've smuggled into bed.

I freeze when the radiator groans. "Keep doing that, *querida,* and we're gonna have a very awkward situation."

My eyes sting as they wrench open, rapidly blinking away the bleariness until I can make out my surroundings. I'm in my bedroom—unsur-prising considering I've barely left over the past week—but there's something distinctly...*different.*

First of all, judging by the amount of light flooding the room, I managed to get more than three measly hours of restless sleep for the first time since Monday. Tormenting dreams of banging fists and slurred threats have kept me wide awake.

Secondly, my door is cracked open as though someone's come and gone, and I always sleep with it firmly shut.

Thirdly, and most worryingly of all; the thick forearm banded tight around my waist that's attached to the large body flush against my back, presumably the owner of the hot breath tickling the back of my neck.

Oh, and the rock-hard *thing* I do not want to think about digging into my ass.

Crap.

Painfully slowly, I shift onto my opposite side, my eyes half-closed as if that will prevent the sight I know I'm about to see. Yet even though I'm expecting it, my lungs still empty when I'm greeted by nothing but gold, and the memories of last night come rushing back in one overwhelming wave.

Nick turning up and me feeling so much better at the mere sight of him that I threw up a wall of bitter rage to ward it off because I didn't want to feel better. The horrible words we spat at each other, none of which I meant, none of which I'm holding against him because I was looking for it, egging him on, hoping he'd snap because it's easier to be angry at someone who's returning the energy. My fight giving out at the glimmer of concern that never faltered, even when he yelled at me. Me breaking down in his arms for God knows how many hours while he held me, hushed me, soothed me until I must've passed out.

Sitting up as quickly as my weak body will allow, I rake my hands down my face and over my hair—as if that'll fix anything—and shuffle until there's as much of a gap between us as my small bed will allow. Drawing my knees up to my chest for comfort, I rest my cheek atop them facing Nick, clearing my throat before croaking a completely casual, "Good morning."

Yawning, Nicks rolls on his side, an arm lazily crooked behind his head, and I have to avert my gaze because no one should be allowed to look that good the moment they wake up, or sound as good as he does when he rasps a greeting in return. Fiddling anxiously with a corner of my duvet, I frown at Nick's attire of a wrinkled t-shirt and jeans with the zip and top button undone, and I definitely do not look at bulge saluting me. "You slept here?"

Nick cracks a sad smile. "Didn't wanna leave you alone."

"Oh." God, I'm not awake enough for this. "Thank you."

I didn't know a body could simultaneously tense and relax but mine does when Nick's arm flops toward me, a thumb swiping what I'm sure is an extremely puffy undereye. "How do you feel?"

Mortified. Uncomfortable. Like I'm in desperate need of a long shower and a therapy session. "Fine."

Nick messes with my hair, smoothing out the tangles carefully, his expression tight with concern. "Will you tell me what happened?"

I hesitate; I'm yet to say it aloud. I'm scared if I do, it's going to come out silly, like I'm overreacting and making a mountain of a molehill because, really, nothing happened. Dylan turned up out of nowhere, banged on my door a couple of times and yelled some unintelligible things, and I got spooked. A long-lasting spook, extended by the fact he won't stop calling me—no matter how many numbers I block, a new one always pops up.

My reluctance, however, is no match for Nick's patience; he traces miscellaneous shapes along the slope of my neck, lulling me into a false sense of security until I relent. I tell him what happened in a quiet voice with a heavy dose of dismissal, backing it up with an 'it's not a big deal' that makes us both flinch.

Nick's hand drifts as I speak, floating across my shoulder and down my arm, tapping the back of my clenched fist until it opens and I let him lace our fingers together, the move as confusing as it is comforting. "He touch you?" It's a stiff question laced with dread, as stiff as the set of his shoulders as he scans every visible inch of me.

"Didn't even speak to him. I pretended I wasn't home." I neglect to mention I cowered in the corner for thirty minutes until a neighbor chased him away.

"I'm sorry," Nick sighs after a long moment of tight-lipped silence. "About that and about last night."

"I'm sorry too. I shouldn't have taken it out on you."

"I can take it." He squeezes my hand, a dejected tilt to his lips. "I prefer you yelling at me over you ignoring me."

I wince. "I'm sorry about that too."

"We don't have to talk about it," there's no need to clarify what *it* is, his tone says it all, "but I want to."

"We don't have to," I agree, wriggling my hand from his grip so I can fuse it with my other in my lap. "I get it, really. You don't have to worry about me becoming all weird and clingy."

"I wasn't worried about that."

"Okay." I swallow, nervously rolling my lips together. "Really, it's fine. We can go back to the way it was before."

I brace myself for a nod, a relieved smile, a few muttered words of agreement followed by Nick getting up and skedaddling so I can die of humiliation slash wallow in peace. That's not what I get though. Instead, I get Nick rolling to prop himself up on an elbow, cocking his head at me with something almost challenging in his gaze. "I don't wanna do that."

Confusion creases my brow. "What?"

Nick opens his mouth to deliver the clarification I desperately need, and I almost whine and kick like a toddler when an alarm suddenly goes off, interrupting him. I swear internally while he curses aloud, digging his ringing phone out of his pocket, silencing it, and swearing again. "I have to go."

My shoulders slump with an unexpected amount of disappointment. "Oh."

Nick squeezes my calf as he clambers over me. My cheeks heat as he fastens his jeans, flashing a glimpse of tan, toned, tattooed lower stomach. "I have work."

Huh. I didn't even know he had a job. "Where do you work?"

It's almost awkward, the way he clears his throat, and he definitely seems a little uneasy as he says, "The Paper Trail."

"The bookstore?"

Nick coughs, overly focused on his feet as he shoves them into shoes. "Uh huh."

Oh, God. Why? *Why?* Hot, sweet—most of the time—and he works in a *bookstore*? Be still my freaking beating heart. "I like that place. It's cute." Super cute, and very un-Nick, so contradictory to the dark and mysterious aesthetic he has going on with all its jewel-tones and plants and quirky, kitsch decorations.

Nick grunts as he perches on my bed again, gently looping a hand around my ankle. "Can I come back later? Please?"

Chewing on my bottom lip, I nod, and whatever uncomfortable conversation we're bound to have suddenly seems worth it for the bright smile he graces me with.

~

"Marry him."

My groan echoes around the living room. "Luna."

"He teaches you self-defense. He beat up Dylan. He brings you coffee. He works in a *bookstore*." She flicks a finger up with each sentence, her voice becoming squealier and squealier as she counts all the reasons why I simply must become the next Mrs. Silva. "He's fucking perfect."

From the opposite end of the sofa, Kate hums a noise of agreement. "And he made you come."

"*Yeah.*" Luna snaps her fingers, shooting Kate an approving look, the antithesis to the scowl I send her. "That too. Top of the list."

"Both of you, stop it."

"Look me in the eyes and tell me you didn't have scandalous, angry sex after you finished yelling at each other last night."

"I just told you that we didn't!"

"And how are we to trust you," Luna tuts, "after you waited an entire week to tell us about your Thanksgiving shenanigans?"

"Jesus Christ." My head hits the back of the sofa with a thud as I slump against the cushions, wishing they'd swallow me whole. I knew spilling the beans about what happened would incur a bombardment of teasing commentary. That's why I kept my mouth shut. Even before anything happened between us, mocking quips weren't uncommon and suspicion was rife, particularly from the blonde portion of our trio; Luna couldn't, and clearly still can't, wrap her head around the concept of us just being friends—something about 'the way he looks at me' or something silly like that. Kate, as always, played her cards a little closer to her chest, kept her analysis of Nick and I's relationship to herself, but now that the cat is out of the bag, everything else is pouring out with it.

"Oh, come on, Mils," she sighs, swishing a hand through the air. "You know he likes you."

"No, I don't, actually."

"And you like him."

"*No, I don't, actually,*" I repeat, kissing my teeth in annoyance when my friends chuckle. "I don't!"

Not a lot, anyway. A perfectly normal amount that barely, *barely*, breaks the boundary of how much you like a good friend.

Whatever amount equates to letting him eat me out on a kitchen counter.

While Kate huffs her belief, Luna sighs dreamily, her temple knocking against mine as dramatically pats beneath her completely dry eyes. "I can't believe our Mils is gonna be the one to tame Nicolas Silva. I might cry."

"Oh, shut up." I shove the little drama queen away, and she flumps onto Kate with a squeal. "If anyone's been *tamed*, it's you."

Pale eyes narrow. "Take that back."

"Don't worry." Kate abdicates from the Amelia Torment Campaign and hops aboard the Ridicule Luna Bandwagon. "Girlfriend looks good on you."

Luna groans, hiding behind her hands but not quick to conceal a glimpse of a smile and a definite blush. Suffice to say, we got the shock of our lives when Luna arrived back from Thanksgiving break toting the very thing she'd always sworn against; a boyfriend. And not just any; she bagged the man made of the most boyfriend material in all of Sun Valley—Oscar Jackson. I'm not particularly close to the guy—we haven't had many opportunities to bond considering his lips are usually occupied attacking Luna's—but I know he's nice. And not nice in the dismissive compliment kind of way you assign to someone you barely know or when you're trying to be polite, but the text-book definition of the word you use for a genuinely good guy. Just short of shy but quiet, for sure. And an undeniably safe choice.

Not one of those words would be the first you used to describe Luna but they work, weirdly, and they're happy, clearly, so aside from the odd dose of gentle ribbing my friend definitely deserves, I'm free from objections.

I'm not going to lie though; after she broke the news, I escaped to the privacy of my shower and spent an hour half-laughing, half-crying as I compared the oh-so-drastic outcomes of our holiday weekends.

I'm about to continue the heckling when the doorbell rings, and all three of us turn in unison to frown at the front door. Two subtle kicks to my thigh urge me to answer—I'm the closest, that's our rule—and I rise with a sigh, throwing a question over my shoulder as I cross the room. "Did we order food and forget about it again?"

A husky chuckle I'd know anywhere greets me as I open the door. "Not sure you can find me on DoorDash, *querida*, but thank you for implying I'm good enough to eat."

Yeah, I most definitely did not order a six-foot-four Brazilian man equipped with a smirk and a plastic bag stamped with the logo of our local Chinese takeout, but I did forget about it. Kind of. I partly forgot, partly assumed he wouldn't show up again, at least not tonight.

Unlike the other times Nick has been here, he doesn't wait for an invitation to come in; he simply barges past me and heads for the kitchen, sparing the girls a wave before bumbling around like he owns the place.

It takes me a second to reboot. Another to close the door, and one more to turn around and gape at the man snagging cutlery from the drawer, and stacking up an impressive amount of foil takeout containers. My gaze swings from him to my friends, and I stifle an embarrassed groan at their reactions to this unexpected situation.

Luna's risen up on her knees to get a better view of the show, her hands cupping her cheeks and her mouth pursed as she holds in what I'm sure is an ear-splitting squeal. Kate's adopted a similar position but she looks like she can't decide whether to be amused or confused or concerned. She settles on the former as she gets to her feet, yanking Luna up with her. "We'll be in our rooms if you need us."

Nick quirks a brow, waving a hand at the mountain of Chinese food. "I brought enough for everyone."

A tiny noise escapes Luna, like the sound of a whisper of air leaving a balloon, and I watch as she subtly waggles five fingers in my direction, another thing added to her list. "Well-"

"We're fine," Kate cuts her off with another hard yank. "Thank you, though."

Nick lifts his chin at them as they scuttle from the room—one a hell of a lot more reluctantly than the other—and then, we're alone.

I feel like, at this point, I should be beyond feeling awkward around Nick. Yet here I am, dithering like a loser, unsure of where to look or how to act. Clearing my throat, I pad toward him, my fingers curling around the edge of the tiny island separating the kitchen from the living room. "What is this?"

"Food," the smart-ass replies.

I offer him a deadpan look. "Why, Nick?"

"I told you I was coming back over." Cracking the lid of what looks like sweet and sour eggplant, he slides it toward me, following it up with a portion of stir-fried broccoli—one day, I'm going to ask how this man knows all of my orders to a T. "And I thought you'd be more agreeable on a full stomach. Less likely to flee."

Despite myself, I laugh. When he offers me a fork, I take it, and we both dig in.

I manage a grand total of six bites before the suspense gets me. "So?"

Nick pauses shoveling beef noodles into his mouth. Chewing thoughtfully, he swallows and sighs. "I shouldn't have said it wasn't a big deal. I get that it was a dickhead thing to say but you were clearly panicking and I wanted to calm you down."

"I wasn't-"

"Yes, you were," he stops my lie before it can fully form. "And that's okay, I get it. It was out of nowhere and it was a lot but it happened and you didn't have to run away. You didn't have to avoid me all week either."

Nick rounds the counter, intimidating as he stalks toward me but not in a scary way—in a way that sends tingles of anticipation down my spin. Coming to a stop, his hand curves over my waist, the other resting on the slope of my neck—his favorite spot—and he uses the grip to tug me closer. "Here's the thing, Amelia. I like what we did. I wanna do it again, among other things. And I think you wanna too but you're letting that pretty little head get in the way."

"It's complicated, Nick." So freaking complicated for so many reasons, none of which I can properly recall as lips brush my fluttering pulse.

"Uncomplicate it."

"Cass-" Nick's groan cuts me off, and he retreats from kissing my neck, displeasure evident in his gaze. "I can't lie to him."

"It's not lying if he doesn't ask." Soft lips kiss forehead in a surprisingly tender move. "We'll be careful."

Careful; code for sneaking around. It should infuriate me, the implication that whatever's between us will be a secret but in an odd twist, the thought relaxes me. Takes the pressure off. Makes the somewhat preposterous idea of me and him a little less...daunting.

And, if I'm honest, it sounds fucking *fun*.

I swallow hard, my breath stuttering as all the contact starts to go to my head. "I don't want a boyfriend."

A soft chuckle tickles my cheek. "I'm not trying to be your boyfriend. I just think it would be a waste."

"What would?"

"I'm attracted to you," he states like the fact is common knowledge and doesn't scramble my insides as much as his mouth brushing the corner of mine does. "You're attracted to me." The opposite corner tingles as it receives the same treatment. "What's the harm in having a little fun?"

God, he's making it all sound so easy. "So, we would be..."

"Whatever you want to be, *querida*."

I'm not sure what that is, not until it comes flying out of my mouth like some gut instinct desperate to be heard. "I want a distraction."

A pause. A shared breath loaded with hesitation and anticipation as he scans every inch of my face before finally, his lips touch mine. "Whatever you want."

24

AMELIA

IT TAKES LESS than two days for me to realize that maybe I'm not cut out for a casual, secret, distracting, friends-with-benefits relationship.

I'm not a jealous person. Really, I'm not—when I'm with someone, I trust them unless given a reason not to. However, I've never been with someone like Nick who attracts women like flies to freaking honey. We're in the library, for God's sake, and no less than four girls have sauntered up to him in the span of a single hour. I'm so distracted by it, I haven't absorbed a word of the textbook sprawled in front of me—studying is a foreign concept right now. All I'm capable of is excessively clicking the top of my pen while trying to put a leash on the weird, unfamiliar green monster writhing in my gut.

"You know," a voice murmurs in my ear as a pen jabs me in the ribs. "If you wanna keep your little experiment a secret, you're gonna have to practice the whole subtle thing."

I slide Kate a glare. "I don't know what you're talking about."

Almost as soon as I told the girls about the newest development in my life, I regretted it. Not that I actually told them; Nick and I'd barely sealed the deal before they were barging into the room, blurting false apologies for interrupting us. Well, one of them did; the other shrieked "*I fucking knew it*" whilst doing a little dance on the spot and making lewd noises.

No prizes for guessing who that was.

It makes my life a little easier, them knowing, since it means I don't have to sneak around in my own home but on the contrary, it makes it a helluva lot harder to lie.

"Relax." Kate nudges me, discreetly jerking her head toward where Nick sits on the opposite side of the wide library table, Cass by his side. "He's not doing anything."

Which is true. He isn't. In an utterly un-Nick fashion, he's not sparing the entourage crowded around him more than a polite smile. In fact, I'm pretty sure he's directing them to Cass. I'm wracking my brain trying to recount a time when he's turned someone down, and apart from that girl who got real familiar with my ribcage, I'm coming up empty. My rational mind can acknowledge that, and appreciate it.

The irrational part, however, is a different story. It insists on reminding me that the exact parameters of our… *situationship* have yet to be defined. For all I know, he could be allowed to do whatever he wants with other women. I could be allowed to do whatever I want with other men. I am hopelessly out of my depth here and it's throwing me off.

Clicking my tongue, I flop back in my chair. "You're supposed to be on my side."

"I side with the facts, baby," Kate coos, patting my thigh. "And your guy is too busy mooning over you to entertain anyone else."

Ignoring the mushy feeling her reassurance incites, I grumble, "He's not my guy."

Kate snorts, re-directs her gaze toward Nick, and snorts again. "He sure as fuck isn't anyone else's guy."

"What're we gossiping about?"

We both jump as Ben plops himself in the empty seat on my other side, the book he was searching for hitting the table with a loud thump. "Nothing," we answer too quickly.

Pale green eyes narrow and flit between us, droll sarcasm tingeing his tone as he drawls, "That wasn't suspicious at all."

"You find what you were looking for?" Kate, God bless her, smoothly changes the subject, easily distracting the kid by tossing a pack of Red Vines his way. That's the thing about Ben; he's the human equivalent of a golden retriever puppy. Inquisitive, persistent, and you wave a treat in his face and everything else is forgotten. Every time, it works like a charm, and now is no exception—snagging a handful of red licorice ropes, he eagerly goes off on a tangent about his newest assignment.

Ben's major makes perfect sense to me. Something about the

perfectly windswept blond hair, the cocksure attitude, and the ripped jeans, colorful Converse, oversized shirt combination he favors simply screams 'yup, I'm a musical prodigy.' Just last night as we gathered in the guys' living room for an impromptu pizza-and-movie night, he'd whipped out his ukulele—a battered old thing covered in Sharpie-scribbled lyrics and faded stickers—and added to the illusion, serenading us with at least half of Harry Styles' discography. It felt like we were in some cliche coming-of-age movie about the importance of friendship and Ben's melodic voice was the soundtrack.

While I likened his voice to a lullaby mere hours ago, and as much as I've grown to love the kid because I really have, I'd cut out his vocal cords if it meant he stopped repeatedly humming the exact same notes. Well, to my ears, they sound the same. According to Ben, they're entirely different, and Kate and I have got to choose what sounds better or else it'll be our fault when he fails his final composition of the semester.

"Stop making that noise," I beg, gesturing to the Red Vine he's gnawing on, "or I'm seriously going to ram that down your throat."

I shouldn't be surprised when Ben finds unintended dirtiness in that threat. "Don't tease me, Tiny." He winks, waving the long piece of candy like a lasso. "You know I'm working on my gag reflex."

God, my own damn gag reflex is triggered by the image that evokes.

Ben snickers as Kate and I shiver and dry-heave dramatically, but all three of us sober up when a shadow falls over our section of the table. A yelp escapes Ben as a hand lands on the back of his chair and yanks so it's teetering on the back two legs, attempting to tip him off but he holds on tight. Dropping his head back, he scowls. "Can I help you?"

Nick wiggles the chair again, another attempt to dethrone Ben. "Scram, kid."

"Excuse *me*."

Ignoring the indignant screech, Nick waves an A4 notepad in my direction, quirking a smile that's far from innocent. "Need a proofreader."

Ben tries to swipe the notepad, pouting when Nick evades him. "I can read too, you know."

"You can?" Nick drawls sarcastically, proving the third time's the charm when he angles the chair again and Ben finally tumbles out. Waving a dismissive hand at the kid mumbling profanities and discreetly waving a middle finger his way, Nick claims the recently vacated seat. "I'll keep that in mind next time I need a nursery rhyme corrected."

The laugh in my throat dies when Nick shifts to face me. I don't like the look on his face at all; it's not the look of a guy who's simply wandering over to ask for help on an essay. It's way too freaking smug for my liking.

Nick tosses his notepad on the table but neither of us is paying attention to it, both well aware that it was a ploy. As he did with Ben, he grabs my chair too but he doesn't chuck me out of it. He hooks a hand around a leg and carefully drags me closer until we're basically thigh to thigh. Glancing around nervously, a relieved puff of air escapes me; Cass has wandered off somewhere, none the wiser when Nick slinks an arm around the back of my seat, not quite touching me but dangerously close to it.

I swallow hard when fingers lightly brush my shoulder, burning through the material of my sweatshirt. "Not gonna lie, Amelia," he twirls a strand of hair around his finger and tugs, "you're hot when you're jealous."

"I'm not jealous." I'm very aware that I should shrug him off, that we're too close for public observation, yet I'm powerless to do anything but titter awkwardly. "You can do whatever you want."

Nick makes a noise deep in his throat as his tongue runs over his teeth. "Can I?"

My first instinct has me opening my mouth to deliver a snapped 'yup,' but at the last second, I think better of it. Quietly, I admit, "I don't know." Like I said, I'm entirely out of my depth here. "Maybe we should, uh, set some rules? Like boundaries or whatever? So it doesn't get... messy."

Even messier than it already has the potential to be, I should say.

"Rules," Nick muses absentmindedly, still fiddling with my hair. He likes doing that, I've noticed, and I have no objection. In general, he's a lot more touchy-feely than I expected—I have no objections to that either. "I can do that."

Okay. Great. Right direction.

Testing our luck more than he already is, Nick leans closer until it's impossible to see anything but him and that freaking dimple-popping smirk. "You gonna tell me what these rules are or do I have to read your mind?"

Rolling my eyes, I playfully shove him away, and it's right on time too; Cass saunters over, squinting at our proximity, and I get that feeling you get when you're a kid and you're caught doing something naughty. "Your mother never teach you about personal space, Nicolas?"

"Your mother never teach you about paranoia?" Nick retorts, slumping casually in his seat. To everyone else, it looks as though his arms simply drop to his side; no one else can see his hand as it clamps on my thigh. "Relax, Cass," he croons, and I don't know how the hell my brother misses the sly wink he aims my way. "She's helping me with something. Apparently, I need to brush up on my grammar *rules*."

I'm aiming for confident as I stride into The Paper Trail later that day, clutching a paper takeout bag from Greenies and armed with a newfound sense of clarity.

Somewhere between pretending to study whilst being discreetly pawed beneath the table and slogging through a work shift with an inexplicable case of the jitters, I came to a conclusion; I'm in control here. Whatever I want, that's what Nick said. The rules, our boundaries, they're up to me. He's handing over the reins, and I should take them instead of being awkward and nervous and constantly doubting everything when he's yet to give me a reason to. I want to go back to how it was between us before the fateful kitchen incident because I was comfortable then and that was fun, and it's supposed to be fun, this thing between us. A welcome distraction. It'd be a crying shame if I wasted it because I can't get out of my damn head.

It struck me as I finished up work that Nick is always the one dropping in on me, catching me off guard, and that doesn't feel fair. It probably adds to the skittish energy I've been adopting in his presence lately. So, I'm balancing the scales a little.

Guided by the coworker behind the register, I find Nick tucked away at the back of the store. He's at the far end of an aisle, sandwiched between two towering walls of books, a stack balanced in the crook of his arm that he's working on depositing amongst the shelves. He's utterly absorbed in what he's doing, pausing every so often to skim a blurb or flip through a couple of pages, and briefly, I linger. I've remarked many a time on how Nick is a man worth admiring, and apparently, rings true even when he's doing something as mundane as working.

And as I stare, I find myself thinking WWLED; What Would Luna Evans Do?

Whistle.

I freaking wolf whistle in the middle of a bookstore.

An immediate cringe follows the noise but I hide it as Nick's surprised gaze snaps upward, his expression melting into an ear-to-ear grin that's entirely too amused and freaking *twinkly* for my liking.

Depositing the remaining books on a random shelf, he closes the distance between us in a couple of long strides, his hands settling on my waist the moment he's within reach. "Did you just whistle at me?"

You're a dipshit, I silently reprimand myself as I contemplate whether or not the bookshelves are light enough for me to topple but heavy enough to crush me and put me out of my misery. "Maybe."

An internal groan echoes around my silly mind as the freaking dimples come out to play. "Are you drunk?"

"Shut up," I mumble, my face screwing up in embarrassment.

Chuckling, Nick pries my hands away when I try to hide behind them, holding them firm as he leans in and kisses me too gently for my brain to handle. "It was cute."

This is what fucks with me, I realize. The softness. When he's sweet to me—and only me, through his own admission. That's what throws me off the most, what causes the flip to switch to awkward. I can handle the flirty player version of Nick—if that Nick fucked me over, I'd survive it. But this Nick? The one a girl could get attached to? I'm not so sure.

Kate would say I'm catastrophizing. Lu would chastise me because 'expect the worst, get the worst' is her mindset. In a rare twist, I listen to them both. Pushing any worrisome thoughts aside, I re-bolster myself, mentally pump up my confidence, and I groan. "I wasn't aiming for cute."

If Luna had done it, no way would it have been *cute.*

However, I quickly decide cute is perfectly okay when Nick kisses me again with the same sweet reverence. It doesn't last long, though, before I'm spun and pressed up against a bookshelf, moaning a stifled noise when Nick deepens the kiss with a lash of his tongue.

In a matter of seconds, I'm wrecked, gasping for air as my knees wobble and my head spins and the bundle of nerves between my legs aches for attention, every graze of the seam of my jeans against it as Nick's hips rock into mine damn near maddening. The bag of food in my hands drops to the ground as they scramble for purchase on the large body pinning me in place, finding it in his hair—I have to rise on the very tip of my toes to reach, and Nick assists me with an oh-so-helpful palm on my ass balancing me, kneading the soft flesh through my jeans. He's doing exactly what our agreement entails, he's distracting me, but now is one of those rare times I need a clear head.

Nick groans as I wrench myself away, keeping him somewhat at bay with a hand planted high on his chest. "We have to talk."

I bite my lip to stop a laugh when the grown-ass man pouts. The action backfires, though, because it draws his attention to the very place I'm trying to avert it from. Groaning again, Nick dips his head, grazing the corner of my mouth before trailing to my jaw and peppering kisses that make me sigh. "So talk, *querida*. I'm listening, I promise."

I wrack my brain for the list I carefully curated earlier but with him sucking on the sensitive skin where my neck meets my hair, I'm having a helluva lot of trouble conjuring it up. "No sleepovers," I eventually manage to grind out, punctuated by a whimper as teeth nip my ear lobe.

"Veto," he grunts, the hand not on my ass drifting to the waistband of my jeans, fingers toying with the top button. "Try kicking me out of your bed at night, *querida*. I dare you."

What was I saying earlier about control? Yeah. I have it. Sure. Uh-huh.

I try again. "We don't tell anyone."

"We already covered that one." He makes his way back up to my mouth at the same time his hand drifts south. My breath catches as slowly, he unbuttons my jeans, drags down the zip, and when he finds no objections, slips his hand inside the stiff denim.

You're in public, rationale screams, yet nowhere in me can I find it to care.

Neither I nor the thin fabric of my panties put up a fight as Nick gently nudges brushes a knuckle against my throbbing clit. "What else?"

Good question. God, he's really blowing my plan to shit, all my focus diverting to his hand cupping my pussy. "No sex."

The golden rule. I'm not going to kid myself and pretend that sex won't lead to me getting attached; it will. I freaking know it will. I'm a chronic monogamist and if I don't have one hard boundary, I'll crumble. It's non-negotiable and I brace myself for...maybe not an argument, but definitely a complaint.

It doesn't come.

"Okay," Nick agrees way easier than I would've expected, even rewarding me with a hard press of his thumb. "Next?"

"No dates."

Aside from the no-sex rule, that's the one most steadfast; dates imply dating, and that's a confusion my impressionable mind can live without.

I didn't think that would be the rule to cause Nick hesitation but it does; infuriatingly, he pauses everything, drawing back slightly to peer down at me. "What're we counting as a date, Amelia?"

I squirm, trying to grind against his hand, but he's unrelenting. A moan-sigh-groan hybrid leaves me. "I don't know." Believe it or not, I'm not a dating connoisseur. "Dinner. Movies. That kind of stuff."

Nick contemplates that for a too-long, exasperating moment. I almost fall to the floor in relief when he kisses his teeth, almost out of frustration, and starts tracing my clit in slow, tight circles, gaining speed the more I moan and writhe.

It's a short-lived relief; right as I reach the edge I'm quickly guided to, Nick slows his pace and reduces the pressure, enough so I'm still hovering but I can't quite get there.

"Bringing you dinner?" he asks, his voice rougher, breathier, than usual. "Does that count?"

"No." I'm hardly going to object to hand-delivered food, especially considering there's a burger from Greenies at our feet with his name on it. Through the pounding of blood in my ears, I swear I hear a muffled 'thank fuck' in response.

"And boxing?" When I shake my head, I'm rewarded with a harsh kiss, a harsher, toe-tingling touch. "Coffee?" My head shakes again and doesn't stop when his final question is, "This?" and his pleased hum spreads warmth through my chest.

"Good to know." I mewl when a hand twines in my hair and yanks my head back slightly so my gaze can collide with a fiery gold one. "I like doing all of that, *querida*," Nick all but growls, "but if I wanna take you out, I'm gonna. Makes my cock hard imagining you getting all dressed up for me."

Oh, God.

"Someone could see us," I protest but it's weak, and I use the same excuse as earlier because it's all my muddled brain can come up with. "It's too messy."

"Someone could see us right now." Mouth pressed to my temple, Nick slips two fingers inside of me. "And I like messy."

Choking on a scream, I bury my face in his neck, nodding frantically, agreeing to God knows what, but I don't care. I think we're done, I think I've remembered all those goddamn rules that have turned out to be pointless, I think the tight coil in my lower belly is finally going to be allowed to snap.

And then Nick issues a directive of his own.

"No one else," he murmurs, the scissoring of his fingers inside of me almost frantic. "Just me and you, *querida*."

He waits for my jerky, frantic nod, before crooking his fingers and smashing his thumb against my clit, and finally, I explode, my cries muffled by the palm that cements itself over my mouth.

Nick barely gives me a chance to catch my breath before stealing it all away again. Looking all too proud of himself, he leans back, a wholly indecent glint in his eyes as he licks his fingers clean. "Thanks for dinner."

25

NICK

I FROWN at my phone as a text from Amelia comes through telling me exactly what I don't want to hear; she's busy.

There goes my plan for the evening. Technically, I already have a plan—I'm in the middle of it—but I would've happily ditched. Seeing Amelia undoubtedly beats freezing my ass off on ice-cold bleachers and watching the guys swinging baseball bats around. It's fucking December, for fuck's sake. Baseball season is, like, two months away. Even preseason training hasn't kicked in yet. There's no reason they need to be fucking around practicing on a Friday night, and there's even less of a reason for me to be here considering I don't play the damn sport, yet here we all are.

"A mandatory roommate outing," Ben had called it.

Fucking bullshit, is more like it.

Irritated, I scowl in the guys' direction—the three of them are crowded into one batting cage, Jackson gently coaching a bat-wielding Ben while Cass sits on the grass with his back against the net, sucking on a beer and occasionally chiming in with shouted notes of his own. I should probably go over there and join in instead of sulking on the sidelines like a loser yet I can't stop my focus from drifting toward my phone again.

Nick: going out?

Amelia: yeah

My fingers hover over the screen as something hot and unfamiliar curls in my chest. Obviously, her going out without me isn't a big deal. We're a week into December and despite the fact we've both been rammed with busy schedules, I'm yet to spend a single winter's night without her, so it's probably healthy to spend one apart. Normal, or whatever. There's probably something in her little rulebook about that.

I don't like it, though. It makes me antsy. Uneasy. It irrationally casts my mind back to all the other times she's gone out recently and it hasn't gone very well on account of a deranged ex. And yeah, it makes me a tiny bit pathetically jealous of whoever's occupying her time.

While I'm mulling over a response that doesn't make me sound like a freak, three little dots pop back up.

Amelia: wild night

The two words are accompanied by a picture, and just like that, my bad mood dissipates. Amelia grins at me through a photo, Kate and Luna on either side of her pulling faces at the camera. They've got some kind of blue face mask shit smeared on their faces, hiding my favorite freckles. In plain sight, though, is the dark purplish-red mark my teeth left on her neck a couple of nights ago, peeking out from behind the collar of her pajama top.

My dipshit-level smile quickly fades when Ben plops down beside me, the bat in his hand clattering loudly to the ground. "What're you grinning at?"

Quickly clicking my phone off, I slide it into my pocket with a shrug. "Nothing."

Ben doesn't miss a beat before accusing, "Liar."

I ignore his goading tone in favor of snatching a beer from the six-pack Cass left by my feet, using the heel of my hand and the lip of the bleacher to pop the top off because the genius didn't bring a churchkey. Ben follows suit but after a single failed attempt, he tips the bottle toward me with puppy-dog eyes. I sigh and do it for him.

You'd think that would earn me a bit of a reprieve from the interrogation brewing—it doesn't. Beer spills down my chin as a surprisingly powerful elbow to the ribs knocks me askew. "Someone didn't come home last night."

God, he's like a cross between an annoying little brother and an overbearing mother. "Mind your own business."

Unsurprisingly, Ben does no such thing. "And when *someone* did come home this morning, *someone* was wearing the same clothes they left in yesterday."

"Do you have a point?"

"All I'm saying is Amelia's never gonna fall in love with you if you keep fucking around."

I almost spit out my damn beer, *that word* all but triggering my gag reflex. "Do you have a head injury I don't know about? Or are you naturally deluded?"

"I *have* a theory."

"I don't care."

"I think you're in love," Ben sings, and once again, bile rises in my throat. It's a helluva exaggeration. I'm not in love. Fuck me, I could barely admit I liked the girl until recently—that's a feat in itself.

And I genuinely fucking like her, which is why it ticks me off when Cass and Jackson wander over, the former crooking a disbelieving brow. "Who's in love?"

When Ben jerks his head toward me, Cass barks a laugh. "Fat fucking chance," he says, and I bristle. "Pretty sure you have to have a heart to fall in love."

It's not a new joke. I've heard it before; I've made it before, laughed at it before. But for some reason, it hits a little sour. And oddly, I'm not the only one who feels it.

Sucking in a hissed breath through gritted teeth, Jackson grimaces. "That's kinda harsh, Cass."

"*I'm* harsh?" Cass blinks at us in bewilderment, stabbing an accusatory finger my way. "Omega Chi have a picture of you taped over the dartboard in their living room because you fucked and ducked so many of them. A girl egged your car because she asked you out and you *laughed*. You banged a girl on her birthday, and then you banged her sister twenty minutes later."

"Fuck off," I cut off his deprecating rant, "you know that last one wasn't on me." I was trashed—I thought they were the same person.

"All I'm saying," Cass continues, hands raised in a display of false innocence, "is you're not exactly the type of guy you bring home to mother."

"And you are?"

"*I* don't run scared at the first whiff of commitment."

My jaw clenches as I scramble for an argument and come up empty. Cass isn't wrong—everything he's saying is backed up by cold, hard facts, and for the first time, I resent this reputation I've earned. How it makes people see me. Fuck, Amelia sees me like that, right? Probably, and I can't even blame her.

As I sit there listening to Cass joke and gripe about how I'd be the last person he'd let near his sister, I'm wondering how the hell I can prove to him, and to her, that she's the last person I want to hurt.

As hard as I try, I can't pinpoint the exact specifics of how I went from shivering at the batting cages to shivering on the ground outside a bar. Alcohol was involved, that much I know for sure—when a six-pack of beer proved insufficient in drowning out the erratic thoughts buzzing around in my head, I moved on, and I convinced the guys to move with me. But I think I might've moved too far—I've drunk myself into a state even I can admit is excessive.

Yet even now, my brain won't turn off.

Amelia this, Amelia that. Amelia, Amelia, *A-fucking-melia*, it wouldn't, *it won't*, stop. It's like the drunker I am, the worse it gets. I keep finding myself thinking about silly shit, like how I need to start buying oat milk because it's the only kind she likes. And how I should probably start stocking the kitchen with a fuck ton of sugar because she goes through that shit in her coffee like crack. And shampoo, I need to find out what shampoo she uses, and conditioner, so I can keep some in my bathroom. And I truly go down a dark hole when I start panicking about what the fuck to get her for Christmas, if I'm even supposed to. I want to but I don't know if that's against the rules and fuck me, I don't know the first thing about buying shit for girls who aren't related to me.

I can only be grateful that when it got to the point of me wanting to articulate those thoughts, I had enough clarity left in me to barrel out of the bar like a bat out of hell—if sober thoughts are drunken words, God knows what trouble drunken thoughts would cause, and I wasn't willing to find out amongst the present company.

Obviously, the better option is mumbling aimlessly to myself while collapsed on the dirty sidewalk with my head between my legs mere feet from the front entrance teeming with life. At one point, I swear I hear someone call out for me but I firmly ignore it, writing it off as a rum-induced hallucination. But then I hear it again, definite this time, a feminine voice crooning my name, and I bristle.

"Not happening," I mutter beneath my breath, an honest to God *hiss* escaping me when a hand lands on my arm. I jerk upright, ready to snap until I see a cloud of red hair and green eyes tight with concern, and I melt like a fucking ice cream on a summer day.

Contentment settles in my chest as I sigh her name. Reaching up, I swipe a thumb down the bridge of a freckled nose, grazing downturned lips before sloppily cupping her jaw. "Beautiful girl."

When Amelia frowns, it takes me a second to realize I'm not speaking English. And when I repeat the sentiment in the language we both understand, pale cheeks redden. I grin, goofy as fuck, but I don't care. I fucking love that blush, and I love it even more when I'm the reason for it.

Eyelids falling to half-mast, I loll toward her as dainty fingers sift through my hair, her soft, sighed breath grazing my skin. "What're you doing out here?"

"Thinking."

Amelia hums low and quiet, a corner of her mouth twitching. "It's cold out here, Nick."

My eyes go wide. Shit. She's right. Hurriedly scrambling to my feet, I shrug off my jacket—a beat-up old leather thing that used to be my dad's. As I scan her outfit, a pained groan echoes through the night air. "What the fuck are you wearing?" I whine needlessly because I can see exactly what she's wearing; I just wish I couldn't.

Fucking pajamas. Thin, *white* pajamas with tiny little hearts printed all over them.

Never thought I'd simultaneously find something cute and sexy as well, yet here she is.

"I was asleep when Cass called." Amelia begrudgingly accepts my offered jacket. Not that I give her much of a choice—I bundle her up before she can object. "I didn't exactly have time to change."

My face scrunches. "Cass called you?"

"Said you guys needed a ride." Looking me up and down, she dryly adds, "I can't imagine why."

A noise I've never made before escapes me—a goddamn chortle—and I would be embarrassed if I wasn't so fucking drunk, and if it didn't earn me the best laugh in the world.

Hands itching to touch her, they slip beneath my jacket to grip her sides and drag her closer. I huff when she weakly protests, one pretty eye twitching as she nervously darts a glance toward the people milling around. We're shrouded in the dark where we are, and even if we weren't, no one's paying attention to us. *And* even if they were, I wouldn't give a shit. Amelia does, though, either way, and I hope my lips brushing hers will distract her enough.

It does—for a too-short second and then she's using a hand on my chest to gently push me away. "You taste like a distillery."

She tastes like salty, buttery popcorn and sugar, an odd combination that I want more of, but she denies me. Instead, she frowns and cocks her head in that way she does when she's thinking hard about something, and it makes my mind race.

"I didn't do anything." I nuzzle the side of her face in an attempt to ease the tiny kernel of panic sprouting in my chest. "Promise."

When I pull back, that frown has only deepened. "I wasn't thinking that."

I exhale my relief. That's good. Part of the reason I fled outside was I got so panicked about the girls flocking around us—all of them discreetly but speedily diverted in Cass' direction. I was paranoid that someone would see and get the wrong end of the stick and it would somehow get back to Amelia and I'd be screwed.

"And," I remember to add, because it's been fucking bugging me, "I'm not gonna bang your sister."

There's a long pause before Amelia coughs. *"What?"*

"And please don't egg my car." I sigh, remembering that mess. "That really sucks."

It's hard to read her expression—I'm not sure if it's actually tough to decipher or if I'm too drunk to do it—but I think it might be amused. Or it's confused. Irritated, maybe? Whatever it is, her tone is soft and genuine as she assures me, "I wasn't planning on it."

"Good." Satisfied I haven't accidentally ruined everything, I try for a kiss again, pouting and whining like a fucking child when she evades.

"I have to get the others," she explains gently before turning on her heel and heading towards the bar entrance.

I stop her before she can even make it two steps, an arm looping around her waist and hoisting her back. "Please," I dip my head to mumble into the crook of her neck, "don't go in there like that."

Amelia twists around in my grip, tipping her head back to glare at me defiantly. "Why not?"

Tugging on the hem of shorts that barely cover her fucking ass, I answer honestly. "I'm too drunk to get in a fight."

Almost on instinct, she adopts an argumentative stance, but when she opens her mouth, it's a surprised laugh that comes out. "You're gonna fight someone for staring at my ass?"

"*Querida*, I wanna fight people for staring at your face."

Amelia's face scrunches up as she futilely tries to hide a smile. She spins out of my grip, not giving me any time to grumble before she grabs my hand, tugging me after her as she heads for her car parked on the other side of the street. "That's a little dramatic. I can't control how people look at me, Nicolas."

Yeah, well. I think I've proven she makes me a little fucking dramatic.

Shoving me into the back seat—a wise choice considering if I was in the front next to her, I wouldn't be able to keep my hands to myself— Amelia clutches the door, leaning down to peer in at me. "I thought all those boxing lessons were so I could fight for myself, hm?"

"Yeah." I clumsily hook an ankle around hers, essentially tripping her into my awaiting grip. She catches herself before our heads clunk together, two palms braced against my chest. Whatever reprimand she prepares dies on her tongue when I lean forward and admit, "And so I could spend time with you."

26

AMELIA

"Where's lover boy?" Kate leans against the kitchen counter, watching while I whip up a complicated, elegant meal of Kraft mac 'n' cheese.

Rolling my eyes, I nod back toward my room. My plans to drop Nick at home with the other three were dashed when he point-blank refused —the others had barely clumsily clambered out of my car when my phone dinged with a demand not to leave without him. He was being so freaking cute, all pouty and wide-eyed, I couldn't, nor did I want to, say no. "Showering."

"Without you?" The cheeky comment ends in a yelp as I flick hot pasta water in her direction.

The joke isn't completely unfounded—the man did offer. Several times. Profusely. But the lingering scent of rum and cigarettes isn't exactly an aphrodisiac, nor is the fact I spent the last hour rubbing his back while he hunched over the toilet bowl, so I scampered from the room yelling promises of food over my shoulder.

Plus, even if he wasn't drunk, sexy shower antics—which I'm pretty sure was the only thing on his mind—are completely off the cards. The girls are both home, and while Luna has no qualms about her sexual escapades bleeding through the walls, Kate and I have a pact about never doing that to each other. And, not that I'm holding out hopes for some big romantic hoopla, I don't really want my first time with Nick to be eavesdropped on by my roommates—there's enough pressure and anxiety there as it is.

It didn't occur to me until tonight that I've never seen Nick drunk. Drinking, yes. Tipsy, maybe. But precariously wobbling, perpetually flushed, and slurring words of nonsense? Nope. Watching him fumble about and hearing sweet words constantly whispered in my ear and feeling soft hands coasting all over my skin... Well, it made me wonder whether Nick gets truly plastered all that often. Because if he does, it's a wonder he's garnered that reputation of his—Drunk Nick is a big freaking softie.

A rambler too, and I can't decide which I like more.

"God, you've gotta stop grinning like that," Kate groans, dramatically banging her forehead against the door of the upper cabinet closest to her. "I can't be mad at him for crashing girl's night when you're grinning like that."

Honestly, I didn't even realize I was grinning, not until I consciously will my lips to flatten and find it to be a surprisingly hard task. Crooking a brow, I query a silent, 'better?'

Kate grunts at my lackluster attempt, a tad hypocritical considering she's not exactly scowling either. There's a definite upturn to her full mouth, a hint of a pleased crinkle in the dark skin around her eyes. "You look really happy, Mils."

"I am." For the first time in a long time, I really am.

"But are you sure you're okay with the whole casual, sneaking around thing?"

"Considering it was my idea, yup." My last relationship was a shitshow and the one before that...well, I'm not in a hurry to jump into a new one, not any time soon. "I like it like this."

"You like *him*."

"He's hard not to like."

"Say that again in the morning when I'm sober enough to remember it."

Kate and I turn as Nick lazily saunters into the room. Eyes still a little glazed and smile still adorably dopey, he's changed into the sweats and t-shirt he quickly took to leaving here. "Just in case," he'd told me with a relaxed shrug, and I had to pretend I wasn't hyperventilating out of nerves and girlish excitement.

I sigh at his wet hair soaking the neckline of his top, shrieking when it suddenly soaks me too as Nick wraps himself around me like the world's friendliest bear. "You're dripping all over me."

Humor rumbles in his chest as he dips his head, purposely brushing wet curls against my cheek. "I think that's my line."

The exaggerated sound of Kate retching fills the kitchen, echoed by Nick's laughter in a cacophony of erratic noise that does something weird to my chest. It draws Luna out of hiding too; she skids into the room, a blur of blonde hair and resentment at the thought of being left out.

"Well, this is all very domestic," she croons haughtily at the sight of Nick and I tangled together. Sidling up to Kate, she bumps her hip, and the two exchange a conspiring look that I hate with every fiber of my being, before she cocks her head at me. "You couldn't have brought Jackson back with you?"

I adopt a deadpan look, gesturing to the man clinging to me. Nick's inability to stifle his drunken affectionate tendencies is explanation enough but I can't resist adding teasingly, "You two could do with a night apart."

"Hey, Pot," Luna taunts mockingly. "It's Kettle. You're black."

Skin heating, I roll my eyes at the comment. Nick's chuff of mirth tickles my cheek before he releases me, stalking towards the girls and not giving them a chance to evade before shaking his head like a wet dog, dispersing droplets of cold water all over them. Kate shrieks, protecting her hair with one hand while the other shoves him away, and Luna cackles, snatching up a dish towel and whipping it at him. The trio dissolves into a racket of sibling-like bickering and half-hearted vitriol but I can't make out a word of it over the volume of my racing thoughts.

This is not a picture I ever became accustomed to when Dylan was in my life. He never joked around with my friends, never made an effort to get along with them. A pang of something acrid thuds in my chest when I consider how a guy I'm only partially, *barely*, connected to tries harder than my long-term boyfriend ever did, and with that comes a whole horde of other comparisons. Dylan's performative affection, only deigning to show it when others were around to witness, or when it was what he wanted. Not one single instance can I recall when I was around a drunk Dylan and I didn't feel...not always scared, but always anxious. He freaked out if I so much as made eye contact with a man, and toward the end, he was even picking out my clothes.

Nick isn't stingy with affection. Everything is an excuse to touch me, even before anything more than friendship occurred between us, and so rarely is it... I don't know, leading? It's not always a means to an end like it seemed to be for my ex, something he did begrudgingly for the sake of getting into my pants. But Nick... It's like he showers me with affection simply because he likes the feel of my skin beneath his fingertips, and God, is that dangerous for a touch-starved woman like myself.

Their drunk personas couldn't be more different. I don't feel unsafe or uneasy with Nick under the influence. I don't feel like I'm walking on shards of glass, unable to help from getting ripped to shreds no matter how carefully I tread. He doesn't change into a person I don't recognize; he softens and melts into the version of himself he keeps tucked away that makes my heart putty in his hands no matter how many walls I erect around it.

And the comment Nick made earlier, him not wanting me to go into the bar, it didn't come from the same place that something like that would've come from within Dylan. There was no aggression or blame behind it, not toward me. It wasn't possessive, it was protective, and it took me such a long time to learn the difference that my eyes burned at the recognition.

They're burning now too, something I don't notice until the sudden silence creeps into my consciousness. Blinking rapidly, my gaze darts between the people staring at me curiously. "What?"

Luna flicks the dishtowel—the one she was previously snapping at Nick's ass—in my direction. "You zoned out for a second."

"Oh." I shrug as I turn to the stove again, my nose twitching as it suddenly itches. "Sorry. You guys hungry?"

They take their sweet time accepting the subject change. When the quiet starts to make me squirm, I peek over my shoulder and catch them exchanging a round of looks, a silent conversation transpiring that I hate as much as I like—them getting along is great and all but it seems dangerous for them to be in cahoots.

I'm dishing vibrantly orange, cheesy pasta into bowls when eventually, a collective sigh rings out. The girls collect their dinner without a word, but with plenty of prying side-eye, and I'm readying to carry mine and Nick's to our tiny excuse for a dining room table when a calloused palm smoothes over my shoulder, another curving around me to grab one of the bowls.

"Thank you," the murmur washes over me along with the faint scent of rum combined with my coconut-scented body wash and something distinctly Nick. Almost instinctively, my head lolls to the side, my cheek rubbing against his knuckles in search of comfort I don't want to ask for.

Lips and sweet, drunk, foreign words brush my temple. "*Gosto mais de você do que desejo.*"

"I don't know what that means."

Nick laughs. "Me neither."

~

I'm curled up on one of the many ridiculously comfortable sofas scattered around The Paper Trail skimming through a book plucked from the stack beside me—a shipment of Brazilian-authored novels came in and Nick cheekily assigned me the task of sorting them into original and translated since I'm here anyway—when a heavy body flops onto the cushion beside me, disturbing me with a yelp.

"Been looking for you." Cass eyes me suspiciously. "What're you doing here?"

I will my expression to remain neutral as I wave the very obvious book in my hand. "Reading."

Snatching it, Cass holds it up for inspection. "*As Três Marias?* Since when can you read Portuguese?"

I poke my tongue out at his impish expression. Yeah, fine, I wasn't reading. I was lazily flipping through the pages, tracing the illustrations and skimming for words I might recognize, coming up embarrassingly empty. I wonder if Nick would teach me some if I asked. When he came over earlier and spotted me flicking through it, softness overtook his expression as he confessed it's one of his mom's favorites.

Cass tosses the book back to me, wiggling his dark brows. "Thought you didn't read anything without a shirtless man on the cover."

My foot connecting with his stomach earns a grunt. "Did you come here to harass me?" I neglect to ask how he knew I was here for fear it'll come out with a guilty edge.

I'm unprepared when Cass sobers suddenly, swallowing my unease when he straightens and clears his throat while digging around in his pocket. When he deposits a crumpled white card adorned with flowing cursive spelling mine and my dad's names, I suck in a breath. "It's a formality." Cass eyes me carefully. "Mom said the same rules as Thanksgiving apply."

AKA I can refuse but Cass has full permission to kidnap me if I do. Not that I would. I do hesitate though.

I don't know how I forgot about the Morgans' annual Christmas party. It's a yearly thing, and I attended dutifully every year for a decade, as did my dad; it was one of the rare things he always carved out time for. I used to spend hours with Lynn hand-making the invitations like this one, damn near going cross-eyed with the concentration it took to perfect the pretty, intricate handwriting, but I still loved it. And I loved the actual party; I can't imagine a kid who wouldn't love what was essentially an early Christmas with all their friends and family and presents and food galore. It's excessive in the best possible way, with everyone dolled up and gorging themselves and getting drunk. Thinking about it sends a tingle of excitement rushing through my blood, but it's tainted by anxiety. Deja vu washes over me as I weigh up my choices—or lack thereof.

I won't be able to avoid anyone like I did over Thanksgiving. Everyone will be milling around the house and completely inescapable. Imagining everyone staring at me, whispering, *knowing*, makes bile bubble up in the back of my throat, causes phantom pangs to erupt in the knee that's long since healed, incites unwanted memories of the worst months of my life.

But… I can't not go. I can't expect my dad not to go when I'm the reason he's been apart from them for so long. I can't take the kindness they're showing me and throw it back in their faces. *Again.*

Pasting on a brave face, I nudge Cass' thigh with my foot. "I wouldn't miss it for the world."

My brother groans as his head falls back. "Thank fuck. I swear to God, they're so fucking boring without you." A heavy hand lands on my head as he ruffles my hair, affectionate but annoying. "Don't worry. I'll save you if it gets too much. And Nick will be there if you need a distraction."

Oh, Cassie. You have no freaking idea.

27

NICK

I'VE NEVER BEEN a fan of romance books.

Not modern romances, anyway. I blame my dad; he raised me on the classics, made me a literature snob from a young age, and everything else seems to pale in comparison. And in all these idealistic stories detailing a perfect happily-ever-after, people like me are the villain. I'm the sleazy guy the main character gets fucked over by before being swept off their feet by the love of their life. I'm the distraction, the place-holder, the temporary blip before the universe rights itself. I'm the asshole catalyst that triggers a metamorphosis and changes them forever, steers their life in a new, better direction while I end up miser-able and alone and lamenting over the one that got away.

Right now, though, surrounded by a sea of romance books, I don't feel miserable. I'm definitely not alone. And in all honesty, I have very little intention of ever letting the girl kissing the life out of me escape.

A growl of frustration leaves me when I try to slip a hand up Amelia's skirt and I'm hindered by sheer black fabric. I liked her outfit when she floated in here and brightened my day with only a smile—I'm never going to complain about a short skirt, even if the turtleneck and cardigan she wears with it deprives me of seeing my marks on her pale neck. But I didn't foresee how fucking annoying the tights would be.

"How pissed would you be if I ripped these?" I murmur against her lips as I cup between her thighs, the heat of her pussy seeping into my palm.

Amelia shivers, grinding against my hand, and I would take that as a green light if not for the jerky shake of her head and the reprimand in her breathy tone. "I am not going to class in crotchless tights, Nicolas."

Fuck me, she's not going to make it to class if she keeps calling me *Nicolas*.

I press closer to her, one hand braced against the—thankfully really sturdy—bookshelf at her back, the other creeping upwards. The pads of my fingers glide up her waist and curve over a tit, a tortured groan escaping me when all I feel is the thick material of her bulky-ass cardigan. "You're wearing too many clothes."

"My sincerest apologies for being cold," she quips sarcastically but she deftly slots large, round buttons free from their fastenings. If ripping her tights would piss her off, I reckon she'd be fuming if I wrecked her top, so I take what I can get, palming her through the damn dark green *turtleneck* that I can't believe I find sexy.

Through the thick fabric, I can just about feel a pert nipple straining for my touch, and I want nothing more than to whisk her somewhere more private than between the crowded shelves of my workplace and undress her slowly, worship her properly. But I've got about ten more minutes until my coworker notices my quiet absence, she's got maybe double that before risking being late to class, so I'm going to have to pretend a quick grope is enough for me.

When dainty fingers coast beneath my sweatshirt, skimming the sensitive skin of my lower stomach, I come to the hopeful realization that maybe it's not enough for her either.

I groan her name when she undoes my jeans, her eyes locked with mine as she confidently slips a hand past the stiff denim. "Amelia," I can barely speak as smooth fingers trace the outline of my cock, painfully hard as it always strives to be when in her presence, "what're you doing?"

"You always touch me," she damn near purrs. "I never get to touch you."

I hiss a breath when she grips me—a little too gently for my liking but I have every intention of teaching her my preferences and taking great pleasure in doing so. Like an eager, horny teenage boy, I thrust into her hand. "You have full permission to touch me whenever the fuck you want, *querida*."

Even if I am slightly worried about finishing my shift covered in my own cum—I'll cross that bridge when I come to it. Literally.

Or I won't cross it all.

Stroking agonizingly slowly, Amelia rises on her toes and whispers in my ear, "Are there cameras in here?"

I shake my head, my eyes all but rolling to the back of my hand when her grip tightens. My boss is a little old lady whose knowledge of technology barely surpasses Facebook—the extent of security around here is nothing more than the lock on the front door. I'm tempted to quip that Amelia wasn't concerned about cameras every time I've had my hands down her pants in this very spot but any concerns, jokes, or intelligible thoughts vanish when my pretty girl drops to her knees.

Ah, merda.

I act on barely restrainable instinct. As she works my jeans down my hips, bundles the hem of my shirt up near my bellybutton, and peppers kisses along the waistband of my boxer briefs, I unclip the weird spiky claw thing holding her curls hostage and toss it aside. Gathering silky strands in my fist, I cup her jaw, tilting her face up to me. "You don't have to do anything you don't want to do," I assure her, my cock pulsing in protest that I ignore.

"I know," Amelia offers her own soft reassurance in return. "I wanna."

My cock gets impossibly harder as I trace full, glossy lips with my thumb, the mere idea of them being wrapped around me, leaving a mess of saliva and shiny pink lip gloss, enough to drive a guy to the brink. "Then go ahead. Suck my cock, *querida*."

God, the things I would do to take a picture of her face in the seconds that follow my crooned command. Eyes hooded, her cheeks pinken, the tiniest tremor in her hands as they tug my underwear down until the rock-hard length of me is set free.

A bone-deep satisfaction settles when Amelia's expression morphs into what I can only describe—while running the risk of sounding like a cocky asshole—as awestruck. Teeth tugging her bottom lip into her mouth, she tentatively brushes a finger from root to tip, the barely-there contact enough to coax a pearly bead of pre-cum to leak from the head of my cock.

I can't help myself. "Where's my confident girl gone?"

Amelia's gaze snaps to mine, pure determination replacing any hesitance in the blink of an eye. Bold once again, she licks her lips and grips me tighter than she did a moment ago. Without breaking eye contact, she leisurely takes me into her mouth, and she doesn't stop until I hit the back of her throat, evoking a hissed curse that makes her hum in satisfaction, the noise traveling up my cock and almost bending me over like a punch to the gut.

My knees threaten to buckle at the feeling, the sight, the fucking *sounds* coming from her as she bobs up and down on my cock at a furious pace that I'm not even setting. I still have one hand tangled in her hair—the other is braced against the bookshelf again to keep me from fucking collapsing—but it's all her, all my wild fucking girl. Every time she rocks forward, she pulls at my hips, urging me to slam into her and I'm powerless to do anything but thrust and groan her name far quieter than I'd prefer.

Wicked tongue flicking and throat swallowing eagerly, she's sucking me off like it's her life's mission to make me come embarrassingly quickly, and Jesus Christ, she's close to accomplishing it.

Fuck me, I can't believe this is happening.

Caught between disbelief and awe, I gaze down at Amelia in a haze, lost in pure fucking bliss, oblivious to everything but her. I have no idea how long passes before a white-hot telling heat shoots up my spine but I hold off, reluctant as fuck to let this end.

Amelia dashes any chances of that when she cups my balls, nails gently scraping the sensitive skin. She moans around me, the noise vibrating through my entire fucking body. "Fuck, *querida*, I'm gonna come."

Bright, teary eyes smolder at me. *So come*, they seem to say.

With a long groan, I do as she says, spilling down her greedy throat, and she laps up every last drop.

The second she slides off with an audible, sloppy noise, her throat bobbing in a deep swallow, I'm tucking myself away with one hand and yanking her to her feet with the other, crushing us together in a searing, desperate kiss. She yelps in shock but sinks into me easily, a palm settling right over my pounding heart. "Jesus *fucking* Christ."

She smiles against my lips. "This distracting thing is fun, hm?"

The sun has barely risen and I'm already in danger of thoroughly embarrassing myself. You don't have to be a frequent gym-goer to know popping a boner mid-workout is frowned upon, and I'm teetering on the edge of breaking the unspoken rule. It's not my fault, though.

All the culpability lies with the barely clothed redhead vigorously attacking a man donning focus mitts.

She's killing me, for fuck's sake. Teeny tiny shorts hidden by a billowing t-shirt—*my t-shirt*. Dripping in sweat. Hair in a state of disarray, partially because I've put us through our paces this morning but you can bet your ass I mussed it up good and well before we rolled out of bed.

It's all payback for waking her up early, I think. Usually, I'm better at sneaking out for my early morning workouts—I've been training twice a day this month—but my stealth faltered this morning. I made it up to her, obviously, but I reckon she's going to keep torturing me and throwing me side-eyed daggers until I get at least three coffees in her.

"You don't have to join me," I'd assured her as she rolled out of bed with a barrage of curses.

"Lying in bed alone doesn't sound very appealing," she'd snapped back, such a fucking grump but I couldn't help but smile.

Moody or not, I'm glad she's here. I like when she's here. I like watching her do something I love, watching her start to love it too. She's gotten good—it's selfish but it puts me at ease knowing she can throw a decent punch if she, God for-fucking-bid, ever needed to. *Again.*

She looks stronger than she did when we first met. Less frail, less angular. More confident too—she stands a little straighter, doesn't hold herself like she's waiting for the right moment to disappear. Bit by bit, the protective shell she keeps herself tightly wound up in is melting away, and I have no idea what's happening exactly to thaw it, but I'm not tempting fate by asking. And I'm sure as fuck not making any sudden movements lest it shoot back up again.

I thought watching her come apart on my fingers, on my tongue, was the hottest thing in the world but I've been proven wrong. Watching her slowly, *achingly slowly*, trust me is far superior.

It's as exhilarating as it is terrifying.

It's a struggle to focus on my own workout—skipping doesn't compare to watching Amelia attack a man at least three times her size—but I manage it. And then I have to wait another agonizing few minutes while Amelia finishes raining calculated punches down on Luka. A fellow punching-bag fanatic but while I box for fun, Luka's on his way to being Sun Valley's very own heavyweight success story.

He's a nice guy, for the most part. A bit of an arrogant prick but I suppose it comes with the territory. His reputation with women would give mine a run for its money but he's all business with Amelia, nothing but respectful as he barks out combinations and corrections. When they're done, he bops her on the shoulder before helping her undo her gloves, all smiles as he mutters something that makes Amelia smile bright in return.

"Your girl's not bad," he tells me with a wink when I wander over.

Slinging an arm lazily around Amelia's sweaty shoulders, I ignore how she tenses slightly, and I ignore how she opens her mouth to correct Luka, cutting her off before she can. "What can I say, she's got a good teacher."

Her lips clamp shut, quirking upwards as she rolls her eyes playfully. They're mid-roll when they suddenly redirect, narrowing into slits zoned in on me when Luka asks, "Excited to see him in action this weekend?"

Ah, shit.

I know I'm in trouble even before Amelia questions in a meticulously neutral tone, "What's this weekend?"

"He has a fight." Luka finds way too much satisfaction in Amelia's cluelessness and the death glare I fix on him. "You didn't tell her, Silva?"

I ignore him as I tug Amelia gently. "C'mere for a sec."

Sparing Luka a wave goodbye, she's just short of willing as she follows me into the locker room, her expression too blank to be natural as I sit her down on a bench. "It's fine." She clears her throat, doing a shit job of acting unbothered. "If you don't want me to come, it's fine."

"I do," I rush to answer, jerking open my locker and fishing around until I find what I'm looking for. I got her tickets weeks ago—I've been chicken-shit about handing them over. I know she said before that she wanted to come to my next fight but a lot has changed. For one, I've become the king of overthinking.

"It's not a big deal or anything," I explain over a tight throat as I hand her the tickets. No one actually comes to these things to see me—my part is some amateur exhibition shit, like the amuse-bouche before the main course—and her expecting anything else would be fucking embarrassing. "But there's an open bar and the guys are coming so it might be fun."

I can't read her expression, her face dropped to stare at the tickets. "Four?"

"In case Luna, Kate, and Sydney wanna come." I figured Luna wouldn't be able to bear a night away from Jackson, and I doubt Kate would miss an opportunity to watch me cop a punch.

The quietest sigh leaves Amelia, her head shaking almost imperceptibly, and I've never wished I could read her mind more. Tipping her face up to me, she reveals a soft smile. "That's really sweet. Thank you."

I sag with relief. "So you wanna come?"

"Yeah." Amelia smiles, standing and looping her arms around my waist. "I really do."

28

NICK

IT'S a testament to the volume my friends are capable of reaching, the fact that I'm able to hear their arrival over the loud music threatening to burst my eardrums.

Tugging off my headphones, I turn as they tumble into the locker room, a tornado of excited, intoxicated energy—looks like they've already taken advantage of the open bar, as they do every time they come to one of these things.

"There he is!" Cass hoots, leading the guys in a messy chant of my name, and I can't tell whether I'm amused or horrified by the attention. Hands slap my shoulders and aim fake punches at my ribs while voices chat my ear off but I barely register their presence. Like a magnet, my attention slams to the woman swaying in the doorway looking unsure as to whether she's welcome.

When I summon her over with a jerk of my head, Amelia wobbles in my direction, her lopsided smile tipsy and bordering on shy. "You came." I feign surprise, pretending I didn't see her mere hours ago, that I didn't watch her try on what felt like a hundred pieces of clothing before settling on her current outfit—a knee-length dress such a dark shade of green, it's nearly black in a shiny material that's almost as soft and silky as her skin. The chunky black boots on her feet mean that when she comes to a stop—about half a foot too far away—she barely reaches my chin instead of barely reaching my shoulders.

Some of her timidness drips away when, discreetly so the guys don't notice, I close the gap between us, brushing my hand against hers. Her pinky hooks around mine, squeezing quickly before releasing. "The girls are here too. They say good luck."

"Nicolas Silva doesn't need luck," Cass scoffs playfully, hooking an arm around my neck and giving me a shake. "You're gonna kill him."

I roll my eyes but I make no attempt to shove him off. I'm in a good mood, pumped full of adrenaline, and even Ben's yippy voice can't pierce it. He's flitting around like an over-excited puppy—the annoying kind, a little ankle-biter—and cooing over the small arena housing the event, fawning over the other boxer, assuring me not to worry because I'm still his favorite, and I must be high as fuck on pre-fight jitters because I laugh at his antics.

"How much have they drunk?" I mutter to Jackson, the only other sober person in the room.

A wince is the only answer I get.

"Don't worry, I'll make sure they don't break anything." Jackson's gaze flits from the guys to Amelia and back to me, the corners of his eyes crinkling as his lips turn up. "I'll keep an eye on her too."

I don't trust myself not to say something incriminating—even a thanks feels like it could drop me in hot water—so I keep my mouth shut. A short hum of acknowledgment is all I offer before I shift my attention to Tweedledum and Tweedledee, resisting the urge to let it fall back to Amelia because suddenly, I'm overly aware of prying, inquisitive eyes.

Only when I hear a throat clear, quiet but pointed, do I risk a sideways glance and meet a curious green gaze. "What was that?" Amelia murmurs under her breath, jerking her head toward Jackson who's currently trying to referee a mock fight between the tipsy menaces we call friends.

My hands itch to smooth out the furrow in her brow but I resist. "No idea."

"Did you tell him?"

I quell the tiny spark of irritation brought on by her narrow-eyed accusation. "No."

"I think he knows."

"Yeah, well," I shrug, ignoring the way my chest pangs at her blatant disapproval—I have no right to be hurt, we both more than willingly agreed to the secrecy. "Like Kate says, we're not actually masters of subtlety."

Frown falling, Amelia lets out a conflicted groan. "I don't know how I feel about you and her suddenly being best friends."

I snort. Far from it—we've simply come to an understanding. Formed a mutually symbiotic relationship founded on the knowledge that we both have Amelia's best interests at heart. She's an easy person to get along with—a wicked dry sense of humor, an admirable protective streak, and a slightly terrifying intuition—but like her best friend, it takes effort to get there.

"If you're so worried about people finding out," God, I hope her alcohol consumption has dulled her senses so she doesn't catch the minor note of bitterness, "why did you come back here?"

"I wanted to wish you luck." It's pathetic that a fucking pinky finger gets my blood pumping but as it wraps tightly around mine again in the only contact she's willing to risk, it does. She's not exactly stingy with her affection—I think it isn't something that comes easy to her. Like she's not used to such displays, like it was something she was reprimanded for before. Shit, a couple of months ago, I wasn't used to it, it didn't come easy to me, and now I can't keep my hands off her. And when that energy is returned, I revel in it.

Amelia smiles sweetly up at me but a brief flash of concern crosses her features, her gaze flitting over my face and bare chest. "Be careful, okay? You just got pretty again."

God, I fucking hate my friends and their insistence on being here. And I hate our fucking secrecy pact too. All I want is to kiss the concern right out of Amelia, taste whatever's softening her disposition but I can't. All I can do is hang onto that single finger, and I hate that too.

∾

Everything is going perfectly until it isn't.

The moment I step into the ring, a familiar feeling of powerful control rushes over me. *I know what to do*, a voice in the back of my head reminds him. *I got this.*

And I do have it. Round after round, I have it.

Until my opponent opens his big, bloody mouth.

I've fought Brett Reynolds before. There are few people in the world I can say with full confidence that I utterly despise, and he's one of them. A bleeder with a glass jaw who relies on dirty tricks and evasive maneuvers. A cocky, rude jackass who fucking begs to be knocked down a few pegs, and I'm more than happy to do it. I do it for four rounds before the guy has had enough, spitting blood as a result of that last uppercut and sneering at me, "Got some pretty girls cheering for you tonight, Silva."

At first, I brush it off. I ignore the words, finding humor in the gargled way they sound due to his mouthguard. Goading tactics aren't uncommon and they're not unfamiliar to me. But, to my opponents' chagrin, I've never had anything worth getting all riled up over, nothing important enough to pin as a sore spot.

Until now.

Brett waits until I swing again, evading me by some stroke of luck and spinning around to hiss in my ear, "The redhead looks real worried."

Don't fucking react.

"I won't fuck you up too bad, pretty boy." Red-stained teeth glint at me. "Just enough to get some tears out of your girl. But don't worry, I'll cheer her up nice and good."

"Shut the fuck up."

Four words and he knows he's got me.

I make the mistake of giving in to the lure of distraction, of stealing a glimpse in Amelia's direction. It's only a split second but the lapse in concentration costs me. Brett notices, his tone foul as he leers. "Shit, look at her. She's a hot little thing. Bet every guy in here wants a piece of that."

My next punch is sloppy, miscalculated, fuelled by anger instead of technique, and Brett dodges it easily. He's on my ass in a second, catching me off guard when he aims below the belt. I backpedal with a curse, realizing too late that I've backed myself into a corner, barely ducking in time to avoid the full force of his offensive punch; it glances my cheek, not damaging but rattling. Frustration bubbles up, steering the left hook that I throw at Brett's stomach, closely followed by the right hook meant for his chin. Both land, but the wave of triumph that crashes over me dries up all too quickly.

"I gotta know man," Brett wheezes, the shot to his liver knocking the breath out of him but that smarminess goes nowhere. "Is she as wild a fuck as she looks?"

My blood runs cold, freezing me in place.

"Nah, don't tell me." He cracks a sickening grin as he glances toward Amelia, a blackening eye dipping in a wink. "I'll find out myself."

I'm on him before I can think better of it. Punch after punch is thrown and landed, none of them regulation but I don't give a fuck, I want fucking blood. Rage blinding me, I can't even see Brett but I hear his grunt of pain, I feel when he starts to fight back. Slimy fucking worm that he is, he manages to slip from my grasp, and my right kidney aches as gloved knuckles connect with the sensitive spot on my lower back.

I spin around, ready to go for him again, but I get yanked away. Restrained by either arm, voices yell at me to calm down but I can barely hear them over my own yelled threat. Spitting on my mouthguard, I repeat on a loop, "Talk about her again and I'll fucking kill you."

You're disqualified, someone is telling me, shouting in my ear that I'm banned for a length of time I don't catch but I couldn't care less. Brett's bloody face is so fucking worth it. I'm shaking with anger as I get dragged from the ring, away from the raucous crowd, down the familiar hallway leading to the locker rooms. A clamoring of noise follows in my wake.

"Jesus fucking Christ, Nick, what was that?" Cass is yelling, Ben is yelling, even fucking Jackson has raised his voice above a gentle murmur for probably the first time in his life, but I'm not focused on them. Nor on Luna or Kate or Sydney as the former shoots me a discreet, wide-eyed thumbs up, the latter shifts nervously from one foot to the other, and the middle wears an expression way too fucking all-knowing for my liking.

It's Amelia who holds all my attention, as she so often does. Lingering on the edge of the group, she looks unsure of what to do, and my first instinct is to go to her. Shaking off the security guards gripping either side of me, I take a step toward her.

She takes a real fucking loud step back.

Eyes wide, she casts a pointed glance toward our audience, and I hate it so much it makes me sick. I hate the secrets, I hate her ex-boyfriend, and for one long, angry second, I hate how much of me I've let her have when she doesn't even want it, not really, not enough.

Her mouth forms my name but if she says it, I don't hear; the bitter laugh that leaves me overrides everything else. I take off, storming into the locker room, the door slamming off the wall with a loud bang as I barrel through. Tossing my headgear aside, I unlace my gloves with my teeth and rip them off. I pace the length of the room in a vain attempt to calm down, barely doing a single lap before a tornado swirls into the room.

"What the hell, Nicolas?"

I glare at a seething Kate. "I'm not in the mood."

Undeterred, she strides towards me, not stopping until she's close enough to cuff me upside the head. "What is wrong with you?"

"What's wrong with *you*?" I retort, rubbing the spot she whacked. God, put her in a ring and she'd win any day.

"What happened?" Kate adds to her endless list of questions yet she cuts me off when I open my mouth to respond. "Hit me with that 'nothing' bullshit and *I swear to God*, Nick. Tell me the truth, and it better be damn good because if you scared the shit out of her for nothing, I will fuck you up."

Guilt vanquishes my anger in a single sentence.

Fuck.

"I scared her?" Of course, I did. *Of fucking course, I did.*

When I sink onto the bench separating one row of lockers from another, Kate sighs down at me. "I think she was scared *for* you more than anything."

"He was talking shit about her," I explain with a wince, preemptively adding, "Don't ask me to repeat it."

There's a pause before Kate makes a noise of acknowledgment, the wooden slats beneath me creaking as she sits beside me. "You looked like you were mad at her."

"I'm not. I'm…" A defeated breath leaves me. "I'm mad at the situation."

I don't need to explain further; thank fuck for those seemingly telepathic abilities of Kate's. Shifting closer, she sets a hand on my knee, squeezing gently in a gesture as placating as her tone. "You know she's giving you everything she can."

I do know, and I feel like a dick for wanting more anyway.

"Give her time, okay? She'll get there. Don't mess it up before she does."

All I can do is nod because I can't find the words to tell her that I'm actively doing everything in my power not to fuck this up, yet I'm failing anyway.

29

AMELIA

"So, we all agree that was hot as fuck, right?"

"Ben," I chastise with a hiss, elbowing my *way* too ecstatic friend. Although, I can't find it in me to argue.

That was, in fact, hot as fuck.

All night, I've been silently remarking on how the man who's not quite mine is so damn hot. And maybe not-so-silently fawning too—I blame that on the open bar—but half of the people here have their jaws on the ground, tongues lolling, so it's not suspicious. I think it would be more suspicious if that tanned, tattooed, glistening body and the menacing, predatory darkness swirling in golden eyes and the cocky, earned strut weren't working for me.

But now is not the time to acknowledge all of that. Now is the time to be pissed because, in all his God-like glory, Nick is ignoring me. He's been ignoring me since he stormed off after that brawl broke out. I have no idea what happened but I gathered pretty quickly that it wasn't the norm—while the crowd was delighted by the bloody display, the referee and the security guards, and a handful of suit-clad men were none too pleased. They banished him to the locker room, and I tried to talk to him once our friends dispersed under the command of the big, scary guy stationed outside the door, but despite my efforts, I got shooed away too. Kate slipped in there before The freaking Mountain arrived but whatever they talked about, she's remaining tight-lipped, only deigning to confirm he's okay.

So, I've resorted to being irritated instead of worried. I let Ben drag me back to the bar and pump me full of sugary, deceivingly easy-to-drink cocktails and talk my ear off about how hot all these brawny, fighting men are because then, it's harder to fixate on the exasperated disappointment that contorted Nick's face before he stormed away.

"Come on," Ben whines beside me, almost falling off his stool as he slumps across the bar. "Look me in the eyes and tell me your panties weren't even a little bit wet."

I grimace. "Please don't talk about my panties."

"Seconded," Cass chimes in with an exaggerated gag, knocking back the rest of his Aperol Spritz in what I know is an effort to swamp cloying disgust.

The three of us are the last of our group lingering. The couples ditched before the penultimate fight of the night and I'm starting to think I should've gone too. Clearly, if the string of texts left unanswered has anything to say about it, Nick doesn't want to see me. Which is perfect; I don't want to see him either. Nope. I'm fine and dandy with my good friend, the mojito, keeping me company.

Or at least, I'm fine until Cass' phone vibrates and he loudly announces with no short amount of excitement that Nick is on his way. Then, I revert to cowardice; chugging my drink, I high-tail it away so fast, arguments are impossible and my shouted explanation that I'm getting an Uber home is probably lost in the wind.

Chilly air caresses my bare skin—I forewent a jacket in the name of fashion knowing damn well I'd pay the price—and coaxes out a shiver as I clumsily stumble into the night. Eerie silence greets me, a stark contrast to the constant buzz indoors, but I convince myself it's a welcome change, well-needed considering my brain is loud enough.

Wrapping an arm around my middle like that'll ward off the cold, I request a ride as fast as humanly possible and forward all the driver's information to the girls; getting murdered and dumped in a ditch somewhere would be my luck. Before a barrage of texts berating me for going home alone can come through, I switch my phone to silent.

"Five minutes," I mutter to myself, hopping from one foot to the other in an attempt to generate some heat. "All that stands between you and your bed."

"Talking to yourself, babe?"

I startle so badly I almost trip over myself. Skin flushing for reasons other than impending frostbite, I twist in the direction of the unfamiliar voice. I recoil on instinct when I recognize the guy leaning against the wall a few feet away, sucking on a cigarette and seemingly immune to the cold in the same flimsy shorts he wore in the ring earlier and a thin sweatshirt. I can't for the life of me remember Nick's opponent's name but I definitely remember the sneer he wore as he taunted Nick with words I couldn't hear, every inch of his face lined with cruelty. He sneers now too, and I back up a couple of steps. "Just waiting for someone."

This time when I shiver, it has nothing to do with the temperature and everything to do with his low snicker. "Your boyfriend on his way?" Straightening, he flicks the cigarette away. "Hope so. I could go for a second round."

A scoff leaves me before I can think better of it, a retort close to follow because come on, the guy barely survived the first round. "Doesn't look like it."

The guy groans in a way that makes my skin crawl. "Feisty little thing, hm? I like it."

A vehement, wholehearted '*ewwww*' pings around my brain.

Fucking. Men.

I'm debating whether I should tuck tail and run or give the creep a piece of my mind—the rum coursing through my bloodstream is advocating for the latter—when a different, and honestly preferable, option presents itself.

"Your memory can't be that fucking short, Reynolds," a voice drawls as a hard body materializes at my back. A warm, possessive hand lands on my hip. "Leave her alone."

I might be drunk and annoyed but it's nowhere near enough to pretend I'm not relieved by Nick's presence, and it's certainly not enough to prevent me from tucking myself against his chest like a true damsel in distress, one hand curving behind me to clutch blindly at a thick thigh.

Hostile energy rolling off the two of them and threatening to suffocate me, I brace myself for a fight. I figure the guy—Brett—is going to get the round two he clearly wants, so I'm readying to chuck myself aside and out of harm's way

My preparation is in vain.

One second, Brett's eyeing me up like a predator. The next, he's gone. More accurately, I'm gone; in the blink of an eye, I'm whisked away by frantic hands, steered around the corner, and ushered toward the parking lot situated at the opposite end of the building at a speed nothing short of urgent. I'd go so far as to say I'm one wrong move away from being chucked over Nick's shoulder like a sack of potatoes.

"What're you doing?" I inject as much indignance as possible into my question but the twang of relief is undeniable.

Nick glances back the way we came and I use his inattention to shrug his hand off. "Don't want that guy anywhere near you."

I resist the urge to growl like a feral dog. "*Nope.*" Skidding to a stop, I cross my arms over my chest and adopt as nasty a glare as I can conjure up. "You don't get to do that. You can't pretend I don't exist and then swoop in acting all jealous."

"That's not-" Nick cuts himself off with a shake of his head and a frustrated sigh. "What the hell are you doing out here alone, Amelia?"

Keeping up the rabid animal routine, I bare my teeth, hackles raised. "Waiting for my ride."

"I'm your ride."

"Hard pass." My scoff is a little meaner than intended. "I called an Uber."

"Amelia-" Nick reaches for me again but now that danger is no longer imminent, I bat him away.

"Touching privileges are for people who don't ignore me."

Cursing roughly, Nick shoves his hands into his pockets—he changed into gray sweats at some point, which is a really sneaky move on his part—and nods toward his truck parked nearby, a hint of desperation about him. "Can we talk inside, please? You're shaking."

My barked 'no' is betrayed by a downright violent shiver. "I told you, I'm waiting for my ride."

"Amelia," Nick utters my name in that low, lilted way that has a particularly strong effect on me, "you are not getting in a random car alone and drunk off your ass. We can talk, or we can not. Either way, I'm driving you home."

It's not fair, how with a handful of concerned words, he can make me forget that I'm mad at him. It's like he cast a freaking spell, hypnotized me somehow, because next thing I know, I'm climbing into the passenger seat of his truck, letting him strap me in, and accepting the sweatshirt he drapes over my bare shoulders and the kiss he drops on my forehead with absolutely zero complaints.

Pathetic little woman.

~

We don't talk on the way to my place. Despite his earlier wishes, Nick doesn't say a word to me, not even when we pull outside a McDonald's —another dirty tactic. The silence is broken when he orders my regular meal, and then by the sounds of me munching on a veggie wrap and slurping a soda.

I don't know if it's a strategy, the combination of softening me up with greasy food and breaking me down with the sheer anticipation of an impending conversation, but even if it isn't, it kind of works.

By the time he parks outside my apartment building and shifts to face me, I'm a squirming ball of suspense. "I'm sorry," he starts softly, and I quietly curse myself for melting a bit at just that, for thinking 'yup, that's enough, nice effort, buddy.'

Pathetic, weak woman with floor-level standards.

Nick continues, "I didn't mean to ignore you. I was angry and upset and I didn't wanna accidentally take it out on you."

"Okay." I gnaw on my bottom lip, mulling over my words lest a soppy 'I forgive you' comes flying out prematurely. "Angry and upset about what?"

Nick tenses, averting his gaze to a nameless spot on the windshield as he kisses his teeth loudly. "Brett," *of course*, "said some nasty shit about you."

"About me?" I blink at him blankly. "Why about me?"

"He knew it would rile me up."

"How?"

His gaze slides to mine. "I didn't tell him if that's what you're getting at."

"It's not." I frown at the audible bitterness in his tone. "Why do you sound like you're mad at me?"

A bear paw of a hand settles over mine where they're clasped in my lap. "I'm not. I'm frustrated."

I let him disentangle my hands, let him entwine one with his instead. "About?"

"I'm not tryna push you, okay? I just wanna be honest," he says, and God, if he's wanting to incite a heart attack, that's a nice, ominous way to go about it. "What Brett said really fucking wound me up. I needed to calm down and..." He trails off, his throat bobbing in a hard swallow, his next words like gravel. "I wanted you."

Like a day breaking, it dawns on me. "And I..." I don't know what I did, really. Freaked out, maybe. Stepped away the moment his attention flicked to me because I didn't trust myself not to fling myself in his arms and fuss over him like the girlfriend that I'm not, revealing our arrangement at the first hurdle.

I grasp for the best way to finish my sentence without embarrassing myself but it turns out I don't need to; Nick needs no further explanation. He squeezes my hand, a sad smile gracing his handsome face. "It's not fair but that pissed me off more so I acted like a dick. I'm sorry, Amelia."

"I'm sorry too." It causes a literal pang of pain in my gut, knowing I had a hand in making him feel worse, accidental as it was. "Do you..." I swallow hard, knowing the question on my tongue is a dangerous one but asking it anyway. "Do you *want* to tell people?"

"The secrecy was your idea," is his irritatingly vague response.

"I just think it would do more harm than good." Harm to other people, harm to me. Because what this is, it isn't going anywhere. We both know it and getting attached—more attached than I already am—would be foolish. Telling people about an arrangement that has an unknown expiration date? That's a recipe for another embarrassing heartbreak, and I've had enough of them. Sooner or later, Nick will get bored, I'll find my way into another doomed relationship, and balance will be restored. It's inevitable and pretending otherwise is only going to make the fallout worse.

For what feels like forever, Nick stares at me silently. I stare back, and it feels like I'm looking right at the end of this short-lived, wonderful thing, and I'm thinking 'hey, it was fun while it lasted,' and I'm wondering why the concept of the finish line hurts quite a bite.

When he sighs, I prepare for him to put me out of misery—or maybe drop me right in it—but a smile throws me off-kilter. "You're right," he surprises me by saying, bringing my hand up to his lips and kissing my knuckles. "Forget I said anything."

I slump in relief, and I can't tell whether it's his dismissal of the subject, or whether it's because he hasn't dismissed me.

30

AMELIA

"Sorry I'm late," I breathe the apology as I rush into class, shooting the lecturer an apologetic glance as I flop into the seat my friends have saved for me.

I knew I wasn't going to make it on time the second I waltzed into the bookstore an hour ago, my totally pure intentions of dropping off lunch and having an innocent rifle through the shelves dashed as soon as golden eyes landed on me. I swear, every time I go there, I never mean to stay yet every time, I find some frivolous reason to, and today was no exception. I got delayed by... *things*. Actions that belong on the pages of deceitfully innocent books and that should not happen in between the shelves during broad freaking daylight.

By the time I managed to pry myself away, the class I intended to use as my excuse to leave had already started, and then I got flustered and decided I needed a real excuse for being late other than 'sorry, I was sucking dick,' so I took an unnecessary detour and snagged coffees and pastries for me, the girls, and our lecturer who is thankfully a saint. It's a miracle, really, that the one class the three of us happen to share is led by the most chill faculty member in this whole university.

Although, as two beady gazes fixate on me, I start to wish we had a grouchy old battleaxe opposed to chit-chat.

Kate and Luna share matching knowing smirks as I hand over the goods that maybe double as a bribe in exchange for their silence. I should've known it wouldn't work. Chewing thoughtfully on the useless white chocolate brownie I smuggled her, Kate muses, "You look a little... ruffled."

At least she attempts subtlety.

Luna, the little shit that she is, brandishes lip gloss the same shade as the one I wore before it was smudged beyond repair. "You've got blowjob lips."

"*Luna*," I hiss, snatching the gloss and praying her voice isn't as loud to everyone else's ears as it is to mine.

"Happens to the best of us, baby." She waves off my embarrassment with a toothy grin, ripping into the cinnamon roll I wish I had chucked in the bin with gusto. "Now that you've deigned to join us, I've been thinking-"

"That's dangerous." My well-deserved quip earns me a pinch on the thigh, and I jolt so hard I almost drop my pastry on the floor. Rude—you don't mess with a girl's caramel pecan swirl. "That wasn't very holiday spirit of you."

"Like I was saying," Luna ignores me, "I was thinking we should go on a trip."

Kate and I exchange rightfully wary glances. "A trip?"

"A road trip," she clarifies. "Us, the boys, Sydney. It would be fun. Jackson's grandparents have a place up at Big Bear so we could take a couple of days off and make it a long weekend." She blurts out her proposal in one, rushed breath with too many hand gestures and gaze suspiciously dipped to the peppermint hot chocolate warming her palm.

I narrow my eyes at her shady behavior. "Sounds like you put a lot of thought into this."

Just as I thought, she folds at the mere thought of an interrogation. "Fine," she sighs. Her head rolls to the side as the puppy dog eyes come out to play, long lashes batting and her bottom lip jutting out. "Jackson and I wanna head up there for Valentine's Day but his grandparents don't want us being there *alone*."

"So we're your sex buffers?" Kate snickers. "And here I thought you wanted some quality time with your friends."

With a broken sigh, I clutch at my chest dramatically. "I'm wounded, Lu."

A whining noise escapes our friend. "Please, please, please, *please*," she whimpers, hands clasped beneath her chin. "Jackson showed me the house and it looks so fucking beautiful and it's *huge* so, really, it'll be like staying in a hotel for free and he said he never goes there because he doesn't like his grandparents but he wants to take me and it's my first Valentine's day with a boyfriend and-"

"Oh my God, if we agree will you shut up?"

Luna perks up at Kate's half-joked question, making a dramatic display of fake zipping her lips shut and throwing away an imaginary key.

"Fine," Kate relents, but I'm positive a big chunk of her reluctance is faked—she's a romantic at heart, and a weekend away with her girlfriend is hardly a hardship. "As long as you're sure Jackson will still hold your interest by then. Two months is, like, a decade in your little head."

"I resent that." Luna tugs one of Kate's braids—she's swapped the stark white for an umber shade the same color as her natural hair—with a scowl before setting her sights on me. "And you, little one?"

Oh, I'm a hard *yes.* Getting off campus for a few days with my favorite people? What the hell kind of argument am I going to have against that? Being trapped in the same house as Cass and Nick might prove to be a challenge but I'm working on my optimism.

At my nod, Luna squeals as quietly as she's capable of, whipping out her phone at the speed of light. A handful of seconds later, my phone vibrates in my pocket.

Luna: *clear your calendars, ladies. Valentine's weekend, Big Bear road trip, presence mandatory*

Ben: *is this some kind of orgy proposition? because if so I'm totally in. begs first crack at nicky*

Nick: *In your dreams, kid. Blonds aren't my type.*

Me: *cute couple alert*

Ben: *right?!?!? that's what I've been saying*

Nick: *Jealous, querida?*

Me: *in your dreams, nicolas*

Cassie: stop flirting with my sister

Ben: fight fight fight

Kate: compare dick sizes later, boys.

Luna: yeah put them away. Who's in?

A round of agreements fill the group chat, earning a triumphant hoot from Luna. Before I know it, we have dates set aside, car logistics figured out, and assignments on who's bringing what handed out. Apparently, we're an efficient bunch. In theory, anyway.

Cassie: just us or can we bring people?

Me: don't tell me Cassie's thinking of bringing a date.

Cassie: ha. funny.

Cassie: can the baseball guys come?

Cassie: Jay's been asking about you, Tiny.

"Who's Jay?" I ask Luna, frowning at my phone as Jackson confirms the baseball guys can join us.

"He's on the team with them," she tells me. "The guy who kinda looks like he belongs in a Twilight movie?"

I sift through the sparse memories I have of Cass' baseball friends. "The super pale guy?"

Luna clicks her fingers in confirmation. Huh. Weird. I've exchanged maybe four words with the guy—definitely not enough to make an impression. I'm in the middle of typing out a reply to Cass when my phone vibrates again, a private message this time.

Nick: Jay, huh?

Me: might need someone to keep me occupied since you'll be busy with Ben

Nick: *Keep teasing, Amelia. See what that gets you.*

I squirm in my seat, biting my lip so hard I taste blood. Clocking my slightly dazed expression, Kate leans over to get a look at my screen, and a low laugh escapes her. "Oh, sweet Mils. You are so screwed."

~

Contrary to Kate's belief, I don't 'get it' when we arrive home to find Nick waiting outside our apartment. Unless the 'it' she was referring to involves him kissing me sweetly, offering my friends a friendly greeting salute, and striding inside the moment the door's open, beelining for the kitchen.

"I'm cooking tonight," he tells us, plopping a bag of groceries on the counter before rooting around in the cabinets and I swear, sexual orientation or relationship status be damned, the three of us swoon. None of us excel in the culinary department—I have four recipes that I rotate regularly, and one of those is pancakes—and, in case it isn't abundantly clear already, the way to our hearts is undoubtedly through our stom-achs. "Everyone okay with *feijoada*?"

I have no idea what that is but I'm guessing it's Brazilian and therefore—if I learned anything from the treats Ana whipped up at Thanksgiving—it's probably freaking delicious, so my nod is more than eager. The girls mimic me and, with a happy squeal, Luna bounds toward Nick, peppering him with questions and offering her assistance, and I can only hope he clocks me and Kate's matching winces. If not, he'll realize very, *very* quickly that a kitchen becomes a million times more deadly when Luna Evans is in it.

There's a dual sigh of relief when, clever boy that he is, Nick slides a tower of tinned black beans Luna's way, instructing her to drain and rinse them, a task even she can't make dangerous. Proving his smarts again, he keeps one eye on her as he fries off bacon and sausage, explaining that he's making a cheat version that would send his mother to an early grave, and the joke would earn him a laugh if I wasn't entirely focused on resisting the urge to break our golden rule.

Gray sweats, curls damp like he's fresh from the shower, *and* he's cooking? Not freaking fair.

Beside me, Kate sighs. "He's full of surprises, hm?"

I hum a strained noise. Understatement of the century.

"Not very friends-with-benefits behavior."

I keep my mouth shut, scared of what might come out.

"Never thought I'd say this but he'd make a great-"

"Don't," I plead. *Don't verbalize the first thought that springs to mind any time he does something nice because it's making what's supposed to be fun and easy so much more complicated.*

My inner turmoil must be written all over my face because Kate drops the subject. Patting me on the shoulder, she squeezes into the kitchen too, quickly getting assigned a job as well. The trio more than fills the small space but none of them look particularly put out by the close proximity, and soon, a comfortable buzz of conversation rolls over the small apartment and makes my heart freaking *ache* because it looks so damn *right*.

Well aware that having a breakdown every time my friends and Nick interact isn't normal, I suck in a steadying breath and join them. The tight quarters give me no choice but to cozy up behind Nick, my arms sliding around his waist, my cheek flat against his back. "If you're trying to deter me from teasing, you're going about it the wrong way."

That husky laugh I adore too much vibrates through me. "I figured you were sick of takeout."

Hands slipping beneath his top, I drum my fingers against the hard stomach I'm met with. "An hour ago you were all 'me caveman, no touch my woman.' Where'd that energy go?"

Nick turns in my grip, shifting so he's leaning against the counter next to the stove and not at risk of burning his perfect ass to a crisp. A slow, slick smile lifts his lips. "Did you just call yourself *my woman?*"

From somewhere behind me, snickering erupts. "She definitely did."

I cast a glare over my shoulder at my smirking friends before refocusing on my, no, *the*, smirking man. "That was not the point."

Heat scorches through my clothes as Nick trails his touch downward, palms curving over my ass with little regard for our audience as he dips his head. "I'm saving it," comes his drawled whisper, too quiet for eavesdropping but loud enough to seize my attention in a vice-like throttle. "What better way to show Clay you're off limits than having him listen to you screaming my name all night?"

Good freaking God.

"First off," I cough out the words, painfully aware of my red cheeks giving away just how much of an effect his words have on me, "you know his name is Jay." The shit-eating grin on his face proves so. "Secondly, there will be no *screaming*. There's gonna be a lot of people around." *And ample chances for us to get caught,* I finish silently.

I don't articulate a 'thirdly,' though I certainly think it. It's hard not to dwell on the notion that these grand plans are months away; who knows if *this* will still be happening. And it's odd my brain didn't immediately catch on the moment the plans were proposed, that I assumed we'd still be... *us*.

There's no opportunity to overanalyze; a strong pat on my ass cheek keeps my mind firmly set in reality, as does Nick's roguish grin. "We can practice being quiet this week."

My head flops back with a groan. God, I've barely thought about the upcoming undoubtedly challenging few days ahead; Christmas with our families. We literally leave for Calton in the morning yet it's barely crossed my mind, I've been so busy with school and work and, well, Nick. My suitcase lies unzipped on my bedroom floor, random clothes haphazardly chucked in because any and all attempts I've made to pack have been thwarted by a needy, handsy giant baby of a man.

"Are you nervous?"

About creeping around for days protecting yet another destructive secret? "No," I lie.

"I am." I must not hide my surprise very well because Nick chuckles. "I gotta meet your dad, *querida*."

Great. I didn't even think about that. "He'll like you."

"You think?" At my nod, Nick hums—a little thoughtful, a lot roguish. "As long as he doesn't find out I've been knuckle-deep in his daughter."

31

AMELIA

THE ONLY TIME of year I ever voluntarily wake up early is when the Christmas holidays roll around.

It's my favorite time of year, the happiest time, and I like soaking up every available minute. The past few years have been a little different, a little less shiny with holiday spirit, but things are back to normal. This year, I'm up with the sun, perched on the steps of the Morgans' back porch, mind wandering aimlessly as I gaze at the oak tree strung with twinkling lights.

"Hey, stranger." At the sound of a blessedly familiar voice, I glance up, a grin damn near splitting my face at who I find looming over me.

At first glance, my dad and I look nothing alike. All the standout physical features, like my hair and my eyes, I, unfortunately, inherited from my mother. But the wide smile, the slightly upturned nose, the creamy skin; that's all my dad.

"Hey." I accept the offered steaming mug of coffee held in his outstretched hand, enjoying the warmth as it awakens my chilled fingers, and pat the space beside me. When he plops down, I rearrange the blanket draped over my legs so it covers us both. When he slips an arm around my shoulders and drags me into a tight sideways hug, I sink into him with a sigh. Five months apart and I didn't realize how much I needed a good dad hug until now. "When did you get here?"

"Late last night." A hand cups the side of my head as he drops a kiss on my temple. "You were dead to the world."

My face scrunches in a silent apology. In my defense, I had a busy Christmas Eve-Eve; somehow, I got roped into helping with all the cooking necessary to prepare us for the subsequent chaotic days, and trust me, a day spent in the kitchen with Lynn and Ana is pretty much equivalent to a day spent completing a freaking triathlon. I passed out the moment my head hit the pillow. Not even Cass crawling into my bed at some point in the night woke me up—he sacrificed his room and bunked up with me so Dad could stay here instead of in a hotel. This morning, his monster-truck-esque snoring did jolt me from an otherwise peaceful sleep.

"I met Nicolas."

Do not blush. Compose yourself. Deep breath. Then speak. "Yeah?"

Dad hums. "Nice boy. You two are close?"

Despite the alarms going off in my head, the corner of my mouth lifts. "We are."

"Does he have anything to do with you and Dylan breaking up?"

"What?" I choke on a mouthful of coffee. "No!" Spitting the word frantically, my brow pulls in a frown; I'm almost positive my break-up has yet to come up in conversation. "Who told you?"

Honestly, I know the answer before Dad admits my eldest brother is the culprit.

Of course. I shouldn't be surprised James has already found time to snitch on me; he's a loud-mouthed gossip with a serious lack of a filter. He and Luna would be a force to be reckoned with.

"When did that happen?"

"Uh," I run my thumb over the rim of my mug nervously, "Halloween."

"Forgot to tell me?"

"Slipped my mind."

"Amelia."

Swallowing a huff, I drag my gaze up to meet his. Very rarely does Patrick Hanlon get to whip out the infamous fatherly 'I'm not impressed with you, young lady' expression so when he does, he makes it extra fierce. I sigh. "I'm sorry. It..." *was a giant, embarrassing clusterfuck,* "didn't end very well and I kinda hate talking about it."

"What do you-"

"Good morning, beautiful." Look at that; saved by the very Morgan

225

who dropped me in shit in the first place. "And good morning to you too, Tiny."

Dad snorts at James' silly joke as the big snitch plops down beside me. Stealing the mug from my hands, he takes a loud, noisy slurp. "Jesus, Mils, do you want some coffee with your sugar?"

I snatch my beverage back, throwing a sharp elbow at his stomach. "If you don't like it, don't drink it."

"Someone's crabby this morning," the eldest Morgan coos. "Cassie's dysfunctional nose keep you up all night?"

"Sleep next to a buffalo, see if you wake up in a good mood."

"I heard that," Cass grumbles as the back door swings open once again and he joins us on the rapidly crowding steps. He slaps us both upside the head before stealing my poor coffee, my cries of protest going disregarded.

"Get your own," I hiss and grab it back, scowling at the lukewarm dregs.

Fucking brothers.

Smushed amongst three bickering siblings, Dad sighs, his face twisted in half a nostalgic smile, half a grimace. "Feels so good to be home."

"Amelia, can you do my hair like yours?"

Unsurprised by Sofia's request, I smile at her mirrored reflection. She's been casting longing glances at me the whole half hour I've been styling my curls; I admire her patience, to be honest. Vacating the chair in front of the vanity, I pat the empty seat.

Sofia almost falls over her own feet in her haste to take my place, and my smile widens as I run a hand through her dark hair. It's thick, like mine, but not quite as wild, not in need of as much help, and it doesn't take long to fix a few curly strands into a loose braid secured by a silky ribbon—dark purple to match her dress. "There," I exclaim, tugging the end of the braid gently. "Gorgeous."

It's a simple as shit hairstyle—pretty much the only thing I can do besides a ponytail or a bun—but to an eight-year-old, it's worthy of an excited squeal and a sweet hug of thanks. Sofia twirls from side to side in front of the mirror, admiring her reflection, and I do the same.

There's not a dress code, as such, for the annual Christmas Eve affair, but we make an effort. We shed the matching pajamas and slip into something slightly more presentable; I've donned the same dress I wore to Nick's fight but I had to layer a high-neck, slight sheer black top underneath it in an attempt to hide the growing collection of hickeys adorning my skin. I swear to God, the man's a vampire. Neck, chest, boobs, they're everywhere. I look like a white tablecloth someone's artistically splattered red wine all over.

I'm nervously tugging the neckline higher when knuckles rap against my bedroom door, pausing our self-appraisal as we turn to the noise but it's a welcome interruption. I don't know anyone who would be disappointed by the sight of a ridiculously good-looking man leaning in the doorway, dressed in dark, perfectly tailored trousers and a shirt —*dark green, fuck me*—with the sleeves rolled up to reveal mouth-watering forearms.

Deep dimples wink at me as Nick assesses us thoroughly. "*Merda*, ladies," he drawls, and Sofia giggles. "Are you trying to make the rest of us look bad?"

Charmer.

My eyes roll but I'm blushing something fierce, unreasonably tempted to do an exhibitional spin like Sofia does, her dress floating around her like a ballerina's as she preens for her brother. There's a definite pang in the general vicinity of my ovaries at how Nick devotes his full, loving attention to her, muttering compliments in a language I don't understand and chuckling as she swats him away when he tries to ruffle her hair. "*Mamãe* is looking for you, *minha anjinha.*"

Excitement for the evening's festivities must have the little girl in a chokehold because she flits from the room without any arguments, shouting her thanks over her shoulder as she thunders downstairs. Nick doesn't spare his fleeing sister a parting glance; he's too busy stalking toward me like a predator approaching its prey.

"Nick," I warn as hands land on my hips, sliding along the silky fabric of my dress to palm my ass. The door is wide open, for God's sake; anyone could walk past and have a clear view of the show.

Nick shushes me gently, teasingly, fingers kneading. "I'm just looking."

And look, he does. *Admire* would be a better word, as much as that acknowledgment makes me squirm. He greedily soaks up every inch of me, the intensity of his gaze doing odd things to my belly, to the treacherously pounding bruised organ in my chest. Dragging down the collar of my top, Nick smirks. "Something to hide?"

I swat his hand away. "They're not gonna disappear if you take your eyes off them."

"I like looking at them," Nick coos with a wriggle of his brows, leaning down to press soft kisses along my neck. Straightening up, his lips connect with my forehead. "You're beautiful."

You're killing me. "You look average." *You look so handsome I want to cry.* "Did you copy me on purpose?"

A palm comes down on my ass so hard, I'm positive the sound can be heard throughout the house. If not the slapping sound, then definitely the squeal that accompanies it. Soothing the sting with stroking motions, Nick crooks a smile. "You're gonna pay for that."

Promises, promises.

~

People have been arriving for hours yet the traffic shows no signs of slowing down; Lynn Morgan's Christmas Eve extravaganza is the neighborhood equivalent of The Oscars.

Every time someone new arrives—which is every four freaking seconds—I'm inevitably met with surprised squeals and exaggerated exclamations of my name. If it wasn't so painful, it would be hilarious; I'm almost positive I've never spoken to half the people claiming it's so good to see me again and lamenting over how much they missed me.

However, the sympathetic, knowing glances they try and fail to hide kill any and all chances of humor. No one says anything directly but the blatant pity in their voices is unmaskable. And the longer the night drags on, the more people I reacquaint myself with who've witnessed me at rock bottom, and the more anxious I become. The guys do their best to offer me relief but I'm reluctant to accept their help; they're having a great time and I don't want to ruin it. Besides, it's hard to keep track of them in the hubbub; the last I checked, Cass was on a mission for ice, James was flirting with anything breathing, and, most worryingly of all, Nick and Dad were engaging in a conversation that looked dangerously akin to bonding.

So, I save myself. Slipping out the front door and into the quiet, peaceful night, I plonk myself on the porch steps with a blanket stolen from the living room, mimicking the way I started the day. I'm nursing a much-needed, very strong rum cocktail when the glass almost slips from my hand, a timid voice sending shivers down my spine. "Amy?"

My suddenly burning eyes open and close in a series of slow, confused blinks as I try to determine whether or not the man hovering in the driveway is really there. He's looking at me like he's seen a ghost, and I'm looking at him the same way.

Light brown hair.

Blue eyes.

An easy smile that used to make my heart flutter something fierce.

Sam.

For a brief, impossible second, I swear it's him. And then, my brain kicks into gear and the man calling me by a nickname I haven't heard in years comes into focus.

His hair isn't long like Sam's was, and he doesn't have the sun-bleached streaks. His eyes are the same but also not; they look older, older than Sam ever got. And that's not his smile either. Close, but so different. "Hi, Zach." I have to force the words out.

My throat doesn't want to speak. It wants to scream and cry and beg for forgiveness I don't deserve.

As though he knows, Zach's tone is gentle. "It's been a while."

Four years, give or take.

"It's good to see you." *Liar.* "I didn't know you'd be here."

I smile weakly. "Cass invited me." *Obviously.*

"I didn't know you two were in touch again."

My shaky shoulders rise. "Long story."

Zach nods slowly, and my vision blurs again because God, he looks so much like *him.* "How've you been?" I cringe before the question even fully leaves his mouth and surprisingly, Zach does too. "Sorry. I hate that question, I don't know why I asked it."

"It's okay." I laugh but it does nothing to ease the tension gripping my body. He's being kind, too kind, and I'm waiting for the other shoe to drop. I'm waiting for him to mention the accident. His brother. Waiting for him to blow up. But he doesn't; he smiles and chats nonchalantly about mundane things, never once broaching the subject that hangs over us like a dark cloud and makes my chest feel like it's about to explode.

He's dead because of me, I want to yell, and the words cut me like knives, accompanied by vivid memories of a boy who once meant everything to me.

Bumping into him at school, embarrassingly flustered by the older boy paying attention to me. Cass teasing me for having a crush on one of his friends. A clumsy but perfect first kiss. Screaming until my voice gave out at endless baseball games. The license he was so proud of getting, his car, *driving…*

"Amelia?" Warm fingertips brushing my cheek break me out of my nightmarish reverie. Concerned golden eyes snap me back to reality with a jerk. A calloused thumb brushes underneath my eyes and comes away wet with tears I didn't realize I'd spilled. *Shit.*

Nick perches beside me, concern written all over his face, and my stomach plummets. Over his shoulder, I spot Zach, looking as guilty and forlorn as I feel. "I'm sorry, Amy, I didn't-"

"It's okay," I interrupt, my voice cracking. "I'm okay." Even to my own ears, I don't sound convincing, and Nick must agree because he doesn't move a muscle other than to clasp my shaking hands tightly in one of his.

I can't find it in me to pull away, not even when Zach's gaze flits between the two of us, piecing something together, and the guilt doubles in a nauseating way. "Zach-"

"You look good, Amy." It's his turn to interrupt, his words heart-breakingly genuine. "I'm happy for you."

I don't even have time to reply. In a blink, he's gone, disappearing into the night, his whirlwind arrival and departure giving me emotional whiplash. If not for Nick sitting quietly beside me, staring at the spot he vacated, I would've wondered if he was ever there at all.

"Do you want to talk about it?"

Words can't describe how much his soft tone, inquisitive but not demanding, settles me. "Not tonight." *Not tomorrow, either. Not ever, if I had my way.*

Soft lips brush my temple. "Do you want me to get Cass?"

I scrunch my nose as I shake my head. God, no. He'd take one look at my puffy eyes and the mascara undoubtedly streaming down my face and descend into panic. I wonder if he knew Zach was coming tonight. Probably not, or he would've warned me. And been glued to my side like a guard dog all night.

Silence surrounds Nick and me, interrupted only by the sounds of the party bleeding into the night air, and the longer we sit, the more my thoughts begin to contradict themselves.

I want to tell him.

Not everything. Just something. Enough to explain what he saw. He's so freaking honest with me all the time, and I like how that makes me feel. I want him to feel like that. Before I can talk myself out of it, the words spill out. "His name's Zach."

Nick's hand tightens around mine. "You don't have to tell me."

"I know." That right there, those six words, are why I want to tell him. "I was... *involved* with his brother." I cringe at my own wording. *Involved* is not the right word to describe what Sam and I were, it doesn't even come close, but the other ones, the ones that really detail how I felt about him, refuse to come out. "He's not around anymore."

It's another vague understatement but the way Nick stiffens tells me he understands. Snaking an arm around my shoulder, he drags me close, chasing the empty, cold ache in my bones away with his presence.. "Thank you for telling me."

It's right then, with those words warming my cheek, that I realize the idea of telling him what happened all those years ago doesn't terrify me quite as much as the fact that I want to tell him.

32

AMELIA

OF ALL THE things I missed about Christmas in Carlton, being awoken at the crack of dawn by two overgrown children jumping on my bed like it's a trampoline is not one of them. The inflexible wood creaks beneath their vigorous bouncing, and they must momentarily forget that the weight of them accounts for about ten of me; I go flying in the air so high I'm surprised I don't crack a hole in the ceiling.

I swear to God, sometimes it's hard to believe Cass and James are fully grown adults and not Sofia's age.

It's still dark outside but we trudge downstairs anyway, only barely avoiding a broken neck as we jostle each other on the staircase, the three of us clad in rumpled matching pajamas. Eyes bleary, I head to the kitchen while the boys harass whatever poor souls are in the living room. Making a beeline for the coffee machine already working overtime, I'm halfway through my first cup when my brain finally kicks into gear and I realize that, despite the early hour, the Silvas are already here.

No force in the world could stifle the laugh that bursts out of me when I catch sight of the man slumped over the kitchen counter, smothering a yawn with one large hand.

Matching obnoxious pajamas are a long-standing tradition in the Morgan-Hanlon household. Every year, they're more ridiculous than the previous, and this year is no exception. When they were first dished out, I wanted to punch whoever chose the bright red onesies covered in a slightly terrifying reindeer pattern and scratchy tinsel, floppy antlers attached to the hood to complete the look. Now, as my gaze runs over the giant body somehow stuffed into one, I'm wondering where to send a thank you note.

"Don't say a fucking word, *querida*," Nick warns in a delightfully husky morning voice, antlers wobbling as he drops his head, cradling it in his palms.

"Wasn't gonna." I think the simple act of standing here, sipping my coffee and smirking, will rile him up sufficiently.

God, how can a man be hot and adorable at the same time?

Nick groans. "This is what I get for bringing you breakfast? Mockery?"

That perks me up more than any coffee could. "Breakfast?"

It's then that I spot the Tupperware sitting on the counter beside him; I was too distracted by the scarlet humanoid reindeer to notice it before. Sidling over, I snatch it up and crack the lid, practically drooling when the scent of cinnamon and brown sugar wafts out. Oh, the wondrous glory that is *rabanada*—like if French toast and churros had a baby. I wholeheartedly gorged on it the last time we were here, singing its praise at the top of my lungs, and it clearly didn't escape Nick's notice.

Quickly glancing around to check we're alone, I let myself simper like a smitten fool, attempting a kiss that I should've known could never be chaste. Nick holds me in place by the nape of my neck, kissing me hard and just long enough to fluster me entirely. When we separate after an entirely too risky length of time, it's his turn to smirk.

A little in the name of Christmas, and a lot because I'm weak, I let us linger on the edge for a moment, staying in his grasp when he cups my cheek sweetly, leaning into his touch. Nick's expression softens as he leans in again, stealing another soft peck. "You feeling better today?"

I nod, and it's surprisingly truthful. Sleep might've been riddled with flashes of what was once a nightmarish reality but when I woke up this morning, I wasn't as rattled as I had been when I went to bed. I can't pinpoint why, exactly, but I reckon it has a lot to do with the man who sat by my side for who knows how long last night, his mere presence lightening the weight of my thoughts and making them a little less suffocating.

Mischief glimmers in Nick's eyes as he runs a thumb along my bottom lip. "If you need a little distracting, I know a great make-out spot by the park."

I laugh, tempting fate for a third time, kissing him again because I can't help myself. "Duly noted."

~

"I think you might've actually killed me," I groan, slumping in my chair and resting my hands on my decidedly round stomach. Death by Christmas dinner; what a way to go. Since our Thanksgiving was oh-so-very American, Lynn handed over the reins to Ana for this holiday dinner and Jesus Christ, did she deliver. The dining room table is—or *was* before we demolished everything—a sea of Brazilian delicacies, none of which I can adequately pronounce, all of which I devour with gusto. I think I've gone up two sizes in the space of a single dinner, and I do not give a shit.

From across the table, Ana grins, unsympathetic to my strife as she slides more *pavê* in my direction. I'm incapable of refusing it so I literally remove myself from the situation; when Lynn starts gathering dishes and toting them off to the kitchen, I stand and help, despite the slight physical exertion making my full stomach heave.

Balancing my plates, *plural*, in one hand, I reach for Nick's with the other—he managed to snag the seat right beside me, and it was as welcome a distraction as it was unwelcome. His ankle has been hooked around mine since we sat down, and he untangles it with a disgruntled huff that only I hear. And only I feel his fingertips brush the inside of my wrist as I take his plate from him, only I know that the innocent smile on his face, as if he has no idea that the simple touch sends my heart racing, is entirely fake.

He knows.

Resisting the urge to *accidentally* spill leftovers in his lap, or to *accidentally* plop myself in his lap, I join Lynn in the kitchen, stacking the dirty dishes next to the sink. "Need help?"

Lynn snickers, jerking her head back toward the dining room. "Ask the boys. They're the ones cleaning this all up."

I cast a glance at the unsuspecting men still seated at the table, chatting merrily, and then at the enormous mess we've all managed to make. *Godspeed, boys.*

Hopping up on the counter, I try very hard to listen to what Lynn's saying and to not think about what happened the last time I was in this position. Vaguely, I recognize a question about enjoying my dad, so I nod and smile. "Thanks for inviting us. I know Dad loves being here too."

"No thanks necessary, sweetie," Lynn sighs, propping a hand on her hip, "this is your home. You're always welcome here, you should know that."

Her words tug at the guilt permanently laced through my heart, extra strong after last night's turn of events. After everything I put them through, their lack of resentment still shocks me.

"I-" My voice breaks and I pause to clear my throat. "I never apologized for leaving like I did. I should've left a note, and I should've called. I wish I had but-"

"Amelia," Lynn cuts me off, at my side in a flash, a soothing hand rubbing the length of my arm. "You don't have to apologize for that or explain. You were hurting."

"We were all hurting," I protest. "Cass was hurting and I left him." In the worst, most selfish way possible.

An earnest, solemn shadow falls over Lynn's face. "I'm not going to lie and say that he wasn't a mess when you left because he was." I visibly deflate, my chest damn near cracking in half, but Lynn continues, rubbing comforting circles across my back. "But he understood why. Honestly, sweetie, it wasn't a total shock. You were miserable here."

I was. I was so freaking miserable, I didn't know what to do with myself.

"None of that matters, Amelia." The words are spoken so fiercely, I doubt anyone would dare challenge them. "All that matters is you came back."

Despite the somber tone of conversation, I can't help but huff a weak laugh. "Technically, your son dragged me back."

"That's my boy."

Nick's being weird.

All day, he's been his regular, flirty self, flitting around happily snapping pictures with an ancient-looking camera, but from the moment we gathered in the living room to hand out presents, something changed. I might've thought it was pre-gift giving anxiety if I hadn't added a rule to our list; no presents. A quick, definitive decision fuelled by me being the world's worst gift giver, my empty bank account, and because we've been crossing lines left, right, and center lately. I thought instilling a rare boundary would help keep my brain on the straight, narrow, and relationshipless.

My gaze sporadically strays toward him as the room slowly fills with wrapping paper and words of gratitude, a dejected feeling settling in my chest as he pointedly avoids eye contact. If I didn't know any better, I'd think he looks nervous.

It's when the pile of gifts beneath the intricately decorated tree dwindles to a couple that the puzzle pieces begin to slot into place. Everyone else is busy unwrapping or messing around with their new belongings; I'm the only one who notices Ana nudging her son and casting a pointed look at the small bundle. That's when I realize it's not nerves I sense; it's awkwardness. Nick's mom got me a present and he feels weird about it.

I try not to be hurt by his reluctance as he scoops up what looks like a wrapped box. Handing it to me silently, he gingerly sits beside me, his leg bouncing rapidly and jostling mine. I resist the urge to frown at his odd behavior, smiling at Ana instead. "You didn't have to get me anything." *Thank God I got something for her.*

Ana waves me off with a scoff, looking the complete opposite to her son as the sound of ripping paper again echoes off the walls. When I lift the lid off an unlabelled box, my breath catches in my throat.

A pair of dark green boxing gloves sit neatly inside, a roll of hand wrap the same color tucked beside them. Underneath them, a Brazilian cookbook peeks through. Sitting prettily on top is a colorful woven bracelet.

"The book is from me and Sofia made the bracelet," Ana explains, and I suck my bottom lip into my mouth with a sharp breath. "The gloves were Nico's idea."

Casting the man in question a sideways glance, I swear golden skin is tinted pink, and his nonchalant shrug is definitely stiff. "Now you can stop stealing my shit."

Would it be weird to burst into tears? Definitely.

Do I want to anyway? Definitely, and I hope it's not obvious as I gush my thanks to the Silva matriarch. The moment Sofia steals her attention again, I shuffle closer to Nick, my voice little more than a whisper as I remind him, "We agreed on no presents."

"Did we?" is his droll reply. "I'm a terrible listener."

He's aiming for humor but that weird edge in his voice and his mannerisms is still prominent. Clearing his throat quietly, he shifts, and then something else lands on my lap. When he offers no explanation, I quirk a confused brow at Nick. "You already gave me a present."

"I did."

"So this is?"

Full lips twitch. "Another one."

If we weren't trying to be discreet, I'd throttle him.

Instead, I settle for quipping snarkily, "Next time you decide to ignore the rules, can you at least tell me? That way I don't look like a bitch when I don't get you anything."

"I can think of plenty ways for you to make it up to me," Nick replies in a suggestive, thankfully quiet voice but I still catch a hint of nervousness, his legs still shakes when it nudges mine. "Shut up and open it."

"Romantic," I mutter beneath my breath, doing what he says, though, because who can resist presents?

I can't tell which of us is more uncomfortable as I peel back the wrapping but Nick goes completely still as a small paperback is revealed. "Everyman," I read the title aloud. It's an old book, clearly tattered and worn from use. When I flip through, I note a bunch of scribbles in the margins, a myriad of highlighted quotes. One in particular catches my eye; *I will go with thee and be thy guide, in thy most need to go by thy side.*

It takes me longer than it should to clock why those words sound so familiar; it should be easy to recognize a quote I sleep on top of every night, etched on the skin covering Nick's ribcage.

"It was my dad's favorite book," he explains, a definite tremor muddying his words. "And mine."

Maybe this can be your favorite too, are the words written on the title page, and in a rare occasion, I'm stunned into silence.

He got me a book.

An important book that clearly means a lot to him, if his behavior is anything to go by.

Shit.

I want to cry again and I'm not sure if it's because this is so fucking sweet and thoughtful and meaningful or if it's because in the entire year I was with Dylan—I hate that my mind goes there but it does—nothing he gave me or did for me ever made me feel quite like this.

I don't know what to say. A simple 'thanks' feels decidedly hollow. So, I don't say anything.

Resting back against the sofa cushions, I draw my knees up to my chest and let them lean to the side, acting as a barrier so no one sees when I slip the hand not tightly gripping my new book between Nick and me. I poke his thigh until he gets the hint, tangling his fingers with mine. When I look up at him, I hope my gaze conveys how much his gift means to me. When he looks down at me, I wonder what the hell those indecipherable emotions swirling in liquid gold mean.

If either of us were capable of paying attention to anything except each other, we would've noticed Ana watching our entire exchange with a smile.

33

AMELIA

"Are you sure you have to leave?"

Despite the fact I knew the answer before I asked the question, I'm still disappointed when Dad nods—Dr. Hanlon is undoubtedly desperately needed to sew some poor hapless soul back together. There's no telling how many lives were lost without him running the show over Christmas. The hospital probably couldn't function without him for an hour, let alone the four whole days he's been gone.

Clearly, I'm not bitter at all.

Dropping the newspaper he's reading, Dad sighs, hands stretching across the dining table to grip mine. "You know I wish I could stay."

I smile weakly; I do know. He hates leaving me as much as I hate it, he always has.

One time, when I was thirteen, he booked an entire week off after I got my appendix taken out; the man cried because we got to eat dinner together every night. On my sixteenth birthday, he got through a full night on-call without any pages and he spent the morning after practically skipping around the kitchen. When he made it in time after a particularly hectic shift to watch Cass' first high school baseball game, he was the loudest parent in the stands. The longest he's ever taken off was after the accident. Four whole months of him doting on me and driving me to physiotherapy and holding me while I moped and cried.

That's why I don't hold a grudge; while my dad might've missed a lot, he was *always* there when it mattered most.

I can know all of that and still miss him before he's even out the door.

Dad stands, rounding the table to tower over me. A gentle hand strokes my hair. "How about I try to come visit you next semester?"

There's an unmissable emphasis on 'try' but I perk up anyway. "Really?"

He stoops to kiss the top of my head. "No promises," *obviously*, "but I should be able to swing it."

It's like a switch flicks; I go from feeling sorry for myself to beaming, and I'm not sure what that says about me, how simply offering to try is enough. "I'd love that."

"He can stay with me," Cass offers as he struts into the kitchen—he was gracious enough to let me and dad have breakfast without his presence.

Dad and I laugh in unison. "Not a chance."

The rest of the family tricks in, bidding their goodbyes to Dad. My face is smushed against his chest, arms wrapped tight around his waist, when the doorbell rings. Everyone exchanges confused glances. "Are we expecting someone?"

Shaking her head, Lynn slips from the room, footsteps heading toward the front door.

It all happens so fast.

I hear the door opening. A sharp inhale that seems to echo off the walls. Stifled arguing, like Lynn's trying to hold back from yelling, which is weird because I don't think I've ever heard Lynn raise her voice unless it's aimed at her sons and me and something silly we got up to.

Curiosity drives me into the hallway. I frown at the sight of Lynn crowding the door with her body, blatantly trying to hide whoever's standing there from view. For a split second, she shifts, and I catch a glimpse of the secret she's so desperate to conceal.

A vaguely familiar woman stands in the doorway, smirking at Lynn. Rusty blonde hair—obviously dyed—is pulled back into a neat bun. She's dressed impeccably, brown pantsuit and white shirt immaculate, cream heels making her a good head taller than Lynn, and I almost laugh at the juxtaposition of her crisp outfit versus our rumpled, border-line dirty pajamas.

When green eyes flicker to me, my laughter dries up and briefly, I stop being able to see, hear, feel anything.

Because those are my green eyes staring at me. Those lips quirked into an amused grin are mine. The blonde slicked-back hair that should be vivid, curly red is mine too.

I know without a doubt who this woman is before she even opens her mouth.

"Hello, darling."

~

Chaos erupts around me.

People are yelling, demanding that she leave, but the only thing I can hear is her voice. Sickly sweet and cloying, ringing in my ears like an awful warning siren.

Hellodarlinghellodarlinghellodarling.

Suddenly I'm six years old again, sitting on my driveway watching *her* drive away.

Hands grip my waist and pull me back into a hard chest, surrounding me with the citrus-and-spice scent of someone I think I should probably push away but my mind won't, *can't*, focus on anything but the woman in front of me. A hand, separate to the ones on my waist, slips into mine, warm and comforting, and another belonging to a third owner drops on my shoulder.

Her gaze is flicking between me and the people around me, and I'm struck with a strong urge to wipe that self-righteous smile, like she's enjoying the havoc she's created, off her face. The hands on me tighten the tiniest bit, as if they know.

"Get out." The voice is so quiet yet so harsh, and it takes a moment for me to realize that I'm the one speaking.

Two perfect eyebrows raise. "Is that anyway to talk to your mother, Amelia?"

Mother.

Sounds like a curse when she says it.

"I think you made it pretty clear you have no interest in that particular job."

She laughs. Her whole face shimmers with amusement, affirming my suspicion that she's genuinely finding pleasure in this sick little scene of her creation.

I wonder if I look half as furious as Lynn does right now, still standing half in front of the door, still blocking the woman who dares call herself my mother from crossing the threshold.

I hear my dad coming around the corner, asking what's going on and I try to move. I try to stop him from seeing the woman who ruined him, but those damn hands hold me back. It's like he hits a wall, the way he suddenly stops in his tracks, his eyes widening almost comically. "Diane?" His rasping voice breaks my heart in two.

It seems to have the opposite effect on the she-devil. "Hello, Patrick," she purrs, fingers wiggling in a little wave.

Dad responds, asking her something, but I can't hear it over the roaring in my head. It's so loud, so overwhelming, so unapologetically *hateful*.

And then suddenly, it's gone.

Drowned out by soft whispers of a language I don't understand yet they calm me all the same.

Despite the circumstances, despite our audience, I can't help but slump against Nick, my free hand curling around one of the ones settled on my waist. Warm breath brushes my cheek, warm lips a second later, and it's enough for my focus to clear, just in time to catch the end of a spat sentence.

"...although, even without you, it seems she's had plenty of *attention.*" Diane stares pointedly at the hands gripping me protectively, and my cheeks flare with nothing but pure rage. Before I can say anything, though, a body moves half in front of me, a shield from her gaze, her words, her insinuations.

"Get the hell out of my house." Cass is *livid*. Wracked with rage toward a woman he's never even met, rage on my behalf, the hand in mine shaking with it, although that could be my own trembling. On my other side, James shifts, mimicking our brother's stance, leaving only a sliver of space between them.

Diane pays them no mind; I remain the sole focus of her attention.

"Don't you want to know why I'm here, darling?" That fucking voice; so sugary, so deadly. I don't answer her, and I swear I see a flicker of annoyance cross her features before they revert into a cool mask. "I saw you," she continues, her gaze darting behind me. "At the grocery store."

Nick stiffens and so do I.

The day before Christmas Eve, we were sent on a grocery store quest

—Lynn had a last minute panic over whether or not she'd stocked the house with enough booze to get us through the holiday—and Nick drove us to one a few towns over.

To waste time, he claimed.

To freely feel me up between the aisles, I know.

Vaguely, I remember messing around and noticing some woman staring at us. At the time, I assumed she was some random spoilsport judging us for being too loud. I didn't even look twice. The receding sound of tapping heels and a hint of a vaguely familiar face were all I took away from that brief encounter.

Apparently, I should've paid more attention.

"I thought, maybe, now that we're both adults, you'd like to have lunch with me. Let me explain."

It takes a moment for Diane's words to settle in, so heavy in my mind it's like I can see them.

And then, in a whiplash of emotion, the anger lifts and I laugh.

Loud, bitter cackles wrack my body, eyes watering and stomach cramping with the force of them. "You're kidding, right?" My voice cracks slightly, as cracked as Diane's perfection mask; she looks completely and utterly bewildered.

"You abandon me, abandon *us*," I gesture wildly at Dad, who's watching me with an odd combination of pride and confusion, "and you don't call, you don't text, you don't even send a fucking postcard for fourteen years, and now you want to have *lunch*?"

What I'm saying isn't funny yet I'm powerless to cease chuckling because this whole thing is so preposterous, so fucking hilarious. Like an episode straight out of some over dramatic soap opera.

Completely cutting your child out of your life, pretending she doesn't exist only to pop back up when she's an adult... Fuck me.

"I tried to get in contact, Amelia." My name sounds so wrong rolling off her tongue. "After your accident and that boy..."

Just like that, the hilarity dissipates.

"Don't you fucking dare," I hiss, skin flushing so red it feels like I'm on fire. "You don't talk about him."

Diane rears back as though I've slapped her. "Darling..."

I hold up a hand to cut her off, like a parent scolding her child, ironically. When I move forward, Nick does too, never breaking contact, and I'm glad for it because I genuinely feel like the only thing holding me back from jumping the wretched woman is his anchoring touch.

There's little doubt in my mind that if I did start swinging, he'd coach me from the side lines, calling out notes on my form.

Looking Diane dead in the eye, I hope to fucking God she hears me loud and clear when I state exactly what she is to me. "You mean absolutely nothing to me, and I don't want you to. Get the hell out and stay away from my family."

She looks shocked. Genuinely shocked, as if she really expected me to run into her arms crying tears of relief and begging her to be my mom.

Surprise, bitch, I goad internally. *I have a mom. She's currently five seconds away from slamming the door in your perfect, prissy little face.*

Diane's gaze flickers to Dad, an essence of pleading to her expression. When he meets her gaze head on and scoffs loudly, I've never been so proud of him.

And when she only hovers in the doorway for a split second longer before turning on her heel and striding down the driveway, I've never been so proud of myself.

Because, this time, when the screech of tires echoes down the street, I don't watch her drive away.

The tree in the Morgans' backyard wasn't only used for slightly dangerous, bruise-creating recreational activities; it was something of a haven to a young me. If I sat at the right angle, the thick trunk hid me from the view of both houses, leaving me to sulk in privacy over silly things, like my older brothers got my new clothes dirty or they cheated at a game.

Right now, my reason for sulking doesn't feel so trivial.

The ground beneath me is freezing cold, as is the air against my bare skin, but I don't mind. The privacy is worth it, being able to float into thoughtless oblivion is worth it.

It doesn't last very long, though.

My eyes crack open at the sound of dead grass crunching beneath heavy footsteps, and I'm greeted by the sight of Nick bathed in wintery sunlight. There's something to say about the fact that, even in dire circumstances, I can't help but admire him. Concern suits him, I've learned. "Cass said to give you space."

"Looks like you didn't listen."

"I told you." Dropping to the ground beside me, he leaves a healthy distance between us. Letting me come to him. "I'm a terrible listener."

I breathe an amused noise. *Liar.*

In spite of his wry tone, Nick's gaze is all serious as it burns the side of my face. His hands fidget where they rest on his lap, his whole body twitching slightly, actually. Only when I reach out and link our hands does the surprisingly soft-centered man settle, a sigh of utter relief escaping him. In a single, strong tug, I'm on his lap, my forehead pressed to the slope of his neck as he buries his face in my hair. Hands rub my back soothingly, silently, providing comfort whilst I struggle finding adequate words to describe how I feel.

"Fourteen years," I croak, and arms tighten around me. "There were so many times in fourteen years when I might've needed her and she picks *now* to show up. I don't get it. *Why?*"

It's a rhetorical question and Nick knows it. Nothing I say is meant to be replied to, none of my ranting and raving, and he knows that too. Without a word, he listens as I spill every thought that clogs my brain, recall the limited memories I have of that woman, very few of which are happy because the only time she ever really paid attention to me was when she was scolding me simply for being a fucking child.

No, darling, you'll get your dress dirty.

Girls don't play rough like that.

That's not very ladylike.

Fuck, if she saw the way I grew up she'd probably have an aneurysm.

The best memory I have of her—possibly the only positive one—is when she left me crying on the driveway. Because by doing that, she consequently left me in Lynn Morgan's care. Lynn, the woman who brought me to dance classes and collected me from my school and gossiped with me about boys and coached me through my first period. My mother left me and I found my mom.

The world really does work in mysterious, fucked up ways.

"You should talk to her."

My head snaps up so quickly I narrowly avoid clocking Nick in the chin. "Why would I do that?"

"You have questions, *querida*," he says like it's obvious. "Ask them."

Not quite sure I'm hearing things correctly, I clamber to my feet, gaping down at him, wide-eyed and open-mouthed. "Are you serious?"

Apparently, he is; rising too, he nods.

"I don't have *questions*, Nick," I spit, forcing myself not to yell because while the tree might hide us from view, it does nothing to quell our voices. "I have complaints. I have anger. I have violent tendencies that involve wanting to break her nose for everything she put my dad through."

"Amelia," Nick frowns when I dodge his attempts to draw me close, "I'm just trying to help."

"Well, don't." Anger burns in my chest, begging to be released. It doesn't matter that most of it is brewing for Diane; Nick is about to be the hapless victim, and I don't think I could stop it if I wanted to.

Wrong place, wrong time, wrong decision to push.

Nick doesn't know shit about what I'm feeling. He didn't watch that woman walk away, completely uncaring about the crying child at her feet. He didn't listen to my dad cry himself to sleep every night for a month or watch him walk around like a zombie for much longer or over-hear the heartbroken conversations he had with Cass' parents.

I'm allowed to be angry. I don't owe *her* anything, not even a measly conversation.

So, I snap.

"You're not my brother, you're not my dad, and you're sure as shit not my boyfriend so back the fuck off. I don't need you."

Nick does what I tell him, literally. Stumbling back a step, his head reels as though I slapped him clean across the cheek, and I wonder if that would've hurt both of us less. Because the distraught look on his face hurts, it physically makes my chest ache, so bad I have to drop my gaze to the ground because I can't bear feeling guilty right now on top of everything else.

When he sucks in a breath, I don't stick around long enough to hear what he has to say.

34

NICK

SHE LEFT.

Packed up her shit and hopped on a flight before the dust had even settled without a word of goodbye.

I didn't even know she was gone until Cass brought it up. According to him, she went back to San Francisco with her dad. And that means she's with Kate too, since her family's place is nearby. That knowledge is of little comfort to me; at least I know she's not sitting in her apartment alone letting her own brain destroy her but it would be a whole lot better if she'd answer her fucking phone and let me know she's okay herself.

Amelia is ignoring me. For a little bit, I convinced myself that it wasn't just my calls she was screening, that she was shutting everyone else out too. That fantasy died when I saw her name flash on Cass' phone and I had to listen to their hushed conversation, fists clenched and chest tight as I stifled the urge to snatch his phone and beg her to speak to me.

It's taking everything in me not to blow up her phone with a million texts and calls but I won't. I can't. *He* did that and fuck if I'm ever giving her a reason to compare me to that asshole. I've resorted to begging Kate for updates, each one less reassuring than the last.

She's fine. She's okay. All good.

I don't know if it's under Amelia's orders or if it's Kate being Kate but the most detailed information I've pried from her is that they flew back to Sun Valley this morning, and the ambiguity is fucking killing me.

Whatever the case, Amelia is making her point perfectly clear; she doesn't need me.

Fuck, that hurt.

I keep trying to convince myself that she didn't mean it. That she was angry. That I simply picked the wrong time to offer advice and she snapped. All of the above are true but the look in her eyes... something in there was serious.

I knew I shouldn't have pushed. One look at her sitting under the tree, steam practically coming out of her ears, and I fucking knew. But I did anyway because she was sitting in my lap, looking and sounding so broken, and if there was something I could possibly say to fix it, I was going to.

Wrong call, clearly.

But still, I don't think I deserved that. Her snapping at me like that for trying to help. It was shitty timing, I should've let her stew longer, but I thought that talking to Diane, asking her all the questions she was quietly asking herself, might help. Be healing or some shit.

You would've thought I asked her to forgive the woman and let her move back in the way she went from zero to sixty so fast, and I can't help but wonder if it's partly because she can't handle the fact that I care enough to want to help.

Every time I think we're getting somewhere, she pushes me away. Actually, she shoves me away. Kicks me. Punches me right in the gut. And then she turns on her tail and sprints in the opposite direction. The night of Christmas Eve, on the front porch, I genuinely thought I was getting somewhere. That maybe she was finally understanding she's not just a distraction to me, that she was finally *trusting* me.

And then her mother shows up and back in her head she goes.

I want to pummel whoever messed her up so bad she can't let me in, and since I assume decking her mother would be frowned upon, I'm going to have to settle with smashing Dylan's face in again the next time the rat pops up.

"Nico, are you even listening to me?" My sister's indignant voice snaps me from my thoughts, little feet kicking at my shins from the opposite side of the table, and I cast her an apologetic glance.

When I offered to take Ma and Sofia for lunch, it selfishly had everything to do with needing to get the hell out of the house before I cracked up. Everywhere I look, whether the home has Morgan or Silva on the lease, I see her.

"*Desculpa, minha anjinha.*" Pasting on a smile, I focus on my family. "What were you saying?"

Satisfied by my attention, Sofia launches into a spiel again, chattering excitedly about things I hate that I can't concentrate on properly. I try, I really do try, but if my one-track, Amelia-oriented mind was bad before, it's only worsened tenfold. And, apparently, as much as I act like I'm listening, nodding along and chiming in with vague additions when appropriate, it's clear I'm not fooling anyone.

"*Você falou com ela?*" Sofia whines as Ma switches the conversation to our native tongue; my little sister's Portuguese is pretty good but she's nowhere near fluent enough to keep up with the speed at which we talk. I have a feeling that's the exact reason for the change.

"*Quem?*" I feign ignorance, faking a sudden interest in my greasy diner breakfast.

"*Não se faça de bobo, Nicolas,*" Ma tuts. "*Querida,*" she drags out the word mockingly, a faint amused smile playing across her lips as she arches a brow.

That fucking nickname. I should've known it would get me in trouble. With Amelia, ignorance is truly bliss; she has no clue what the term of endearment means or if she does, she doesn't care. Ma, however, knows. She knows intimately what it means because it's what my dad used to call her.

I didn't do it on purpose, I swear to God. It just came out and it stuck and it's screwed me over royally because the second my mother heard it, she heard wedding bells too. And when she heard about the book... Fuck, I'm surprised she hasn't given me her goddamn ring.

Shrugging in a vain attempt at nonchalance, I act like the answer to Ma's question doesn't feel like a punch in the gut. "*Não.*"

"*Você a chamou?*"

"*Obviamente.*"

Golden eyes narrow at my snapped tone but there's sympathy lurking in my mother's gaze. "*Você deveria ter ido com ela.*"

I scoff at her declaration. "*Ela não precisa de mim.*" She told me as much herself.

"*Você é um tolo.*"

While Sofia covers her mouth and giggles, clearly picking up the meaning of that last declaration, I gape at Ma in disbelief. How am I the fool in this situation? I'm doing exactly what she told me to, I'm backing the fuck off, yet when I tell Ma as much, she scoffs, expression rife with indignance. "*Ela estava brava.*"

"*Estava tentando ajudar!*"

"*Ela não queria ajuda!*" Ma whisper-yells, clearly exasperated. Shaking her head with a huff, she softens her tone before continuing in English, "She didn't want advice or pity. Nico. She just needed comfort."

I slump defeatedly in my seat. I thought I was comforting her. Ma, sensing my turmoil, leans across the table to slip her hand into mine. "Just because you would jump at the chance to talk to your father again doesn't mean she would do the same for Diane."

And just like that, it clicks.

I compared the two. Used my own experience with my dad and assumed Amelia would feel the same. Forgot momentarily that Dad didn't choose to leave us like that awful woman chose to leave Patrick and Amelia.

Shit.

Ma sits back slowly, turning her attention back to Sofia who's been entertaining herself with a mess of sugar packets. But when I fish my phone out of my pocket and fire off a quick text asking Cass if he wants to leave sooner than planned, I don't miss her triumphant smile.

It's past midnight when I finally make it to Amelia's place.

The apartment block is quiet, the only other person venturing out this late is her neighbor, a lanky, bald guy who eyes me suspiciously as we cross paths on the stairs. It's a weird feeling, getting wary looks from a suspected drug dealer. Bit of an ego boost, to be honest.

The first couple of knocks on Amelia's front door go unheard, or ignored. I know she's here; Kate deigned to tell me as much. She also said Amelia hasn't left her room since they got home. And that it's just my girl home tonight so if she murders me in a vicious rage, my body probably won't be found until tomorrow afternoon.

Too many minutes pass with no response, and while I don't want to give up, I don't want to be the asshole banging on her door all night either. A sick twist of rejection writhing in my stomach, I start to leave but as I do, a light flickers on inside. Through the thin wood, I hear shuffling and murmured curses, the sounds getting louder the closer she gets, and I'm full on fucking holding my breath in anticipation,

The door swings open and there she is, hair ruffled, eyes heavy with sleep, slight body drowning in my clothes. The invisible anvil that's been sitting on my chest since the moment she stormed away from me suddenly disappears; it genuinely feels easier to breathe with her in my sights.

Amelia is mid-yawn when she registers who her midnight guest is, and her mouth abruptly slams shut, settling in an unhappy straight line. "What are you doing here?"

Holding up the bag of treats clasped in my grip—I came prepared with all her favorites because to not would be very unwise—I offer a tentative smile.

She doesn't return it. "I told you, I don't-"

"Need me?" I cut her off. Any attempt to hide the bitterness in my voice is a weak one. "Yeah, I heard you the first time. Loud and clear. And I know I'm not your boyfriend but I am your friend so take the damn food and talk to me."

Her eyes widen but her lips remain grimly set, like she can't decide whether to be surprised or pissed. Whatever emotion she settles on, it allows her to take a step back and open the door a little wider, and I grip that meager offering with both hands.

I slip inside before she can change her mind, feeling another wash of familiarity as I head for the kitchen. Amelia follows quietly, arms crossed protectively over her chest as she eyes the food I unload on the counter quizzically. Red Vines, ice-cream in that godawful banana flavor she inexplicably enjoys, her regular order from the takeout place around the corner. A quiet explanation, I say, "You forget to eat when you're stressed."

Her puzzled gaze shifts to me, and I can't tell if she's confused because she has yet to realize that she tends to skip meals on bad days or if she didn't realize I notice. Judging by her paler-than-normal pallor, I think it's safe to say her eating habits have gone to shit the last couple of days.

A blink-and-you'll-miss-it flash of gratefulness lightens her expression, gone before I can truly appreciate it. I soak it up all the same, taking it as permission to dish her up a hearty portion of that eggplant shit she loves. A little more tension eases from my body when she digs in eagerly.

I wait until she's finished her first helping before speaking. "So," she winces through a mouthful as if she knows where this is going, "how was your flight?"

The one you got on without so much as a goodbye.

Slender throat bobbing in a nervous swallow, she shrugs. "It was fine."

I am so fucking sick of that word.

"How's your dad?"

Amelia shrugs again, not even bothering with words this time. Not even bothering to look at me for even a second.

A frustrated huff leaves me as I rake a hand through my hair, briefly massaging my scalp like that will ease the headache brewing beneath. "Can you please look at me, Amelia?"

To her credit, she only briefly hesitates before obliging. "My dad is fine. I'm fine. You didn't need to come here.'"

"I know I didn't." Resting my forearms on the counter, I lean down until we're at eye level, a rarity for us. "I overstepped when I pushed you to talk to Diane. I shouldn't have butted in and I'm sorry."

I could leave it at that.

I probably should leave it at that.

Apology done and hopefully accepted, and we can go back to normal.

But I can't.

"You hurt me, Amelia. Leaving without saying goodbye, saying what you said. That really fucking hurt."

Guilt flickers across her face but it's like she's intent on not giving me an inch lest I take a mile. It's gone as quick as it appears, her face is so maddeningly clear of any expression as she asks, "Why are you here, Nick?"

I'm smart enough to read between the lines; she's not asking why I'm in her apartment. She's asking why I'm here when she's trying her best to shut me out.

"Because I want to be." *Because I care about you.*

Tilting her head at me in that way that drives me out of my mind, her mask of indifference goes nowhere. "What if I don't want you here?"

My heart drops to my stomach. My mouth goes completely dry as if I've been deprived of water for a month, yet I still manage to croak out, "Tell me to go and I'll go, *querida.*"

Don't tell me to go, I silently beg. *Please don't fucking tell me to go.*

Amelia's gaze drops again, her voice so quiet it's like she doesn't want me to hear her, not really.

But I do.

And when she says, "I think you should go," I listen.

35

AMELIA

"FUCKING HELL, AMELIA."

Drumming anxiously against the steering wheel, I focus on the road ahead, refusing to meet the somewhat shell-shocked gazes of my friends. Even Jackson—always the stoic, impartial third party—is staring at me like I ran over his puppy. Or maybe he's staring at me like I'm the puppy that got run over. I can't tell.

"Did Lynn hit her? I bet she hit her."

A pained screech echoes from the back of the car as Kate twists in the passenger seat and reaches behind her to pinch Luna. "Ow! What the hell?"

"Seriously Lu? That's your first question?" Kate glares, enraged on my behalf but honestly, I'm stifling a laugh. Luna almost hit the nail on the head; a handful more disrespectful comments from Diane and the answer to her question would've been a resounding *hell yeah*.

Before the two can erupt into their usual bickering, I clear my throat loudly, flashing them—or more specifically Luna—imploring, pleading eyes in the rear-view mirror. "Can we not talk about it?"

It's for their sake more than mine; there's no telling what will set me off these days and I'm sick of snapping at people I care about.

Luna pouts but she keeps her inquisitive lips shut, even though it blatantly pains her to do so.

Small miracles.

I knew when I agreed to collect Luna and Jackson from the airport—

she shocked us all again by toting the boy home for Christmas—I'd have to spill the beans sooner or later. What I didn't expect; Luna announcing something was definitely wrong with me within four seconds of reuniting. I swear, she can *smell* drama.

At the risk of experiencing severe consequences if I dare to withhold information, I told her, with Jackson present and all because he already knows most of the nitty-gritty details of my life; there's no harm in him being privy to one more. And, as announced by the man himself, he knows about Nick and me.

The whole damn time, he's known, and Luna swears up and down she didn't tell. At his own admission, he figured it out himself, and he's so damn nice that he never breathed a word. I reckon he would've kept it to himself until the end of time if I hadn't accidentally tripped over my words when mentioning Nick and cast panicking eyes at his reflection in the rear-view mirror and he'd simply nodded and uttered a quiet, "I know."

See—*nice.*

"So did Nicky fuck the sadness out of you?"

"Jesus Christ, Lu!"

"What? I'm changing the subject! Hey, stop hitting me!" The latter shriek is aimed at Kate who, when I give her the nod, whacks a palm across Luna's thighs.

You see, in my retelling of the turbulent Christmas holidays, while I included Nick's sweet gift-giving, I may have skimmed over the part of the story that involved me blowing up at him. And the part where I fled the state without so much as a goodbye. And the part where he came to my apartment, sweet and worried, and I told him to leave. *And* the part where he actually left so I bundled myself up in bed and cried my freaking eyes out.

He apologized. He genuinely apologized and the one apology that should've been so easy to accept, that I could trust the man issuing it enough to accept, I stomped all over. I had the audacity to feel sad when he left, to expect him to stay even though I told him to do the opposite.

Pathetic.

Although I haven't breathed a word, I suspect Kate knows more than she's letting on. When she got home from Sydney's this morning, she actually knocked on my bedroom door before coming in. Privacy isn't really a thing in our apartment; the only time we ever knock is when someone's had an overnight guest.

The look of surprise on her face when she found me in bed alone said it all; she knew he was coming over. So, she knew something happened. And she expected us to have made up.

I don't know how to feel about the disappointment that clouded her expression when her expectations weren't met.

Luna, however, is blissfully ignorant, as proven by the way she stares at me with big, gossip-hungry eyes. "No," I sigh, a hand scraping over my flushed cheeks as if I can rub the blush away. "He did not... do that."

He could've if I'd let him. Whatever comfort I needed, he would've provided, I know that. What I don't know is why I pushed him away so viciously. I wasn't angry anymore, not at him. The second I got on that plane, my annoyance with him fizzled out. My head cleared and I realized my outburst was a product of overreactions and miscommunication. But for some fucked up reason, I ignored him, and the only explanation is that I was scared. I *am* scared.

Because if I let him in and he bails, it will fucking ruin me. I know it will.

And I'm not sure a Nicolas Silva heartbreak is something I can recover from.

I'm deep in a pit of wallowing when my bedroom door creaks open and a head peeks around the edge. However, it's not any of the heads I'd expect.

"Hey." Jackson smiles softly, a little awkwardly. "Can I come in?"

Smoothing away my instinctive frown, I nod—*Gilmore Girls* reruns can wait a couple of minutes. Jackson inches into my room, leaving the door ajar behind him before stiffly taking the seat at my desk.

I fidget as I scoot upright, equal parts intrigued and concerned at his sudden want for a private conversation. He's a great guy and definitely a good friend—he proved that yesterday when he admitted to keeping his mouth shut about me and Nick—don't get me wrong, and practically a roommate at this point, but it's not like we *talk*. Except for now, apparently.

"You know my mom left when I was a kid too, right?"

Well, shit.

I'm not sure what I was expecting but it definitely wasn't that. "No, I didn't know that."

"Oh." Jackson fiddles with the ends of his long hair, and my gut tells me he assumed a certain rowdy blonde spilled the beans. "Well, she did. When I was twelve. My dad wasn't around either so my younger sisters and I got dumped with our grandparents."

"Shit, Jackson, I had no idea." God, I can't even imagine what that must've been like; at least I was young enough to not really remember the woman who left me, and I always had my dad. I never had younger siblings to worry about. Judging by his tone when he mentions his grandparents, it doesn't sound like Jackson really had anyone.

"It's okay." He waves off my concern. "I'm over it. Only good thing that woman ever did was leave."

Yeah, I know the feeling.

"I, uh, wanted to tell you. In case you need someone to talk to who gets it, you know."

Okay. Yeah. If I were Luna, I'd give up my wild ways for this man too. "Thank you, Jackson. Seriously."

Jackson shrugs—clearly his favorite form of communication—off my thanks, standing and heading for the door, silently conveying that the swift conversation is over.

My fingers hover over the keys of my laptop, ready to hit play as soon as Jackson vacates the room. Except, he doesn't.

Because at the last minute, I break. "Hey, have you talked to Nick?" Jackson stops in his tracks, and something about the look on his face sends dread plummeting in my stomach. He looks like he's been caught in a lie, in a secret, and he doesn't need to say a thing. "He didn't come home last night, did he?"

The shake of his head only confirms what I already know.

"Oh." The single utterance is pathetically dejected, even to my own ears. "And the night before?"

"I'm sorry, Mils, I haven't seen him since I got back."

"Has anyone?" Because I'm starting to panic a little, beyond the selfish fear that he might've spent a night in a bed other than his own or mine. A day without anyone hearing from him? That's cause for concern, right?

As if sensing my rising anxiety, Jackson's brown eyes go wide, a frantic hand going to his pocket and whipping out his phone. "He probably crashed at a friend's place. I'll ask Ben."

Right. Crashed at a friend's place. God, sometimes I forget that people outside our friend group exist.

They're embarrassingly agonizing, the few minutes that pass where the only sound is my heavy breathing. My heart jumps into my throat when a text tone sounds. Jackson's sigh of relief is like music to my ears. "He's home."

Thank fuck.

I huff my own breath of relief, a sheepish snicker escaping. However, it gets caught in my throat when I notice Jackson frowning at his phone, the screen not-so-discreetly turned away from me.

My gaze darts between him and whatever he's doing a crap job at hiding from me. "What?"

"Nothing," is his too-quick reply.

Sighing, I cock my head at him. "You really want me to get Luna in here?"

As suspected, he folds like a cheap lawn chair. A wince crinkling his features, he reluctantly hands his phone over.

Ben: *Yeah, he's here. Rolled in an hour ago looking thoroughly fucked. Back to his old habits I guess :(*

It takes four reads before the words sink in.

Oh. Okay. Guess I deserve that.

"Amelia..."

Shoving Jackson's phone back at him, I force a smile. "It's fine."

His expression reeks of doubt but that's fine too. I wouldn't believe me either, not with the way my hands are shaking and my voice is cracking.

It's my own fault, though. He told me I was hurting him and I hurt him again so what did I expect? This whole time, I've been pushing him away, unconsciously or not, it doesn't matter. I shouldn't be surprised that I finally succeeded.

"Are you sure?" The words are careful, slow, as though Jackson already knows the answer and he's preparing for the fallout.

I nod stiffly. "We were messing around. No strings attached and all that." Which is true. That's what we decided. That's what *I* decided.

Why the fuck did I decide that again?

In a soft, gentle voice, Jackson asks, "Do you seriously believe that, Amelia?"

No, I yell internally.

"Yes," I lie aloud.

Because that's what I do best, evidently. I lie and avoid my feelings, uncaring that I hurt people in the process because at least I don't get hurt.

Except right now, sitting on my bed with Ben's text seared in my mind and hot tears in my eyes, it really doesn't feel like I'm not getting hurt.

There's a man in my bedroom. I can make out his outline as he sneaks in the doorway, the light from my laptop illuminating him eerily. He's walking on his tip-toes, like one of those cartoon burglars, and I have to resist the urge to laugh at the absurd picture my young friend is creating. "Ben?"

A strangled panicked noise escapes his throat as he jumps about a foot in the air, hand flying to his chest. "Holy shit, Tiny. You scared me."

Snorting, I prop myself up on an elbow. "*I* scared *you*?"

"Kate said you were asleep." Shrugging off his jacket, he chucks it on my desk, kicking his shoes off too.

"And what, you decided to watch? Very Edward Cullen of you."

"I'm taking that as a compliment." Without any invitation, Ben flops onto my bed, wriggling under he's tucked under the sheets beside me, almost knocking my laptop off the bed in the process. "I wanted to check on you," he explains, busying himself setting my almost ruined electronic carefully on the floor.

When pity flashes in his eyes, I groan loudly, slamming my face into my pillow. "Cass told you?"

Wrestling the pillow from my grasp, Ben tucks it behind his head so I'm left defenseless, forced to take his concern. "He tried. I'm not fluent in 'distraught big brother' yet. I heard the words '*Amelia*', '*mother*', and '*shitshow*' and kind of put the pieces together."

Groaning again, I let Ben jostle us around until he's got his arms wrapped around me, hugging me tightly to his chest as his hands rub my back, reminding me of different hands on other occasions, and my chest squeezes painfully.

"So, did you punch her?"

My barked laugh is muffled in his chest. What, was everyone hoping for a nice holiday brawl? "No. I wanted to, though."

A huff of disappointment blows warm air on the top of my head. "Damn. I bet Jackson ten bucks you punched her."

"Sorry to disappoint."

Ben makes a dismissive noise, his arms tightening around me. After a few moments of silence, he starts humming a soft tune, something I can't quite place but it acts like a lullaby, soothing me into a drowsy state until my eyes flutter closed.

"Hey, Tiny?" Ben whispers into the quiet darkness. "I'm sorry your mom's a twat but I love you, if that makes you feel better."

Forcing my eyes open, I tilt my head and offer Ben a sleepy smile. "I love you too, kid."

"Love me like 'friends' love me or love me like you'll be my surrogate one day? Because I think our genes would create very beautiful babies. Very pale babies, with very green eyes."

"Find a man who can put up with you and we have a deal."

He scoffs. "What if I want to be a single parent?"

"There is no way in hell I'm letting you take care of a baby by yourself." Pretty sure that falls somewhere under child endangerment. Ben can barely take care of himself. I watched him eat dry ramen last week because he was too lazy to boil water.

"Yeah, probably a good call." Ben's chin finds my head, hands still stroking me to sleep. "I'm really glad you kicked me out of Greenie's that one day."

"Me too, Benny. Me fucking too."

36

AMELIA

I HATE THIS HOUSE.

Genuinely despise it with every fiber of my being.

Bad things happen to me in this house, especially when a drunken night is brewing, so it really blows my mind that I keep allowing myself to be dragged back here. The fine art of guilt-tripping has something to do with it.

The girls said if I didn't go, they weren't going because hell if they were letting me spend New Year's Eve alone. Cass as good as said if I didn't show up—I swear to God, I've never attended as many parties as I have this semester and it's all his fault—he'd turn up at my apartment and kidnap me. Ben seconded that motion.

Two different tactics—both very effective.

So, for the sake of my friends, I peeled myself out of bed and let Luna doll me up even though the last thing I feel like doing is stumbling around the house of the guy I'm avoiding. Or maybe he's avoiding me. I don't really know. Both, probably.

An hour of lackluster partying passes and I already wish I told my friends to take a hike.

Another and I'm contemplating fleeing. I would, too, if I didn't have my own personal entourage keeping track of my every move, trying and failing to coax me into having a little fun.

It's too hot in here. There are too many people. And there's nothing to do other than drown my self-made sorrows in rum and cola, exceptionally heavy on the former since Ben made them. While everyone else enjoys themselves, I cower in the corner, sipping and sipping and sipping, getting drunker and drunker and drunker, acting like I'm not constantly scanning the room for Nick when, really, that's all I'm doing.

I'm unsure whether I'm relieved or disappointed when I keep coming up empty but I'm completely sure that when I finally find him, I wish I hadn't.

Because Nick is not alone.

He's lurking at the opposite end of the crowded living room, intermittently hidden by swaying bodies, but once my gaze locks on, he doesn't leave my sight. Nor does the owner of the perfectly manicured hand caressing his muscles.

Oh, you have got to be kidding me.

It's that *girl*. The one who bodychecked me in the pub that one night. Jen-who-fucking-gives-a-shit. I don't give a crap about her name; all I care about is the way she's simpering at Nick with big doe eyes, and he's not even trying to push her away. In fact, I'm pretty sure he's shifting closer, leaning down so she can whisper God knows what in his ear.

Any doubts I might've had about Ben's text being legitimate suddenly fly out the window, replaced with outrage because here I am, feeling fucking awful about hurting him and there he is, getting someone else to lick his wounds. I'm so pissed that it hurts and I'm *drunk* and that should numb the pain but it's only making it worse. And then there's the voice in my head, the one that feels like tiny jabs of a knife in my brain, reminding me that I've done this all to myself.

And I don't think there's anything I can do to fix it.

And it doesn't look like he wants me to.

God knows how long later, I stumble upstairs, a feat that takes a helluva lot longer than it should since my limbs stopped cooperating about two drinks ago. It turns out there was something I could do; I could get disgustingly inebriated until I didn't have to fight the urge to seek out Nick in the crowd because my vision became too blurry to see anything.

The downfall to that; jealousy feeds off alcohol, and I provided it with a feast.

I don't know if it's the not-so-little green monster making me nauseous or the mix of spirits sitting heavy in my gut but either way, my spinning head urges me to take a break from the festivities. From the eyes assessing me carefully. From pretending to have fun to appease those eyes and not ruin their night like I ruin everything else.

Staggering down the hallway, I blindly twist the first doorknob my shaky hands find, and I don't know if it's fate or karma that sends me tripping into Nick's room. It's like instinct brought me here. An internal GPS programmed to eternally point me in his direction.

Fun.

It's empty, thankfully—I wouldn't be able to handle anything else—and I relish the relative silence when I shut the door behind me, letting my gaze drift around a room I'm not all that familiar with despite how intimately familiar I am with the man who occupies it.

Our sleepovers occur in the sanctity of my room. The only times I've been in here were tainted by dramatic events and too much booze—now included, I guess. I've never had the chance to properly take in the bookshelf stuffed to the brim, the desk overflowing with stuff, the large, neatly-made bed.

Choosing the lesser of all evils—or so I think—I collapse into the desk chair, slumping with a heavy exhale. When my gaze snags on the stack of recently developed photos, the only tidy portion of his desk, that exhale gets caught in my throat. I know I shouldn't snoop but is it really snooping if the first photo is of me?

And the second.

And the third.

The fourth is a sweet, blurry shot of Kate and Sydney, the next a drunk Ben doing a cartwheel in the middle of the street, an event I remember vividly since the kid almost broke his neck and got run over in one fell swoop. All of my friends, *our* friends, feature but as I carefully flick through, more often than not, it's my own face staring back at me. My permanently smiling face, eyes bright but never quite looking straight at the lens, always more focused on something slightly above it.

Melancholy settles in my bones, makes my entire body throb painfully. Forcing myself to my feet, I trudge into the bathroom where I know there's a stash of aspirin. I crouch down, opening the cabinet under the sink and rifling for what my aching head demands.

What I'm met with knocks me flat on my ass.

A fully stocked basket of toiletries hides near the back. At first glance, there's nothing extraordinary about it. The only reason it catches my eye is because, honestly, I wouldn't expect Nick to keep amenities for his overnight guests—surely that would rack up quite the bill over time—but it makes sense, I guess.

Like a hotel leaving mints on pillows, I snark silently, liquor making me petty.

When I delve deeper, unable to help myself, my throat goes dry.

Everything is brand new and unopened. Shampoo, conditioner, curl cream, not only the same brand I use but the exact scent. A miniature bottle of the perfume I favor tucked in beside a box of tampons. A broken laugh escapes me when I spot a toothbrush and Denman brush, both the same shade of dark green.

The first tear burns as it falls, origin unknown. Whether it's a happy or sad one or utterly distraught is a mystery, although it's more than likely all of the above and more. It's not alone for long because soon, I'm sobbing so hard, I swear I can be heard over the music thumping downstairs.

I needn't have worried about Nick breaking my heart. I did it to myself.

~

I cry all my makeup off. I cry until my cheeks, my neck, my chest, everything is soaked with tears. I cry until my ass goes numb from sitting on the cold bathroom floor for so long. Yet when I'm done crying, when I run out of tears, I make no effort to move; I simply rest my sodden cheek against my knees and stare at the open undersink cabinet, at the basket mocking me.

"Are you okay?"

I flinch at the voice, both the last yet the only I want to hear. My aching eyes cringe at Nick hovering in the doorway. Hands shoved in his pocket, his expression is carefully blank as he follows my line of sight, the only reaction the bob of his throat as he swallows.

"How long?" *How long have you had a secret stash of my stuff hidden in your bathroom?*

It's odd how a simple shrug can cause such a profound pain in my chest. "A while."

A while. So nonchalant. So casual. Like he does it for everyone when I know, *I know,* he doesn't.

I hug my knees tighter to my chest in an effort to alleviate the icy chill his vacant demeanor is causing, tucking my head to hide from him.

When Nick repeats the question I forgot he even asked, I nod, and he huffs. "Words, Amelia."

"Yes." The word is snapped, a tiny scowl playing across my face as I tilt my head toward him against my better judgment.

Nick nods stiffly, and it might be an intoxicated illusion but he looks relieved. He looks sad. And I almost forget that I'm mad, that we're mad at each other. "I didn't think you'd come."

Almost.

My haughty laugh echoes around the room. "That makes it okay, then." When his brow furrows in genuine confusion, I laugh again. "I saw you with *her.* Jean or whatever. And I know you didn't go home after you left mine, or the night after."

Without hesitation, Nick drops to his haunches in front of me, honest to God flames writhing in those golden irises. "I didn't go home after yours," he spits but it's not anger souring the words, it's frustration, "because I got so shit-faced, I passed out in my car. I spent the entire day in the gym and then I crashed at Luka's because I didn't feel like explaining to Cass-" Nick sucks in a breath, shaking his head quickly. "I was in a shit mood and I didn't wanna go home."

"But-"

"Enough," he cuts me off. "Nothing happened with *Jean or whatever* or with anyone else. Whatever you think you saw, you got it wrong. Maybe you're too drunk to remember but we have a deal."

Have. Present tense.

I throttle the hope that flutters in my belly before it gets out of hand, opening my mouth to say God knows what but I'm interrupted once again. "I'm not arguing with you like this. Take a shower, take a nap, I don't care. Just sober up."

Nick doesn't wait for a response before retreating into the bedroom, leaving the door ajar in his wake. Banging and rustling sounds along with a few muttered foreign curses before another door slams shut, leaving me alone with nothing but suffocating silence.

Slowly, with wobbly legs, I clamber to my feet. I'm on autopilot as I do what he says, showering quickly and not daring to use the stuff beneath the sink because I fear I'm not welcome to it anymore. Wrapped in the towel that was hanging on the back of the door, I pad into the bedroom, unreasonably disappointed when Nick's really gone, foolishly having hoped he'd be waiting.

Obviously, he isn't but there is a pile of clothing sitting on his bed. I slip into the t-shirt and boxer briefs all too eagerly, completely enveloped by the smell of citrus and spice as I burrow beneath his sheets. If I close my eyes, I can almost imagine he's lying beside me, and that's what lets me drift off, what helps me sleep better than I have in days.

~

The buzzing of my phone combined with obnoxious shouting jerks me awake. I groan as I roll over, burying deeper beneath the covers like that might ward off the freaking marching band causing havoc behind my temples. While the room may no longer be spinning, I've clearly traded off one problem for another; sleeping off the alcohol has welcomed not only a rum-induced hangover but an emotional one too.

Terrific.

Forcing open an eye, another groan escapes me but it's one of relief this time. Someone a lot wiser than me anticipated my current dilemma; on the nightstand sits a glass of water begging to be drunk, the two white pills sitting beside it eager to be swallowed.

Not deigning to open my eyes beyond a crack, I prop myself up on an elbow, chasing down the aspirin with greedy gulps of water while begrudgingly checking my incessantly vibrating phone. It's well after midnight so I've missed the main event, not that I care. I didn't want to celebrate in the first place but I do feel guilty that I disappeared without a word. Although, no one seems particularly concerned.

Cass' messages are a jumble of words that bear no resemblance to the English language. Ben's are no better, the only distinguishable thing being a snap of him and a bong. There's a couple of Kate asking where I am but it's when I get to Luna that the lack of a search party makes sense; a creative, artistic thread of winky faces, various suggestive emojis, and a woefully misspelled encouragement to 'get it' lead me to believe that they know exactly where I am, although the reasoning might be lost.

"You're awake."

Water sloshes down my chin as I jump at the sudden declaration, my eyes opening wide for the first time since I woke up as they dart to the man hunched over the desk, an open book balanced in one hand. God, has he been here this whole time?

The question was meant for my mind only but when Nick replies, I gather I accidentally mumbled it aloud. "Didn't feel like partying," he drones, an edge to his voice when he adds, "didn't want you throwing up in my sheets either," as though he's annoyed at himself for being concerned.

As though the ruined sheets would be the least of his priorities and he doesn't like that.

The chair creaks as Nick shifts, silent as he stares, and I swallow hard over a scratchy throat. "I'm sorry."

A dark brow lifts. "For?"

"Everything."

"Like?"

I stifle yet another groan. He's making me work for it, and I deserve that, but I don't like it. "Snapping at you. Ignoring you. Kicking you out."

Kissing his teeth, Nick drops his head back to stare at the ceiling, as if he can't bear looking at me. "Why did you do it?"

I suck in a deep, ragged breath. "I got scared." *There. I admitted it. Baby steps.*

"You got scared," Nick repeats slowly, letting the words fall off his tongue. "Scared of what?"

Him.

Myself.

Us.

The frightening amount I like him.

I have plenty of reasons but they get caught in my throat, choking me as much as the horrible tension between us that only I can fix but I can't.

"Okay then." With a loud, disappointed sigh, Nick gets to his feet, and I panic as he heads for the door.

Scrambling off the bed, I take a timid step toward him, finally finding my voice but I think it's too late, "Nick, wait-"

"No." Nick spins around, teeth gritted and jaw so tense it could shatter. "I need to leave because you are everywhere, all the time, and I can't fucking think straight. I can't fucking *breathe*, Amelia. I can't stop wanting you and *I hate it* because you don't want me."

Shock freezes me in place.

He...

What?

I can't stop wanting you.

I want to ask what exactly that means. I need clarification, affirmation, more than I need air. But I'm too busy drowning in the flood of emotions hitting me like a tsunami, threatening to sweep me off my feet, clogging my throat.

He waits, a strained, desperate look in his eyes but I don't know what to say. Actually, I do know but my mouth is being awfully uncooperative tonight.

To his credit, he waits longer than I would've before giving up.

Broad shoulders slump in utter defeat. "I can't do this anymore," he whispers, so quiet yet deafening in their meaning, and it's like an invisible fist slams into my gut. I've been preparing myself for this to end since before it even began yet as it arrives, I squeeze my eyes shut and pray it's all a dream.

Footsteps inch toward me but I keep my eyes closed, even when hands sweep my hair back and cup my cheeks. "I can't sneak around," he continues, and I bite down on a pathetic whimper, "and act like I'm not falling for you because it's not fucking working. It's too hard, Amelia."

My heart stops. The rapid beating ceases as it becomes a vestigial organ in my chest along with lungs that refuse to suck in air.

Falling for you.

Falling for me.

He is falling for me.

Lips brush my forehead before his touch disappears. "I'm yours, Amelia, but I can't do this anymore."

He's falling for me and he's leaving.

A couple more steps and he'll reach the door, one more and he'll be out, and a handful after that, he'll be downstairs, lost in the crowd, lost to me.

I don't think; I just move. One second, I'm frozen on the other side of the room. The next, I'm throwing myself between him and the door. "I know what I want," I blurt out, frantic hands bunching his shirt because maybe if I literally hold him hostage, he won't leave.

A slow, tentative glimmer of hope lights my favorite pair of eyes, an endearing tremor in my favorite voice as it asks, "And what's that?"

"You."

37

AMELIA

EVERYTHING GOES STILL.

One, single word hangs in the air between us, so impossibly loud that everything else fades into nothingness.

"I want you," I clarify when the silence drags on too long, my cheeks heated as I lick suddenly bone-dry lips. "I'm done acting too."

Nick says nothing and for a terrifying, indecipherable length of time, I'm sure I waited too long. As he scans my face, searching for something, I fall deeper and deeper into a spiral of self-loathing and regret.

And then whatever he's looking for, he finds it.

Full mouth morphing into a devastating smile, Nick's entire face brightens, and it's like the sun comes out. "C'mere, *querida*."

Something akin to a relieved sob escapes me as I launch myself at him. He catches me easily, hoisting up and wrapping my legs around his waist, a supporting arm banded under my ass. His other hand buries itself in my hair, palming the crown of my head as he dips to capture my lips with his. If I wasn't perched in his grip, I'd sink to the floor, every ounce of tension seeping out of me the moment he kisses me.

Home, I realize. That's what kissing Nick feels like. Safety and peace and home.

He mumbles something against my lips, not in a language I understand but I don't think he even realizes, too lost in whatever's going on in his head. I get it; when his tongue tangles with mine, it's hard to think of anything else.

When Nick pulls away, I whine in contempt, the noise soothed by another chaste peck before he deprives me again. "We should talk."

I stifle a groan but don't quite manage to hide the distasteful crinkle of my nose. "Probably."

Nick's eyes dart around my face, taking in every detail before settling on my lips, a groan tearing from between his. "Fuck it."

The words have barely been spoken before he's descending on me once again, torturing me with a desperate kiss, full of angst and pent-up emotion and so much damn frustration. Nipping at my bottom lip, he coaxes a moan out of me that has the hand on my ass squeezing tighter.

Fingers toy with the hem of my borrowed t-shirt and all it takes is a jerky nod from me before the fabric is gone, yanked over my head and tossed aside, leaving me bare from the waist up. There's something powerful about watching a confident man suddenly be reduced to a horny teenage boy, and there's something hilarious about that happening all because of a pair of naked tits. Nick greedily soaks up the sight of my bare chest, knuckles grazing over each breast until my nipples salute him. Groaning, he casts being gentle aside and palms me with zero hesitation, kneading my tits until my thighs clench around him in a useless attempt to mute the throbbing between my thighs.

Nick's rough touch and the downright feral glint in his eye is so sweetly contrasted by the gentle way he deposits me on his bed, his gaze never leaving mine as he straightens, steps back, simply looks at me. "What do you want, *querida*?"

"You." Folding my legs beneath me, I rise up on my knees. "All of you."

That's all the permission he needs.

Rapt, I watch as Nick slowly sheds his loose black shirt so we're both bare-chested before unbuttoning his jeans and shoving them down, and I all but lick my lips at the strip show. Ordinarily, I'd visually explore his tattooed chest, studying each and every image meticulously inked on golden skin. Tonight, though, the impressive bulge taunting me behind plain black boxer-briefs holds, and deserves, all my attention.

An impatient whine catches in my throat as Nick approaches too slowly, kisses me too slowly, joins me on the bed and scoots us upward until my head hits a pillow too slowly. I hiss when he kisses down my neck and along my chest, taking his sweet time nipping at my sensitive skin. It's leisurely, the way his lips linger on my chest so he can freshen the fading marks there and it's purposeful, how his fingers join the party and pinch my nipples into peaks. When I moan his name, he shushes me gently, hot breath skating over my skin in the most maddening way. Gazing up at me through hooded eyes, he sucks a nipple between his lips, tongue lashing the aching peak while fingers tweak the neglected one, his hands and mouth working in tandem until I'm a writhing, panting, *dripping* mess begging for more.

He's barely even touching me and I'm already teetering dangerously close to the edge.

Somehow, despite the lack of breath in my lungs, I manage to choke out, "*Please.*"

Nick hums and the vibration shoots through me, sends me arching off the bed, my hands grappling for purchase in his thick hair. I use my grip to drag him upward, kissing him hard enough to steal his breath, see how he likes it for a change. I do my own roaming, trailing a hand over stomach muscles that tense beneath my touch, inching toward the underwear I desperately need to be gone. When I palm him over the thin material, his breathy groan tickles my cheek, satisfaction warming my chest when his erection twitches under my attention."Please," I repeat."I need you now."

If I knew before that four simple words could bring a man to his knees, I would've used them far more often.

With a flick of his hand, his underwear is gone. Mine isn't far behind, dragged down my legs hurriedly as Nick rises, strong thighs straining as he rests back on his feet but as miraculous as they are, they don't hold my attention.

No, that would be the rock-hard, thick cock the size of my fucking forearm hanging between them.

I've seen Nick in all his naked glory before. I know that he's packing, the same way I know my fingers don't meet when I wrap them around his dick, nor can my mouth take all of him without some serious struggle. All of this, I already know.

But when I learned all of that, I was never worrying about whether or not it would fit inside my vagina. Now, as I marvel at the fucking weapon fisted in Nick's hand, I am very fucking worried. I am a woman of science. Scientifically speaking, anatomically speaking, this isn't going to work. *That* is not going to fit inside me. Not without hurting like a motherfucker, surely.

"Stop looking at me like that," Nick growls, slowly stroking his cock, eyes practically glowing as they focus on the bare apex of my thighs.

"Like what?" I stutter as he spreads my legs, fingers caressing my skin reverently.

An unmistakably cocky aura floats around him. "Like I'm about to break you in half."

A nervous titter escapes me because that's exactly what I feel like is about to happen. Nick's demeanor softens, the playful arrogance melting away as he plants a hand on either side of my head and hovers over me. "Do you wanna stop?"

I start to shake my head, catching myself when he tuts and verbalizing the thought, "No."

"If I hurt you, tell me and I'll stop, okay?"

When I whisper my agreement, he kisses me gently.

A split second. That's all he allows me before the amorous, sex god Nicolas Silva I've heard countless rumors about rears his pretty head, and I am ruined.

∾

Something wicked twists Nick's features in a terrifying yet endearing and most definitely attractive way and I just know; I'm so fucking in for it.

"I promise, *querida*," he hums against my neck as he begins a downward journey, his breath scorching against my stomach as he continues, "I'll make it so good for you. Been waiting too long not to."

Propping myself up on weak elbows, I watch with bated breath as his tongue lashes, his teeth scrape, his lips suck. Right as he gets exactly where I want him, where I need him, he pauses. "You already wet for me, Amelia?" I don't have to answer; he finds out himself, an almost pained noise ripping from him. "Course you are." He kisses the inside of my thigh. "Always so wet for me."

Nick doesn't make me beg again. He wastes no more time, pushing two fingers inside of me and plucking every intelligible thought from my head as he crooks them just right. At the same time, his lips lock around my clit, sucking with a ferocity that matches the movements of his hand, and *Jesus fucking Christ, I think I'm going to die.*

When a third finger breaches me, rubbing against the sensitive patch inside me that has me gasping for breath and my legs shaking uncontrollably, my head drops back, my eyes screwing shut. I need to block at least one stimulant before I fucking explode—the relentless sight of him is too much for me to handle.

Nick disagrees.

A hand wraps around my throat and yanks my head upward, grip tight enough that I couldn't escape if I wanted to, ensuring I have a perfect view of everything he's doing to me. And if his silent command to watch wasn't clear enough, he all but growls, "Eyes on me, *querida*."

It might be the words, it might be the quick, tight circles his tongue draws around my clit, but regardless of the cause, I shatter. An utterly ruining orgasm tears through me, a silent scream aching in my throat, and the sensation is made all the richer by the fact Nick never shifts his gaze from mine.

A minute, maybe two, passes before he finally allows my body to collapse like it desperately wants to, and he only does so because he finds a better use for his hand. With a bruising grip on my ass cheeks, he lifts me closer to his mouth, giving himself better access and driving me to the brink again before I've recovered from the last fall. My nails dig into his scalp as he keeps going and going and going, offering me release after sweet release, pausing only to whisper how perfect I am, how good I am, asking for more and taking it until I beg him to stop.

I draw in a shaky, quivering breath when he finally relents, kissing his way back up my body, and I watch in a daze as he licks his glossy lips clean, the corners quirked devilishly.

That wasn't even the main event and I'm exhausted yet somehow, I power through. Call it horny determination, or being dick-notized. I push at him until he lifts off me slightly, balancing on one elbow as I stretch toward the bedside table, wrenching open the drawer I suspect houses condoms, and rightfully so. With shaky hands, I pass one to Nick, and I can't tell if it's comforting or petrifying that he's shaking too as he rips open the condom and sheathes himself quickly. "Are you sure?"

"Yes." Honestly, I don't think I've ever been more sure about anything in my life than I am about this. About him.

Powerful bravada abruptly vanishing, Nick drops his forehead to mine, his voice full of hesitant hope that makes my heart surge. "This is it, okay? No more rules. No more secrets. No going back."

I arch to brush our lips together, hating myself for ever giving him a reason to doubt. "I know."

Nick adjusts himself, the blunt way his cock nudges my entrance so wildly contrasting to the reverent way he cups the slope of my neck. "Mine?"

Wrapping my legs around his hips and my arms around his neck, I urge him closer, and we gasp in unison when he slips inside me ever so slightly. "Yours."

It's a testament to his restraint, how slowly he enters me. Agonizing slowly, to the point where I can't tell if the tingling pain stems from the overwhelming stretch of my pussy trying to accomadate his fucking giant cock or if it's an intense ache for more.

Gritting my teeth, I dig my heels into his lower back, and we moan together when he finally fills me completely.

"Fuck." His head drops to the crook of my neck, his lips brushing my collarbone. "Fucking ruined me, beautiful girl."

Sweet words and a couple of slow, testing thrusts are the gentle introduction to what I can only describe as blissfully brutal. Nick pounds into me, every thrust relentless and powerful and reaching deeper than I knew possible, hitting unexplored fucking territory. Bowing off the bed, I close the miniscule distance between us, my nipples grazing his chest and creating more stimulation than I can handle.

I've never been a particularly noisy lover. The occasional moan and whimper, sure. But screaming and crying and cursing like I'm doing now? No, that's brand new and reserved solely for Nick.

I'm fucking *loud*, as loud as the headboard banging against the wall, as loud as the dirty, sloppy sound of Nick slamming into me relentlessly. It's all too loud but when I turn my head to muffle at least one of the obscene noises we're creating in a pillow, the hand on my neck yanks me straight again. "Don't you dare."

Strangled words leave me with a sob, "Someone could hear us."

"I don't give a fuck. Let them hear. Want everyone in this house to know how good I fuck my girl."

"Oh, *God*."

"*Boa menina*." Quicker and quicker he trusts, louder and louder I get, and when a calloused thumb rubs my clit punishingly, I'm a goner. "You gonna come for me, *querida*?"

I am. I do. Downright violently, thrashing beneath him like a wild animal. My pussy squeezing and spasming around Nick brings him to his own release and the force of him coming sparks a whole new round of tremors within me, leaving the two of us breathless, groaning, destroyed messes.

Breathing heavily, Nick collapses on top of me, trying to catch his weight so he doesn't crush me completely but I don't let him. I like him crushing me. I like being smothered by his heat and surrounded by the smell of him.

I like feeling safe.

38

AMELIA

I DIDN'T MEAN to fall asleep.

I fully planned on getting dressed and sneaking out long before anyone else in the house woke up. Although I meant it when I agreed to no more sneaking around, I really, *really* don't think the greatest way for Cass to find out about my new relationship is by walking in on me naked in his best friend's bed. Especially taking into consideration what I undoubtedly look like right now; the phrase *thoroughly fucked* comes to mind.

I learned very quickly that Nicolas Silva does not do just one round —all of ten minutes passed before he was inside me again, hands gripping my hips hard enough to bruise while I bounced on his lap. After round three, I assumed he was done but I made the mistake of joking about him having great stamina for an old man. Next thing I knew, I was face down, ass up, my hair bundled in his fist while he slammed into me from behind. Only when the party downstairs wound down, the music muffling our antics coming to a halt, did the sex stop.

The touching and the kissing did not.

The hickeys on my chest aren't alone anymore; they have friends scattered across my collarbones, my stomach, trailing over my hips to the inside of my thighs. I can't say for sure but there's a high probability that there's a few dispersed across my back and shoulders too. I think there's even one on my ass. The part of me that isn't reveling in the sick pleasure his little marks are evoking is kind of concerned about blood clots.

It's safe to say we tempted fate last night. We loudly threw caution to the wind. When his head was between my thighs for the umpteenth time, somewhere in the back of my sex-addled mind, I acknowledged that we were pushing it. I decided that no matter how much I wanted to, no matter how late—or, more accurately, how *early*—it was, I couldn't stay over.

So, when I wake up to the sound of voices in the hallway and the smell of bacon sizzling, I panic. "Shit." Squinting against the bright morning sunlight, I grab my phone and swear again when I see the time. 2PM. "*Shit.*"

As fast as my aching body will allow, I wriggle out of Nick's grasp and roll out of bed. The naked man who fell asleep half on top of me after promising he wouldn't stirs with a groan but I ignore him, too focused on gathering my clothes strewn across the floor while simultaneously coming up with a plan on how the hell I'm getting out of here without being seen. Considering I can barely move without the dull throb between my thighs summoning a hiss, my options are severely limited.

A sleepy, sarcastic chuckle freezes me in place. "One night. You lasted one night."

Spinning around, I find Nick watching me with narrowed eyes, expression rife with disappointment. Disappointed but not surprised, and my heart aches at the realization that, on some level, he was expecting me to flee. And I am, technically, living up to that expectation but not the way he thinks.

"I'm not running," I insist in a low voice, paranoid despite the voices in the hallway having moved downstairs. A frustrated groan leaves me when Nick's expression remains unconvinced. "*I swear*, I'm not running."

To prove my point, I stop the frantic clothes retrieval and leap back into bed, crawling until I've hovering over Nick, knees planted on either side of his hips. "I. Am. Not. Running." I punctuate each word with a chaste kiss, drawing out a smile. "But if Cass finds me here looking like *this*, I don't think either of us will leave this house alive."

Hands grip my bare hips before I can move away, keeping me in place and pulling until my naked chest crashes against. Nose brushing mine, his hands inch up my thighs, golden eyes aflame. "What a way to go, hm?"

"Don't even think about it." Despite the aroused shiver tickling my spine, I slap his wandering paws away, pinning him with a warning look that hopefully conveys the fact my vagina is off limits for two to three business days while it recovers from the damage done last night.

The smug smile Nick tries and fails to pass off as innocent confirms my message was read loud and clear. Palm stroking up the length of my spine, he applies pressure to my shoulder blades until I'm almost horizontal atop him, until it's as easy as a flex of his neck for him to kiss me softly. "Stay."

When I try to argue, he kisses me again, harder this time, only retreating when I'm limp in his grasp. "He's already awake, *querida*. There's no way you're getting out of here without being seen. Unless you wanna risk your brother asking why you're limping out of here, stay."

Nick is right, obviously, but I scowl anyway, resenting the proud smirk lighting up his face as much as I find it attractive. *Cocky bastard.*

Smoothing out my furrowed brow with his thumb, his smirk softens to a smile. "Stay," he repeats for a third time. "Please."

God, I've really got to work on strengthening my resolve because if it keeps melting the moment this man utters a plea, I'm in so much trouble.

Sighing dramatically, I sink into his chest, pressing a kiss to the ink etched on his collarbone. "Fine," I relent with more despondency than I actually feel. "Only if you smuggle some food in here because I'm starving." Endless rounds of sex really takes it out of a girl; I think I burnt more calories last night than I have in any workout ever.

Nuzzling the top of my head, Nick snickers. "I can think of something much better to eat."

Jesus Christ, this man is insatiable. Rolling from his grasp—he must believe I'm not going to bolt before he lets me, albeit reluctantly—I flop onto my front beside him. "Get your mind out of the gutter, Silva."

"Don't ask impossible things of me, Hanlon," is his quipped retort. As though going a moment without touching me is simply incomprehensible, Nick strokes my back again, and something akin to a purr rumbles in my chest as he absently draws shapes. Vaguely, somewhere in the back of my exhausted mind, I register that they're not so random;

he's connecting my freckles like they're constellations to be charted. "You going back to sleep?"

I hum sleepily in reply, my eyes already closed.

A quiet chuckle washes over me and when I crack an eye, Nick's right there in front of me, suspiciously solemn. Tucking a strand of hair behind my ear, he offers a nervous smile. "I meant it, okay?" *No more rules. No more secrets. No going back.* "I'm all in."

All in.

Two words with so much meaning.

"Nicolas Silva," I drawl through a tempered yawn, "are you asking me to be your girlfriend?"

Golden eyes flash and my heart skips. "I'm not asking."

I laugh and Nick swallows the noise, kissing me leisurely like he has all the time in the world and as we lie there, limbs tangled and breath shared, I feel something I haven't genuinely, completely felt in a long time.

I'm happy.

～

Hot, thick steam floods the bathroom as gentle hands carefully work the knots out of my hair. Nick really did a number on my curls last night; I did a double take when I spotted myself in the mirror, horrified at the mess atop my head. Luckily, he was more than willing to fix the damage he caused, and I wasn't going to say no to a free head massage.

I almost burst into tears again when he cracked into the stash of toiletries beneath his sink, and I'm still stifling them as the scent of products he bought solely for me surrounds us.

"I love your hair," Nick murmurs so quietly I almost don't hear him over the din of hot water pelting down on us. "That was the first thing I noticed about you."

I say nothing, too entranced by the way he's stroking my scalp softly, lulling me into an almost dream-like state despite the fact I've slept most of the day away.

"It was longer then." A hand travels from my head to the slope of my waist and back up to my collarbone, where he presses a kiss. "I like it short."

So do I. Dylan didn't; anywhere close to my shoulders and he said I looked too 'manly,' according to him. When I cut it to my collarbones at the end of last semester, he threw an Oscar-award winning tantrum.

Dipshit.

Pushing my ex from my mind and focusing on the wonderful man behind me, I tilt my chin so he can see my raised brows. "Exactly when was that?"

I don't expect him to really answer; I anticipate an eye roll and a sarcastic comment. So when he utters the following words, it's enough to jolt me back to full consciousness. "July, I think."

"*July?*" Months before we met. Eyes wide, I gape at him, mind reeling trying to figure out how he noticed me yet, before he opened his big mouth, I never noticed him.

Hands snaking around my waist to rest on my stomach, Nick drops his head to my shoulder, his soft smile palpable against my skin. "I was at Greenies with Jackson. You were working. He was drooling over Luna and I couldn't keep my eyes off the little redhead cursing out the old man who kept trying to cop a feel."

My barked laugh drowns out the roar of the shower. "I remember that day."

"I'm sure *he* does too. You poured hot coffee in his lap."

Damn right, I did; the old creep pinched my ass. My outburst earned me a month of the dreaded weekend shift but it was so worth it.

With his confession, everything falls into place. Everything suddenly makes sense. His slightly panicked reaction when he found out who I was, what I meant to Cass, and why Cass was a little weird. How he knew how I take my coffee. All the little quips and jokes Ben consistently makes but I never quite get.

With a smirk that rivals Nick's infamous one, I turn in his arms, looping mine around his neck. "You've been pining for me."

Now, I get the eyeroll I was expecting before. "No."

Shrugging me off, Nick shuts off the water and steps out of the shower. I shiver immediately at the loss of heat, both from the running water and the human radiator of a man, but I'm not cold for long; Nick tugs me after him, engulfing me in a large, fluffy towel. "Oh, come on! Admit it!"

Ignoring me, Nick wraps a towel around his waist and heads for the bedroom. I move to follow him but my reflection in the slightly foggy mirror catches my eye. Downright startles me, actually.

I can't get over how utterly content I look. Bright eyes, skin glowing, an embarrassingly wide smile. Somehow, despite the dark circles underneath my eyes from lack of sleep and the dripping wet messy hair, I look better than I have in months. More alive. *Why the hell did I try to run from this man again?*

The bruises peppering my skin catch my eye too, and it astounds me how different they make me feel compared to the bruises I had the last time I was here. Those ones stemmed from anger and jealousy and bitterness.

These ones are the opposite. These ones only remind me of a man who makes me feel safe and comfortable and....

Loved.

What a terrifying concept.

Smiling like a fool, I practically skip back into Nick's bedroom. "You know," I lower my voice now we're not shielded by the sound of the shower, eyeing him greedily as he tugs underwear up thick thighs, "if you'd spoken to me instead of stalking me, maybe I would've been pining too."

A grunt and clothes being chucked in my face is the only response I get.

Snickering to myself, I dry off and dress. I'm using a spare t-shirt to dry my hair when a loud exhale sounds.

"Fine," Nick admits, husky and sweet and worthy of all the affection he lavishes me with. "I was pining a little."

39

AMELIA

"You brought booze to a baseball game?"

Luna pauses her not-so-stealthy uncapping of her hilariously bejeweled flask to shoot Nick a glare. I avert my gaze, propping the straw of my drink between my lips innocently and hoping I added enough orange soda to mask the smell of alcohol.

Nick's suspicious stare swings my way, eyes narrowed as he snatches the to-go cup from my hand, cracks the lid, and sniffs. "Vodka, *querida*? Really? It's barely the afternoon."

Neither Luna nor I mention that we've been sneakily necking shots since 10AM. Purely a self-preservation tactic, of course—it's harder to be cold and bored with vodka coursing your bloodstream.

"I'm sorry," Luna snorts, "are we getting morality lessons from *Nicolas Silva?*"

Snickering, I grab my drink, patting Nick's thigh and taking a long gulp out of teasing spite. "Five o'clock somewhere, baby."

The 'barely afternoon' light dances in his eyes as he pretends to scowl at me, tugging on my ponytail playfully. His fingers linger on the nape of my neck a second longer than can be considered friendly before dropping, and I wish I could say my shivering was from the slight chill in the air but I'd be lying.

"Do you know how *long* these games are, Nick?" Luna chimes in again, swishing her drink to mix the cola she bought from one of the concession stands with her smuggled-in vodka. "Perky asses can only entertain a girl for so long."

"Here, here." I clink my drink against hers in a cheer, snickering again when Nick side-eyes me with a warning glare.

I'm kidding—mostly—but Luna is right; baseball games are long, and today is no ordinary game. It's a pre-season exhibition game, a chance for competing teams to size each other up but they slap a fundraiser on top of it to quell any unsportsmanlike behavior.

If I'm being totally honest, I have no idea what they're fundraising for. I'm here for Cass, hence why I've got his name slapped on my back, one of his team hoodies keeping me warm. Luna's donned one of Jackson's, while the both of us wear caps detailed with Ben's jersey number. I want to support this odd little family we've created, and I definitely don't want to give my brother a heart attack, hence why I gently shuck Nick off with a meaningful look before anyone clocks the possessive touch.

Luna might be drinking to pass the time but I'm drinking to soothe my trembling nerves. Because tonight, come hell or highwater, I am introducing Cass to my boyfriend. Or, more accurately, I'm re-introducing his best friend to him as my boyfriend.

The last few weeks with Nick have been, at the risk of sounding like a corny fool, something damn close to perfect. Like an invisible wall between us crumbled, I stopped second-guessing every move, every word—I stopped doubting him and myself. But it's all tainted by the fact Cass still doesn't know.

I swear on my life, I really have tried to tell him. Countless times I've worked up the nerve but something always interrupts us. A last minute practice, a phone call, an oblivious roommate bursting into the room. The fifth time Ben ruined my painstakingly prepared speech, I almost throttled the kid.

Nick's being a saint about it. As wonderful, understanding a saint as he is a boyfriend. None of the guilt I feel about harboring a secret I promised I wouldn't stems from him, it's all of my own making. He gets that I want to do it right and not drop a bomb on him randomly. That's not to say he likes it because he doesn't, not one bit, and he reaffirms that knowledge when he pouts like a big baby at being told to keep his hands to himself.

Tonight, though, I'm going to tell him. Win or lose, come hell or highwater, I'm going to confess. And because it's tradition around here to hit up Greenies after a game, my shining solace is that celebration or commiseration, Cass will be nice and liquored up, and I will be too.

"Hey, can you see them?" I have to yell at Luna to be heard over the noise around us; Sun Valley's only stadium is buzzing with people, not an empty seat in sight, what sounds like a million voices melding together to create a loud, unrelenting hum.

Eagerly searching the field for our boys, it takes a moment until we find a cloister of familiar looking figures. Gaze catching on the player with the number six etched on his back, I instantly grin. Alcohol making me brave, I hook my fingers in my mouth and whistle loud in the way he taught me. Cass' head snaps to me in an instant, a matching grin already on his face like he was waiting for me, like he knows exactly what I'm about to do.

Making a fist, I gently tap it against my cheek twice in a punching motion before extending my pointer finger toward him. Even from a good distance away, I see his expression soften as he repeats the motion back to me. Our little pre-game ritual.

Knock 'em out.

"That was cute," an accented voice croons in my ear the moment a whistle blows and Cass' attention is drawn elsewhere. Rolling my eyes, I shift to ask Nick if he's really mocking a sacred childhood custom but when my gaze snags on something over his shoulder, my lips clamp shut and settle in a grimace.

When me and Luna first sat down clad in gear representing our guys, there was a very distinctly negative murmuring aimed in our direction that definitely came from the haggle of jersey chasers lingering nearby. Clearly, if the nasty looks they keep shooting us are anything to go by, they think we're encroaching on their territory and I strongly believe that if not for the glorified bodyguard pasted to my side, the over-whelming stench of Victoria's Secret body mist wouldn't be the only thing choking us.

But while Nick's presence might be the only thing preventing a catty brawl over men I have no interest in, when I recognize one of the girls eyeing us up downright viciously, I wish he'd spontaneously evaporate.

God, I really should remember the name of the girl who wants to bang my boyfriend, huh? It would be better if, when cursing her out in my head for smirking at my boyfriend like she's seen him naked—which she has—I could refer to her as something other than *bitch*.

"Ignore them." Nick's mouth says *them* but the hint of awkward, unnecessary guilt in his tone screams *her*; he knows exactly who's got me all riled up.

Huffing, I refocus my glare on Nick and utter the understatement of the year. "I don't like her."

The little bastard chuckles, white teeth gleaming as he grins. "You're jealous."

"You," I poke a rock-hard pectoral muscle, "are not allowed to mock, Mr. *I Want To Punch People For Looking At You*. Look at how *she's* looking at *you!*"

I'm being a freak, I'm well aware, but the words simply refuse to be swallowed. Hell, it's taking enough effort to keep my voice at a low whisper instead of an indignant yell. I blame the vodka, which is also urging me to plant a big, smacking kiss on Nick and stake my freaking claim despite what a terrible idea I know that is.

Bad vodka.

Knuckles brushing my cheek as he tucks a wayward curl behind my ear, Nick turns my own words back on me. "I can't control how she looks at me, Amelia."

Touché, motherfucker.

Brazen now the game has begun and is occupying most people's attention, Nick's touch lingers, his thumb brushing the hollow of my throat. "Do I need to prove how pointless your jealousy is?"

It's borderline embarrassing, how goddamn tempted I am to yelp a 'yes, sir' and drag him to his truck for a quickie but before I can break like the weak, horny woman I am, a throat clears loudly beside us. "Rein in the horny, guys," Luna scolds, but her smirk is far from chastising, "unless you want a baseball bat to the skull."

Nick and I spring apart—I don't know when we became so close, practically nose to nose. *Oops.*

In hindsight, getting smashed before divulging a potentially relationship-ruining secret was probably not the best idea. It's a shame that only dawns on me once I'm past the point of no return.

Honestly, I was at that point for, like, three hours. I forgot how hyped baseball games got me, and I forgot how damn good Cass is; no wonder he's such a freaking hotshot around campus. Just as inebriated and exhilarated, Luna battled me for the title of loudest supporter as we cheered for our guys and heckled the shit out of the other team, all the while sucking down spiked sodas. At one point, when we reached the height of our rowdiness, Nick actually moved to sit between us, a hand clamped on each of our shoulders to stop us from clambering atop the seats to really amplify our taunts.

It was all fun and games until the sporting portion of the day came to an end and the horde moved to Greenies, and the reality that I needed to be eloquent and careful when telling Cass about Nick, not slurring and stumbling, set in.

There have been few times in my life where I've been grateful for the grease-riddled food Greenies provides, and this is one of those times; it's prime alcohol-soakage. I polish off a burger and fries in record time, pinching some of Nick's too when I think he's not looking. *Think* being the operative word. Nick shoots some serious side-eye my way, the arm slung around the back of my seat shifting to tap my shoulder, but he doesn't stop me, and if we didn't have an audience, I'd kiss him for it.

Although, we don't really have an audience. The others were crushed in the booth with us but they've gone their separate ways, leaving the two of us tucked in the corner alone. I can barely make out Cass in the flurry of admirers crowding around him, so I'd bet he can't see me. So, I suppose there's no harm in shifting an inch closer to Nick, leaning into his side, craning my neck to kiss his.

Way less preoccupied about being caught than I am, Nick yanks me even closer, a groaned laugh brushing the top of my head. "God, how much did you drink? You reek of booze."

"Relax, old man." I wriggle upright, his skin warm beneath my fingertips as I pinch his cheek. "Let the youth have fun."

"So mouthy when you're drunk, *meu amor*."

If I was sober, the new term of endearment would undoubtedly send me into a spiral. But I'm not; I'm drunk and I want to kiss my boyfriend but I can't, and when I suddenly spot the reason why, I jump to my feet and clamber over Nick's lap, muttering that I'll be right back and yelping when a parting slap stings my ass.

Suck it up, I silently command myself as I follow Cass outside to the smoking area, cornering him before another adoring fan can. "There you are," he slurs when he spots me, face lit up with a smile. Chucking an arm around my shoulders, he gives me a shake, and consequently causes the pint of beer in his hand to slosh down his arm. He doesn't notice; it appears he's trying to catch up with me and Luna. "My good luck charm."

Slapping his chest, I force an eye roll. "Oh, please. You're that good all by yourself."

"True," he admits cockily with a dramatic shrug, quickly reverting into sweet big brother mode, "but it's still nice to have you back."

Oh, hell.

I steel myself against the nerves and guilt whirling around in my gut; I can't lose my nerve again. I need to tell him now or I fear it'll start feeling like I never will.

Shucking him off, I poise my confession to escape, but in true fashion for whenever I try to freaking speak, someone else beats me to it. "I have a question," Cass drones, and something about his thoughtful, slightly suspicious expression makes me sweat.

I fidget under his gaze, or maybe as a result of the oddly accusatory note in his tone. "Shoot."

"You and Nick both disappeared on New Year."

Oh, he so fucking knows. Or suspects, at least. I'm hoping for the latter because at least that'll cushion the blow a little, right? "I don't hear a question."

Cass crooks a brow as if it's obvious. "Where were you?"

"In his room." *Truth.* "Talking." *Half-truth.* A justified half-truth because I doubt 'we were fucking like rabbits' would go down well.

Cass leans toward me in a way I'm sure is meant to be mildly intimidating in a brotherly interrogation kind of way but really, it results in him spilling beer down himself again. "Just talking?"

"Yes." The bold-faced lie tastes acrid but I can tell him we're dating without divulging the more intimate details. "I was too drunk and a little upset and Nick took care of me." *Three truths to counteract the lie.*

As he scrutinizes me, as I become more and more sure he sees right through my minor deception, I'm about to add one more truth, the most important one, to the list.

And then Cass opens his mouth and my stomach hits the ground.

"Thank God." He drops his head as a booming, relieved laugh leaves him. "Thought I was gonna have to kill him."

"That's a little dramatic." I steal his beer, sucking down a hearty sip to clear the lump in my throat, the bitter liquid emboldening me enough to play a dangerous game. "Would it really be that bad?"

Another laugh, painfully sarcastic this time. "Yeah, Amelia, it would be *that bad*. He's my best friend and I love the guy but I know how he treats women," I cringe, "and I'm not letting him do that to you."

He's different with me, I want to say but true as that may be, it's a foolishly cliché, naive thing to say that would only make Cass more resistant. "I'm a big girl, Cass," I claim instead. "I can handle myself."

"I'm not saying you can't." Cass sighs. "Listen, I know he had this weird crush on you before he knew who you were but it's different now. He knows you're my sister and that crossing that line is not okay. He wouldn't do that."

"Yeah." I laugh despite the pit in my stomach. "You're right."

40

NICK

SHE DIDN'T TELL HIM.

For the hundredth time, she didn't tell him. It's been two weeks of broken promises and desperate excuses and I get it, I really do get it, but that doesn't mean I'm not fucking *tired* of it.

Silence fills my truck, the tension between us damn near suffocating, and I sigh knowing I'm the one who has to break it. The conversation with Cass rattled her, I can tell in the way she's chewing her bottom lip hard enough to draw blood. "You're freaking out over nothing."

Amelia gapes at me in disbelief. "*Nothing*? Did you not hear me? He said he would *kill* you."

"He was drunk, *querida*, and being dramatic." *Must run in the family*, I quip silently. "Do you even want to tell him?"

"Of course, I do," she answers without hesitation.

"It doesn't seem like it."

A soft, sad noise escapes Amelia, a whisper of a sound yet it breaks my heart anyway.

Body tense with the effort of keeping my gaze straight ahead, I ignore my mind screaming at me, begging me, to look at her. I can't look at her because if I look at her, I'll touch her, and when I touch her I can't think straight, let alone articulate meaningful words. Despite my frustration, I work to keep my tone even because I don't want to yell at her, I don't want to chastise like a dick when she's trying her best, I just need to vent. "I can't even kiss my girlfriend in public, Amelia. I can't even kiss you in front of *our friends*. That's not normal."

"I know." Her voice is little more than a shaky whisper. "I..." Slender throat bobbing in a harsh swallow, she dips her head. "I just got him back, Nick. I can't lose him again so quickly."

Soft as they are, her words hit me like a train. A thought that's been eating away at me right from the beginning, one that I shoved to the back of my mind because my head aches even considering it, rushes to the forefront.

When, *if*, she tells him, and if he makes her choose, I'm never going to be her first choice. Or his. She doesn't see that if this whole thing goes to shit—I hope to fuck it doesn't—I'm the one losing everything. Not her.

Dropping my forehead to the steering wheel, I shut my eyes and force a few deep breaths in the hopes that'll clear the throbbing ache in my chest and behind my temples.

"I'm sorry." A dainty hand lands on my back as lips brush my cheek. Finally giving in because it's too fucking hard not to, I tilt my head and latch onto the wide eyes blinking at me worriedly. "I don't want you to lose him either."

Sighing, I smooth out her scrunched nose with my thumb, tracing the bottom lip she's gnawed raw. "I told you I don't want to sneak around anymore."

"I heard you. Nick, I promise I *will* tell him. Tonight just threw me a little."

I want to believe her. Fuck, I want to believe her so much. And I do but I don't because as convincing as the resolute glint in her green gaze is, her track record is working against her. I trust her but I'm not sure I trust her reasoning behind staying quiet. I want her but I don't want this half-assed arrangement we have, and if I need to do something slightly drastic to hammer that fact home, I will.

In one smooth movement, I sit back and lift Amelia onto my lap, a squeal escaping her as her thighs settle on either side of mine. She inhales sharply when I dip beneath her hoodie, stroking her bare skin until it's pebbled with goosebumps. My other hand drifts down to cup her ass, the material of her leggings soft against my palm. "Do you know how fucking hard it is to keep my hands off you? To watch other guys flirt with you, *touch you*, when I can't?"

"No one was-" I cut her off with a harsh laugh. God, she's so fucking oblivious sometimes; half the baseball team, half the damn diner, was chasing after her tonight. Trying to make her laugh, offering to buy her drinks, 'accidentally' rubbing up against her. Fuck me, I almost shattered the beer in my hand half a dozen times, I was gripping it so hard trying to stop myself from doing something I'd regret.

Or, more likely, from doing something Amelia would yell at me for.

Lips brushing her neck, I greedily breath in the heady scent of coconut, tongue darting out to trace her pulse. "You think you're the only one who gets jealous?"

Amelia hums a non-response, too busy watching as I breach the waistband of her pants, slipping a hand in her panties and wasting no time dragging a thumb over the bundle of nerves always begging for my attention. Fighting a smirk when her hips begin to writhe, I press harder, tracing circles I know are too slow for her liking. "You want me to touch you, *querida?*"

She moans agreeably, head jerking in a nod, and I kiss my teeth in mock annoyance. "What did we say about words?"

"Please." *Boa menina.*

"Please, what?" I taunt, dragging my teeth along her jaw. Amelia whines, my shirt bunching between her fists as she wriggles closer.

"Please touch me."

I do. Slowly, and it's as painstaking for me as it is for her. As one hand works between her thighs, the other traces each and every inch of her skin I can reach, lingering on the spots I know are stained purple. At my own leisurely pace, I touch the girl who refuses to acknowledge herself as mine until her head drops to my shoulder, her soft moans ringing in my ear. "Nick, *please.*"

As quickly as I tugged her onto my lap, I remove her, swiftly depositing her back onto the passenger seat, clicking her seatbelt into place, and starting the truck before she even registers what's happening. "No."

Out of the corner of my eyes, I see her gaping at me, swollen lips parted in an expression of confusion, surprise, and a whole lot of frustration.

Good.

The ten minute drive back to her place passes in complete silence, charged by pure sexual tension. Only when my truck rolls to a stop outside her place do I finally turn to her, fighting back a grin once again at the sight of her mussed hair and pretty glare.

"What the fuck was that, Nicolas?"

"If I can't touch you in public, I'm not touching you in private." When she scoffs in disbelief, I reach over and grip her chin between my fingers, face as solemn as I'm capable of setting it. "I'm serious, Amelia. If you don't tell him, I'm out. I'm not sneaking around anymore like we're doing something wrong when we're not. You deserve so much fucking more than a quick fuck in a parking lot, *meu amor*, and if you won't let me give you that, then I'm done."

As my speech settles in the air around us, the air becomes stifling again. When bright eyes become watery, a bottom lip wobbling danger-ously, I curse myself internally. For a harrowing moment, I'm convinced I took it too far. And then, Amelia cups my cheek, sliding a thumb along my cheekbone. "For the record," she sniffs, "you deserve more than this too."

So give it to me, querida.

"Glad you think so." Already disregarding the newly introduced rule, I shift to kiss her palm. "According to your brother, I deserve to die alone in a hole."

Her watery laughter fills the truck, as little humor behind it as there is in her subsequent unnecessary apology, "I'm sorry I let him talk about you like that."

"Don't be. I've given him a reason to." God, I knew the no-touching thing would be difficult but I didn't expect to fail so damn quickly; I can't seem to resist tangling my fingers around hers, moving them from my cheek to my lip as I spout the most cliché shit but I need it verbal-ized, "This is different."

And fuck, does something in my chest roll when she confirms with complete confidence, "I know."

I am the first to admit that for someone enforcing a strict ban on physical contact, I am indulging in a fuck-ton of physical contact. In hindsight, it wasn't my greatest idea, announcing a plan born of desperation that I can't exactly go back on; I realized that about thirty seconds after she climbed out of my truck and I was left dithering like a dickhead wondering if I was allowed to follow her upstairs. Logically speaking, no touching equates to no sleepovers, and an internal dilemma began as I tried to recall the last time I slept by myself, let alone in my own bed.

Luckily, our relationship does not revolve around logic. It's unclear whether Amelia took pity on me or whether she simply wasn't too fond of sleeping alone either but when she beckoned me after her, I followed like a lovesick puppy. And I'm pretty sure that's what I am.

Lovesick.

I'm not an expert on the matter, God knows that, but if I had to put a name to the goddamn warm, fuzzy feeling constantly plaguing me, I'd call it love.

I almost told her when we crawled into bed last night. And again when she got up for class this morning, a pathetic whine leaving me as she wriggled from my grasp, the confession poised to be used as a bribe to stay. And when I was roused a couple of hours later as she crept between the sheets again, her freezing cold skin jerking me awake, I was so fucking close to whispering it in her ear as I lazily rolled on top of her, lending her my body warmth and drifting off again.

The three little words are once again perched on the tip of my tongue as I doze on the girl I—*fuck it*—love, as she combs gently through my hair, her voice a low murmur as to not disturb as she talks into her phone.

Kissing the chest I'm sleepily nuzzling, I shift so my lips can graze the slender throat vibrating with words I'm not yet awake enough to decipher. Fingers dig into my scalp, pulling slightly to stop my antics.

"Dad," I hear that boner-killing word loud and fucking clear, "gimme two minutes, okay?"

Waiting until she clicks the call on hold and carefully sets her phone aside, I groan and drop my forehead to her collarbone. "There's something very wrong about you being on the phone to your father while I'm on top of you."

"I figured the alleged lack of touching would keep things PG." Amelia smoothes my hair back from my face, laughing and speaking softly as though she's paranoid her dad might somehow hear. "I didn't think you'd be so shit at your own rule."

"I'm amending it," I grumble. "No coming."

Using her grip on my hair, Amelia wrenches my head backward and arches a brow. "If I don't get to come, neither do you."

"It'll be worth it when you tell Cass and I can fuck the life out of you without feeling like a criminal."

Freckled cheeks tint pink—exactly what I was hoping for. I roll off her with a chuckle. "You want me to leave?" I ask when she reaches for her phone again.

Instead of nodding like I expect, Amelia pauses. Her head tilts like she's considering it, tongue darting out to wet the corner of her mouth. And then, like a light bulb goes off in her pretty little head, her face brightens and she practically lunges for her phone. Before I can question her, she's taking her dad off hold and blurting, "I have something to tell you."

What are you doing? I mouth but she waves me off.

"Dad, I have a boyfriend."

Oh, *fuck*.

Choking on a protest, I throw myself at her but she evades, leaping off the bed and scuttling to the opposite side of the room. I stalk after her, a dainty hand on my chest barely keeping me at bay, my hissed complaints going ignored. If I was smart, I would shut the fuck up and try to listen in on her dad's reply but my gut is screaming at me to hang up that damn phone before she blurts out *who* her boyfriend is and I end up with another important man in her life rooting against me.

When Amelia bursts out laughing, I freeze. "How did you know?"

"*Know?*" I wheeze too loudly before I can stop myself. "Know what?"

Amelia slaps at my chest with wide eyes, but the mirth lurking in them goes nowhere. No matter how hard I strain, her dad's garbled voice is too faint to understand. At least that means he's not yelling, I guess.

Silver linings.

"Yeah, he's here now." I shrink away, half-expecting Patrick to crawl through the phone and throttle me, but I'm soothed when my favorite version of Amelia's smile comes out to play, the one that appears when she stops overthinking and actually lets herself be happy. "He is. He's really good to me."

As quickly as it descended, the dread coiled in my gut fucks right off.

I can't help it; I break out smiling like a fool. A lovestruck fool. Amelia keeps talking but I don't hear a word, too busy gazing at her with fucking stars in my eyes.

She told her dad. She fucking told her dad. Her *dad*. One of the most important men in her life knows because *she told him,* and as far as I'm aware, there was no screaming about how I'm not good enough for his little girl.

Not that he'd be wrong about that.

The moment she hangs up, I'm on her. Scooping her up, I tote her back to bed, carefully flopping down with her beneath me and cupping her face with all the reverence in the world. "Why'd you do that?"

It's a rhetorical question, almost. I think I know the answer; this is her way of proving that she's trying. Actions speak louder than words, and all that shit.

"Because I wanted to," she states too simply. "Although, does it really count as telling him if he already knew?" When I frown, she smoothes out the grooves of my forehead. "Our mothers."

I groan—enough said. I should've known that if my mom caught on, Lynn wouldn't be far behind. Judging by Amelia's sunny demeanor, there's some unspoken agreement that it won't get back to Cass until she decides to let it.

41

AMELIA

Today is not my day.

As soon as I woke up, I felt off. All day, there's been an aching weight crushing my chest and making it hard to breathe but I can't for the life of me figure out the source. My brain feels itchy, like I've forgotten something, but whatever it is is a complete mystery to me.

The malfunctioning lungs, the sudden memory loss, both are attributing to a particularly shitty mood, hence why I'm stomping around work like a disgruntled child, a dark cloud of frustration hanging over my head. To make everything even worse, it's Luna's day off; instead of reveling in a good rant with my best friend, I'm stuck throwing my negative energy into wiping down sticky counters and scowling at handsy men. Plus I get the pleasure of spending my shift with the grouchy bartender old enough to be my dad who only speaks to my boobs and the ditzy waitress with the hand-eye coordination of a toddler.

Lucky me.

Only once does my bad mood lift. Right as the dinner rush comes to a blessed halt, my phone dings.

Nick: *My bed smells like you.*

Despite my sour temper, I grin at the message. In a wondrous, well-needed turn of events, Nick's had the house to himself for the last few days; the others have gone on some bonding retreat for baseball so we're taking advantage of his empty house.

Well, not *full* advantage—I still have yet to tell Cass so Nick's inane rule is still in place. But we get to sleep in his much bigger bed for once, and that's definitely a win.

Nick: *It's giving me a hard on.*

Sweet to nasty in a millisecond.

My man.

Before I can reply, a pointed cough draws my attention. Slipping my phone back into my pocket, I paste on a fake smile, readying myself to apologize to whatever customer is undoubtedly about to berate me for daring to use my phone during work.

The smile is overridden by a glare the moment my gaze lands on the woman sitting smugly at the counter, her expensive purse gingerly propped on a counter I suddenly wish I hadn't just scrubbed clean of spilled soda. "What the fuck are you doing here?"

At my deservedly harsh words, Diane's face twists into a disapproving grimace. "Language, darling," she reprimands. "Honestly, I don't know who raised you to be so rude."

I clutch the counter tightly in an effort not to put my handy new fighting skills to use and punch her square in the face. "Certainly not you."

Raising a brow, her upper lip curls in haughty disdain as though it irritates her that I'm sticking up for my father; it's a skill, really, how she's managed to convince herself she's not the villain in our story. She kisses her teeth and flashes a fake smile that rivals mine. "I'll have a coffee, please. Black, three sugars."

Never in my life has it been so hard to pour a cup of damn coffee.

I slam a mug on the counter and fill it with steaming hot liquid, contemplating pouring it in her purse instead—that's better than wanting to chuck it in her face, right?

When I'm done, I step back. I want her to leave. Or, better yet, I want to physically throw her out myself. But fuck, I'm kind of curious too. I want to know why she's here, how she's here, if I wasn't clear enough last time about how much I don't want her in my life or if she's too dense to understand. Settling on the question most prominent, I ask, "How did you find me?"

Diane's mouth twitches in satisfaction as she digs through her purse, fishing out her phone and tapping on the screen. When she turns it my way, my face falls at the sight of a familiar article, recognizing it easily because I witnessed the written words being spoken aloud. I was there when the journalist approached Cass about the article after that exhibition game. I stood beside him, beaming with pride as she piled on the compliments and told us she wanted the inside scoop on the future star player of the MLB.

How the hell *she* got her hands on it, I have no idea; I didn't even know it was out yet.

"Wonderful interview," Diane coos, unwarranted sarcasm dripping like acid. "Sounds like he's a talented man." Studying my reaction, she taps her phone screen again and a photo appears. It's of me and Cass at the game, one that I didn't even know was being taken but I can guess is my boyfriend's handiwork; I didn't see anyone else flitting around the field with a camera. We're tangled up in a hug, him spinning me around, both laughing our asses off, both so damn happy. "He mentioned you a lot. His 'good luck charm'. *Adorable.*"

I didn't think it was possible, but my anger intensifies. I hate that she knows who Cass is. I hate that she used him to find me, that she's using him and something he's so damn proud of as ammunition against me. I *hate* that she thinks she deserves to have an opinion on him. Before I can stop myself, I'm snatching the phone from her hands and dumping it back in her bag. I would've preferred to smash it against a wall, but I don't want to make a scene. Not yet anyways. Shoving her purse into her arms, I demand, "Get out."

Diane taps her nails against the side of her still-full mug. "I'm a customer, Amelia."

I correct her swiftly, "You're a bitch, Diane."

Gone is the smugness, replaced by an enraged sneer, nostrils flaring in a delightfully unladylike move. "I'm your mother."

"No, you're not." God, she really is dense. "My mother is wonderful and kind and did an amazing job raising me, and that sure as shit isn't you."

Diane opens her mouth to argue but clearly thinks better of it.

Pressing her lips together, she relaxes her uptight posture and sighs. "I didn't come here to fight with you. I came to explain."

For the first time since walking through the door, Diane drops the mask and lets some sliver of real emotion break through.

Desperation.

She looks, and sounds, desperate.

My curiosity spikes against my will—what could possibly drive this awful woman to show actual emotion? Sucking in a breath, I nod stiffly, permitting her to carry on.

Perfect nails tap a nervous rhythm on the counter as Diane clears her throat. "I was very young when I had you."

"And I was very young when you fucked off. What's your point?"

"I wasn't prepared to be a mother."

"I wasn't prepared to be motherless."

"Amelia, *please.*" Diane pinches the bridge of her nose in irritation. "I was young and clueless. Your father was always studying or working." I tense automatically at the mention of Dad; ironic how her solution to a supposedly absent husband was becoming a definitely absent wife and mother. "I was lonely. I wasn't ready to be a mother or a wife and I didn't realize until it was too late."

Six years. It was *six years* too late before she realized her life was one big mistake.

When she reaches for my hand, I jerk away, and I swear, something akin to hurt crosses her features. "I'm getting married, darling, and I want you to be there. I want to get to know you."

Remarried, I correct her silently. She's getting *remarried.* Fuck, it's like Dad never existed.

"I don't know how to make myself any clearer, Diane," I start, relieved as hell when the words come out strong and clear. " I don't want you in my life. I don't *need* you in my life. I already have a mother. I've been perfectly fine without you for over a decade, and I will be perfectly fine without you for the next. Do not come near me or my family again or, I swear to God, you'll regret it."

Surprise floods Diane's face, like she never fathomed her visit ending in anything other than me forgiving her. "Amelia, I'm trying to make things right."

"I don't care." She made her bed and now she has to fucking lie in it. She doesn't deserve to make things right. If I've learned anything the past couple of months, it's that not everyone deserves a second chance. "Don't test me, Diane."

Because I know it will only irritate her more, I don't watch her walk away; I turn my back on the woman who did the same to me. It's only when I hear the click of her heels walking away, the clang of the front door closing, do I let myself breathe.

There's a business card sitting on the counter when I turn back around. Hands trembling, I snatch it up with the sole intention of chucking it in the trash but something catches my eye, the address printed neatly on white cardboard.

Phoenix.

All these years, she's been in *Phoenix*. I always assumed she high-tailed it to the other side of the country where there was no chance of her ever bumping into her forgotten family again. Never in a million years did I expect her to settle a measly drive away. God, no wonder she ran into Nick and I around Christmas; we're practically fucking neighbors still.

Head shaking in disbelief, I can't help but laugh; not only did she leave, she did a pretty shit job of it.

As soon as my shift ends, I sprint out the door, leaving Leery and Dopey to lock up. I'm not entirely sure they know how, considering they share about three brain cells between them, but that's not my problem; I'm focused on going home, indulging in a long ass shower, and begging my boyfriend to fuck me despite the fact I'm a massive coward.

I barely make it five steps out the door before someone barks my name, scaring the ever-loving shit out of me. My high-pitched screech echoes down the street, keys brandished like a weapon as I spin to face my potential attacker.

"It's just me, Mils."

It's just me, Dylan says.

Just me, said so casually like the prospect of him posing a threat is unthinkable.

My ex-boyfriend—otherwise known as the man I could go my entire life without seeing again and be perfectly content—frowns in genuine, laughable confusion when I don't relax, my keys still ready to gouge his

EJ BLAISE

eye out if he so much as breathes wrong. The universe is clearly working against me today; I'm not taking any chances.

When Dylan steps forward, I step back, and his frown morphs into an icy glower. "I want to talk."

"No, thanks."

His jaw ticks, a silent warning. "You've been busy, babe."

I cringe. "Don't call me that."

"Why?" He spits. "Only Silva allowed give you nicknames now?"

Dylan's climbing fury is a palpable thing, and what little self-preservation instincts I have urge me to get the hell out of here but I can't. I'm frozen in place like I so often am when I'm the frequent victim of his rage. And something in my gut tells me that running for my car right now would be akin to running from a hungry predator; a really fucking foolish move.

"I gotta say, I'm surprised he's not bored of you yet. Not like you're anything special."

"Is that why you won't leave me the fuck alone?" I snap before I can think better of it; while my legs might've ceased functioning, my mouth clearly hasn't. "Because I'm *nothing special?*"

It's the wrong move and I know it.

In the blink of an eye, a hand locks around my arm, and as I realize not a soul besides us lingers on the dark street, it dawns on me how fucked I am. Bravado eviscerated by his painful grip, it's replaced by the overwhelming need to flee because something is so very wrong. God knows I've seen Dylan angry before, irate like he is right now but there's an eerie calm about him too. And it's the calculated composure that truly terrifies me. "Please," I beg, hating myself for it. "You're hurting me."

"I don't fucking care."

Sharp pain emanates from the back of my head, shooting down my spine in the most sickeningly uncomfortable way, and it takes a moment to register he's slammed me against the wall of one of the many buildings lining the street. Hard, jagged concrete digs into my back as I blink away the dark spots dancing in my vision, overly aware of a sticky substance dripping down the nape of my neck.

"I treated you well, Amelia, and this is how you repay me?" He's not shouting, and I wish he would because this sinister poise is worse. "You're a worthless, broken, pathetic little slut."

302

For the second time tonight, I make the wrong decision.

"Bullshit." One tiny word is shocking enough to catch us both off guard. Dylan's grip slackens and I take advantage of it, shoving him away as hard as I can. "You treated me like shit. You cheated on me. You fucking abused me, Dylan. If anyone is pathetic here, it's you."

I don't see his fist coming.

I just feel it slamming into the side of my face, my cheek exploding in pain. The force of it senses me tumbling to the ground, the skin of my hands and knees splitting as I hit the uneven sidewalk hard. Pain shoots up my left knee, the one I injured all those years ago, and the almost nostalgic agony makes my eyes burn. I'm only down for a split second before a hand drags me upright my hair, before I'm shoved against the wall again.

"You need to stop fucking talking, *baby*," Dylan sneers, "and I'm gonna make you."

He descends on me and, for some reason, it's his tongue trying to tangle with mine that really ignites my fight or flight, something in my brain registering that unless I make him, he's not going to stop.

With all of my might, I raise a knee and slam it into his groin using as much power and fury as he doled out on me. A sick thrill rushes through me when Dylan crumbles to the floor with a wounded wail, but I don't stop to revel in my handiwork. I sprint toward my car, a sob of relief escaping me when I realize that somehow, I managed to keep hold of my keys. Throwing myself inside, I slam and lock the door, my hands trembling and my eyes unfocused as I ignite the ignition and peel away without a backward glance.

Drive, I tell myself when my brain gets fuzzy, when the feel of something warm and wet dripping down my cheek becomes unignorable, when I glance down and see my jeans ripped and bloody at the knees and red streaks smeared across the steering wheel from my stinging palms. *Just drive.*

I don't know where I'm going until I get there, until some of the tension eases from my shoulders and I slump against the steering wheel, the word *safe* echoing in my brain. Safe yet I can't bring myself to move.

I have no idea how long I sit in my car—time isn't measured in minutes in here, it's measured by the increasingly painful throbbing in my face, my hands, my knees, my lungs, *my fucking brain*—and I have no idea how long passes until knuckles tapping gently against the window make me jump in my seat, my hands flying instinctively to the door to check the door is still locked.

"*Querida?*" A sob builds in my throat. "What're you doing here?"

He sounds so happy to see me and I hate that I'm about to ruin it. When I unlock the door, I hate that I flinch when he opens it. I hate that I drop my head to use my hair to shield my face, covering the rips in my jeans with my hands. And most of all, I hate that when I start to cry, burning hot tears of pure fucking shame because I can't believe I let this happen to me again.

Over the sound of my own wailing, I hear Nick ask what's wrong and it only makes me cry harder. The emotions I try so hard to rein in explode in a series of anguished sobs that wrack my body from head to toe. In between whimpers are strangled words, my attempts to explain but they're completely unintelligible.

"Amelia," Nick utters name and it sounds like a plea, it makes me cry harder. "*Meu amor*, I can't understand you."

When I lift a hand, exposing my torn knees, and tuck my hair behind my ear, exposing my bleeding, probably bruised cheek, Nick chokes on a gasp. When I turn to him, his eyes widen in shock, gaze trained on my cheek. All it takes is three barely audible words for shock to turn to fury.

"He hit me."

42

NICK

AMELIA'S SOBBED confession resonates throughout my entire body, tensing every muscle and making me sick to my stomach.

I don't have to ask who *he* is. The blatant fear in her eyes, a look I've seen too many times, says everything.

I want to kill him. Run him over with my car. Pound my fists into his face. Wrap my hands around his throat and squeeze until he looks as blank, *as lifeless*, as she does right now sitting on my bed, bleeding and shaking. Picturing her sobbing in her car, flinching from my touch, caked in dried blood is enough to have me reaching for my car keys and bolting out the door, but I don't. Not yet. It took me twenty minutes to coax her inside with promises of safety. I'm not leaving her. I *can't* leave her.

The lack of joy in those emerald eyes, so unusually dull, hits me like a punch to the gut. That pain intensifies, reverberating through me like a gunshot, when they focus anywhere but on me. She stares at the floor, hiding her face, hiding the silent tears dripping down her cheeks.

Her cheeks. Her beautiful pale cheeks, one of them so swollen, painted in strokes of purple and yellow.

Rolling my shoulders back in an effort to release the fury holding me taut, I creep towards her slowly. When I'm close enough but not too close, I drop to my knees in front of her, cautiously inspecting her wounds. "*Querida*, I think you should go to the hospital."

The cut on her cheek isn't as bad as I first thought—the darkening bruise is the real problem—and while her hands and knees are cut to shit and must sting like hell, I think the dried blood is making everything look worse. Or, at least, so I try to convince myself; putting a less serious, less heartbreaking spin on her injuries is hurting my head but I need to do it. Otherwise, I'll fucking lose it and I don't think she can handle that right now.

Strong. Calm. For her.

What really worries me, though, is the way she keeps rubbing the back of her head and wincing, and the disconnected haze in her eyes. My gut instinct screams concussion, and I'm painfully aware that I have no idea what he did to her; she could be hiding a million bruises or broken body parts.

A freckled nose scrunches in pain as Amelia shakes her head vehemently like I knew she would.

"Please, *meu amor.*" Another urgent refusal, and I sigh, wondering if this is my karma for refusing to let her take me to the hospital all those weeks ago. "Okay, "I relent, my hands itching with the urge to touch her but I deny them. "No hospital tonight."

In the morning, though, I'm not posing it as an option.

Making a mental note to set alarms so I can check her head throughout the night, I gesture at the scrapes littering her body. "We need to clean these."

No reply; she just stares blankly at the floor. A sigh scrapes my throat as I slowly stand, intending on digging out some clothes for her before running downstairs to grab that goddamn first aid kit that's gotten too much use lately.

I don't get very far. A hand latches onto my t-shirt, honest to God, I swear the sound of my heart breaking is audible as Amelia peers up at me worriedly, eyes lined with red and glossy with unshed tears. Quietly, in a voice so hoarse it must be sore, she begs, "Please, don't go."

I wish I could say my smile is reassuring but I know it's not; a grimace is a more accurate description. Keeping my grip gentle despite how badly I want to cling, I transfer her hand to mine. "I'll be right back."

A long minute passes before Amelia reluctantly releases me. When she does, I make quick work of getting her something to change into. Leaving her with a soft order to shower, I bolt downstairs at the speed of damn light and gather what I need.

I'm so quick, the shower is still on when I shuffle back into my bedroom, and I pace outside the ensuite door, rage and worry warring for dominance in my head, as I wait for the shower to shut off. While I have a chance, I shoot off a couple of texts, the same short messages for all three recipients—Amelia's worried roommates who will probably freak if she doesn't come home and the brother who will definitely freak if he wanders in here in the morning and finds her tucked in bed with me.

Me: *Amelia's at the house, had a run-in with Dylan. I've got her.*

By the time I toss my phone on my desk, the rush of running water has stopped. I give it another few hellish minutes before gently knocking, rasping her name.

The door swings open and there she is, ruined work clothes discarded, hair damp and scraped back from a freshly cleaned face. I was right about the cut; definitely no need for stitches, thank fuck. Her palms, too, the blood was definitely making them look worse. God, but her legs though. The skin of her knees is torn to shreds, and when she crosses the room to clamber onto my bed, I notice she's limping a little, favoring her left leg—I mentally add that to the list of reasons why she needs to see a damn doctor.

Cautiously, I creep toward her, crouching at the foot of the bed with the first aid kit beside me, excruciatingly aware when she flinches or tenses at my every movement, loathing how numbly she watches me dig through the first aid kit.

I find some solace in Amelia closing the distance between us of her own volition, however slowly and skittishly she may do it. Scooching until her legs hang over the side of the bed, she rests her hands on her thighs, fingers drumming an erratic rhythm.

"Can I?" I question softly, holding up a cotton ball soaked in antiseptic solution. Again, her small nod is a minor consolation. As tenderly as I possibly can, I get to work making sure her cuts are clean, unnerved by how soundless and still Amelia remains the whole time.

I can't help but remember when she did this for me. How there was underlying solemnity in the room but it was also rife with electric tension, so much raw energy floating between us, a promise of what was to come.

Now, it's all dull. Dimmed. It's fucking sad, that's the only word for it, and I'd give anything to make it better.

"He showed up after work."

My movements still as a tiny voice pierces the silence. Not wanting to scare her back into that horrible, unresponsive shell, I work to keep my face impassive, to not shout no matter how much the mention of him makes me want to roar and yell and tear some shit up. "What happened?"

Not until I'm finished cleaning her up does she answer.

Amelia crumples, physically and emotionally, as she recounts what happened through heaved breaths and heart-wrenching sobs. Everything he said to her, every hand he lay on her, *everything*. By the time she finishes, we're both trembling—her with fear, me with pure, unadulterated rage.

Hands balled into fists, I stand slowly, shaking with the need to flatten that fucking monster. Blazing hot fury clouds my senses and I have to work hard to stay still, to not fly out the door because if I do, I really, really think I'm going to kill him.

One glance at Amelia sucks the rage right out of me.

She's shaking like a leaf, a bruised, trampled leaf, and more than anything, I want to comfort her. I want to make it better, even a little bit. Breathing hard, I sit beside her, leaving a too large gap between us and mentally chatting a continuous reminder that I have to let her come to me.

I almost burst into fucking tears when she does.

My arms wrap around her without hesitation when she crawls onto my lap and buries her face in my neck, her hot tears scorching my skin. "Please don't do anything reckless," she whimpers. "He's not worth it."

No, he isn't. But she is.

Giving her all the time in the world to pull away, I gingerly cup her uninjured cheek, an honest to God fucking *whine* of relief ripping from my throat when she not only lets me, but leans into me. "Look at what he did to you." The anguished whisper hurts my throat.

Amelia presses closer to me. "I'm so tired, Nick."

Somehow, I know it's not physical fatigue she's talking about.

It's *him*.

And if something doesn't change, it's always going to be him.

~

A slamming door jolts me to drowsy consciousness.

Instinctively, my gaze drops, and I exhale the anxious breath caught in my throat when I find Amelia sleeping soundly, still wrapped around me. Coaxed by exhaustion, she drifted off easily last night. I wasn't so lucky—troubled thoughts kept me up, and by the time my eyes drooped against my will, faint light was spilling into the room and birds were chirping.

That can't have been more than a couple of hours ago yet here I am, wide awake, carefully disentangling myself from Amelia and hurrying out of my room, intent on intercepting the owner of the muffled shouts sounding throughout the house before they wake her up too.

As I'm closing the door behind me, Cass appears at the top of the stars, face twisted in wild panic and about to bellow again.

I interrupt before he can, firm and quiet and a little fucking pissed, "She's sleeping."

Glancing from me to the door I'm guarding and back again, Cass' mouth opens and closes as he decides which question to ask first. Eventually, he settles on the simplest, "What happened?"

"A lot," I reply, shoving my hands in my pockets. "I think she should tell you herself."

My vagueness annoys him, I can tell, but he swallows it down. "How bad was it?"

A flashback of her last night, terrified and bleeding, makes me flinch. "Bad."

Cass swears and scrubs his hand across his jaw in frustration. It's obvious that he's desperate to see her, shifting on his feet and staring longingly over my shoulder, looking like he might bodycheck me out of the way any moment. Stepping in his line of sight, I shake my head firmly. "Let her sleep." The brisk command has him narrowing his eyes, adopting the same look Amelia does when she's gearing up for an argument. Folding my arms over my chest, I return his determined stare, not moving a damn inch. "She had a long night, Cass. Let her sleep."

He's not happy about it, his harsh gaze confirms that, but he listens. After scrutinizing me for a long moment—in which I can almost see the cogs turning in his head as he tries to piece together something I really hope he doesn't figure out on his own—before he grumbles his reluctant agreement. When he stomps back downstairs, I follow.

"Is she okay?" Ben and Jackson stand when we enter the living room, both looking tired and stressed. Ben looks particularly wrecked—eyes red-rimmed and puffy, hair sticking up all over the place like he's been raking his hands through it for hours. I'm in no place to judge though; if I looked in a mirror right now, I'm pretty sure an equally fucked appearance would stare back at me.

"She's asleep," Cass states flatly, shooting a subtle glare my way. I resist the urge to roll my eyes at his pissy attitude. He can be snarky with me all he wants, I don't give a shit. Cass' feelings are the least of my fucking worries right now.

Nonetheless, when he storms in the kitchen, I go after him, sighing when he avoids looking at me, choosing to scowl at the counter instead. "Look, man, I'm sorry." He scoffs at my clearly insincere apology. A burst of annoyance flares and I snap, "Stop being a fucking child and look at me."

A flicker of surprise crosses his face as he turns to me before his scowl returns, twice as furious, steam practically coming out of his ears. "Excuse-"

"You didn't see her, Cass," I interrupt, fighting down the urge to yell. "You didn't see the blood or the tears or the fucking terrified look on her face. I *did*. So instead of throwing a tantrum, listen to me when I say give her fucking space."

Cass' face drops. The hard lines etched across his forehead smooth out as his expression morphs from one of anger to guilt. "Fuck," he exhales heavily, "You're right. I'm sorry." Lifting a hand, he sets it on my shoulder. "Thank you. For being there. Seems like you're always there when she needs someone."

More like I'm always there after to clean up the mess, always a minute too late. "Don't thank me. She's my best friend, Cass."

Cass jerks slightly, blinking rapidly before he attempts a weak chuckle. "Shit. Knocked out of first place by my own sister, huh?"

"What do you guys call it again?" I cast my mind back to being at the Morgans' place when Cass and James were joking about everything else becoming insignificant to their mother as soon as Amelia walked into the room. "The Tiny Effect?"

"That's the one." Cass smiles but it's half-hearted, something else clearly weighing on his mind. "Nick?"

"Yeah?"

For too long, Cass simply stares at me. "I don't get why she came here."

Fuck.

It's not a question yet it is.

She could've gone home to the girls like she did last time. Could've gone back to Greenies. Could've gone to the damn hospital like she should've done, which she's going to do even if I have to drag her there. She knew Cass wasn't here, she knew I was the only one here, yet here she came.

And I think Cass wants to know why as much as he doesn't.

I don't know if it's luck or good karma or what but I'm saved from answering when a furious, shrill voice suddenly makes us both wince.

"*I swear to fucking god I'm going to castrate him.*" Luna's shout booms around the kitchen a good ten seconds before she blows through the doorway, a murderous glare twisting her face that makes both Cass and I take a hefty step backward.

"Have you killed him yet?" she demands in a completely serious tone, hands planted firmly on her hips. When I shake my head, she growls like a wild animal, eyes flaring dangerously, and I'm worried I might be the next target of that terrifying fury. "Well, fuck, are we going or what? I'm going to stick my foot so far up his ass, he'll taste Nike for a week."

"Sweetheart," Jackson appears out of nowhere, smoothing his hands over his girl's shoulders, "calm down." Fuck, even I flinch when Luna shifts her death glare on him but Jackson doesn't miss a beat. Whispering what I'm assuming are calming words in her ear, he steers her back into the living room, gently shushing her grumbled threats all the way. *What a match.*

Our conversation seemingly forgotten—for now, at least—Cass follows them out, offering Kate a weak smile as she slips quietly into the room, a stark contrast to Luna. Where Luna is a ball of fiery rage, Kate is a sea of barely contained calmness, the only clues to her distress being the heavy, tired look in her dark eyes and the deep furrow of her brow. "Is she okay?" she asks the question of the day, a question that has no simple answer.

When I shrug, she takes a step closer, hands twisted together in a nervous knot. "Are you okay?"

Finally. Something I can answer. "No."

One word is all it takes for her to close the distance between us and pull me into a cautious hug. It's a little awkward for a moment, both our hands hovering without touching each other, until Kate sniffles quietly and I crush her to my chest. The two of us stand there for a long moment, ignoring the whisper-yelled promises of murder coming from the living room, shedding silent tears for our girl sleeping above us.

43

AMELIA

"Where's your security detail?"

Scowling at Ben's greeting, I drop my textbooks loudly onto the table he and Kate occupy—narrowly avoiding crushing his fingers and earning a glare from the librarian—and flop into the seat beside Kate.

It's not my young friend's words that bother me; it's his smirk.

His *fake* smirk.

All week, he's been playing up to his role as the comedian of the group, trying to lighten the heavy mood for my benefit but it's so unbelievably forced. His smile never reaches his eyes, his weak jokes fall flat, and his voice freaking trembles with stifled tears as he tries to pull a laugh out of everyone. Everything about him is lackluster compared to usual, and out of everything that has happened as a result of last week's shit show, that gets me the most; if I managed to suck the life out of him then things must really be screwed up.

"Ditched them after class," I answer Ben's earlier question with an annoyed sigh. 'Ditched' is an understatement. 'A mad dash for freedom' would be more accurate.

The run from lecture hall to library winded me something awful but it was worth escaping out from under the thumb of my very large, very conspicuous, *very annoying* newfound bodyguards. Between the two of them, Cass and Nick haven't allowed me a moment alone since that godawful night that has everyone treating me like a bomb about to go off, since they tag-teamed dragging me to the hospital despite my protests. As I suspected, I was completely fine, but that did nothing to dull their overprotectiveness.

Nick is bearable. Irritating but bearable. His 'protection' comes in the form of squared shoulders and a hand glued to the small of my back as he escorts me around the place, shooting hard looks at anyone who dares bump into me. And ordinarily, that would be fine. Welcomed, even.

If he wasn't touching me like he's afraid I'll shatter.

If that wasn't his only way of touching me.

It's not fair, him getting me attached to his attention, him swaying me to the dark side of public displays of affection, only to snatch it away so suddenly.

The real problem, however, is my brother.

Cass has taken on the role of guard-dog, and he never lets it drop. I feel like I'm in fucking WITSEC when he's around—get the man some dark sunglasses and an ear piece and he could pass as a Secret Service agent. I don't think I've had a normal conversation with him all week; everything revolves around whether I'm feeling okay, if my head hurts, if I've thought more about reporting *him*, the latter of which I always have the same damn answer.

No.

I can't, and I don't get why no one understands my reasoning.

If doing fucking nothing provokes him into attacking me, I don't want to know what would happen if I actually made a move against him. I don't want to know what his friends would do. And I certainly don't want to know everyone in this damn town's opinion on the matter —God knows they'd have one once they found out, which they would.

I already fled one home in a quest to not be the local subject of pity. I can't do it again.

All I want is some normality. A life that doesn't revolve around fear or worry or goddamn secrets—to add insult to injury, telling Cass about Nick has been abruptly shoved to the backburner because I am one hundred percent sure the aggression he's feeling towards my ex-boyfriend would end up being taken out on my current one and I've had enough gore for one week.

I've had *enough* for one week. Enough for a fucking lifetime, actually.

I haven't slept properly. Haven't eaten anything that wasn't practically shoved down my throat. My life revolves around college and work because those are the only times my mind is busy enough to semi-forget the raging storm of shit around me, the brief few hours I can ignore the poorly concealed gazes filled with pity.

"I can't do this shit anymore," I groan, cradling my aching head in my hands. "I am actually losing my fucking mind."

Kate rubs my back soothingly but lightly, barely touching me because apparently, I'm fucking radioactive these days. "They're trying to help."

I snort loudly, digging my knuckles into my eyes until I see stars instead of sad eyes. "I don't need help. I need some space to breathe."

Slumping back in my seat, I flick my hair out of my face for a split second until I remember the ugly bruise on my cheek and quickly let my curls fall forward again before it catches anyone's eye. If there's anything worse than my friends' dejected looks when their eyes land on the mark, it's the curious, slightly judgemental looks I get from everyone else.

With a sigh, I redirect my attention to the mound of homework beckoning me, intent on using it as a distraction from Ben eyeing me cautiously and Kate biting her lip in the way she always does when she's trying to keep her mouth shut.

She doesn't try very hard.

"You know they'd probably loosen up if you stopped this whole act."

Through gritted teeth, I ask, "What act?"

A shrewd expression accompanies Kate's exasperated tone as she waves her hands in the air. "This whole 'I'm fine' bullshit."

"I am fine!" *I have to be fine.*

"Amelia, you were *attacked*." Kate's whisper is too loud, too honest, *too much*, making me flinch and glance over my shoulder to check no one overheard. "You can't pretend like everything is normal."

"No, I can't, because I have six fucking reminders hovering over me every hour of every day." With an angry huff, I shove my books back in my bag.

Peace and quiet.

That's all I wanted.

Kate and Ben's pleas for me to stay are drowned out by the

screeching sound of my chair scraping against the floor as I stand up. No matter what I do, no matter how much I insist I'm fine, everything always revolves around that night, around *him*. It's not enough that I had to live through it; I have to fucking relive it too.

Slinging my bag over my shoulder, I lean closer to Kate and Ben in an attempt to gain some semblance of privacy in the very public space in which Kate's chosen to start up this conversation again. "What happened isn't the problem." I have to fight to keep my voice lowered, hands shaking because I'm frustrated and *done*. "All of you suffocating me is."

I don't wait for either of their replies before storming out of the library, barely resisting the urge to slam the hefty doors behind me. I hurtle outside, desperate for some fresh air to make me feel less trapped. Closing my eyes, I exhale a breath of pure exhaustion and let the cool air ease away some of the tension, wrapping my arms around myself and wishing they were someone else's.

Tiring.

This week has been so fucking tiring.

Keeping up a smile in an attempt to stop all the fussing. Putting up with said never-ending fussing and feeling guilty for not appreciating the fact that it means I'm loved. Pretending like it doesn't kill me to watch my friends walk on eggshells around me and treat me like I'm broken.

Someone bumps into me but I take no notice, not until a hand settles on my shoulder and I flinch away automatically, eyes flying wide open. The instinctive fear is quick to dissipate, though. Anger bubbles up in its place when I find golden eyes glinting with ever-present concern.

"God," I huff before he even has a chance to open his mouth, "*of course* you're here right now. Who snitched, Kate or Ben? No, wait, let me guess, you guys went ahead and put a fucking tracker in my phone. Do you want me to wait here while you call Cass or would you prefer to trail twenty feet behind me like a real stalker?"

"*Querida...*" Nick reaches for me but stops halfway, second guessing himself like he has been all fucking week, making me want to scream at the top of my lungs because maybe that's the only way someone will listen to me.

But I don't.

I keep my voice low and steady as I slap his hovering hands away.

"No, don't *querida* me." He doesn't get to dodge my affection all week and then whip out the cutesy nicknames. "Ben can't even look at me without tearing up, Kate and Jackson tiptoe around like the slightest movement will set me off, Luna and Cass are probably going to be convicted for murder and end up in fucking jail. And *you*." I stab a finger at his chest, following the movement visually because if I look anywhere else, there will be tears and I'm sick of crying. "My own boyfriend won't even fucking kiss me. You barely look at me. I get it, I'm damaged goods and you didn't sign up for all the baggage but fuck-"

Soft warm lips connecting to mine cut me off mid-sentence.

Instinctively, I melt into him, a soft sigh escaping me as his hands find my hips, until my mind catches up with my actions and I jerk my head back. "You can't do that," I hiss yet I make no effort to move away, enjoying the comfort I've been seeking for days too much to give a shit about anything else. "I'm mad at you."

Nick's smile is rueful, fingertips grazing my neck as he smooths my hair away from my face. "I know," he says quietly, breath tickling my cheek as he kisses the bruised skin gently, wearing an honest, truly apologetic expression. "You're not damaged, Amelia, and I'm sorry I made you feel like that. But," I reel back, narrowing my eyes at the sudden twinkle in his eyes, "can you be mad at me in the car? We're late."

"Where are we going?" I ask for the hundredth time, struggling to keep the childish whine from my voice.

Nick's only reply is a sly grin and a kiss brushed against my knuckles, the same as it has been for as long as we've been driving. For the first hour, I hounded him relentlessly like an impatient child, even resorting to begging. When that didn't work, I gave up, sulking silently and scouring the road signs whizzing past us for hints. When the sun began to set and darkness engulfed everything in sight, I forfeited all efforts and nodded off, soothed by the warm hand in mine even if I was annoyed as hell at the owner.

Now, however, I'm wide awake and ready for interrogation round two.

"Nick." I tug on his hand to get his attention.

He takes his eyes off the road for a split second. "Yes, *meu amor*?"

"Where are we going?"

"It's a surprise."

"I hate surprises." Not entirely true—more like I've had enough surprises to last me a while.

Unperturbed, Nick's lips curl at the edges, giving me a perfect view of those damn dimples that almost make me forget anything else. "You'll like this one."

With a huff, I slump in my seat, ripping my hand from his so I can cross my arms over my chest, and Nick only chuckles, settling a hand on my thigh. Ten, twenty, thirty minutes pass, our silence only broken by the crackle of music coming from the radio.

I hate to admit it but I feel more settled than I have all week. Yeah, I'm still annoyed at Nick for his recent distant behavior and his current secretive kidnapping act, and confused about the sudden total attitude change, but I can't deny that being around him, alone with him at last, has me feeling calm as hell.

Silently cursing my lack of control, I rest my hand on top of his, letting him twine our fingers together. The comforting motion of his thumb stroking my hand has me drifting off to sleep again, head lolling against the window. I don't even notice the cars come to a halt until Nick murmurs, "We're here."

Blinking rapidly to clear the sleepy haze, I lean forward to squint out the windscreen, eager to discover where they hell Nick has taken me. A quaint building looms before us, illuminated by the soft glow of porch lights, a sign hanging over the door. *Monterey Bay Inn.*

"Monterey?" God, no wonder it felt like we were driving forever; driving here is almost equivalent to our road trips back home for the holidays. "What're we doing here?" Confused, I shift in my seat to face Nick only to find him already gazing at me.

"I know I've been distant this week," he starts, hand holding mine tightly, "and I'm sorry. I didn't want to make you uncomfortable and I was trying to give you space. But I realize that was the wrong call so…" Trailing off, he gestures at the building before us. "Here's Plan B."

Before explaining further, Nick hops out of the truck and darts around to wrench my door open, unbuckling my seatbelt and lifting me out. Fingers nervously fidgeting with the ends of my hair, he blurts out in a single rushed breath, "You're not fine, Amelia. You're hurt but I think you're too scared to be or you don't want people to see you like that so I booked a room here for a few days. No one knows you're here, I told them you went to your dad's place, so no one's gonna bother you. If you want, I'll stay but if you wanna be alone, that's okay too. I'll go home and collect you at the end of the week. It's completely up to you but I think you need to stay and just hurt for a little."

Silence follows Nick's lengthy speech, a silence I'm incapable of piercing because I can't do anything but stare at him, stunned.

He…

He's right.

As much as I hate to admit it, he's right.

God, I'm so damn sick of crying but my body has yet to get the memo because here I am, teary-eyed, nose burning, swallowing down yet another lump in my throat.

Peace and quiet is what I've been begging for all week, and peace and quiet is what he's given me.

All of my annoyance, my frustration, everything suffocating me is suddenly wiped clear by the salty tang in the air, by the sound of gently lapping waves hidden by the dark, by for a little while, I'm free from heavy gazes and stifling concern.

My heart swells as I glance between Nick and the inn, melting at the sincerity written all over his face. I know without a shadow of a doubt, he'd suffer through another couple of long, lonely road trips without any complaints if it made me happy.

And that's exactly why I loop my arms around his neck and shrug with false indifference. "I guess you can stay."

A brilliant, heart-race-increasing beam lights up Nick's face. Hands slide down my back, leaving warm sparks in their wake, and dip into the back pockets of my jeans, urging me closer. "Thank fuck."

For the second time today, I'm cut off by lips meeting mine. Nick swallows my impending laughter, kissing me with less caution, as though he's been longing for me this past week as much as I've been for him.

Every part of me relaxes into him. I swear my whole body sighs in relief as though it knows I'm safe and secure and something else that I don't let my mind settle on for too long because it's an emotion that

EJ BLAISE

inspires fear in me as much as it does comfort, an emotion that I'm not sure I'm completely ready for.

It helps, though. The way he makes me feel, the way he looks at me, makes everything else fade away and seem insignificant. He *helps*.

Conflictingly, that fear-mongering emotion in his eyes helps.

44

AMELIA

"I hate you."

Nick's laughter echoes around our home for the next few days, his lips twitching into a smirk as he pulls a beanie down over my head. "Stop whining."

"It's the middle of the night."

"Amelia, it's 6AM."

"*It's dark outside,*" I hiss through pouted lips, batting away Nick's hands when he attempts to wrap a scarf around my neck, bundling me in yet another layer. Not only am I awake hours before I'd prefer, I'm wearing enough clothes to comfortably walk around outside in freaking Antarctica. When I asked why I needed to wake up at the crack of dawn and spend the day looking like the Michelin Man, Nick silenced me with another insufferable *'it's a surprise.'*

It's a good thing he's handsome. And that he came prepared with copious amounts of strong, sweet coffee and pastries when he woke me up.

The birds have barely begun chirping when Nick drags my yawning form outside, his camera swinging around his neck and a disposition that's way too cheery for this hour. A chilly wind tickles my cheeks and despite my contempt for his merriment, I huddle closer to Nick, and when it hits me that we're strolling hand-in-hand in public without a care in the world, my mood suddenly lightens. With a relenting huff, my grumpiness ebbs and I wrap my free hand around his arm, resting my

EJ BLAISE

head on his shoulder, letting myself revel in the fact we're acting like the couple we are for once.

It's so ridiculous that something so normal can make me feel like I'm floating. I don't even care that I have no idea where we're going; I'm enjoying strolling with my boyfriend without feeling the need to glance over my shoulder every two seconds.

As the sun begins to rise, it bathes everything around us in soft, golden light, finally allowing me to see beyond the dimly lit path we're following. Waves crash gently against the rocks below us, the soothing sound accompanied by the screech of seagulls flying above us. The ocean is dotted with the shadows of early morning surfers scoping out the first icy waves of the day, the sunrise making the whole image so unbelievably picturesque.

Just like that, my aversion to waking up at the crack of dawn is canceled out completely as I'm struck by how peaceful, how pretty all of this is. How it's exactly what I needed.

I'm so busy gazing out to sea that I barely notice Nick coming to a halt. Not until he nudges me to grab my attention do I realize we've reached our destination. Dozens of boats occupy the marina we've come to a stop before, swaying gently in the wind and waves.

Side-eyeing Nick, I raise a brow. "Please tell me we're not going fishing." It would be kind of funny if, for all his observancy, he failed to notice I'm a vegetarian.

"No, *meu amor*," he rolls his eyes, huffing a sarcastic noise as he herds me toward one of the boats looming close to us, a stark white vessel on the smaller side with the words, '*Monterey Bay Whale Watching*' painted across the hull, "we are not going fishing."

"Whale watching?" I glance at Nick, his apprehensive smile warming me more than any layer could.

"Whale watching," he confirms as he wraps his arms around my waist. "Thought the fresh air would be good for your head, and it's pretty peaceful out there. Plus," he clears his throat in the most adorably nervous way, "I thought it was about time I took you on a date."

Heart beating thunderously, something foolishly happy grips me by the throat. "A date, huh?"

Nick hums, leaning forward to brush his nose—perfectly warm because, like I've said before, the man is a living furnace—against mine. "We've got a lunch reservation too."

322

"Oh," I sigh. "You really should've led with that. Then I wouldn't have been so grumpy."

"You're cute when you're grumpy." Tossing me a wink, Nick grabs my hand and together, we clamber onto the boat. The people already onboard greet us excitedly, all looking relaxed and jovial and making me wonder if I'm the only non-morning person in the whole bay.

It doesn't take long before we get going; after a quick welcome spiel and before I know it, the coast is becoming a faint dot in the distance. The further out we sail, the stronger and icier the wind gets and I'm begrudgingly grateful for Nick's obsessive bundling, as grateful as I am for him standing flush behind me, acting like another layer. Chin resting on head, his hands sneak around my waist and join mine where they're stuffed in my coat pockets, fingers lacing with mine like a living pair of gloves.

I'm ashamed to admit we don't even attempt to make small talk with the other people on the boat. We're wholly occupied with each other. Not in an indecent or obnoxious way, though.

Well, maybe a little.

"I like kissing you in public," Nick murmurs in my ear, and my cheeks redden for reasons beyond the biting wind. Slight embarrassment aside—Nick truly has zero inhibitions when it comes to PDA—I can't help but agree. Something about being able to kiss him freely after hiding for so long is downright exhilarating.

As Nick dips his head to add substance to his claim once again, my attention is suddenly drawn elsewhere, toward a round of excited shouting. "Look!" One of the crew members hollers loudly, gesturing at a random spot in the ocean. Following his pointed finger, I can't help but gasp at the group of dark blobs dipping beneath waves sparkling in the sunlight.

Half a dozen whales, I think, swim a stone's throw away from the boat. God, they're *huge*. Sleek and streamlined as they glide through the water effortlessly. Majestic, that's the word that comes to mind.

Feeling like a giddy child, I break out of Nick's grasp and hurry to the railing where everyone is congregating, gripping the frigid metal tightly and bouncing on the balls of my feet, genuinely awestruck as I watch the whales sporadically break the surface. I tear my gaze away only to check if Nick is enjoying this as much as I am, glancing over my shoulder as the camera pointed in my direction snaps a picture with a definite click. Groaning with a cringe, I cover my face, not even daring to imagine how awful I look, all flushed and disheveled with my hair probably flying in a million directions.

Tutting his disapproval, Nick drops his camera, letting it hang around his neck as he pries my hands away. "My fucking beautiful girl," he whispers way too loudly for my liking before leaning in for yet another public display of affection.

Despite my self-consciousness, I freaking simper. "You are unbelievably sappy today."

"You love it."

"Yeah." I let my head fall back against his chest when he spins us to face the ocean again, his lips lavishing my cheek with affection. "I really do."

~

Releasing a tired but happy sigh, I tilt my face towards the sun, basking in the warm rays as they thaw my chilled bones. A few hours out on the open sea have me shivering despite the layers, but it was so damn worth it. God, I really loved that.

My gaze shifts to the man strolling alongside me, and I sigh again. After our morning adventure, Nick made good on his promise of lunch, leading me to a cute pub right by the ocean and treating me to the best meal I've had in a while. And a handful of drinks. With the combination of a full belly and a clear, slightly intoxicated mind, I already know I'm going to sleep well tonight.

As we walk back to the inn, taking the same ocean path as this morning, I take advantage of him being entranced by the view and thoroughly, unashamedly check him out. God, he's hot. Scruffier than usual, which I think is only adding to the hotness. He's got a whole beard thing going on lately, and his hair is a little longer than normal too, dark curls peeking out from underneath his beanie, and I'm loving it.

Sensing my gaze, he turns to me with the smile I've learned is reserved only for me, the light catching his honey eyes so perfectly it makes me sigh a third time.

So pretty. And all mine.

"You're staring," he teases, coasting one hand down my arm while the other pushes open the front door of the inn.

Since there's no point denying it, I shrug, shouldering past him and dashing for our room, already anticipating how good hot water battering my cold skin is going to feel. The moment the door closes and locks behind us, I'm stripping off, leaving my abundance of clothes scattered on the floor as I bolt for the bathroom. When I get down to my underwear, I glance back at Nick, whatever I was going to say abruptly gets caught in my throat.

He's staring at me intently, hungrily, in the way I freaking crave. But the moment he realizes he's been caught, he averts his gaze and clears his throat, pretending to be busy messing around with his camera.

A wicked idea springs to mind. "Nick?"

He hums a nondescript reply, still fiddling with his camera, still avoiding looking at me.

"Nick," I repeat more assertively. Painfully slowly, Nick raises his gaze, throat bobbing in a hard swallow as he tries and fails not to blatantly check out my almost naked body. "Are you going to join me?"

"I don't think that's a good idea."

Taking a small step toward him, I cross my arms over my chest, subsequently drawing his attention to the lacy bralette doing little to hide anything. "Why not?"

"Amelia…" he warns quietly but it's not me he's warning; it's himself. I know what he's thinking; it's written all over his face. He doesn't want to push me or make me uncomfortable, and I appreciate that more than words can convey.

But it's been too long since he touched me in any way other than gentle. And I love gentle, I do, but I'm so sick of it.

I want him to touch me like he wants me.

Breathing his name for a third time, I close the distance between us, his skin scorchingly warm beneath my palms as I slide them along the curve of his neck. To my delight, he doesn't hesitate in greedily palming my barely covered ass, groaning as he kneads my flesh. "I need you." Molten gold irises flash dangerously at my proclamation. "So, will you stop treating me with kid gloves and just fuck me already?"

In the blink of an eye, I'm upside down, thrown over Nick's shoulder like a sack of flour. A low groan rumbles deep in his chest as I wriggle in anticipation, a surprised squeal spilling from my lips when a stinging slap cracks across my ass cheek.

Fucking finally.

Blood rushes to my head as I'm placed back on my feet, and I feel as giddy as I did earlier as the sound of running water fills the bathroom, as I watch him strip away his clothes and the rest of mine with hasty eagerness.

When we both stand naked in front of each other, Nick exhales deeply, gaze reverent as it sweeps over me. "Are you sure?"

"Yes."

One word is all it takes for his lips to smash against mine with unbridled, desperate power. His hands are everywhere, all over me, all at once, touching and teasing and persuading moans from my lips as he leads me under the hot spray, twirling me so my back is crushed against his front.

Nick makes quick work of coaxing a first orgasm out of me. With his hand between my thighs, I almost buckle as the pleasure I've been deprived of for too long washes over me. So long, too long, without him touching me, without me touching him. A handful of thrusts have me melting against him, begging for more, my hands reaching up so I can bury them in his hair.

"Do you want to come, *meu amor*?" His breath tickling my neck only heightens the sensation, as does his teeth nipping my earlobe.

My mind gets fuzzy as I get dangerously close to the edge, my thoughts completely consumed by Nick. "What about your rule?" *Shut up, Amelia. Holy fuck, shut up.*

The pressure of his fingers inside me increases as Nick growls, "Fuck that. I wanna hear you scream my name."

And I do. Fuck, I do. I scream his name so loudly that if I wasn't so lost in ecstasy, I'd probably feel bad for the other inhabitants of the inn, probably be a little embarrassed.

But I can't bring myself to give a shit.

The orgasm rips through my body, prolonged by teeth scraping my neck, one hand massaging my breast, the other rubbing furiously between my legs until my knees truly give out and the only thing holding me up is the arm hooked around my waist. Blood pounds in my ears, drowning out the sound of our ragged breathing and running water. *Fuck, I missed that.*

I whine in protest as Nick lets me go and moves to get out of the shower, grabbing his arm and pulling him back to me. "What're you doing?"

"Getting a condom, *querida.*"

"I'm on birth control." I blurt out the words without even thinking, an obvious invitation laced within them. Nick freezes in place, eyes wide and undoubtedly dark, filled with barely controlled lust. My words float in the air between us, palpable and loaded, like a physical line we're about to cross.

I've never had sex without a condom before, never trusted anyone enough, and something about the way Nick's looking at me tells me same goes for him. But I trust Nick. Completely, unequivocally, *scarily.*

"Are you sure?" He asks that question again, voice husky and low and trembling. I can't tell if the shaky voice is because he's nervous or if it's from the effort of holding back.

Something tonight has me feeling bold, probably a mixture of my overwhelming need to be close to him and the way he's looking at me like I'm the only thing in the world that matters. Moving until our chests are flush, I wrap my arms around his neck. "Don't you want to come inside me, Nick?"

The words barely leave my mouth before I'm attacked with a kiss and plucked off the ground, my legs immediately wrapping around his waist. In one swift movement, my back hits the shower wall, his hand sliding between my head and the hard marble to act as a cushion as he buries himself inside me. "*Merda,* I missed being inside of you."

The feeling is most definitely mutual.

He slams into me relentlessly, both of us moaning each other's names and muttering curse after curse until I can't distinguish between my voice and Nick's. I move my hips against him, kissing him with every-thing I have. He tastes like the hot chocolate we drank on the way home and the salty ocean wind we spent the morning swaying in and I can't fucking get enough, I don't think I'll ever get enough.

His thrusts get harder, deeper, and I can't help but let my head fall to his shoulder with a cry. The second I do, he stops abruptly, coming to a standstill inside me. The hand cupping my head moves to my neck, thumb stroking my jaw in a tender move that completely contradicts the hold he has on me. "Eyes, Amelia."

Panting heavily, I lift my head and nod, gazing at him through lidded eyes. Satisfied, he starts to move again, picking up speed until I can't breath, until all I know is the way he feels inside me, hitting the same mind-numbing spot again and again.

Not long passes before the coil in my lower belly tightens again and I explode around him, nails digging into his shoulder as my mouth drops open, my moans getting stuck in my throat.

He doesn't stop, not for a second. If anything, his movements get more furious. His grip on me tightens, fingers digging into my ass as he fucks me relentlessly, his breathing getting more and more erratic, his thrusts getting sloppier. "Come with me, *querida.*"

"I can't," I moan, barely able to get my eyes open anymore. I'm spent, thoroughly spent, but he's not having it.

"You will."

The hand encircling my neck slides between us, moving down and down until it settles on the sensitive, throbbing bundle of nerves. I thrash in his grasp as he rubs agonizing, constant circles, the line between pain and pleasure blurring in the best way possible.

We unravel together, chanting each other's names like a prayer as he spills into me with a groan. I collapse against him, my legs threatening to slip from his waist as I lose all control over my limbs, only kept in place by his strong arms. We stay like that for a moment, breathing rapidly, two wet, exhausted bodies stuck together in every way possible.

I hiss quietly as Nick pulls out of me, the dull throbbing between my legs suddenly becoming apparent. Kissing my shoulder softly, he sets me down on shaky legs only to immediately pick me up again when my legs crumble beneath me. "I think you broke me."

Nick laughs huskily, securing one arm around my waist to hold me up, using the other to smooth my wet hair back from my face. His smile morphs into a more serious expression as his intense gaze darts around my face, taking in every flushed detail before settling on my eyes. "You are the best fucking thing that's ever happened to me."

If I wasn't already a melted mess, I definitely would've become a puddle on the floor and disappeared down the drain. With a dopey smile on my face, I kiss him again, pouring every emotion I'm too scared to express verbally into it

He is perfect.

Legitimately perfect.

The best person I've ever known.

Slumping against him, I intertwine my fingers with his and bring them to my lips, kissing his knuckles quickly, my voice trembling as I admit, "You're the best thing that's ever happened to me too."

45

NICK

She's toying with me.

There's a wicked gleam in her eyes as she rolls her hips against mine teasingly, fingers digging into my shoulders to steady herself. Bare thighs settled on either side of mine, she lifts herself up slowly, achingly fucking slowly, hovering above my tip momentarily before slamming herself down so every inch of me is buried inside of her.

Her name spills from my lips in a half-groan, half-plea, one of my hands coasting up her naked back to grip her by the nape of the neck. She grins lazily at me, her own hands slipping from my shoulders and wrapping around my waist, pulling me close until our bare chests are smashed together, hearts thumping in tandem.

Amelia likes it like this. Being on top, being in control, fucking herself slowly on my cock. I have zero fucking complaints. How could I, when I have this beautiful fucking girl writhing on top of me?

My beautiful fucking girl.

Her naked body is a fucking sight to see, skin all smooth and glistening, breasts full and fucking begging for attention. Cheeks flushed, lips swollen and parted slightly, hair floating wildly around her like a fucking halo. Eyes, green and bright, wide open and trained on me, occasionally flicking down to watch where we join. "So fucking perfect."

Her breathing quickens as her pace does, grinding faster and faster, no longer moving languidly against me. My hands find their way to her hips, dwarfing her small frame, helping keep a rhythm as I flex my hips to meet her movements.

Nothing in the entire fucking world will ever come close to feeling as good as this. No barrier between us, I can feel all of her, every damn thing, and I can't get enough. There's something so fucking satisfying about knowing I'm the only one to ever have her like this. That I get to be one of her firsts, and her one of mine.

Three days of being here, splitting our time between sightseeing and holing ourselves up in our room earning noise complaints and I *still* can't get enough of her. She's fucking addictive.

Her movements become frantic, hips bucking wildly, nails tearing a path down my back. "That's my girl," I coo in her ear as she clenches around me, her whimpers of pleasure spurring me to thrust harder. "Come for me, *querida*."

With a loud cry, she shatters in my arms. Her eyes roll to the back of her head as she spasms on top of me, my grip on her the only thing keeping her erratic movements steady. Her breathy moans tickle my cheek as her forehead falls against mine, eyes hooded with lust blinking wearily.

I'm not far behind her, those fucking eyes boring into mine enough to have me emptying into her with a groan.

Panting and spent, I collapse backwards on the bed, dragging Amelia with me, her sweaty, limp body clinging to mine. She curls up on top of me, dainty fingers trailing up my chest to trace the tattoos inked there. Tilting my head to get a better look at her, I brush her tangled curls away from her face, letting my fingertips linger on her freckled cheeks.

"Well, good fucking morning to you too."

My shy girl returns in the blink of an eye. The little vixen who was just bouncing on my cock with reckless abandon disappears as Amelia rolls away with a sheepish squeak. Standing on shaky legs, she wobbles to the bathroom, grumbling something I'm sure is insulting beneath her breath. I'm so busy leering at her bare ass, one cheek stained with my handprint, that when a phone rings, I don't check who it is before answering.

Rookie mistake.

I realize my error a second too late when my rasped greeting is met by a triumphant screech. "I fucking knew it!"

Cringing away from the assault to my eardrums, I squint at the caller

ID, swearing softly at the worst possible name. "Kate!" Luna shrieks again. "I told you she wasn't at her dad's house!"

Faint rustling and definite snickering is accompanied by a barely audible 'no shit, Sherlock,' before a third voice joins the conversation. "You guys suck at subtlety," Kate states wryly, distinctly smug.

"So we've been told," I respond dryly. "Is there a reason you're calling?"

Both women clear their throats, and I tense when I imagine them swapping those glances that make it seem like they can read each other's minds. "Sorry, lovebirds." It's Kate who speaks, tone smooth and serious. "Cass' getting antsy. Figured we'd warn you because the boy is one missed call away from tracking Amelia down."

Raking a hand down my face, I wonder how the fuck my morning went from perfect sex with my girlfriend to stressing about her brother. "Does he…"

"Suspect you whisked his sister away on a romantic vacation?" Kate finishes for me. "Nah, don't worry. Your secret's safe. Ben asked where you were and Cass told him you were probably on some sex bender." *Technically, he's not far off.* "You're lucky I'm the only one with a brain around here," Kate teases, and I'm inclined to agree.

Indignant shouts erupt in the background and Kate scoffs, shouting a snarky reply to Luna's protest. "Oh, please. It took you forty-eight hours to even notice she was gone."

She mutters something else under her breath that I try very fucking hard to pretend I didn't hear. Something about being too busy doing *things* to Jackson that I definitely do not want to fucking know about.

"Thanks for the heads up," I steer the subject away from anything involving my friend and his dick. "We were planning on leaving today anyway." The 'family emergency' I used as an excuse to clear us from work and class can only last so long.

"Good," Kate grunts. I'm about to hang up, figuring that's the conversation done, when a question whispers through the phone. "Hey, Nick?"

Anticipating what she's about to say, I reassure her, "She's okay, Kate. I promise." Or at least, she's getting there. Smiling real smiles and laughing real laughs, happy, normal things that shouldn't send my heart thumping a mile a minute but they do.

"That's not what I was going to ask, dumbass," Kate sneers, her eye roll honest-to-God audible. "Don't interrupt me."

Rolling my lips together to quell a laugh, I wait as Kate clears her throat, any humorous urges dying where her unsteady voice sounds again, "Thank you."

~

"Well, that was fun while it lasted," Amelia laments with a wistful sigh, casting me a half-hearted smile as we reluctantly scale the stairs of her apartment building.

"Say the word and we can go back," I say, only half joking. It puts me on edge, being back, as inevitable as our return was. I'm fucking terrified that Amelia is going to revert into that awful shell of a girl she was before we left, drifting like a ghost. Barely speaking, barely eating, barely fucking *moving*. It physically hurt to see her like that, and I don't think I could take it happening again. I don't think either of us could.

A stilted laugh leaving her, Amelia brings our clasped hands to her lips, kissing the back of my mine as she mutters, "I wish."

The closer we get to her apartment, the slower her steps become. As much as I was dreading coming home, she was tenfold. The whole drive, she was fretting about whether or not the others will still be intent on tiptoeing around her, whether they'll be mad at her for running away, that latter worry remaining no matter how many times I corrected her; technically, I kidnapped her.

"Hey," I call softly when we reach her front door, tugging on her hand until she faces me, apprehension darkening her pretty face. "It'll be okay, *querida*. Be honest with them. You didn't like how they were treating you, so tell them."

Despite her obvious anxiety, Amelia croons wryly, "So old and wise,"

"Brat," I mutter, kissing the side of her head, waiting for her nod of approval before opening the front door.

I shouldn't be surprised that a mere step across the threshold is all the girls are willing to wait before whisking Amelia into their arms. "You're home!" Luna squeals from somewhere within the tangle of three women. They separate, Lu and Kate each gripping one of Amelia's shoulders, both wearing matching expressions of concern. "We were worried about you."

Amelia stiffens. Throat bobbing as she takes a deep breath, she adopts a determined expression. "Can I talk to you guys?"

The girls nod, mine casting me a sweet smile, before disappearing down the hall. Only when I hear a door shut do I let myself breathe. And only then do I realize The Tiny Effect has been working full force since I entered the apartment; until now, I didn't even notice Jackson stretched out on the sofa, smirking at me in a sly way that completely contradicts his quiet nature. With a sigh, I flop down next to him. "Spit it out."

He doesn't hesitate. "You really love her."

I don't bother denying it. "I do."

"You tell her?"

"Not yet."

"What're you waiting for?"

If I felt like being honest, I would tell him it's because I'm scared shit-less. Scared because I've never said it to someone before, not like this. Scared because I've never felt it before, not like this. Scared because I'm almost completely positive that the moment I let those three words fly, she's going to run.

Shrugging, I settle on the easy answer like the coward I am. "Figure I should probably tell Cass I'm dating his sister first."

"Uh-huh," a single utterance convinces me that Jackson doesn't believe a word out of my mouth, and if it didn't, his next words would, "keep telling yourself that."

Ignoring the obvious taunt, I turn the conversation back on him. "How's it going with Lu?"

Five words is all it takes for my friend's face to light up with what I can only describe as elation. "Couldn't be better," he sighs happily. "She met my sisters."

I whistle, long and low. I knew it was serious between them but *shit*. Big step. Jackson's sisters are like royalty to him—I've known the guy for years and I can count the times I've met those girls on one hand. "Did it go okay?"

"Think they love her more than they love me," Jackson muses, shaking his head with a dopey smile. Huffing a laugh, he knocks me with his elbow. "Both got the girl, hey?"

"Yeah." It's my turn to smile like a fool. "Guess we did."

We're chatting idly about mundane shit when the girls finally reappear.

"She's all yours, lover boy," Luna sings as she saunters toward us, smiling stiffly in an obvious effort to draw attention away from glassy blue eyes but there's no hiding her sniffling as she settles beside Jackson, melting into the man.

Kate's not far behind, looking as afflicted as her blonde friend as she flops in the armchair tucked in the corner. When I frown inquisitively, she shakes her head and mouths, "don't worry."

I don't realize how wound up I am until Amelia appears and my body goes slack. I shift, making room for her to squeeze onto the sofa, an air of confidence and determination around her as she curls up beside me. Her expression is unnervingly peaceful, a stark contrast to the tears threatening to fall.

Slinging an arm around her shoulder, I urge her closer, hauling her onto my lap. "You okay?"

Amelia nods, exchanging indecipherable looks with her friends before clearing her throat. "Can you do me a favor?"

I swipe away the warm drops dampening her undereyes. "Anything, *meu amor.*"

"Will you come with me to file a restraining order?"

The next few hours are a whir of paperwork.

I don't know what happened to the girl who begged her friends not to breathe a word about what was done to her but she was not present when Amelia stormed into the police station, a rigid, resolute woman on a fucking mission.

My strong girl whipped out proof of every harassing text Dylan sent her, relayed every awful word, produced evidence of his physical abuse, pictures that made my stomach roll. "Kate took them," she'd whispered to me, eyes on our clasped hands as though she couldn't bear to look either, "just in case."

In that moment, I briefly loved Kate more than the girl trying not to tremble beside me.

By the time we're done, Amelia is red-eyed and exhausted. My brain is spinning, my phone like a lead brick in my pocket, weighed down by the shitload of legal jargon and important information I jotted down.

The prospect of my truck's silent interior greets us like an oasis, a needed contrast from the bustling, never-ending noise of the station. I open the passenger door and Amelia hops in wearily, crumpling against the worn leather seat. I don't move yet; instead, I drop my head to her shoulder, kissing the curve of her neck. "I'm so fucking proud of you."

Soft fingers leave a trail of heat as they curl beneath my chin, guiding me up for a chaste kiss. "Thank you for coming with me."

"What changed your mind?" I carefully ask the question that's been on my mind all day. From the beginning, she was adamant about not reporting him. I'm glad she reconsidered, but I can't help but wonder why.

"I was explaining everything to the girls," Amelia starts. "How I wasn't fine, I just wanted to be. That I was scared not to be. And Kate said something that stuck." She pauses, smiling wanly, watching her fingers as they tangle in my hair.

"Fear only has the power you give it," she whispers, "and I don't wanna give it any more than I already have."

In lieu of fucking crying like a baby like I suddenly want to do, I joke weakly, "Kate's been spending too much time on Pinterest."

Amelia buries a snivelly laugh in my chest. "That's what Luna said."

My hands run rampant, caressing her back, her arms, every inch of her I can reach. "I'm proud of you," I repeat as I kiss her head.

I love you, I add in my head as I reluctantly let her go and join her inside the car. Twisting the keys in the ignition, the radio hums to life, and I barely register the vaguely recognizable song playing.

Beside me, Amelia suddenly inhales a shuddering breath, and when I glance over she's gone completely still, her tired but happy demeanor plummeting to something cold. "Amelia?" I reach over to palm her thigh, frowning when she recoils. "What's wrong?"

Slowly, she turns to me, eyes terrifyingly blank and skin impossibly pale. "My boyfriend died and I forgot."

46

AMELIA

"Please, Sam."

"Baby, I can't." The deafening noise of the party fades as I stumble out the front door, allowing me to hear the resigned sigh coming from my phone clearly. A couple people wave hello as I pass, and I catch sight of the birthday girl cowering near the bushes, her sixteenth birthday sash caked in vomit. Yuck.

"Please." My tongue, loosened by alcohol, trips over the plea in unison with my feet tripping down the driveway.

"Amy," Sam groans, and I can just picture his face scrunched up in the cute little frown that I love. *"I've had a beer and I have practice at the crack of dawn. I can't."*

I huff and mumble something incoherent that even I can't fully understand, earning another frustrated sigh. Kicking at the grass under my feet in frustration, I scowl at the few specks of dirt that dare ruin the white fabric of my favorite Converse. *"When did you get so boring?"* I whine into the phone, hiccuping loudly, sounding like a spoiled child but I don't care; I'm drunk, cold, and I want to see my hot boyfriend. *"Amy, how drunk are you?"*

My heart flutters at the concern in his voice, a small smile replacing my scowl. *"Come find out."*

I swear I hear the slightest laugh through the phone despite Sam's attempts to cover it with a cough. *"My mom will freak, babe."* I roll my eyes at that— such a momma's boy. *"Is Cass there? I thought he was designated driver tonight."*

Scoffing, I glance over my shoulder in time to see Cass finish chugging his *umpteenth beer—he must be hitting double digits by now—and let out a victory cry as he wins his latest round of beer pong.When he spots me through the window, he grins widely, quickly tapping his knuckles against his cheek and throwing me a wink. I return the gesture before replying to Sam, "He's drunker than I am."*

"You and your brother are a menace to society, you know that, right?"

I grin, eyes still trained on my brother as he switches from beer pong to dancing like a fool with a bunch of the boys. They all have practice in the morning too. Of course, I had to choose the only responsible guy on the team to go out with.

"Menace to society," I repeat thoughtfully, chewing on my lip. "I want that written on my gravestone."

Sam can't hide his laugh this time. "I'll carve it on there myself."

I giggle at his joke before I remember I'm mad at him and my lips fall back into a pout. "So you're not gonna come get me?" I don't need him to come get me, not really. One of my friends is bound to be playing DD tonight since a couple of them have gotten their licenses recently and they're dying to show them off. I just want to see Sam. I've barely seen him outside of school all week because of freaking practice.

I miss my damn boyfriend. Sue me.

"No, baby," Sam says softly, his voice quiet and apologetic, and I almost feel bad for the move I'm about to pull.

Almost.

"Fine." I feign a contemplative sigh and amble further down the drive until the party noise completely fades away. "I'll walk home." I hold my breath, bottom lip between my teeth. There's the briefest of pauses before Sam lets out a defeated laugh and I hear the tell-tale sound of keys jingling.

"I'm on my way."

Swallowing a squeal, I plop down on the sidewalk and smile at my feet. "I love you."

"I love you too, baby."

Twenty minutes later and I'm still in the same position.

It shouldn't take this long. He lives ten minutes away, tops, and it's the middle of the night—even his piece of crap car can get here in less time than that when there's no traffic.

I'm two minutes away from stomping back inside in a huff, convinced he ditched me, when I hear the rumble of an engine and I'm momentarily blinded by a pair of headlights. I shield my eyes as a door slams and a tall figure rounds the front of the car, a handsome face playfully glaring at me. "We're in big shit with my mom, young lady," *Sam scolds as he pulls me to my feet, a gleam in his eyes that assures he's not really mad.*

Batting my eyelashes, I flash him puppy-dog eyes, popping my bottom lip. "I'm sorry."

Immune to my charms after all this time, Sam snickers. "No, you're not."

"Yeah you're right, I'm really not," *I agree, wrapping my arms around his neck.* "I'll grovel to your mom tomorrow about stealing her favorite son away," *I promise before pressing my lips to his.*

He kisses me back for a brief moment before pulling away and making a face. "Since when do you drink beer?"

"Since your buddies on the baseball team decided to give it out for free."

Sam shakes his head, muttering something under his breath about team-mates getting their asses kicked in the morning before pecking me again. Hands slipping down my back, Sam pats my ass before nudging me towards his car. "C'mon, my little wild child. Let's get you home."

I bat at his chest as he slips an arm around my waist, letting me use him as support for my wobbly limbs. "I am not a child. Or little!"

"Hey, I'm not the one who calls you Tiny."

I glare at him as he opens the passenger door and ushers me inside. "Cass is sixteen too, you don't call him a child."

Sam grins cheekily and wiggles his eyebrows. "I don't call Cass a lot of the things that I call you."

Huffing a laugh, I punch his arm lightly, ducking my head to hide my blush. His lips ghost the bare skin of my shoulder before he closes the door, and I wince at the screeching sound the hinges make. This thing is a freaking hazard on wheels but Sam adores it and I adore him, therefore I tolerate the pile of crap.

Sam slips into the driver's seat and said pile of crap starts up with a bang. As we leave the party in our rear-view mirror, I shoot Cass a quick text letting him know I'm safe before tossing my phone in the glovebox.

"So," *Sam glances at me quickly and quirks a brow,* "good night, I'm assuming?"

"Would've been better if you were there."

Sam rolls his eyes. "Excuse me for being dedicated to the game."

"Cass is dedicated," *I point out.* "He still finds time for fun."

338

"Cass is a freak of nature."

Well, I can't exactly disagree with that—Cass has more natural talent in his pinky finger than I have in my entire body, than the team has combined. He could play an entire game drunk and he'd probably still wipe the floor with everyone.

A comfortable silence settles between Sam and I. He hums along with the radio under his breath, tapping his fingers against the steering wheel as he focuses on the road ahead, ever the diligent driver as he always is when I'm in the car.

My head falls against the headrest as I watch him silently, admiring him. God, he's so pretty it hurts. He really filled out this year, his borderline lanky limbs thickening, becoming more defined. He let his hair grow out too, and I freaking love it. There's a couple stray light brown curls falling in his face, and my hands itch to reach out and tuck it behind his ear but I fear my arms won't cooperate. I'd probably bop him in the eye and send the car into a tailspin by accident.

Blue eyes shine at me as Sam side-eyes, a sly smirk lifting the corner of his mouth. "Stop looking at me like that, Amy."

"Like what?"

"Like you want me to sneak you into my room."

I drop my head, again trying to hide a blush, wiggling in my seat as a thrill of excitement pools in my stomach. We had sex the first time a few weeks ago, and now every time he looks at me the way he's looking at me right now I get all... flustered.

"Why don't you?" I coo as sexily as I can, cringing internally as I slur my words and silently cursing Cass for learning the recipe to one of James' godforsaken alcoholic concoctions. I swear, a junior in college and all my eldest brother has learned is how to make severe hangover inducing beverages.

Sam groans, one hand leaving the wheel to rake through his hair. "Because you're drunk, babe."

"I'm tipsy," I correct with a wag of my finger. Sam opens his mouth, probably to argue further but he doesn't get a chance; my abrupt squeal cuts him off. My fingers find the volume control of the radio and crank it all the way up, a familiar song booming throughout the car. "It's our song, Sammy."

Is it borderline embarrassing that I've christened Maroon 5's 'She Will Be Loved' as our song purely because it was in a movie we watched on our first date? Absolutely.

Do I care? Absolutely not.

I belt the words as loud as possible, dance in my seat as hard as the confines of my seatbelt will let me, beaming when Sam goes along with it. He always does. He says it's because he loves me but I know the truth; it's the song he loves. I give him until the second chorus before his tone-deaf voice drowns out mine.

It all happens so fast.

One second, we're singing at the top of our lungs.

The next, Sam's yelling my name, the arm closest to me flying out and crushing me back against my seat. There's an awful screeching sound as the car stammers to a halt, and a motorbike whizzes past, coming dangerously close to smashing right into us.

"Fucking hell," Sam swears loudly after a tense moment, reaching out to turn down the radio."What a dipshit."

I exhale shakily, my hands clinging to the arm still banded across my chest. When he goes to start the car again, I let go of him reluctantly, noting he's trembling as bad as I am. "You okay?" I nod quickly, asking the same question and receiving the same answer. "Shit, that was scary."

Sam grips my thigh reassuringly as we start up again, his driving even more cautious than he was before. Blue eyes meet mine again momentarily, offering comfort as he opens his mouth to speak but whatever he says is drowned out by his name leaving my lips on a scream.

It's like the world slows down.

Glass shatters, metal crunches, my head flies forward and smacks against the dashboard. It feels like we're flying or flipping, I'm not sure, and I don't know how long it lasts but eventually, the world becomes still. Vaguely, I recognize we're upside down.

Blood.

There's so much blood.

I can taste it on my tongue, smell the metallic scent in the air, feel it dripping down my forehead and flooding my eyes. A nagging voice in my head whispers that the blood isn't mine. I think it's right. I don't hurt yet I'm covered in red.

Sam.

My neck screams in pain as I turn to look for him, relief flooding me when I find him still sitting beside me. I say his name, weak as hell, too weak I think because he doesn't hear it. He doesn't react. He stares at me, wide-eyed and terrified. I think I scream and still, he doesn't react. I reach for him but it feels like I'm underwater, or moving through mud, and black spots flood my vision with the exertion.

I blink rapidly, fighting against my eyelids as they fall shut but it's futile. The blackness spreads until there's nothing but darkness.

As I drift towards unconsciousness, all I can think of is the beautiful, pale boy, looking but not seeing.

~

My brother is crying.

That's the sound and image that greets me when I wake up.

There's beeping too, a whole lot of beeping. Too bright lights buzzing loudly. Hushed voices coming from a TV, I think. And I hurt. I hurt really bad, one of my legs and my head throbbing in equal measure. But it's the quiet sobs that I zone in on, the ones coming from the boy curled in a plastic chair that only fits half his lanky body.

"Cassie?" His name scratches my dry throat, making me cough.

Cass sits up so quickly he almost falls to the floor. Wild, watery eyes land on me and widen, almost in disbelief. He's at my side in an instant, the legs of his chair scraping the tiled ground and making me wince. "Holy shit." His arms engulf me, trapping him against his chest as he hugs me hard, probably too hard for someone in a hospital bed.

Why the hell am I in a hospital bed?

A pang shoots through my head as he pulls away abruptly, gaze raking over me as he holds me at arm's length, his face and tone equally fierce. "Don't you ever do that again."

Confused, I rub the back of my head, frowning at the needle in my hand. "What happened?" No sooner have I asked the question than the memories come flooding back.

Accident. We were in an accident.

I feel the blood drain from my face as I squeeze my eyes closed. My hands tremble as I'm hit with a million images, only one of them managing to push their way to the forefront. "Where's Sam?"

Silence. Deafening, terrifying silence.

Streams of tears wet Cass' cheeks, flowing like a river, and he doesn't even try to wipe them away. I've never seen him cry before. Not once. Not even when we broke our wrists sledding one winter; I cried like a baby, he laughed through the pain.

341

A sinking feeling turns my stomach. "Cassie, where is he?"

His sob is all the answer I need yet he provides me with words anyway. "I'm so sorry, Amelia. He's gone."

My head jerks back like he's slapped me. Bile rises in my throat as three simple words obliterate my entire world. "That's not funny."

He's not laughing.

Blue eyes. Looking but not seeing.

"No." One word, said with such determination that Cass visibly flinches. There's no way. It's impossible. He wouldn't leave me, he would never leave me, not like this.

There is no way.

Except Cass is crying and Cass doesn't cry, and Cass doesn't lie either, not to me.

"No," I repeat, again and again until it's no longer a word. It's a cry, a plea, a hysterical scream that has more people rushing into the room in a panic. I make out James' face among the crowd and the word dies on my lips because suddenly, I know.

Cass crying is cause for concern.

James crying is devastating.

A body slides between me and the pillows at my back, tucking me against a hard chest as James pulls me into his grasp, careful not to jostle my bandaged leg but it wouldn't matter if he did; I can't feel a thing. His other arm wraps around Cass, tugging him closer, and our brother holds us as we sob, his smooth voice breaking as he whispers words of consolation. Empty words, because I can't be consoled.

I don't deserve to be consoled.

My boyfriend is dead and it's my fault.

47

NICK

IT's my fault he's dead.

She's trembling so badly, it feels like the truck is shaking with her.

Knees tucked up to her chest, she curls in on herself like she's trying to disappear. Like she's shrinking down to her sixteen-year-old self before my very eyes, re-becoming the young, terrified girl whose entire world shifted in a heartbeat.

Amelia's tears dry up around the same time her words do, when she's finished telling me the awful story she's kept close to her chest for years. A scarily blank expression replaces the aching sadness in her eyes. That shine, that glow, that always forces my gaze to her is gone. It's like she simply has no emotions left, or maybe they're too much for her to handle so she's switched them off. Fuck, after what she just told me, I can't blame her.

I itch to tug her onto my lap, to comfort her, to fucking love her but I don't. I don't think that's what she wants. No, I know that's not what she wants. Judging by the self-loathing lacing her every word, sympathy will only make it worse.

So, I clasp my fidgeting hands in my lap and I wait for her to talk. For her to come to me, if she wants to. Whatever she wants. Whenever she wants.

It doesn't take as long as I expected.

"It was a drunk driver," she says blankly, the only sign of emotion the rasping shakiness of her voice. "They were coming straight at us but

Sam must've swerved or something because he..." Trailing off, she squeezes her eyes shut. "All the impact was on the driver's side. He died instantly."

It takes all my strength not to react. To keep my expression neutral and my hands to myself, my nails biting into my palms with the effort.

Amelia shifts to face me, eyes opening slowly, and the complete and utter agony within their watery depths makes my chest seize. "If you'd seen the wreck." She inhales a deep, steadying breath, shaking her head as if she's trying to empty it of what I can only imagine is a harrowing image.

I understand what she's implying and I wish I didn't.

I should be dead too.

"I was lucky." She snickers sarcastically, her face twisting with bitterness and *hatred* as she spits the words like they taste bad in her mouth. It's self-hatred, enough to make my skin fucking crawl and my heart plummet to my stomach. "A concussion and a dislocated knee, that's all I got."

All. That's all. Like her pain meant nothing. I've seen the damn scar on her leg, faint as it may be; that's a surgical scar. That isn't *nothing*.

I don't point that out; I know better. I wait and see if she's going to carry on. When she doesn't I give her a gentle push. "What did you mean when you said you forgot?"

Wincing, Amelia looks away. "It was his anniversary. The other day, when everything happened with Diane and Dylan, I knew I was forgetting something but I couldn't place it. It was four years since he died and I forgot." Forehead furrowing, she quietens as though she's talking to herself. "I killed him and I fucking forgot and I'm pretty sure all that shit was the universe smacking me down for it."

Before I can stop myself, I grab her hand, squeezing in the hopes it'll make her look at me. It works, and I struggle not to buckle beneath the weight of the guilt in the eyes I love so much. "Don't say that. It wasn't your fault," I say, praying that she lets herself hear me. "Nothing that has happened to you has been your fault."

A frustrated noise escapes her and she rips her hand from mine. "You don't get it," she insists. "The only reason he was driving was because of *me*. If I didn't force him to come get me, he would've never been in that car. If he hadn't swerved, he wouldn't have died."

"Or you both would've died," I counter but I don't think she even hears me. She's beyond reason, overwhelmed by grief, the memories she's shoved down for so long proving too much for her.

Amelia reaches for the door handle and all I can do is click the central lock to stop her from leaving, too terrified to let her out of my sight. She jiggles the handle, slapping at the door with a wail when it doesn't budge, raking her hands through her hair harshly before cupping her face. "I stole someone's *son*," she sobs. "Fuck and his *brother*. We grew up together and now I can barely look at him."

It's so easy to connect the dots now. Why I found her on the verge of a breakdown that night in Carlton with that guy—Sam's brother, obviously—hovering nearby worriedly. Why they both looked so fucking distraught at the sight of each other, like they'd seen a ghost. Why she left Carlton, why she was so distressed at the thought of returning, why *everything*.

She's gasping for air now, a hand pressed to her chest as she cries her fucking heart out, mine breaking at the sound, and I can't take it anymore. I unlock the car but before she can escape, I'm out and rounding the hood, wrenching her door open, and gathering her in my arms. Her wheezed protest is half-hearted and short-lived; as soon as I wrap my arms around her—our earlier position mimicked yet so fucking different—she collapses against me. As her muffled sobs resonate through me and her tears soak my jumper, I constantly repeat how it wasn't her fault and, after an eternity in which I'm not sure she breathes, she settles enough to croak out, "I used to wish I died with him."

Merda.

"He was gone. I couldn't dance anymore. Me and Cass couldn't talk without crying. I started drinking a lot to cope." I stiffen; I did the same when my dad died but shit, I was an adult. Amelia was a kid. Alone and suffering and coping in the worst way possible, and it fucking breaks my heart to imagine her like that.

"I got in with the wrong crowd purely because they were the furthest thing from my actual friends. I was such a fucking mess for *months*. I didn't even go to his funeral. I was too drunk or too high, I can't even remember. I just..." Her forehead digs into my chest as she takes a shuddering breath. "I couldn't do it. I couldn't see the family I ruined because I was drunk and selfish. So fucking selfish. I ended someone else's life so why shouldn't I ruin my own?"

I have to stop myself from interrupting her with my protests about how fucking wrong that is, holding her a little tighter instead.

"James found me one night behind the wheel of my dad's car, drunk off my ass and begging to see Sam."

Oblivious to the fact I've almost stopped fucking breathing, Amelia carries on, telling me how she moved a couple of days later but I barely hear her. I can't stop picturing her, wrecked and sobbing behind the wheel of a car like she was when I found her not even a week ago. It broke me seeing her like that, and it breaks me all over again knowing it wasn't the first time.

Wasn't even the worst time.

If it's this fucking painful knowing everything she's gone through, I can't even *imagine* how much she's hurting. She doesn't fucking deserve any of this shit yet she's so convinced she does.

A fucking awful thought occurs to me.

"Amelia," I croak her name. "Is that why you stayed with Dylan? Because you thought you deserved how he treated you?"

Green eyes meet mine and silently answer my question, so much fucking shame and that overwhelming, sickening guilt lurking within them. She breaks my stare, watching her fingers as they trace invisible patterns on her wrist.

"I think Dylan is my karma."

"That's bullshit," I bark, unable to help myself. "There is nothing that you could possibly do to ever deserve anyone putting their hands on you like that. *Nothing*."

She doesn't believe me, I can tell she doesn't, but that's okay. I'll remind her every day for the rest of my fucking life until it sticks in that beautiful, complicated head of hers.

Releasing another haggard sigh, she tilts her head so her nose brushes my neck, her deep inhale echoing around the car's interior. "The worst part is I'm pretty sure Sam would be so disappointed in me."

"If he loved you half as much as I think he did, that's impossible." If he loved her half as much as I do, it's unfathomable. Gripping her by the chin, I coax her gaze upward. "You're killing yourself with this guilt, *querida*. This isn't healthy."

The saddest smile curls her lips. "I don't know how to turn it off."

"Talking about it might help." Tucking her hair behind her ears, I cup her cheeks. "You can talk to me, *querida*."

Amelia hesitates. She shifts. A couple of long, shaky deep breaths warm my skin. And then, she nods. "Okay."

She spends the next hour telling me about him.

Trapped in my room—we relocated from the police station, resuming our conversation when tucked beneath my sheets—she verbally sifts through the good memories. The ones that make her chuckle and smile wistfully. The ones that evoke happy tears, not distraught ones. The ones that aren't tainted by death and sadness.

I play with her hair as she talks, winding coppery strands around my fingers, tugging occasionally when she steers off track and gets that lost look on her face. I don't say a word; I listen to the beautiful, strong girl curled up in my bed, and I relish in the show of trust her quiet confessions convey.

When she runs out of memories, or maybe when she can't take divulging any more, she wriggles closer, the hand that's been fisting my jumper gliding upward to rest on my cheek. "Thank you for listening."

"You gotta stop thanking me for common decency, *meu amor*." It crushes me that she thinks not being left to sob and suffer alone deserves any praise.

"Don't want you feeling neglected," she murmurs, the note of teasing like a soothing balm to the fucking rip in my emotions. "I'm grateful you're here even though I didn't make it easy."

Covering her hand with mine, I twist to kiss her palm. "I'm not going anywhere."

"You don't know that."

God, the quiver in her voice fucking kills me.

""You don't know either," I point out carefully, studying her conflicted expression. "Do you trust me when I say I don't *want* to go anywhere?"

Satisfaction bursts within me when she nods without hesitation. "Yes."

I'm about to tell her to focus on that trust when a slamming door causes us to jolt apart. "Amelia?" Cass' voice rings out and I swear to God, my heart falls to my ass. "Are you here?"

We must've lost track of time; I was supposed to get her out of here before the guys got back from practice. Or, at the very least, relocate somewhere less suspicious. And it's too late to smuggle her out; her bag and shoes are downstairs, already giving away her presence.

Frantically, Amelia and I scramble to our feet, fixing our rumpled clothes—we didn't do anything other than talk but it sure as fuck looks like we did. She's smoothing down her hair, mouth open presumably to ask how the hell we're going to talk our way out of this, when my bedroom door swings open and the least ideal visitor in the world barges in. "Hey, Amelia's stuff is downstairs, is she-"

Cass stops.

Blinking slowly, forehead creased in confusion, he looks from Amelia to me to my messy bed and back to Amelia again, zoning in on her tear-stained cheeks.

I see the exact moment my friend automatically assumes the worst and confusion morphs into pure fucking rage. In a flash, I'm shoved against the wall, the material of my jumper fisted between Cass' fingers. "What the fuck did you do?"

I don't try to fight him. I could flatten him if I wanted to, he knows it. I do kind of want to, honestly—I'm a little offended that after everything I've done, he still doubts my intentions. But I don't.

I hold my hands up innocently. "Cass, calm down."

Instead of listening to me, Cass proves how freakily similar he and Amelia are; when strong emotions take over, everything else fades away. "What the *fuck* did you do?" he repeats, slamming me against the wall again for good measure, trying to be threatening but only succeeding in irritating me.

One more slam and I'm going to slam back.

Sensing my irritation, Amelia snaps into action. "Stop it," she admonishes, trying to wriggle between us to no avail; Cass doesn't budge. "*Cass*. He didn't do anything."

Scoffing angrily, Cass' glare shifts to his sister. "You're crying."

"Not because of him."

"You were in his-"

"I told him about Sam."

In the blink of an eye, Cass' fire burns out. His face shifts from enraged to absolutely devastated, his hands moving from my chest to Amelia's shoulders, the tight grip he had on me a stark contrast to the gentle way he holds her. A hushed conversation breaks out between them, only pieces of which I catch.

Forgot. Anniversary. Sorry.

So quickly, I'm forgotten. Neither of them notice as I back away despite the fact all I want to do is throw Amelia over my shoulder and drive her ass back to our happy little bubble by the coast.

I don't get very far. My feet hit the bottom step of the staircase and I come to a halt when I notice it's not just my roommates scattered around the living room like I expected; Amelia's are too, along with Sydney.

"Oh, Nicky," Ben sighs. "What did you do?"

"Nothing." Avoiding their gazes, I shuffle into the kitchen, away from prying eyes. My elbows hit the island counter, my palms cradling my head, and I let all the air leave my lungs. A never-ending loop of everything Amelia told me, everything I now know about the shit she's been through, plays in my head. Dylan's face pops up, and for the millionth time, I curse that fucker and all his bullshit.

Thirty seconds of peace are all I get before someone murmuring my name snaps me out of my thoughts. I let out a groan, expecting Ben's teasing or Jackson's unobtrusive but equally annoying prying, surprised when instead, I'm met with a pleasant grin. I've only met Sydney a couple of times yet the way she's beaming at me, you'd swear we were best friends.

"Never a dull moment, huh?" She jokes gently, patting my shoulder.

An emotionless chuckle escapes me.

Copying my stance, curiosity tilts Sydney's head. "What language was that?"

I spare her a sideways glance, quirking a brow.

"You were muttering away to yourself. It sounded like Spanish but it's not, right?"

I grimace; apparently, my internal monologue about how much I want to fucking ruin Dylan Wells wasn't so internal. "Portuguese."

"Oh, yeah. You're Brazilian, right?"

I nod, confused by her sudden interest in me but intrigued at the same time.

"That's cool. I always wanted to speak another language. My parents tried to teach us Bengali but it didn't really stick."

"Bengali?"

Sydney beams at my question as though I've offered her the fucking moon on a silver platter. One word is all it takes for her to launch into conversation, telling me all about her heritage and her parent's attempts to get her speaking their mother tongue but, according to her, she's shit at languages because she's right-brained, apparently, whatever the fuck that means.

I listen to her babbling, reluctantly at first but her cheery, excited tone is hard to tune out. It draws me in, and eventually, I find myself chuckling at her anecdotes, find myself enjoying her company, find myself actually engaging in the conversation.

Just when I find myself thinking I'm grateful for the distraction, I realize that was probably her intention all along. With narrowed eyes and a knowing smirk, I lift my gaze, unsurprised when I find Kate lurking just beyond the doorway, pretending not to watch us. Her nose crinkles when she realizes she's been caught but she's far from sheepish. When I beckon her over with a jerk of my head, she saunters toward us, the picture of innocence as she slips an arm around her girlfriend and asks, as if she didn't orchestrate this entire conversation, "She talking your ear off?"

Observant and cunning. What a combination.

Sydney pinches the hand tangling in her thick, dark hair. "Excuse you. I am *great* company. Right?" When I nod my agreement, she huffs triumphantly. "Nick's gonna teach me Portuguese."

"He is?"

"I am," I confirm; a single real conversation and I'm convinced Sydney could get anyone to agree to anything with the sheer force of her geniality. A dangerous team, her and Kate.

Feigning a grimace, Kate muses, "I'm not sure who I feel more sorry for."

48

AMELIA

"ARE WE NEARLY THERE?"

"Sweetheart, we've only been driving for an hour."

An exaggerated groan comes from the passenger seat where Luna sits, pouting. "Seriously? Feels like forever." Jackson removes a hand from the steering wheel and pats his impatient girlfriend's thigh, lips twitching as she continues her complaints, "My legs weren't made for long car rides."

Nick and I both snort loudly from the backseat where we're squished in with way too much luggage for a long weekend, most of which belongs to Lu. Although, I can't really complain; there are worse things than being forced to snuggle with your boyfriend.

Slouched at an angle so he has a little more room to stretch his legs, Nick was quick to guide my head to his lap the moment we clambered into Jackson's truck. Obviously, I had zero problems with that; with my feet tucked on the seat and his fingers threading through my hair evoking the occasional shiver, I've spent most of our road trip wafting in and out of consciousness. I intend on spending the rest of the drive in the same way, taking advantage of the opportunity for open affection before a weekend of scuttling around in hiding. And I do, my peaceful snoozing only occasionally interrupted by Luna and Jackson bickering like an old married couple. Or, more accurately, Luna bickering at Jackson.

Only when the light pouring in the window suddenly changes,

catching me at the wrong angle and glaring through my eyelids, am I forced awake. Groaning quietly, I shift onto my back and use a hand to shield my eyes. I squint up at Nick, about to ask if we're close to our destination, but the sight that greets me quite honestly takes my breath away.

Holy hell, he's so annoyingly attractive.

He's dozing too, eyes closed and his head tilted to the side, exposing that mouthwatering bone structure; no mortal man should have cheekbones and a jawline like that. The golden light he's bathed in bounces off his head like a freaking halo; I swear the light always hits him right, no matter where we are. He and the sun are best freaking friends.

Unable to help myself, I reach up and trace that perfect jawline, savoring the warmth of his skin beneath my fingertips. I find myself wondering what he'll look like in a decade or two—softer around the edges, maybe with a couple of gray hairs. Probably still as perfect, if his mom is anything to go by.

When my thumb brushes across a soft upper lip, teeth nip at the pad. Lazily, he cracks an eye open. "You're staring."

I shrug, captivated by his eyes glittering in the light. *So pretty.* "I'm allowed to."

Nick shifts to kiss my palm, humming his agreement against my skin.

"You guys might want to tone it down a bit," Jackson calls over his shoulder, the creak of the handbrake sounding as the truck rolls to a stop. "We're here."

A groan of contentment escapes all of us as we clamber outside, the loudest of which comes from Nick when he gets to stretch his poor, cramped legs. I'm readying to crack an old-man joke when I notice him staring straight ahead, brows raised and mouth slightly agape. Following his gaze, my expression immediately mimics his.

I'm not sure what I expected of our abode for the next few days. I've heard through the grapevine that Jackson's grandparents are wealthy, and a spot right next to Big Bear Lake was inevitably going to be something special.

Special is an understatement. *Abode* is an understatement. Hell, *house* is an understatement. The building looming before us is a freaking castle. An enormous wooden structure dusted in snow, surrounded by trees, and looking like something you'd find within the pages of Architectural Digest. It doesn't strike me as somewhere a bunch of twenty-year-olds should be allowed to stay unsupervised; I think us simply standing outside peering at it in awe is decreasing the value.

"Jesus Christ," Nick mutters.

"My thoughts exactly," I agree.

Shaking my head to clear the stupor, I sling my bag over my shoulder and warily approach the intimidating-as-hell mansion. I wave at the rest of our group gathered on the front porch that's bigger than my entire apartment, faltering slightly when I notice the stragglers joining them. Crap. I almost forgot the baseball guys were joining us. They're not staying in the house, thank God. They could definitely fit but I think they have slightly more nefarious intentions for this weekend so they rented a place down the street.

Each of them greets me with way too much enthusiasm considering the extent of our relationship involves me serving them beer and burgers—a pretty good foundation for any relationship but I have a hunch their friendliness is fueled by the beer on their breath.

When one sidles up to me, I internally cringe as recognition hits. "Good to see you again, Tiny,"

My face contorts slightly at the casual use of my nickname as if we're best friends but I'm quick to smooth out my features. "Hey, Jay."

Immediately, I wish I'd pretended to forget his name; he looks all too pleased by my remembering, and he really shouldn't be. I suspect his satisfaction would fade all too quickly if he knew Luna comparing him to a vampire is the only reason his name stuck.

"Here," Jay reaches out a hand, "let me take your bags."

Before I can reply with a 'no, thank you,' a tattooed hand sneaks in my line of sight and snatches my bag away. "She's good."

Nick doesn't spare me a glance; he's firmly focused on staring down Jay in a silent challenge that only a fool wouldn't recognize. God, we really are shit at being subtle.

Jay's amiability slips for a millisecond before he catches it, slotting a smile in place before nodding and flitting off elsewhere.

Luckily, no one else noticed the interaction but I still throw an elbow at Nick. "Smooth."

My sarcasm appears only to embolden him; one lid dipping in a lazy wink, he smacks my ass in a blatant display of possessiveness. "Wasn't tryna be smooth."

353

EJ BLAISE

Oh, we are so not making it through this weekend unscathed.

"Was Cass dropped on his head as a child or something?" Luna hisses as she drags me inside, away from the men droning on about the party they're throwing next door. One look at my girls proved we all felt the same about that; hard pass. "How the hell has he not copped on yet?"

On my other side, Kate snickers. "One too many baseballs to the skull, I think."

"Maybe he should see an optician," even Sydney chimes in. "Nick just groped you in plain sight and he didn't see a thing."

They're joking and while Cass' slightly worrying unobservance may be kind of funny, guilt still claws at my insides. "He trusts us," is the real reason. He doesn't think us capable of what's such a betrayal in his eyes. Of lying to him and roping everyone else into lying too.

"I can't believe you still haven't told him," Ben muses as he twirls around the unsurprisingly massive living room that bears resemblance to the kind of open-plane, sleek homes you see on *MTV Cribs*.

I'm so entranced by the luxurious interior, I don't process my young friend's words. It's not until the girls' shocked chortling seeps into my consciousness do I realize what the hell he just said. When I do, my jaw hits the exquisite hardwood floor. "Wait, *you know?*"

Ben's laughter echoes around the high ceilings. "Oh, *please*. Being in the same room as you two is like watching porn. Of course, I know."

Great. Terrific. Fan-freaking-tastic. Another person lying to Cass on my behalf.

Sensing my strife, Ben nudges Lu out of the way so he can wrap an arm around my shoulders. "Do you have a plan for telling him or…"

"Not really." Every time I make one, the universe pulls a freaking Uno reverse card on me. I really, really wanted to tell him before this weekend. Despite everything that's been going on, despite my relationship being the one perfect thing I have, I would've risked losing my little bubble of safety.

It was Nick's decision to hide it a little longer. A decision born out of pity, I fear, but I was loath to argue. He's been different lately. Laidback and relaxed. Content. I catch him staring at me more than usual—which was already a lot—and often, he'll start to say something and abruptly trail off, like he loses his nerve or something.

It's odd but I'm not going to question it when I'm pretty sure after

354

everything, he wants some peace. An absence of drama, for once. If that's what he craves—and I'm not going to lie and say I don't crave it too—then that's what I'll give him.

Ben's hip knocking against mine drags me out of my thoughts. "You're happy, Tiny. That's all he'll care about."

A girl can only hope.

When the guys filter inside the house, I swiftly change the subject. "So, what's the room situation?"

"Five bedrooms," Jackson replies, and there's a round of impressed whistles. "Take your pick."

Predictably, Luna hurtles toward the grand staircase yelling dibs on the biggest room, hauling Jackson behind her. Kate and Sydney take off too—they're rooming together, obviously. The arm around my shoulder shakes me vigorously, and my brewing stress about sleeping arrangements ebbs. "Guess we're roomies," Ben sings loudly, lowering his decibel as he mutters in my ear, "Although, we both know you won't be sleeping in my bed."

Cass is too busy clapping in delight to notice me thumping his teammate. "So Nick and I get a room each to ourselves." My brother wriggles his brows. "Lucky us, hey?" When Nick fails to react with anything other than a sluggishly lifted shoulder, Cass slaps him on the chest, clearly mistaking his lack of enthusiasm for something akin to disappointment. "Don't worry, man. I'm sure you can find someone to warm your bed."

Mouth quirking into a smirk, golden eyes flicker to me for a split second. "I'm sure I can."

～

"Pink or purple?" Luna muses aloud, holding up two bottles of nail polish to compare against her boyfriend's tawny skin. It's a rhetorical question; the latter is chosen before Jackson has a chance to answer. Setting her empty wine glass on the floor by her feet, she yanks his hand onto her lap, and I stifle a giggle as the man sits dutifully, wincing so often when Luna's haphazard painting edges too close to the white sofas for comfort.

A wistful sigh flutters past my lips. While the rest of the boys headed next door for a drinking session, Jackson had a pretty, blonde excuse to stay, much to his girlfriend's delight. I wasn't so lucky; Nick was Cass' prime target to whisk away and 'nah, I wanna snuggle my girlfriend instead' wasn't a viable option for him. It's fine though. Fifth wheeling for the night is totally fine. So fine that I've been eating my feelings, powering through the hefty Tupperware laden with *brigadeiro* Nick plopped on my lap with a wink before he left.

I chuck another fudgey, chocolatey ball of goodness in my mouth as Sydney scampers over from the floor-to-ceiling window she's been gazing out of, watching the light snowfall as it sticks to the ground. "It's so pretty here," she sighs, joining Kate lounging on the sofa opposite me.

"Fucking freezing, though," is Luna's grumbled addition.

She's not wrong but the picturesque scenery most definitely counter-acts the cold. We went on a dinner procurement mission earlier, taking a stroll by the lake into town, and with the setting sun making the icy water shimmer and glinting off snow-dusted trees, it felt like we were in a snowglobe. I feel like I did at Monterey, and not only because I was bundled up in so many layers, breathing was an issue. I felt calm and refreshed and peaceful and *happy*.

And with a full belly and a fire crackling in the ornate fireplace keeping me toasty, there is very little that could improve my evening. One thing, to be precise. One thing that makes a loud, clumsy appear-ance halfway through our second movie of night just when my eyes are beginning to drift shut.

Briefly, I can't breathe. My sleep-addled brain, for some reason, is convinced I'm being smothered by a pillow. Blinking awake, it's not until my eyes adjust to the dimly lit room that I realize there's a big ass body crushing me. "What the hell?"

Nick pauses nuzzling my chest to flash me a goofy, lopsided grin that, breathing incapabilities aside, makes me freaking melt. "I missed you."

I crane my neck to read the ridiculously lavish standing clock in the corner. "It's only been a couple of hours."

"Too long," he huffs right in my face, and the reek of alcohol assaults my nostrils. Crinkling my nose, I inspect him carefully. Skin flushed, pupils ridiculously dilated, that wonky smile. Oh, yeah; he's hammered. It's a given, in my mind, but still I ask, unable to keep the teasing note from my tone, "Are you drunk?"

"It's not my fault," the man slurs with a whine. "Those guys are so fucking boring. Being dry as fuck must be a prerequisite to become a baseball player."

Dual indignant yells echo around the room and remind me we're not alone. Jackson brandishes a purple-tipped middle finger in our direction while Ben chucks a pillow at Nick, and consequently *my*, head. I don't have time to be concerned about the whereabouts of the third player possibly in their midst; Nick murmurs in my ear, "He won't be coming home tonight."

Innuendo heard loud and clear, I'm caught between being relieved by his absence and disgusted at the cause.

An ice-cold nose nudges my cheek as equally freezing hands slip under my hoodie to graze my ribs, my squeal going entirely ignored as an insistent voice demands, *"Beijos por favor, meu amor."*

Wriggling futilely beneath his icy grip, I play the clueless, monolingual card. "I don't speak Portuguese."

A noise between a growl and a whine rumbles in Nick's chest, his— surprise surprise—cold forehead pressing hard against mine. *"Me beije. Agora."*

Running my hands through his hair, I crook a brow. "If I kiss you, will you go to sleep?" My gut tells me it's going to be a bribe-to-sleep kind of night.

"You sleeping in my bed?" At my nod, Nick beams. *"Sim."*

A chaste brush of lips is what I offer but it's not good enough for Nick. He dives in for more, swallowing my half-hearted protest, gripping the back of my neck to hold me in place as he peppers sloppy, drunk kisses all over my face until I'm squealing and giggling like a silly, besotted girl.

"Jesus Christ." Someone, or possibly everyone, cackles. "And they're surprised everyone knows."

49

NICK

NEVER AGAIN.

I am never drinking fucking wine again.

My head is pounding, my throat is dry and scratchy, my eyelids might actually be glued shut, and I feel nauseous as fuck.

Never fucking again.

I roll over with a groan and reach for Amelia only to be met by an empty, cold spot. Squinting against the offensive light seeping in through the ugly as fuck curtains framing huge windows, I lift my head off the pillow and glance around the room, letting out an embarrassingly whiney sound and pouting like a child when my girl is nowhere in sight.

She was here when I fell asleep; not much about last night is clear—like how I went from chugging beers with the guys to sipping Savignon Blanc with fucking Luna—but I definitely remember her crawling into bed beside me. I remember her closing the door too, in case Cass stumbled home, but it's ajar now. A mouthwatering smell wafts through the opening, erasing the lingering cloying stench of wine and... nail polish? A glance downward reveals my nails painted a particularly horrendous shade of vomit green.

Great.

Massaging my thumping head, I force myself out of bed. I stumble around the room, picking up whatever clothes of mine are scattered on the floor, before trudging downstairs in search of whatever smells so fucking good.

God, am I greeted by a sight for sore eyes.

Amelia stands over the stove, wrapped in a fluffy robe, swaying to faintly playing music as she flips pancakes. Quickly checking no one is around, I sneak up behind her, wrapping my arms around her waist as I kiss her cheek. She jolts in surprise, her lips quickly tipping upward when she realizes it's me. "Morning," she sings loud enough to draw a wince out of me. Judging by her expression, that was exactly her intention.

Her good mood does not rub off on me. "I don't like waking up alone," I grumble against her cheek, trying for a real kiss and pouting when she evades.

"You're supposed to say 'thank you for breakfast, my wonderful girlfriend'."

"Thank you for breakfast, *minha namorada maravilhosa*," I oblige, burying my face in her hair and inhaling her fucking intoxicating scent.

A small hand pats mine where it rests on her stomach. "You speak Portuguese when you're drunk."

"I do?"

"Mmmhmm," she hums with an abundance of mirth. "A lot. We tried to Google Translate but even that couldn't understand you."

Well, thank fuck for that. God knows what I was spouting.

I grunt, leaning in for a kiss to sooth my embarrassment only to be pushed away, a freckled nose wrinkled in disgust. "Shower first, kiss later. You reek of wine."

I grumble unhappily but do as she says. I rush through getting ready and when I hurry back downstairs—teeth brushed, body washed, and clothes changed—I'm ready for my reward. Unfortunately, we're no longer alone; everyone else has emerged from their rooms and Amelia's doling out food like it's a school cafeteria in here.

I beeline for Cass and Ben. The former is practically passed out in his food while the latter strongly resembles a dead animal—Luna hooked him on her wine agenda and the poor kid is clearly paying the price for overindulgence. Coming up behind the pair, I sling an arm around each of their shoulders. "Fun night?"

"Great night," an unwelcome voice chirps out of nowhere, wiping the smug expression right off my face. "You should've come," Jay adds, clearly addressing Amelia, and I stiffen.

Crossing my arms over my chest, my jaw ticks with barely concealed annoyance. "What are you doing here?"

"Heard there was breakfast," the intruder replies, practically dropping to his knees in thanks when Amelia shoves a plate of food in his direction.

A plate slides my way too, along with a warning look, narrowed eyes, and a mouthed *'behave.'*

Begrudgingly sitting beside a barely alive Cass, I mouth back *'I will if he does.'*

Scowling at the counter because I can't openly scowl at Jay, I tune out his constant babbling. Cass comes alive when he gets some food in him and starts droning on about the hot girls he met last night, so I tune him out too, focusing all my attention on the breakfast my girl made.

I jolt when I feel a pinch on my arm and Cass becomes the new victim of my scowl. A skeptical brow raised, he questions, "You okay?"

"Yup." I stab at a piece of bacon. "Just tired."

He eyes my bright nails mockingly. "Long night of pampering?"

"Fuck off. You try saying no to Luna."

Cass grimaces, opening his mouth to reply but it's not his voice I hear say, "She's fucking scary, right?"

I eye the dipshit who's once again unwelcomingly butted in and resist the urge to stab my fork into the back of his hand next. "Watch your mouth."

Wide-eyed, Jay holds his hand up in innocence. "I was—"

"Don't."

"Nick-"

"Did you want something, Jay?" Cass interrupts, shooting me a weird look.

Averting his gaze from me, Jay leans his elbows against the counter, ducking his head and lowering his voice. "Is Amelia single?"

"Yeah," Cass answers aloud.

Not in the fucking slightest, I bark in my head.

"Can I have her number?"

Cass' spine snaps straight, expression turning stoic. "Why?"

"I wanna ask her out," Jay explains slowly, like it should be obvious.

"How the fuck are you gonna ask her out if you don't even have the balls to get her number?" Cass quips.

I fight back a triumphant sneer. *Ha.*

As much as I'd love to stick around and relish in Jay's bumbling protests, I remove myself from the situation before I do something foolish. And because, from the other side of the kitchen, the very topic of conversation is subtly beckoning me over with a raise of her coffee mug.

"That guy is pissing me off," I complain quietly, reaching for the coffee pot she's standing in front of. Not because I want coffee—entirely because it's an excellent cover for being close to her.

"Really?" Amelia drones dryly. "I couldn't tell." She watches as I pour myself a mug, topping up hers too and adding the mandatory three teaspoons of sugar. "He's harmless."

I snort. *Harmless.* Yeah, right.

Risking scrutiny, Amelia flattens a hand against my chest, patting reassuringly. "Stand down, big guy. I'm not interested."

"Of course, you're not," I deadpan, lips twitching as I rake a hand through my hair. "*I'm* your boyfriend."

The enormous round table decorating the back porch of Jackson's fucking palace feels minunscule with my friends plus the baseball guys crowded around it.

No one was particularly keen on inviting them over—Tweedledum, Tweedledee and me were still nursing the remnants of a hangover while Jackson was worried about them destroying the place—but they not-so-subtly insisted on the favor being returned. Which is how we've ended up huddled together, outdoor heaters on full blast, warm blankets slung over laps for extra warmth, and inappropriately cold beers ready to be sucked down.

At least it's not wine.

Honestly, most of the guys, I don't have any gripe with. When they're not obscenely drunk, they're tolerable.

Jay does not fall into that margin.

No matter what, he gets on my fucking nerves. Probably because he's paying way too much damn attention to my girl. Thank fuck she's beside me and he's on the other side of the table because if he was close enough to lay a scrawny hand on her like it's so fucking obvious he wants to, I'd probably rip it off. The longing gazes and the giggling—the guy is giggling like a schoolgirl—are already testing my limit.

I need to touch her. Reassure myself. Soothe that fucking needy-ass possessive streak that's crying out to pull her onto my lap, to touch and kiss her freely.

As discreetly as I can, I scoot my chair closer to hers. Goosebumps pepper her soft skin as I slip a hand beneath the blanket covering her lap, the muscles in her thigh tensing beneath my palm. Ignoring the warning side-eye she shoots me, my thumb draws slow circles on her inner thigh, my free hand reaching for my beer.

To anyone else, it looks like she's shivering because of the cold, not because of my hand inching higher and higher. Only I can see her clinging to the arms of her chair with a vice-like grip. And when she shifts slightly, only I know it's to spread her legs in a silent invitation

That's my girl.

Unwavering, I toy with the edge of her skimpy little shorts. I ridiculed her earlier when she'd skipped downstairs in pajamas completely inappropriate for a night of outdoor drinking—safe to say, as I easily slip inside them, I change my opinion.

A stifled, hissed breath is Amelia's lone reaction when I stroke the outside of her underwear. Ceasing any attempts at conversation, she stares intently at a random spot on the table, biting her lip hard enough to draw blood. Not in the mood for teasing, I shove her panties aside and drag a finger through the slick arousal already gathered at the apex of her thighs, fighting down the pleased groan desperately clawing its way up my throat.

Green eyes, wide and excited, dart to me. That pretty, pert mouth of hers drops open in what I know is a silent moan when I thrust a finger inside of her at the same time my thumb brushes her clit, throbbing and begging for my attention.

Amelia coughs out a choked noise, her chair screeching against the wooden decking as she abruptly shoves backwards. Cheeks flushed, she stands abruptly, and curious gazes flit to her. Thinking on the spot, she grabs her phone and waves it in the air, excusing herself to take an imaginary phone call.

I wait as long as I'm physically capable before downing my beer, excusing myself to get a refill, and hauling ass inside. As expected, Amelia's waiting for me in the bathroom, pacing on shaky legs.

Locking the door behind me, I tease, "Who was on the phone, *querida*?"

"What was that?" she demands, chest heaving, an intoxicating combination of aroused and angry.

"What was what?" I feign ignorance as I switch our positions, pinning her between me and the door. "This?" I dip inside her shorts again, finding her even wetter than she was a few minutes ago. Amelia melts against me, nails digging into my forearm as she grips me tightly, eyes fluttering as she stifles a moan.

I drop my head so we're eye-level. "He likes you."

A flicker of taunting amusement lifts the corners of her mouth. "Seems like it."

Diaba.

Teeth tugging her earlobe punishingly, I work two fingers inside of her easily. A harsh swear flees soft lips. Head falling back against the door with a thud, Amelia clenches around me, bucking eagerly, but I keep my pace slow, taunting her like she did me. "You like him too?"

"No," she stutters breathily, the single word somehow a beg.

The blatant want in her eyes almost fucking floors me.

She likes this.

The possessive streak, my blatant jealousy. She fucking likes it.

Spurred on by her reaction, I add a third finger and increase the pace. "Who's Jay, *querida*?"

She doesn't answer. She can't answer; her free hand is clamped over her mouth to stifle her ecstatic noises. Knocking her hand away, I repeat the question. "*Who's Jay?*"

Amelia cries out. "Nobody."

"Good girl." Grinning wickedly, I draw back so I can see those fucking eyes, lavishing quick, hard attention on that needy bundle of nerves until she's writhing uncontrollably. "Now say my name while you come."

And fuck me, she does.

My name falls from her lips like a fucking prayer as she goes off like a rocket, loud and wild just how I like her. I don't stop pumping as I yank down my sweats because I'm not fucking done yet, and she proves that she isn't either. The second my cock springs free, she's grasping it greedily, blessing me with harsh tugs that make my vision go foggy. When I hoist her up, she wraps her legs around my waist without hesitation, guiding my cock to where she wants it. I'm about to swap my fingers for what she really craves when a voice calls her name.

We both freeze as someone knocks on the door. "Amelia? You okay?"

God, the odds of Jay returning home in one piece are slimming by the minute; I'm going to throttle him.

But I'm going to fuck my girlfriend first.

Amelia narrows her eyes as I grind against her, notching my tip at her entrance, but the hands clawing at my ass urge me closer. Flexing my hips, I push inside of her, and she slaps a hand over my mouth to stifle the groan her warm, wet, tight pussy evokes.

"I'm fine," she calls out shrilly, her breathlessness unmissable as I bottom out inside her.

"Are you sure?" For every meaningless, unwanted word Jay utters, I thrust slowly, drawing tiny, addictive noises out of my girl. "You looked a little flushed earlier."

Oh, buddy. You should see her right now.

"I'm fine, Jay," she insists, and I shove a hand between us, pinching her clit punishingly for saying another fucking man's name while I'm inside her, muffling her whimper with a harsh kiss. My fingers work in tandem with my cock to make my girl come again, to make sure everyone in this damn house knows she's mine. God knows how but she manages to twist her panted moans into a semi-normal sentence, "I'll be out in a minute."

Jay's wary 'okay' and receding footsteps sound just in time. Burying her face in my neck to stifle her whimpers, Amelia falls apart again, damn near taking me with her.

Trembling fingers dance over my cheek, through my hair, sweeping curls from my forehead. She gazes up at me through heavy eyelids and pulls my forehead to hers. "Yours," she promises quietly, and fuck, I could come at that word alone.

Groaning, I grind against her, too slowly for either of our likings. "Someone else might come looking for us," I offer her an out. *Someone less fucking clueless.*

"I don't care."

That's all the encouragement I need. I slam into her, fucking her hard and fast, getting rid of all that pent up frustration. She meets my intensity eagerly, greedy in the way she bucks against me, rips at my skin with her nails, tangles her tongue with mine.

We explode together, swallowing each other's groans of pleasure with a searing, neverending kiss. I come so fucking hard I almost double over, spilling so much cum into her that it drips down her thighs.

A moment of heavy breathing passes as we collect ourselves, attempt to steady our erratic pulses, before I pull out of her and set her gently on her wobbly feet. She glances down at the mess we've made coating her thighs and grimaces. "I need a shower."

I hum my agreement and help her clean up a little, pull her shorts back up. Kissing her temple lightly, I nudge her towards the locked door. "Go. If anyone asks, I'll say you didn't feel well or something."

A hand on my chin guides my lips to hers, supplying me with one last kiss before she opens the door and comically waddles off upstairs, shooting me a glare when I chuckle under my breath.

I clean myself up quickly and tug my clothes back on before rejoining the group, picking up a fresh beer from the kitchen on my way out the back door.

By some miracle, no one bats an eye when I settle back into my seat looking a hell of a lot more ruffled than I did twenty minutes ago and probably reeking of sex. I do spot Jay watching me intently, jaw locked and beady eyes narrowed.

Tipping my bear in his direction, I smile.

Mine, motherfucker.

By the time I've cracked open a third beer, Amelia still hasn't reappeared.

I assumed she'd shower and slink back downstairs discreetly but I don't blame her for choosing not to; as expected, things are getting rowdier and rowdier with each downed round. Jay, in particular, is really indulging; nursing his poor, pathetic broken heart, I hope.

I bide my time, waiting until it gets late enough or these fools get drunk enough for me to excuse myself without suspicion. When words become more slurred than spoken, I decide to take my chances. "I'm gonna head up for the night."

Cass catches me by the arm as I stand. "Check in on Tiny for me?"

I nod stiffly, dropping my head to avoid a host of silent heckles. Ben, unsurprisingly, is not so silent but his loud guffaw dissolves into a howl of pain when I kick his shin discreetly as I pass. Taking the stairs two at a time, I burst into my room, shoulders slumping when I find it empty.

It's fucking freezing in here, though, and I trace the source to the balcony doors being wide open. A peek around the doorway and Amelia comes into sight, curled up on the outdoor lounger underneath a pile of blankets, head tilted up to the sky. I stare at her for a long moment, simply taking in how fucking beautiful my girl is, how lucky I am to even get to call her that, before I murmur her name softly and walk outside.

Amelia smiles when she sees me, shuffling upright so I can slot behind her, humming happily when I kiss her neck tenderly. "Everything okay?"

She nods, eyes still trained on the sky. "Got distracted."

Following her gaze, I can see why. The stars are incredible here, bright and mesmerizing as they wink at us. But the look on Amelia's face as she gazes skyward has the stars themselves beat. "It's so pretty," she remarks happily, entwining our hands.

"Yeah, it is."

When she catches me still peering down at her, she groans playfully. "Smooth."

"I mean it."

Rolling her eyes, she changes the subject like she always does when someone deigns to compliment her. "How do you say star in Portuguese?"

"*Estrela.*"

Amelia repeats the word, tongue tripping over it slightly. I correct her and she tries again, perfect this time, beaming up at me proudly. My suspicions were correct; hearing her speak Portuguese, even one little word, is hot as fuck.

"When was the last time you went to Brazil?"

"Just after my dad died." Her grip on my hand tightens, her gaze softening. "We stayed in Salvador for a couple of months so my mom could be with her family."

"What's it like there?"

"Loud." Even after living in New York, the hustle and bustle of the city my mom grew up in still always catches me by surprise with how vibrant and busy and *alive* it is. "And so fucking beautiful. I lost count of how many rolls of film I went through." Noting how Amelia's gaze brightens with curiosity as I reminisce, I promise, "I'll take you there someday."

"Really?"

Fuck, her hopeful excitement kills me. "You'd fit right in."

"Because I'm loud?"

"And beautiful," I bend down to kiss her pouting lips.

"Charmer." The hand not holding mine slaps my thigh before settling there, squeezing gently. "I'd like that a lot."

"So would I." So fucking much. Picturing her there is easy. Meeting all my family, totally overwhelmed but fucking loving it. Happily rattling off broken Portuguese. Throwing herself into every situation wholeheartedly, no matter how new and unfamiliar. Fuck, the photos I could take of her.

It hits me that even beyond that, imagining her in my life is effortless.

Imagining her not is impossible.

I can't, no matter how hard I try, conjure up a future without her in it.

"Amelia?"

"Hm?" She continues gazing at the sky, absentmindedly stroking my thigh.

"I love you."

50

AMELIA

I FREEZE.

I hate to say it but I freeze.

Stop moving, stop breathing, stop thinking, drowning in the honeyed gaze, so brutally honest and overwhelming, that pins me in place.

Three words have rendered me incapable of doing anything but stare, wide-eyed. Three words hang in the air like bombs waiting to go off. Dangerous, all-consuming bombs with no failsafe, waiting to wreck me.

And then he says my name quietly and those bombs go off, the weight of those words hitting me full force, smacking me out of my stupor.

I sit up so fast my forehead narrowly avoids colliding with Nick's chin. Pure panic bubbles up in my chest as I scramble up and away from him. The freezing metal railing of the balcony grounds me, lets me think clearly in a way that Nick's presence doesn't. I am completely positive that if you compared my face right now to a picture of a deer in head-lights, they'd be impossible to tell apart.

"You what?" I finally manage to squeak out after what feels like a lifetime. Maybe I heard him wrong. Maybe he was talking about the stars. Or Brazil. Or, fuck I don't know, my hair, I know he loves my hair.

Except when Nick repeats it, he's looking right at me, peering into my freaking soul. "I love you," he says calmly, slowly, the way you'd talk to a skittish feral cat.

I keep gaping at him, head tilted and brow furrowed, a wave of confusion washing away the panic and causing me to blurt out, "Why?

Nick arches a dark brow, a hint of amusement dancing within his gaze. "Why the fuck wouldn't I?"

Off the top of my head, I can think of a thousand reasons. Number one of that list; men who claim to love me tend to die. Or lie and become awful, unhinged versions of themselves. Add in the fact that I'm selfish and traumatized and a little emotionally unstable and *so not good enough for him*.... I can't comprehend it.

"Amelia," Nick reaches for me, and it's the plea in his utterance of my name that has me letting him guide me to stand between his legs. "I love you. And every reason you're conjuring up for why you think I don't only makes me love you more." His complete sincerity knocks me back a step but Nick doesn't let me go far, hands locked around my thighs holding me in place.

I force myself to look at him. Force myself to gaze into those golden eyes that shine with so much fucking love it makes me weak at the knees. A look I've seen a hundred times but could never quite place.

And now I can.

And it makes my heart flutter and my pulse pound and every part of me fucking ache with happiness but I can't even enjoy it because intrusive thoughts hit me like a freight train, knocking me from my high before it even hits.

I hate it but I can't stop thinking about the other guys who've told me they love me. One died literally right in front of my eyes, my first love ripped from me in a second. And then the other was *Dylan*. Both ruined me wholly. Both left me with automatic negative associations with the emotion. Both made me terrified to hear it from anyone again, let alone to feel it or say.

Neither had as much of a hold on me as Nick does. If someone goes wrong with him, if this love ruins me... God, I don't think I could take that. No, I *know* I couldn't take that, and since ruin is nothing short of inevitable in my life...

A hand settling on my cheek guides my panicked eyes back to his serene ones. "Relax," he murmurs, the pad of his thumb stroking my cheekbone. "It doesn't have to change anything. You don't need to say it back. I just wanted to tell you."

Every swipe of his thumb erases some worry, helps me to relax into his touch, and painfully slowly, my thoughts begin to rationalize.

He is so fucking perfect.

So patient with me always. Kind but firm. Sweet yet so fucking nasty at the same time. *Loving.* He listens to me. He knows me. *He loves me.*

I don't deserve him, I really don't. I don't deserve to love him, but fuck *I do.*

I'm scared.

I am so fucking tired of being scared.

Which is why I interlock my fingers with the ones caressing my cheek, feeling Nick's breath hitch as I press my other hand to his chest, seeing that look in his eyes intensify as my lips part and I bite the fucking bullet. "I love you."

It's his turn to freeze, his turn to look unsure. Surprise flickers across his face, like the possibility of me saying it back never even crossed his mind. I think he would've been less surprised if I leapt off the balcony and fled.

It makes me sad that he doesn't think I love him. It makes me annoyed at myself that I haven't done enough to prove I do, ashamed because all he's ever done is prove himself and *I* have the nerve to doubt *him.*

I inch closer, brushing my lips against his palm as he tilts his head to look up at me. "I love you, Nicolas."

In a moment that I don't think I'll ever forget as long as I live, Nick breaks out in the most breathtaking smile I've ever seen. "Thank fucking God."

He holds out his arms and I dive bomb into his lap, wrapping my limbs around him and showering his face with a flurry of kisses, murmuring those three words again and again. We're both laughing, both smiling like fools and I sit back to get the full scope of that dazzling beam, dimples and all.

"Say it again?" He requests softly, and my heart squeezes in my chest at the pure vulnerability on his face.

I trace the contours of his face, wiping away his worry like he did for me, whispering against the corner of his mouth. "I love you."

He looks so fucking happy that it makes me happy because I'm the one making him smile like that. I'm the reason his eyes are lit up like two golden stars. He loves me, *he fucking loves me,* and I love him.

We're both in a state of euphoria and it incites an air of determination in me.

Rain, hail, or shine, the second we get home, I'm telling Cass. Fuck, I'm telling *everyone*.

Because I will do anything to keep that smile on his face.

~

Valentine's Day has never been my favorite holiday.

Today, however, is perfect.

Absolutely perfect because I wake up in the strong, muscly arms of the man I love, the man who loves me.

"Feliz Dia dos Namorados, meu amor." A husky whisper tickles my neck, soft lips caressing the sensitive skin beneath my ear. I let out a happy sigh and snuggle further into his embrace.

Meu amor.

He always calls me that but it feels different now. More powerful. Makes my whole body buzz and come to life. I turn in his arms and bury my face in his chest, kissing the taut tattooed skin, murmuring 'I love you' for what must be the millionth time yet it's still not enough.

A rough hand tilts my chin upwards and his lips descend on my mouth, whispering the same words back to me with a smile.

I am so fucking happy it hurts.

His hands travel to my back, slipping under my t-shirt to trail up and down my bare skin lightly. I shiver at the contact, my back arching on its own accord. A giggle slips from me when he coasts further down to palm my ass hungrily, rolling my hips into his so I can feel how much he *loves* me.

Unfortunately, I can hear people stirring in the house and I'm not sure our luck will hold up two days in a row. Extremely reluctantly, I sit up and bat Nick away. "I need to go back to my room."

He groans loudly and paws my ass again, grumbling his protests in my ear. It takes some pleading, a couple dirty promises and many proclamations of love before he lets me out of his grasp and I scamper from the room, checking both ways before I sneak across the hall.

The door swings open before I even touch the handle, revealing a very hungover Ben. "You look great," I praise sarcastically, earning a middle finger and a muttered 'shut the fuck up.'

"What was that?" I cup my hand to my ear, arching a brow. "You don't want breakfast this morning?"

Instantly, his demeanor changes. Out come the puppy dog eyes, a sheepish smile playing across his lips. "I said 'good morning, beautiful, tiny woman who I love very much?'"

Another door creaks open down the hall and Cass' head peeks out. "You're making breakfast?"

Amazing, really, how he can hear Ben and I whispering about breakfast through a closed door but was oblivious to his best friend fucking the life out of me last night next door. Selective hearing at its finest.

With a resigned sigh, I nod. "Give me twenty minutes." Ben smacks a kiss on my cheek as he bounds down the hall, suddenly a lot more lively than he was a moment ago.

I get ready as quickly as I can, changing my clothes and giving my teeth a quick brush before tackling my hair. I stroll out of the bathroom, hands mid-working my hair into a ponytail but they drop to my side when I'm met with the sight of Nick perched on my bed, a proud smirk on his face. On the nightstand next to him sits a ridiculously beautiful bouquet of flowers in a crystal vase surely nabbed from Jackson's kitchen.

"For me?" I gasp, inspecting them with a soft smile. *Girassóis para o meu raio de sol* is scrawled on the note attached to a bunch of sunflowers, attached by a scrap of yellow lace, and while I have no idea what it means, I still freaking melt.

"No, for Ben," is Nick's cheeky response. Standing, he grabs my waist and yanks me to him. "I got you a real present," he adds, "but it's not something you want your brother to see."

Interesting.

"You didn't need to get me anything." Linking my hands behind his neck, I pull his face down to mine. "But thank you. I love you."

"*Eu te amo.*"

"*Eu te amo,*" I repeat, and I'm rewarded with that smile and a chaste kiss that quickly turns rough, relentless. A gasp parts my lips and his tongue slips into my mouth, a deep groan rumbling in his chest. I pull away hesitantly, chest heaving as I catch my breath. "The boys are waiting for me downstairs."

His eyes glimmer dangerously as his hands find my ass again. "We'll be quick."

Yeah, right.

Loving, taunting touches caress my body, easily working me into a wriggling frenzy. Heat pools between my legs, my breath gets caught in my throat, a groan rips from his. Clothes are ripped off and thrown across the room until we're both stark naked. His hard cock presses eagerly against my belly, talented fingers alternating between tugging at my peaked nipples and swiping between my legs.

I cling to him as he picks me up and pushes me against the wall, the wood cool against my hot skin. One powerful thrust and he's inside of me, the rough way he's pounding into me contrasted by the gentle way he kisses me, my moans and mewls disappearing into his mouth.

When he hits that spot that makes me want to scream, I bite down on his lip and his hands grip me hard enough to leave marks. Teeth scraping my nipples send me over the edge, my entire body shaking uncontrollably as I come around him. My orgasm triggers his, a growl-like noise escaping him as he thrusts a final time. Aftershocks wrack my body, triggered by the feeling of him twitching inside me, filling me up, coating my thighs, so fucking dirty and primal.

I slump against him as he walks us to the shower, setting me on my feet as the hot spray rains down on us. I lean my weight on the shower wall as he cleans me up, worshiping my body as he kisses every inch. Fondling my breasts, swishing his tongue across my belly, stroking between my thighs until I'm quivering and moaning again, all while whispering those three words.

He's rock-hard again by the time he's finished. I reach between us to stroke him, thumb swiping at his tip, his head dropping to my shoulder as I tug hard. In the blink of an eye, I'm wrapped around his waist again. His fist tangles in my hair to tug my head back to stare up at him.

This time, when he slips inside of me, it's not fucking. It's not even sex. It's pure love.

And damn if it isn't the best high I've ever reached.

~

"Will you tell us where we're going now?"

"Nope," all four boys answer firmly at once. Watching as Jackson kisses the pout from Luna's lips and zips up her jacket. I have to look away from the easy public display of affection as jealousy bubbles in my chest.

One more day, and then it's all out in the open.

The boys herd us out of the house, shooing us down the steps and towards the small town by the lake. Their excitement is odd, kind of infectious, and we're more than a little curious and skeptical about what they have planned— I think it makes us all a little nervous that our group Valentine's festivities have been left in the hands of the boys.

They walk in front of us, obscuring our view of whatever they're leading us towards. As though practiced, they part in synchronicity. "Ta-da," Ben sings, wiggling his fingers at the... outdoor ice rink?

Yeah. It's a freaking ice rink. Sparkling in the sunlight, mostly empty except for a few lingering couples skating around.

I have to admit; I'm impressed. We were expecting a bar or a trap or something silly and boyish, not a genuinely sweet gesture. And—*aw*—it makes it even better, seeing how damn proud the boys look of themselves.

Luna is the first to take off, squealing excitedly as she links arms with Jackson and he guides her to the shack renting skates. The other couple wander towards a nearby stall selling hot drinks, calling over their shoulders that they'll meet us on the ice.

"Come on, Tiny Dancer." Cass slings a heavy arm around my shoulders. "You'll be a natural."

I guess his logic makes sense—ice skating is like dancing on ice, right?

Following in Kate and Luna's footsteps, we grab skates in our size and lace up before trudging awkwardly toward the rink. Cass steps onto the ice first, holding a hand out to steady me as I follow. I cling to him as he leads me around, essentially dragging me behind him. He's good at it, obviously because he's annoyingly good at everything. After a few warm-up laps, he carefully extracts his hand from mine, a proud smile lighting up his face when I manage to stay upright. "See! Natural!"

Laughing shakily, I shuffle forward a few painfully ungraceful steps. *Natural, my ass.*

I almost get knocked on said-ass when Luna whips by me, gliding around elegantly, easily mistaken for a professional—she's honed her skills over years spent at The Rink At Rockefeller Center—and Ben is hot on her trail because, like my brother, he's good at everything.

Kate and Syd cheer us on from the sidelines, cradling disposable coffee cups in their gloved hands, hooting loudly and clapping their encouragement. Their gazes shift to something behind me and suddenly they burst out laughing.

Frowning, I follow their line of sight. A grin stretches my lips when I see Jackson and Nick huddled close to the railing, clutching each other for dear life.

"Hey, Lu!" I call and skate towards her. Blonde hair flies around her face as her head whips around to look at me, ice spraying everywhere as she skids to a halt. I jerk my head in the boys' direction and she starts cackling loudly. "We've been replaced."

Luna slips her arm through mine and we skate towards them together, whistling loudly as we pass. They scowl and let go of each other immediately, almost falling on their faces as they stagger and stumble wildly like large, clunky newborn deers.

In the end, Cass was right; I do get the hang of it quickly. I even manage to skate backwards, under Luna's guidance. A yelp escapes me as I skate right into a hard body. Warm hands settle on my hips to steady me, sending sparks shooting up my sides. Tilting my head back, I find Nick smirking down at me. "Careful, *querida*," he warns, voice throaty and gruff. "Wouldn't want to bruise that perfect fucking ass of yours. That's my job."

And then he skates away without another word, wobbling his way over to Kate and Sydney, leaving me hot and bothered and squirming on my skates. *Bastard*.

~

Our last day in Big Bear is a slow one.

We spend the morning lazily packing up and cleaning any remaining mess. Now, we're all lounging around in the living room, a pile of suitcases by the door, waiting for Princess Nick to fluff his hair or whatever the hell is taking him so long.

The third time Ben shouts at him to hurry up, Nick finally appears, tutting at Ben as he chucks his bag onto the pile. "Patience, kid." Ben opens his mouth to argue but Nick cuts him off with an annoyed huff, patting his jeans pockets frantically. Pulling out the contents—his wallet and a half-empty pack of gum—he groans. "Shit. Forgot my phone."

Everyone echoes his groan as he tosses his wallet on the coffee table and sprints back upstairs.

"Oh crap." Beside me, Cass rises with a whine, eyeing Nick's discarded wallet. "I owe him money for booze." Snatching it up, he pulls cash out of his pocket with one hand, flipping open the sleek leather with the other.

Out of the corner of my eye, I see something flutter to the floor. I watch Cass bend down to pick it up. I notice him frown as he squints at what looks like a small white square of paper, and when he freezes, nostrils flaring, I sit up a little straighter.

Cheers erupt around the room as Nick slopes back in the room, waving his phone triumphantly and rolling his eyes. When Cass doesn't react, something in my stomach sinks.

"Fucking finally," Ben groans, standing up and dramatically checking the time. "Took your sweet time, princess."

Nick flashes him a toothy grin. "Can't rush perfection."

"Nick?" Cass' voice is as shaky as the hands holding whatever he's gripping tightly.

"Yeah, man?" Nick sidles up to him, clapping a hand on his shoulder. When he notices the object of Cass' attention, he pales. Apologetic eyes flicker to mine as he steps back, wincing when my brother turns to face him.

"Why the fuck is there a photo of my sister in your wallet?"

51

AMELIA

COMPLETE AND UTTER SILENCE SETTLES, so profound that I swear I can hear Cass' thoughts racing around in his head as the pieces of one giant, deceitful puzzle fall into place.

The only thing permeating the quiet; his question echoing off every nook and cranny, hanging in the air threateningly. *Why is there a picture of my sister in your wallet?*

Nick keeps casting remorseful glances my way but it's not his fault, it's mine. I chose to keep everything a secret, and now it's blowing up, like everyone warned me it would.

The photo falls from Cass' shaky hand, the incriminating evidence fluttering to the floor. I glance down and wince at the sight of bare skin. There is truly no explaining ourselves out of this one. There is nothing that hides the fact I am completely naked.

Perched on a bed with my knees pulled up to my chest, my bare back is to the camera, my content face visible as I glance over my shoulder at the man behind the camera. The more intimate parts of my naked body are hidden behind strategically placed limbs but glaringly obvious are the hickies littering my skin, the fucking fingertip-shaped bruises on my hips.

It would be a nice photo. Its reckless position in Nick's wallet would send a little thrill through me. *If* it hadn't landed me in deep, deep shit.

"Cass," my voice comes out weaker than I intended, laced with guilt, and my legs shake as I stand and step toward him, "I can explain."

Cass steps back. Usually warm brown eyes burn into me, suddenly terrifyingly dark and unfamiliar.

"I asked you," he says slowly, voice rife with accusation, confusion painting his features. "I asked you if anything was going on."

"I know." He's right. He did. After the Sam reveal, when he found me in Nick's bed, he asked me point-blank and I swept it away like it was absurd. Like he was a fool for even suggesting it. "*Fuck*, I know, please let me-"

"You lied to me."

He's right, again. I did. Repeatedly. *Excessively*.

Cass looks away from me with a grimace as though the sight of me pains him. Confusion and hurt turn to fury when his gaze lands on Nick, his fists clenching by his sides. In the blink of an eye, Jackson is standing between the two of them, a hand on each other's chests, a human barrier.

Three best friends in a stand-off. Because of me.

I think I'm going to vomit.

A warm hand slips into mine, dark eyes floating into view and offering me comfort that only makes me more nauseous because it's comfort I don't deserve. Avoiding Kate's gaze, I focus on the trainwreck, the wreck I caused.

Cass is vibrating with barely contained anger as he surveys Nick, waiting for him to explain himself like I tried to do. When he doesn't, Cass seeks answers on his own. "How long have you been fucking my sister?"

Every single person in the room collectively winces at Cass' crass words. Except for Nick; he remains a sea of calm, refusing to give Cass the reaction he's baiting him for. The only sign he hears Cass is his fingers twitching at his side, a flash of annoyance rippling through his muscled body.

"Well?" Cass scoffs. "How long has my sister been your dirty little secret?"

Golden eyes flaming as Nick squares his shoulders, a lip curling in disgust. "It's not like that."

"Bullshit," Cass spits and takes a threatening step forward. Nick mimics his movement, his temper flaring dangerously.

Jackson springs into action, gently shoving each of them back. "Both of you, calm down."

The pleading command only seems to rile Cass up more. He knocks Jackson's hand away roughly and turns his furious gaze on him. "Don't tell me to calm down. How would you feel if *he* was fucking around with your sister?"

"That's not what this is." The second the words leave his mouth, Jackson realizes his mistake. With a wince, he glances at me, mouthing a silent apology.

Shit.

A moment later, Cass frowns, his question heard before he even asks it. "How the fuck would you know?"

I swear I can hear everyone's hearts thumping in anticipation as the awful realization slowly hits Cass. "You knew," he drags out the words slowly, like the possibility of them being true is foreign to him, unimaginable.

Jackson's guilty gaze says all that needs to be said.

Cass' head whips towards the rest of our friends, staring them each in the eye accusingly. "You all knew?" There's a pleading note to his voice, as if he's begging them to tell him he's wrong, that no one else knew, that it was mine and Nick's secret that Jackson somehow got dragged into.

I wish they could give him that.

But they can't, and it's like I see his heart break in two as he uncovers another secret. He hides his dejected expression behind a mask of anger, focusing all that rage on Nick. "You need to stay away from her," he demands with deadly clarity, lethal finality. "Stay away from both of us."

Nick meets his demand with a stubborn shake of his head. "I can't do that."

"And why not? What, you're fucking in love with her or something?" he spits sarcastically, snickering under his breath as though the mere idea is ludicrous. He's scornful and angry and completely oblivious to how loaded his question is.

Nick says nothing. He doesn't have to say anything. The look on his face says it all, and I see the exact moment Cass recognizes it.

For a split second, my brother lets his mask break, and all the hurt that shines through makes my eyes water and my chest ache. "You're in love with her," he breathes, and it's amazing how words that gave me an indescribable high when they were uttered for the first time now sink in my stomach like a lead balloon. How I feel a rush of guilt now instead of a spark of joy.

When Nick nods, Cass' shining eyes flit to me. "And you're in love with him." It's a statement, not a question, and I am powerless to do anything but nod shakily. "And you didn't tell me."

"I didn't know how," is my weak, pathetic excuse.

"Amelia, *it's me.*" His voice breaks as he scrubs his hand over his jaw in frustration. God, he looks so fucking heartbroken. *We tell each other everything,* is what his disoriented expression says. I told him about my first kiss, my first time, my first fucking period. *So why not this?*

A beat of silence passes before he steels himself. "How long?"

My answer comes out in a quiet, shaky whisper. "Thanksgiving." The night on his kitchen counter when the lying and pretending and betrayal began.

Months.

We've been lying to him for months. *I've* been lying for months.

"So Christmas, New Year's, this entire fucking weekend, you were sneaking around?" I can only nod, too much of a coward to even look at him. "Did you even go to your dad's place?"

Tears burn my eyes.

He's not even yelling and I hate it. I want him to yell, to scream at me, to curse me out because I deserve it and this silence is a million times worse.

Abruptly, Cass turns on his heel and tears out of the house, the front door slamming behind him. I'm on my feet and flying after him before anyone can stop me, tears streaming down my face as I follow him outside calling his name. "Cassie, I'm so sorry."

"Don't." He whirls around to face me and stabs a finger in my direction. "What if it was the other way around, huh? What if I'd been sneaking around with your best friend for months? What if every single one of your friends had been lying to you for *months?*"

"I know," I cry pathetically. "I know and I'm so sorry."

This is happening all wrong. I was supposed to tell him. It was supposed to come from me in private, not with a fucking audience, *not like this.*

Anger and hurt fight for dominance within my brother's expression. "You know, I suspected something was going on but I brushed it off. I thought 'nah, there's no way. Amelia would tell me." A bitter laugh wracks his body. "I fucking thanked him for *taking care of you*."

"Please, can we talk?" I beg, all but dropping to my knees at his feet. "Let me explain, I..." I don't get to finish my sentence because Cass is stomping towards his car. The door slams shut behind him and before I can comprehend it, he's driving away, leaving me sobbing on the driveway.

This was not supposed to happen like this.

The drive home is solemn.

Kate and Sydney sit up front, exchanging worried glances and whispered exchanges that I don't even bother to try to listen to. I'm sandwiched between Luna and Ben in the backseat, a hand in each of theirs, brushing off the occasional comforting word that I don't want to hear because I don't deserve them.

My mind is racing, so many conflicting thoughts swirling around and driving me insane.

I fucked up. I fucked up so bad. I know that. I should've told him the second something happened, I could've avoided all of this so easily.

The selfish part of me tries to rationalize my actions. Wonders if Nick and I would even be together if I told Cass. He would've been dead set on separating us, at least I was right about that much. My altruistic side wouldn't change a thing; half the things that happened between Nick and I would've never even happened if it weren't for us sneaking around, and sacrificing that is not a risk I'd be willing to take.

But that look on Cass' face... Pure and utter devastation. The last time I saw that look, one of his best friends died. I suppose, in a way, yet another best friend has been taken from him and I'm responsible for it again.

I barely notice when we pull up outside our apartment, only alerted by Ben gently nudging me out of the car. Sydney offers me a sad smile before she drives away, leaving the somber trio to steer me inside. Before I know it, I'm in my bed, cocooned between Kate and Luna with Ben stretched out at our feet.

We sit in awful stifling silence that I think we all hate but no one knows how to break. I want to ask them to go check on Cass but my mouth isn't cooperating, fearful to open in case the only thing that comes out are sobs. Instead, I stay quiet and wrack my brain for fights with Cass, trying to think of our worst ones, trying to minimize this one. There aren't many. Childish, petty, sibling arguments that were solved as quickly as they began.

There was one after the accident when I was spiraling that feels scarily similar to this one. He didn't yell at me. He was quietly angry with me for throwing my life away.

Disappointed. That's what it was.

I left a week after that fight.

My phone goes off, the loud sound jarring amidst the silence. Nick's name flashes on the screen. I don't want to answer it. I think I'll cry again if I hear his voice because I love him and I feel so guilty about loving him and I hate that. Kate takes one look at my panicked expression and answers for me, speaking in hushed tones as she leaves the room.

I feel sick again.

Sick with guilt and self-loathing and fucking shame. The betrayal and disgust in Cass' eyes haunts me the same way Sam's unseeing eyes used to, two markers of my biggest fucking mistakes.

Kate returns to the room and slips under the covers, curling up beside me. "They're home," she informs me quietly, brushing a strand of hair behind my ear, the gesture making my heart ache. "Cass' car is in the driveway." I let out a sigh of relief. He's home and safe, at least.

A tug on my hair directs my attention back to Kate. "Nick told me to tell you he loves you."

Despite the guilt bubbling up in my stomach, I smile.

Luna shifts behind me, propping her chin on my arm. "When did that happen?"

"Couple days ago." It feels tainted now. Barely two days of being happy and in love before I managed to fuck it up.

Luna leans her cheek flat against my forearm, smiling sadly. "I'm happy for you."

Yeah. I was too.

A hand curls around my ankle, and my heart pangs as I stare at the somber expression that so does not suit Ben. "Cass will come around. Give him some time."

Yeah. Maybe.

~

They let me wallow for an hour before dragging me out of bed. It's still early in the evening, too early to sleep, unfortunately; too early to fall into an oblivious slumber and forget for a little while.

Someone makes food that no one really eats because they're too busy staring at me worriedly.

Someone puts on a movie that no one watches because they're too busy staring at me worriedly.

When I excuse myself to my room, they follow me, piling onto my bed, and once again, staring at me worriedly.

It's a relief when they fall asleep—all of us squished together but uncaring—and I get a break from their weighty stares. I stay awake for hours after them, staring unseeing at the ceiling, unable to shut my thoughts off.

Liar, liar, liar.

"Mils?" I jerk in surprise at Kate's whispering voice. Turning my head so my cheek rests against the cool pillow, I meet dark, worried eyes, barely visible in the room only lit by the glow of street lights seeping in from outside since none of us bothered with closing the curtains.

"Yeah?"

"Don't push Nick away," Kate pleads softly. "I know Cass is your brother and you love him and you'll do anything for him." Except tell the truth. evidently. "But Nick is so good for you. Cass will see that eventually and I don't want you to ruin it before he can."

"I don't want to." God, I hope I don't ruin it. I hate that she assumes I will but I can't really blame her—I have a bit of a track record after all. I think it's in my DNA to blow up a good thing while I have it.

"Good." She squeezes my hand, offering me a calming smile, ever the pragmatist. "Take a day to calm down and figure out what you're gonna do but please, call him."

"I will," I promise quietly into the darkness.

One last squeeze and Kate lets go of my hand, rolling onto her other side. After a while, I hear her breathing slow as she drifts off to sleep as well.

I still feel restless. Exhausted, but restless. Like my body refuses to fall asleep like this, with something missing.

Careful not to wake the others, I grab my phone from the nightstand, eyes watering at the sudden brightness as the screen comes to life. My thumbs move deftly across the screen, easily finding Nick's contact. The mere sight of his contact picture calms me, sends a gentle lull through my body. No sooner have I hit send and slipped my phone under the pillow than I'm drifting off to sleep, my mind finally letting my body rest.

Me: I'm okay. I love you.

52

NICK

THE DRIVE HOME feels so much longer than the drive here did.

I spend most of it trying to call Amelia so I can steer her thoughts back on track, to resolve some of the guilt I know she's drowning in, to remind her the blame doesn't fall on her alone. After all, *I* pursued *her*. At first, I wanted to keep everything a secret too. It's because of me that Cass found out this way. This mess is as much my fault as it is hers.

I get her voicemail every time.

When I give up—briefly—I slump in the seat of Jackson's car, ignoring his pointed glances. I don't want to talk about it; I want to stew in anger. Anger at Cass for how crass he made my relationship sound. For making demands. For looking at me like being in love with his sister was a fucking crime, as though it's worse than me just fucking her. For leaving Amelia crumpled on the driveway, crushed beyond belief, without so much as a backward glance.

I last half an hour before my twitching fingers reach for my phone again. Relief floods me when my umpteenth attempt at a call finally connects but it quickly turns to disappointment when it's not Amelia who greets me. "Hey," Kate whispers.

"Is she okay?"

A brief pause is followed by a sigh. "Not really. She's kind of out of it."

"Can I come over?"

"No," is her immediate, firm answer. "I think she needs a little space.

385

You know what she's like when she's upset, I don't want her lashing out and saying something she regrets."

Her suggestion makes sense, I know it does, but that doesn't mean I'm happy about it. It's hard to stay away when I know she's hurting, when every instinct is screaming to ease her pain. "Okay," I agree reluctantly as, after what feels like forever, our house comes into view, along with a familiar car that makes my temper flare. "We're home. Cass' car is here."

"I'll let her know." Another small pause. "You okay?"

"I'm good," I lie, somewhat unconvincingly but unwilling to divulge right now. "Tell her I love her, okay?"

"I will. Please don't beat up Cass."

No promises.

The call drops as Jackson parks in the driveway. We sit in silence for a moment, like we're mentally preparing for the shitstorm undoubtedly ahead. When I reach for the handle, my friend shoots me a tight-lipped grimace. "You ready for this?"

I respond by getting out of the car and slamming the door loudly behind me.

We find Cass standing in the middle of the living room staring blankly at his phone. There's a bag at his feet, bigger than the one he brought to Big Bear and stuffed to the brim, his baseball gloves lying on top of it. I'm a little surprised to see him, to be honest; I thought he'd be upstairs stewing in his room.

Or waiting in mine with a gun.

Cass doesn't look up at us as we walk in, his shoulders tensing the only sign he registers our arrival. "I just got off the phone with my mom."

Fuck.

Slowly, he lifts his head, jaw ticking. "Imagine my fucking surprise when she tells me she knew about this too."

"Cass-"

"What the fuck is wrong with you?" he interrupts with a humorless laugh. "Did you think if you got my family's approval first I'd be okay with this? Was telling them part of a sick little game or something?"

"We didn't tell anyone anything."

"You are so full of shit," he spits, advancing a threatening step.

A rush of exasperated annoyance straightening my spine. His

fucking righteous, holier-than-thou tone is pissing me off. Acting like he knows anything about Amelia and me when he refuses to fucking listen.

"We didn't tell anyone anything," I articulate slowly, trying so damn hard to be diplomatic and failing miserably, "because they figured it out by themselves. Ask anyone—we weren't subtle. Maybe if you weren't so fucking hellbent on convincing yourself I'm a piece of shit you would've figured it out too."

Another step shortens the distance between us to a couple of feet, close enough for Cass to stab a finger into my chest. "That's not fair," he seethes. "I know you, Nick. You fuck around. You don't take girls seriously, you don't take *anything* seriously."

"I'm serious about her."

A scornful noise leaves him. "Yeah, hiding her away from everyone seems real serious. You didn't tell anyone because then it's easier to fuck her over and pretend she doesn't exist. Like you always do."

"*I* wanted to tell you." Frustration fuels my yell. "She was the one who wanted to keep it a secret. She was fucking terrified of how you'd react!" Cass jerks his head back as if I've punched him, exhibiting the briefest flash of guilt, but I don't stop. "This, *this fucking tantrum*, is exactly why she didn't tell you. She knew you would freak out. She was scared and she was fucking right because look *what you did*. You wouldn't even talk to her." My temper gets the best of me and I shove him harder than I should, adopting as menacing a glare as I can muster. "You say I'm bad for her but I'm not the one who left her fucking sobbing on the driveway."

Just like her mom did.

Cass lunges, fist swinging in a sloppy arc toward my face, and I resist the urge to sigh as I catch it easily. Using his momentum against him, I slam him into the wall, my forearm locked across his throat so he doesn't try that shit again. "Fucking calm down."

If looks could kill, I'd be six feet under but I don't relent. "I get that I don't have the best track record with women, okay, but I love Amelia. Frankly, I don't give a shit if you don't believe me. It doesn't change anything. But for her sake, please let us fucking explain."

"I told you not to fuck up her being back in my life," Cass spits in reply.

"I know." It was the first thing he said to me the day they reunited, when we discovered the girl from the diner the boys relentlessly teased me about and his sister were one and the same. I promised I wouldn't then, and I promise the same now.

Except now, Cass doesn't believe me. "When you break her heart," *when, not if,* "she'll run again. And I'll never fucking forgive you."

I could tell him that's not going to happen. I could tell him that she's so much fucking more than someone I love. But he doesn't want to hear that. He won't hear it, not in this angry state of betrayal. While he's like this, I don't think there's anything I can do to convince him.

I let him go. I back up, watching as he shakes himself off, as his expression shifts to something cold and impassive. He doesn't say another word as he snatches up his bag and storms to the door, knocking his shoulder against mine violently on his way past.

"Cass," I call out just before he disappears out the door. "I'm not the one messing with her being in your life right now."

The only response he spares is a hard look and a slamming door.

Two days pass and I'm losing my damn mind.

Two days of not speaking to her. Of only getting updates through Luna or Kate, most of them bleak and alluding to her being glued to her phone trying to get a hold of Cass, and not doing much else. I physically fucking ache with worry but there's fuck all I can do. Like Kate said, if I go there now, if I insert myself into the situation and push too hard, the chances are, it will all go up in flames.

None of us have heard from Cass. Not for lack of trying; his phone must be on the brink of death with the endless messages rolling in but he ignores every attempt at communication. All we know is that he's been staying at one of his teammate's apartments—Luna used that knowledge for evil; she stormed the place in a fury, threatening to castrate the man if he didn't pick up his phone. Luckily for him, Cass wasn't there to face her wrath but fuck, I hope he got the message.

I hope he gets *my* messages. I'm typing out the umpteenth plea for him to at least call Amelia when someone jabs their fingers into my side, and the sweet, dark coffee I'm absently sipping on almost goes flying everywhere. Smacking away Ben's poking hands, I meet his scowl with one of my own. "What?"

"This is pathetic." He nods at the thread of unanswered messages to

Cass. "You really think a thousand messages a day are gonna make him want to speak to us?"

I shrug. Probably not but what's the alternative? Ignoring him and hoping absence makes the heart grow fonder? Fat fucking chance.

Drumming on the kitchen counter, Ben announces, "We're going out." Before I can protest, he slaps a hand over my mouth. "Nope. No arguments. Your moping is making me nauseous and the vibe in here is depressing. We *need* to go out."

I'm not keen. I let Ben know I'm not keen. I put up argument after argument, protest after protest, and somehow I still end up in Greenies, sandwiched between Ben and Jackson like I'm a damn flight risk, knocking back rum like my life depends on it.

The kid is fucking persuasive.

Nursing some fruity cocktail, he chatters about everything and anything yet somehow steers clear of any subject that could lead back to the two people we're trying and failing not to think about. A fucking hard feat considering I've got a one-track mind that constantly loops back around to my girl. Especially when I'm drunk. Double especially when I'm drinking rum.

Fuck, I bet she's forgetting to eat.

Whipping out my phone, clumsy thumbs pull up that Chinese place she likes. It might not be wise for me to personally bring her a shit ton of food, but a delivery man can.

"So, like, I was- *Oh, for fuck's sake.*" Ben groans, snatching my phone away and clucking his tongue disapprovingly, but his glare melts into a simper when he does a double-take at the screen. "As adorable as this is," he half coos, half scolds, "the objective of tonight was to get our minds *off* certain people."

"Shut up." I snatch my phone back, elbowing Jackson when he makes a teasing, crooning noise. "She doesn't eat when she's stressed."

The briefest flash of a sympathetic smile is all I get before my phone is re-confiscated, another drink taking its place.

And another not long after. And another. After that, I lose track, but I know that by the time we stumble outside, we're unashamedly drunk. Like stumbling around, snickering at every-thing trashed—Ben trips over the curb and we bust a gut laughing for ten minutes.

The brisk night air is only slightly sobering, waking me up enough so that when someone bumps into me, I manage to string together a somewhat coherent apology.

An apology I immediately retract when I take the note of who it's aimed at.

Speak—or think—of the Devil and he shall fucking come.

"Look who it is," the bane of my fucking existence sneers with an obnoxious whistling.

It takes every ounce of self-restraint I possess not to wrap my hands around Dylan's puny neck and squeeze. "Fuck off."

He doesn't. Proving his severe lack of intelligence, he encroaches on me, a heavy slap landing on my shoulder. "How's my girl treating you? You get bored of her yet?"

"Shut the fuck up." Edging around him, I try so hard to be the bigger person. To walk away before I snap and flatten the dickhead like he deserves. Only the ghost of Amelia's pleas from the worst night of my life ringing in my ears allows any semblance of level-headedness. *Please don't do anything reckless.*

Dylan, unsurprisingly, has zero interest in being the better man. His survival instincts must be broken because, ignoring the downright murderous intent behind my glare, he gets in my face again, smirking evilly. "I think I'll pay her a visit again soon," he muses, eyes gleaming with a purely disguised threat. "Didn't get the chance to finish our chat last time."

He's baiting me, we all know it, and it's fucking working, but before I can fall for it completely, a hand lands on my shoulder. "He's not worth it," Jackson mutters in my ear.

I agree, like I agreed with Amelia when she said the same thing, but fuck, I don't care. He deserves it. I fucking deserve it, to pummel the shit out of the guy who hurt the woman I love. And I'm about to when Dylan's savage leer shifts to the one person currently keeping his face intact.

"Maybe I'll go see Luna too." Jackson tenses as Dylan licks his lips, throwing his head back and groaning dramatically. "Fuck, you have no idea how many times I thought of her when I was fucking-"

A sickening, satisfying crack rings in the air as a fist cuts off whatever disgusting thing Dylan was about to spout. He tumbles back with the force of the punch but Jackson doesn't let him go far, catching him by the collar and yanking him forward, furious in a way I've never seen. "Watch your fucking mouth."

With a harsh shove, Dylan stumbles away, wiping his bleeding nose on the back of his sleeve—God, I hope it's broken. Regaining his footing, he stares disbelievingly at the blood on his shirt before his narrowed gaze flicks up to us. "You're gonna regret that."

Oh, I highly fucking doubt it.

In the blink of an eye, all hell breaks loose.

One look from their fucking caveman leader and Dylan's witless henchmen spring forward, swinging blindly at us.

Their lack of coordination—as well as their clueless willingness to jump into a fight with someone who spends every fucking day practicing beating the shit out of people and someone else who looks ready to rip heads from bodies—makes me fucking cackle. Fools.

Even floating on a rum-flavored cloud, it's easy to sidestep them, to flatten them in a matter of goddamn minutes. For fuck's sake, I don't even try; one of them trips over my foot. So quickly, everything dissolves into a mess of flying fists and pained wails, none of which come from me. I only wince slightly when my knuckles connect to a cheekbone and split, and when my casualty drops to the floor, I give him an extra enthusiastic kick in the gut for trouble caused. A second later, I'm throwing back an elbow because another dickhead—I swear to God, they multiply like cockroaches—tries to catch me in a headlock. It's that bastard Will, I realize, when he sinks down next to his little friend, and I find a particularly immense amount of sick pleasure in his yelp when my boot connects with his pelvis. *Easy work.*

At the sound of a yelp, I spin around just as Ben cracks Dylan—held upright by Jackson—across the face. Bending at the waist, Ben whines loudly, shaking out his hand wildly. "*Ow.* That fucking hurt."

Dylan groans, agreeing with him apparently.

At the pathetic sound, Ben's grimace quickly turns to a delighted grin, the same one Jackson and I are wearing. The three of us exchange a look, the same sentiment running through each of our minds—*fucking finally.*

With one last dig to the back, Jackson lets Dylan go, shoving him to join the tangled, moaning heap on the ground. I think that last punch might've killed off his last few surviving brain cells because, roaring almost comically, he lunges for Jackson in an attempt to tackle him to the ground.

"Nice fucking try." Snickering, I intercept him halfway with a fist to the stomach, his pained hiss of breath the best sound I've ever heard. Holding him by the scruff of his neck, I lower my mouth to his ear. "Touch *my* girl again and I'll fucking kill you. Although," I jerk my head toward Jackson, "when we tell *his* girl what you said about her, she might beat me to it. Hope you aren't too attached to your balls."

For good measure, said-balls become well acquainted with my knee. Dylan collapses to the ground, the dulcet tones of his whimpers fucking music to my ears as they mix with Ben's triumphant hoots.

Karma, bitch.

53

AMELIA

THE SHRILL SOUND of a doorbell startles Kate and me, pulling our attention away from the television and towards the front door. We exchange confused glances, reaching for our phones to check the time. Past 11PM; a little late for surprise guests.

Reluctantly, Kate rises. "You think Luna forgot her key?"

I snort. "As if she's coming home tonight." Our missing roommate tore out of the apartment about an hour ago after a brief, apparently flustering phone call like a woman on a mission. Specifically, like a woman on a mission for late-night sex.

Peering quizzically through the peephole, Kate's face scrunches in confusion. "Did you order food?"

"No, why?"

In answer, Kate opens the door and reveals a delivery guy laden with food. And I mean *laden*; he's got like three bags in each hand, each one adorned with the logo of my go-to takeout spot. *What the hell?*

"Uh," Kate gapes at the sheer volume of food, "I think you have the wrong address?"

With an entirely unnecessary eye roll, the delivery guy glances at the receipt and recites our address in a bored tone.

"That's us, but we didn't order anything."

"It's for a..." He squints at the lengthy piece of paper. "*Querida*?" Shrugging, he regards us with a blank, unbothered expression. "Everything's paid for. You want it or not?"

Despite his butchering of my favorite word, my heart melts. Of course, it's from Nick.

Abandoning my seat on the sofa, I scurry toward Kate and help her accept the food, kicking the door shut before staggering to the kitchen. When takeout containers cover every inch of kitchen space, Kate and I stare, wordlessly wondering how the hell we're even going to make a dent in everything. "I can't tell if this is really sweet or super ridiculous."

My laugh is uneasy, set off balance by the guilt swirling in my stomach. I've been neglecting Nick, I know that. The part of me that has been hoping Cass would acknowledge one of my million messages and show up, ready to talk, was nervous that if Nick was here, he'd scare him off. Nevermind the fact all I want is for Nick to be here.

And because I'm a massive hypocrite, him not contacting me either has that voice in my head convincing me he's not simply giving me the space I asked for; he's finally realized I'm so not worth the headache.

Then, like always, he does something sweet—but definitely ridiculous—like deliver me my body weight in food to affirm that I am, in fact, unhinged.

"How are we gonna-" Kate's question morphs into a surprised screech that I echo when the front door suddenly bangs open and a whirlwind of fury storms inside.

Luna flails her arms around wildly as she screeches unintelligibly, her rage so all-consuming that she doesn't notice Kate and I watching her with dropped jaws and eyes wide.

Three sheepish men trail in behind her, cowering under her glower. "What's going on?"

Four pairs of eyes snap in my direction, a beloved pair brightening when they land on me. "*Meu amor,*" Nick bounds over, smacking an obnoxious kiss on my lips, "did you get the food?"

Nodding jerkily, I frown when Nick cups my face and something sticky and wet coats my skin. Swatting his hand away and wiping my cheek, I splutter in disbelief at the sight of my fingertips stained red, gasping when I spot Nick's bloody knuckles. "What happened?" Gripping his chin gently, I tilt his face from side to side, checking for injuries and finding nothing but a smug smirk.

"These *buffoons,*" Luna shrieks, "got in a *fight.*"

My head whips towards her lightning-fast. "A fight? What fight?"

Kissing her teeth, Luna holds up a hand in a gesture that screams, 'oh, just you wait.' "They got in a fight," she repeats, slow with maximum venom. "At Greenies. Where. We. *Work.*" Each word, she punctuates with a punch to Jackson's arm. Unbothered, the man simply catches her flailing fist and brings it to his lips, kissing her knuckles. When she whacks him with the other hand, he does the same thing, and she rips them both away with a scowl.

"Dopey Dan was working and recognized this fool," she tells me, jerking a thumb at her boyfriend. "He called me to pick them up because not only did they start a fucking brawl, they decided to drink themselves into the gutter after."

Ah. So that's what that smell is. Something heady and sweet—like rum—mixed with the distinct metallic scent of blood and subtle undertones of Chinese food.

The Yankee Candle of my dreams.

"My co-worker ringing me to pick up my boyfriend," Luna mumbles, pinching the bridge of her nose. "Jesus fucking Christ."

"Trust me, baby." Ignoring her resistance, Jackson tugs Luna into his arms, planting a possessive kiss on the curve of her neck. "He deserved it,"

"Who deserved it?"

The boys all freeze at my question, their proud leering suddenly wiped away. Pulling me into his side, Nick peers down at me apprehensively, like he's afraid whatever he's about to say will piss me off. Throat bobbing as he swallows, he squeezes my hip and utters a single word. "Dylan."

A heavy silence settles and lasts all of two seconds before Luna hollers a victory roar. "You should've led with that!" Skipping around the room, she doles out high-fives to each of the guys, following up with a slap upside the head and an admonishment for not ensuring she was there to witness the glorious event. "I want details."

Ben indulges her, brandishing his bruised knuckles like a trophy. Snatching his hand to check the damage, Kate feigns a stern look that barely conceals her Cheshire Cat grin. "About time," I hear her mutter.

While my friends celebrate, I process silently. Yeah, I'm over the moon Dylan finally got his ass kicked like he rightly deserves. But I also know what he's like; volatile as fuck.

My cheek aches with the memory of his favorite form of *repercussions.*

A hand sneaks into my hair, tugging lightly and directing my gaze upwards to meet a knowing gaze. "I'm bleeding on your floor."

I glance down at the scarlet droplets collecting on the wood under my feet. "Shit."

Nick holds his bleeding knuckles up, adopting a pathetically adorable helpless expression. "Help me clean up?"

~

I wonder if my father would be proud of how adept I've become at cleaning up battle wounds. It's second nature at this point; my fingers work quickly, deftly wiping blood and applying ointments and bandaging carefully.

He'd probably be less proud at how the sight of blood makes my stomach roll.

He definitely would not be proud of me sitting on my patient's lap with his head buried in my neck. "Remember my birthday?" Nick asks out of nowhere, the words muffled as he peppers kisses along my skin.

"Uh-huh."

"You cleaned me up then too."

"I did."

"I wanted to fuck you so bad."

"Nick!" I jerk back, mouth and eyes wide as I slap at his chest.

"What? I did." He smiles innocently, but the glimmer in his eyes is anything but innocent. "You taking care of me, all doe-eyed, in that fucking dress. And then you in my shirt." He groans playfully, eyes flitting skyward as he squeezes my thighs. "I knew I was screwed."

"I knew you were flirting to distract me," *like you're doing now,* I add silently.

"It worked, didn't it?" That it did. It *definitely* did. His playful antics and dirty remarks were enough to make me forget the shitshow that night was, even if just for a little while. It's where the whole distraction thing began.

The mirthful atmosphere fades as Nick skims his uninjured knuckles up my waist. "I missed you."

That seemingly permanent prickle of guilt itches up my spine again. Cradling one cheek, I kiss the other. "I missed you too. I'm sorry."

He dismisses my apology with a frown, cutting off my attempt to explain too with a brisk shake of his head. "Tomorrow," he whispers, tilting his head to capture my lips briefly.

Probably for the best; I think his breath could get me second-hand drunk.

Since he won't let me explain, I turn the opportunity on him. "How about tonight you explain what happened with Dylan?"

Nick sours instantly. "He started it."

Manchild. "Elaborate a little, love."

Lips curling in a snarl, Nick holds me tight as he runs through the night's unexpected turn of events—losing me at times when he unconsciously slips between Portuguese and English but I get the gist. I cringe when he relays Dylan's crass words, a tight, nauseating knot forming in my stomach.

Only when fists start being thrown in his tale does Nick's expression lighten, his stony face lifting into a proud smirk. "I think Jackson broke his nose."

"Remind me to thank him."

Calloused fingers dip beneath my pajamas to tickle my sides. "I kicked him in the balls."

"Snap," I chuckle softly. "So did I."

In the blink of an eye, Nick's face falls solemn again. "I mean it, *querida*. He follows through on his threat and I swear to God, *vou matá-lo.*"

"He can't," I assure him, feeling a flutter of relief. For once, I can say those words with absolute certainty.

Nick grumbles in dissatisfaction. "If he does, he won't be lucky enough to walk away this time."

"No," I lean back, catching his annoyed gaze, "he literally can't." Trailing a finger along his collarbone, I confess, "they granted me a temporary restraining order. I got a court date to appeal for a permanent one. He'll be served soon."

"What?" Nick splutters, blinking rapidly in surprise. "When did you find out?"

"Yesterday." I was too caught up with everything else to properly let the information sink in when I got the call—it was only hours later, when the girls did their routine check-in, that it actually hit me. A single 'you okay?' and I burst into tears, my friends not far behind when I wheezed out why I was blubbering once again. We spent the night curled up in a ball of happy, grateful tears and snotty noses.

Trapping me in a bone-crushing hug, Nick flips us so I'm pinned to the mattress, trapped beneath his body as he attacks me with kisses and murmured triumphant expletives. "I am so fucking proud of you, *querida*."

I blush at his attention and praise, shrugging it off, but I'm kind of proud of myself too—it's nice to know I've done something right lately.

Nice to know I finally get to close a horrendous chapter of my life soon.

I slip out of bed as stealthily as I'm capable of, not wanting to wake the peacefully snoozing man still curled up on my mattress. I'd much prefer to stay wrapped up in the warm cocoon Nick always creates but I have class. Considering how my studies took a nosedive last semester—chaos and drama drama don't lend themselves to a great working environment—I can't afford to skip.

So, like the responsible adult I'm aiming to be, I get my ass out of bed.

Well, I *try*.

I'm barely upright before I'm yanked back down, cradled against a warm chest again, a husky grumble sending a shiver down my spine. "Don't even think about it, *querida*."

Grunting unattractively, I whine an objection. "I have class."

In one swift movement, Nick rolls us both so I'm sprawled on top of him. One large hand settles on my ass, the other on the small of my back, both securing me in place. "I don't give a shit," he mutters, cracking open an eye. Dimples winking, he dips his head to trail teasing kisses along my jaw. "What did I say about waking up alone?"

"Nick." His name comes out as a whimper when his tongue lashes the sensitive spot just below my ear. "I have to go."

"You *have* two days to make up for." His grin is roguish when I first sit up, my knees digging into the mattress as I straddle him, but any mirth disappears when our gazes lock. Grip shifting to my waist, he squeezes gently, thumbs tracing my hip bones absently. "You've been ignoring me."

My teeth catch my bottom lip, chewing nervously. "Not on purpose."

I've been so wrapped up in trying to contact Cass, I've neglected everything else. Those two absent days have been a constant cycle of dialing his number, leaving a voicemail, and redialing, the gaps in between filled with nervous pacing and obsessing over every little thing I did wrong.

I explain it all to Nick and when I'm done, he brushes his swollen knuckles across my cheek, guiding my gaze back to his. "You said you'd let me help," he reminds me quietly.

"There's not really much you can do. This is my mess."

"Our mess," he corrects. "He's mad at me too. Actually, he's madder at me," he grumbles the latter beneath his breath, shifting in a sudden bout of irritation, and at my questioning stare, he relays his conversation with Cass from the other day. I assumed that, same as me, he hadn't seen Cass since Big Bear, and anger and sadness flood me in equal measure when I hear how Cass spoke to him, so dismissive and plain rude.

The hands on my waist pinch my skin lightly. "You're being too hard on yourself. I'm at fault here too, and Cass isn't being fair by not even giving us the chance to explain."

"I get it though." I lift a shoulder weakly. "He's hurt. I wouldn't want to hear my excuses either. But," sighing, my fingers coast upward, sprawling on either side of his neck, "I wish he was taking his anger out on me instead of you. I don't like the way he's bashing you constantly."

"I deserve some of it."

"No, you don't." I stoop to kiss him. "Best thing that ever happened to me, remember?"

I don't get the smile I'm fishing for; I get a thoughtfully creased forehead and a tiny, vulnerable question that makes my heart break. "What if he makes you choose? Between me and him."

"He wouldn't." That, I'm positive about. Cass might not like Nick and I being together but he'd never issue an ultimatum. We weren't raised like that.

Reactive and stubborn, yes.

Selfish and uncompromising, never.

"But if he did, then that's not the person I grew up with." That is a person who'd get his ass kicked by a very disappointed mother. "I wouldn't want someone like that in my life."

A playful, weak grin breaks through. "So, you'd pick me?"

"I wouldn't pick at all." I poke his chest, rolling my eyes when he pouts. "If he would rather cut me out than see me happy with the man I love, then that's his choice, not mine. But, like I said, he wouldn't do that."

Twining my hair around his fingers, Nick tugs me down until we're a breath apart. "That was a really good answer."

I grin. "I've had two days to think about it."

54

AMELIA

WEEKS PASS without a single word from Cass.

No calls, no messages, not even so much as a glimpse of him on campus. As far as the guys can tell, he hasn't been home since the day he stormed out. He disappears completely; the only reason I know he's alive is because Lynn has assured me so.

I'm worried beyond freaking belief but more than that, I'm angry because I think he wants me to be worried. It feels like he's doing it on purpose, like he's taking what I did years ago and throwing it back at me, seeing how I like it, and it's not freaking fair. He's hurt, fine. He thinks we betrayed him, valid. But it's not the same.

Cass being hurt that I lied about my relationship is not the same as my boyfriend freaking *dying*. And if he tries to compare the two, I really think I'm going to punch him in the face.

It is weird, though, how I can have this ominous dark cloud hanging over my head yet simultaneously be so inexplicably happy. Because freaking cumulonimbus has a silver lining.

Nick.

We're inseparable. Like, truly joined at the hip. That couple you make fun of with your friends for being so obsessed with each other? We are that couple, and I don't give a shit.

Call it making up for all that lost time I wasted hiding him away.

I've been on more dates the past few weeks than I have in my entire life, and I strongly suspect it's Nick's tactic to keep my mind off Cass. It works; hard to think about anything else when your hot boyfriend is constantly showering you with love.

Sometimes, I still find it hard to correlate the Nick I know now with the drunk player I first met—and didn't particularly like—months ago. I can't quite imagine *that* Nick letting me drag him around farmer's markets on Sunday mornings, going to brunch with my friends, or strolling through the Antelope Valley Poppy Reserve hand in hand with me, snapping endless pictures and tucking a freaking flower behind my ear.

It's the weirdest feeling in the world, going from disliking affection—because I always had to beg for the genuine kind—to drowning in a never-ending abundance of it yet still not being able to get enough.

And Nick has been doling out a little extra since we arrived in Carlton to spend what's shaping up to be a very awkward Spring Break with our families.

Coming here was always the plan; we amended it slightly. Instead of staying with the Morgans—it's up in the air whether or not Cass is still coming but I figured ambushing him wouldn't be a smart idea—I'm staying with the Silvas.

In their house.

Which my brain is convinced is still *my* house.

Super weird.

There was a full minute after I woke up from napping—the early morning and a long, anxious drive took it out of me—when I was sixteen again. Sleeping in a bed I really considered a spare in a room I barely used. If I squinted hard enough, I could make out marks on the wall where a mirror used to hang, scuffs on the floorboards made by dancing feet.

Dancing I did before the structure tucked down the end of my—*Nick's*—backyard was built.

I swallow hard as I inspect the glorified shed holding considerably more memories than my childhood home, the one place I ever really felt alone. It's changed—I knew that before I stepped foot inside. No longer is it the dance studio of every little ballerina's dreams. It's still floored with hardwood. The walls are still wrapped with mirrors. The ratty old bean bag where a blue-eyed boy used to sit and watch his girlfriend work her toes bloody somehow survived the renovation. But, newly added, there's a punching bag hanging from the ceiling. A weight rack in one corner. A pull-up bar in another that has my mind wandering, imagining a sweaty, straining Nick working out in here.

I should resent the change but I don't. I'm glad the space I once cherished didn't become completely desolate, instead morphing into someone else's little haven.

Strong arms wrapping around my waist don't surprise me; I knew once Nick found his bed empty, he'd come looking, and there's only so many places to hide. I relax into him, clutching the forearms banded tightly across my tummy. "Do you miss it?" he murmurs in my ear, and it strikes me that it's the first time I've ever been asked that. If I miss the second thing I lost in the accident, the hobby I could no longer bring myself to do because it hurt too much, beyond the physical. It's the first time I've ever really considered it, actually; I had something far more important to mourn.

"No," young Amelia would be shocked to hear. "I loved it but it was just a thing I did, y'know?" James—shockingly—is basically a genius. Cass has baseball. I needed something that was mine.

"Hmm." Stubble tickles my skin as Nick's cheek brushes mine. "Your dad's next door."

"Already?" He's early—a rarity. Full of surprises lately, my dad; him exchanging a weekend visit to Sun Valley with a whole week in Carlton was a welcome shock. Twirling around, my excitement dims when I notice the abnormal rigidity of my boyfriend. "What's wrong with you?"

"Nothing," Nick lies.

"Bull." Through narrowed eyes, I inspect him *carefully*, noting the tight set of his jaw, the exaggerated bob of his throat as he swallows, the constant fidgeting with the hem of my dress. "Are you *nervous*?"

Calloused fingers trace the column of my spine before digging into my lower back. "I'm meeting your dad."

"You've met him before."

"This is different. I wasn't your boyfriend then, I was—"

"My distraction?" I tease, winding my arms around his neck, playing with the soft curls at the nape. "Pining? Wistfully waiting for me to fall in love with you?"

"All of the above," he rasps.

I'm not entirely sure it's a joke.

Nick ducks out of my grip, the pressure of his fingertips increasing as he guides me outside and toward the gap in the fence—storm damage no one ever bothered to fix. Wriggling between the warped slats of wood, we amble up to the house. "I want him to like me."

I squeeze the hand held tight in mine. "He does like you."

"It's true," a third voice concurs. Both our gazes snap to the man standing on the Morgans' back porch, hands on his hips and a smile on his face.

I return my dad's grin. Jogging the last few yards between us, I exhale happily when he wraps me in a tight hug. "I missed you." I always miss him but sometimes I forget how much. I never realize how much his absence affects me until he's standing in front of me, presence soothing me from the inside out.

Dad returns the sentiment with a kiss brushed on the top of my head. He keeps me tucked beneath his arm as he extends a hand toward the uncharacteristically flushed man lurking on the bottom step. "Good to see you again, son."

To his credit, Nick doesn't hesitate before accepting my dad's hand, shaking firmly and hitting him with one of his winning smiles, dimples and all. "Nice to see you too, sir."

Dad's laugh is booming. "Patrick, please. Call me sir again and I'll change my mind about liking you."

Oh, I like nervous Nick. I like nervous Nick a lot. He's freaking adorable, flushed and scratching the back of his head as he nods timidly.

Dad doesn't miss a beat; he launches into easy conversation as he hustles inside, quizzing us on class and work and hobbies until the tension holding Nick taut eases. Before I know it, they're laughing like old friends and I'm holding back a groan as they make all kinds of plans.

Apparently, the next time my boyfriend beats the crap out of someone for entertainment, Dad's going to bear witness.

Fun.

When I flick on the kettle and fish three mugs from the cabinet, Nick stops me. "I'm not staying." Dual protests are met with an adamant shake of his head. "I'll let you two catch up."

"I'll walk you out." As we disappear down the hall, I notice Dad making a purposeful effort to busy himself, whistling quietly and pouring tea.

One hand on the doorknob, Nick drags me closer than he dared stand when in the presence of my father, fingers dancing along my hip. I purse my lips at how tentatively he touches me—even without watchful eyes, his usual possessive grip is replaced by a timid ghost of a caress. "Ma said to invite him for dinner."

Chin resting on his chest, I gaze up at him. "He'll love that."

A relieved breath brushes my temple in tandem with soft lips. "*Eu te amo.*"

"I love you," I reciprocate quietly, placing a kiss near the center of his chest—the highest spot I can reach.

The second the door closes behind Nick, a very amused throat clears. Nose scrunching in anticipation, I spin around to find my dad exactly as I expected; smirking like a jackass. "*Love,* huh?"

As I rejoin him in the kitchen, I wonder if I've reached the age where I can flip him off without consequence. "Shut up."

"For the record, I am way too young to be a grandfather."

"*Dad.*" I sink onto a stool with a groan, palming my cheeks like that might stem the raging blush. "Jesus Christ."

Fueled by my embarrassment, he only grins wider, damn near glowing as he slides a hot mug of tea—he's a strictly herbal man —my way.

"So," he starts, and I brace myself for more freaking harassment, "will I be seeing Cass this week?"

Damn. I almost wish he'd teased me some more instead of bringing up *that.*

Slumping against the counter, I shrug. "I don't know. I texted him." A reply wasn't expected yet I was still disappointed when I didn't get one.

Dad reaches over to squeeze my forearm, humor fading. "I'm sorry, sweetie."

Another shrug is all I can manage as I watch steam swirl up from my mug. "It's okay. I messed up."

"Yeah, you did," Dad agrees, all matter-of-fact and way too quick for my liking. "But you'll fix it." He rounds the counter to sit beside me, gently knocking our shoulders. "What you did was hurtful, yes, but it's not unforgivable. You didn't do anything wrong, kiddo. You just fell in love."

Well, it sounds a helluva lot less clandestine when you put it like that.

Corner of my mouth lifting tentatively, I search for clarification on what I already know. "So, you approve?"

"Approve?" Another booming laugh sounds. "He has a good job and studies hard, he takes care of his family, he treats my daughter well, *and* he puts up with not one, but *two* of my kids. Any man who can manage all that is worthy in my eyes. Heck, I might even be a little in love with him."

Despite his jesting tone, I know he's serious, and my heart freaking swells when my presumption is confirmed. "Yes, Amelia. I approve."

One down, one to go.

~

"Fuck me, that smells good."

James' moan is met by a round of chastising and pointed looks towards a giggling Sofia. "Language," Lynn tuts, scowling at her son as she sets a casserole dish on the dining table.

Unsurprisingly, the reprimand rolls off my eldest brother's back; sheepish is not a trait of his. Laughing, he yanks my hair with a wink. "What, Nick can eat Amelia's face off in front of the kid but *naughty language*," he tosses our mother a mocking look, "is gonna scandalize her?"

"I despise you," I hiss, shoving him away. Why, *why*, was I ever delighted to have this big freaking oaf back in my life? "You are a menace."

"*You* need to keep your tongue to yourself."

"James," it's Dad's turn to whine. "For the love of God, shut up."

The chest at my back vibrates with poorly concealed laughter, and I crane my neck to scowl at Nick. "I'm so glad you find this funny."

"I do." He stoops, murmuring for my ears only, "You think they'd be so prudish about kissing if they knew what we did on that counter?"

Kill me. Literally, kill me now.

If I wasn't already convinced I'm a little in love with my boyfriend's mom, I'd fall the moment she claps her hands pointedly and gestures at the food-laden dining table, most of which she had a hand in cooking up. "Everybody sit, *por favor*, before my poor *nora* faints."

Nick's laughter dries up quickfast. He stares at his mother as he pulls out a chair for me, plopping himself in the one beside. "What does *nora* mean?" I ask, only a little because I'm curious, a lot because the word makes nervous Nick rear his head and, as established, I am a big fan of him.

Unease bleeds from the man. Rolling his shoulders, he cranks his neck like he's working out a crick. "*Querida*, I have a feeling you'd prefer not knowing."

"Well, now I'm intrigued," I croon, landing a hand on his thigh as I lean in and bat my lashes at him. "C'mon. Spill."

The kick I'm getting out of Nick's discomfort dies in an instant when his mouth adopts a slow, smug curve. "Daughter-in-law, *meu amor*," he drawls. "That's what it means."

Oh.

Squeaking something unintelligible, I snap forward, hands clasped in my lap. With a chuckle, Nick slips an arm around the back of my chair, gripping the nape of my neck. "Was I right?"

Yup. Ignorance would've been bliss.

Fingers massage my neck. "Don't freak out."

I'd laugh, if I wasn't freaking out. "I'm not."

Nick's *uh-huh* is the epitome of comic dubiety.

With one last squeeze, he releases me, filling his hand with a serving spoon instead and filling the dinner bowl in front of me with something he calls *moqueca*. "It's seafood stew," he tells me. "But Ma made a veggie version for you."

As the others join us around the Morgans' dining room table for a family dinner, there's a glaringly obvious absence. Everyone avoids mentioning it like the plague, filling our focus with the immense spread of food before us instead.

I don't know at what point I'm supposed to stop expecting Cass to appear. I wonder if my guilt will dry up when he inevitably does; don't need to be a genius to know he's staying away on account of my presence.

Lynn is positive he'll show up. "You know our boy," she'd said when I first arrived, tucking me beneath her arm. "He'll come around. Stubbornness just runs in the family."

Yeah, well, optimism does not.

That's probably why when, over the ruckus of eating and conversation, I faintly hear the sound of the front door opening and closing, I

EJ BLAISE

don't think anything of it—I attribute it to my imagination. The footsteps in the hallway, too they're probably in my head.

Something I can't blame on being a conjured-up hallucination?

The appearance of the very man I've been dying to see in the kitchen
doorway.

55

AMELIA

FOR A BRIEF MOMENT, no one moves. No one says a word.

We gape at Cass like he's a mirage. He looks at us in a similar way, almost like he's caught off guard. Which is confusing, because this is his house, and he definitely knew we were here.

On closer inspection, I realize it's not surprise, but apprehension. Nerves. Kind of like how he looks before a big game—jittery and anxious and pumped with adrenaline.

"Well, finally," it's James who breaks the silence, drawling loudly, "look who showed up."

Cass doesn't react with anything more than a tight-lipped grimace I think is supposed to be a smile.

He's staring at me. Not directly at me, but in my direction, focusing on something below my face. It only takes a quick glance to see it's the hand cupping my shoulder—Nick's hand. A soft touch that falls to my lower back as I stand. A source of strength and support as I clear my throat, very aware of the dozen or so eyes trained on me, not meeting any but Cass'. "Can we talk?"

He offers neither a yes nor a no; he turns on his heel and strides outside again, leaving the front door open in his wake as a wordless invitation to follow.

"Where've you been?" I ask the moment my feet hit the wooden porch, arms folded awkwardly around myself.

My brother leans against the railing and shrugs. "Around."

"I was worried about you." Cass snorts, scuffing the toe of his sneaker against the decking. My fingers twitch at my side. "*I was.*"

"Okay," he mutters sarcastically, and for some reason, the single, drawn-out word pisses me off enough to snap.

I get that he's hurt, I understand that, but he's being a child. He's missing class, avoiding his house, avoiding his friends. For God's sake, he missed a game. Enough is freaking enough. "Will you cut the passive-aggressive shit and talk to me?"

"Will you stop lying?" he spits back. "First, you lie about Dylan, then you lie about Nick."

I bristle. "That is not the same thing."

"Isn't it?" he challenges. "They're both pretty fucking big secrets. Life-altering, I'd say."

"They're not the same," I repeat through gritted teeth. There's no comparison between a secret protected out of love and one kept out of shame and embarrassment, and *fear*.

"Do you not trust me or something?" The hint of a forlorn expression, the tiny break in his voice, tugs at my heartstrings and calls on the almost permanent pit of guilt in my stomach.

"Of course I do," I huff in frustration, collapsing on the porch swing, my anger snuffed out by a sudden wave of fatigue and weariness. Fighting with Cass is—and has always been—exhausting. I think that's the main reason our arguments were always such sporadic bouts, quick-burning and hastily resolved; we simply never had the stamina to stay mad at each other.

Or the willpower.

Shifting awkwardly, I shoot my brother a pleading stare. "Can we talk, please? Let me explain?"

For the longest second of my life, he doesn't respond. Studies me without meeting my imploring gaze. Contemplates my request as though it's a life-or-death decision. Eventually, he sighs. "I'm gonna need a drink for this."

Cass returns with a six-pack of beer in his grip. Collapsing beside me, he offers me one and I take it more than eagerly, as eagerly as he cracks open his and sucks down the contents.

For the first time in a month, Cass looks me in the eye, the regret in his gaze staggering. "I'm sorry. I shouldn't have mentioned Dylan."

"Yeah, you shouldn't have." I tuck my knees up to my chest, resting my chin on them. "But I forgive you."

There's a pause—we both fill it by taking a welcome sip of beer—before Cass quietly says, "So. Thanksgiving." It's a timid prompt, one I'm not sure how to answer, so I simply nod. His jaw clenches as he runs his tongue over his teeth. "Was I in the house when you fucked my best friend?"

"Jesus, Cass," I choke, grimacing at his crassness. "We didn't... do *that.*" Figuring he doesn't need to hear what we did do, I continue vaguely, "It just happened. I didn't tell you at first because we were keeping it a casual thing. Which was completely my decision, not Nick's," I add when his expression turns thunderous. "I didn't want anything serious after Dylan, and Nick went along with it."

"I'm guessing you changed your mind."

"More like I came to my senses." Cass raises a questioning brow at my muttered comment, and I take a deep breath, powering through despite how disgustingly awkward this conversation is. "On New Year's Eve, he called me out on my bullshit. He didn't want to sneak around anymore." I smile faintly at my hands, remembering.

I can't sneak around and act like I'm not falling for you because it's not fucking working.

Shifting my attention back to Cass, I try my best to stop grinning like a fool. "I know you don't see it, Cass, but he is so fucking good to me."

Cass drops his gaze, picking at the label on his beer bottle. "I don't see it because you wouldn't let me."

"I know. That was all me as well. After things got serious, Nick wanted to tell you but I kept holding off. There was so much shit going on and I liked having something that was *mine.*"

The faintest of smiles curl Cass' lips, igniting a flutter of hope in my chest. "Control freak," he jokes weakly.

I allow myself to bathe in the smallest display of a ceasefire before persevering, "I promise, we never purposely told anyone else. They all found out by accident. I didn't want to tell anyone else until I told you but," I swallow, hating the repetitive excuse but it's the truth, "it just happened."

"After the baseball fundraiser," Cass says suddenly, randomly, frowning. "You tried to tell me?" When I nod, he slumps forward, resting his elbows on his knees and his head in his hand. "And I basically told you I'd never be okay with it."

A wry smile curls my lips. "I believe you said you'd kill him."

Cass crinkles his nose and reluctantly shifts his gaze to me. "Okay, yeah, that one was my bad."

"And Mom?" he asks. "How did she know?"

My cheeks heat. "The book Nick gave me for Christmas," I say softly. I explain how it was his dad's favorite, how Ana saw it and put two and two together, how she shared her suspicions with Lynn, and the whole thing unraveled like an exceptionally tangled piece of string.

When I'm done, Cass groans and throws his head back against the sofa. "So everyone really just figured it out? Fucking hell, I feel like a dumbass."

"At least you're pretty," I pose a risky joke, testing the waters, crossing my fingers in my lap. Cass scowls at me, but a reluctant smile peeks through.

It takes an hour for me to divulge the whole thing. How it happened was painful to explain because the simple answer is raw sex appeal, and that's not the most fun thing to admit to your brother. I dance around the more salacious details and hope he gets—or that he doesn't get—the gist.

Why it continued, which I think garnered me sympathy points; how can you be mad at your poor sister, desperate for a gentle touch rather than a painful grip?

Through all my story-telling, one theme remains; the blame is entirely on me. Not on our friends, not on Nick, purely on me. I think I can live with him being mad at me, as long as it's me that his anger is aimed at. As long as nothing else is ruined too.

We're exhausted by the time I'm done. Rubbing his tired, overwhelmed-looking eyes, Cass exhales heavily. "I'm not mad because you're with him." He pauses, cocking his head as he contemplates his words, "Well, I was at first, a little. But it was mostly the lying."

"I know, and I'm so, so sorry." Another constant theme of the last hour; apologizing. Profusely. Desperately. A tad pathetically but my pride can take the bashing.

"I was embarrassed," Cass admits. "You guys were literally under my nose and I didn't see it." He pauses again, seeming to shrink in on himself as he drops his gaze to his rapidly bouncing knees. "And I was jealous," comes his quiet, frown-inducing confession. Suddenly, he looks so much younger, so much like the brother from my childhood who got pouty when he caught James and me playing without him, or when Lynn gave me more attention than she gave him. "I just got you back. I wasn't prepared to have to share you so quickly."

When he drags his eyes to meet mine, the intense vulnerability in them makes my chest ache. "If my sister and my best friend are in love and spending all their time with each other, then where do I fit in?"

I strongly suspect the sound of my heart breaking in two is unmistakably audible.

"Cass," I release the breath burning my lungs in a soft sigh and shift closer. "Nothing is ever going to change the fact that we're family. I can love him and still love you, it's not a one or the other kind of thing."

"I know that," he grumbles unconvincingly. Making a noise of resignation, he slings an arm around me and tugs me into his side. I almost weep at the contact, eyes burning as I drop my head to his shoulder.

This is what I was afraid of losing. Comfort. Friendship. *Family.*

"I didn't tell you," I sniff with the effort of stifling tears, "because I was so terrified of losing you."

Grip tightening, he rests his cheek atop my head. "Never gonna happen, Tiny."

~

We're okay.

I think we're okay.

We're laughing and joking and catching up on everything we missed in each other's lives; he's been bouncing around from one teammate's place to another and spending all his time at the batting cages and bars a town over so he wouldn't run into anyone.

We're teetering on a rocky edge, toeing a dangerous line.

A line that I might break with a single request.

Because God knows I *love* pushing my luck.

"I hate to ruin the moment," I start tentatively, earning a pained look from Cass as he cracks open another beer. "You need to apologize to Nick." Cass pauses mid-drink, narrowing his eyes at me but I soldier on. "The shit you said to him wasn't okay. He doesn't deserve you making

413

out like he's using me or taking advantage of me or something. Honestly, if anything it was the other way around."

Cass fakes a gag. "I did not need to know that."

Ignoring his horror, I fix him with a determined stare. "Please."

He huffs, suddenly fascinated by his beer.

"Cassie," I whine, turning to my trusty trio of pouting, puppy-dog eyes, and childhood nicknames. Three things that always had him relenting with a sigh, and it appears they still work like a charm.

"I will. Just gimme some time."

Now, doesn't that sound familiar?

Like sister, like brother.

"I saw Dylan on campus."

"Oh yeah?" For once, the mention of my ex's name doesn't cause me to stiffen and shrink. Instead, I smile, because something about Cass' expression tells me something very specific about Dylan's features caught his eye. Namely, the bruises covering every square inch of his face.

I saw him on campus for a fleeting second and God, in the weirdest turn of events, it brightened my day.

Apparently, if his shit-eating grin is anything to go by, it had the same effect on Cass. "Guessing that was Nick's handiwork?"

"Technically, it was Jackson's. A little bit of Ben's, too. I don't think you ever wanna get close enough to see the bruises Nick left."

Cass grunts a laugh, the delight on his face morphing with a pouty grimace. "Why do I always miss the good shit?"

"You were too busy throwing a tantrum," I mutter under my breath, but he hears me. He shoots me a glare, I smile innocently back. "Too soon?" An annoyed grunt rumbles in his chest but he dips his head to hide a smile, the sight sending a flood of relief through me.

I notice Cass' throat bob as he swallows, scratching the back of his head nervously. "I think it's my turn to ruin the moment."

The same as he did earlier, I groan in protest, slumping forward so my elbows hit my knees, beer bottle dangling from my fingertips.

"Your dad mentioned you saw Diane."

The mere mention of her name has my lips curling up in a sneer, my blood boiling, the most intense feelings of hatred I've ever experienced flushing my skin.

"I'm sorry I wasn't there for you," Cass apologizes sincerely. "If you need to talk about it…"

"I don't," I interrupt. I really, really don't. I'm done, I'm so freaking done with that woman, and if I never see her again, it'll be too soon. I have too many absences to mourn to spend another second thinking about her.

Cass gets it, like I suspected he would. Slumping beside me, he clinks his beer bottle against mine, and we sip in unison.

For the first time in weeks, I feel settled. Unbothered. Unburdened. At ease with myself and my life.

God only knows how long that'll last.

56

NICK

"SLEEP WELL?" Ma pounces the moment I slope into the kitchen, a grin on her face as she sips her coffee. A wry, knowing grin as though she suspects her question has a salacious answer.

Jesus Christ.

"*Sim, mamãe.* We *slept* very well." Literally all Amelia and I did last night was talk and sleep; I wasn't going to fuck her with my mother and sister sleeping soundly down the hall, able to hear every moan and whimper.

I'm waiting until they leave for the day. Like a gentleman.

"*Onde está Amelia?*"

"Showering." Mid-rummage through the refrigerator, I glance over my shoulder and catch my mom pouting at my girlfriend's absence. Honestly, same; it takes a special kind of willpower to leave a beautiful, naked woman alone in your room.

Or a special kind of inanity.

"Everything is okay?" Standing, Ma rounds the counter to set her mug in the sink, brushing a hand over my shoulder.

With Amelia? Perfect.

With Cass? Not so much.

There's an undeniable strain between us. Every move I make, he scrutinizes. Every time I so much as brush against Amelia, he notes. He always has this warning, cautious look in his eyes like he's daring me to fuck up, waiting for me to do something wrong.

When I explain as much to Ma, she clicks her tongue and waves off my comments dismissively. "He is a good brother." I scoff and she fixes me with a knowing stare. "Put yourself in his shoes, Nico. Imagine you were watching a man drape himself over Sofia constantly."

My face twists—the thought alone of someone getting handsy with her in the future makes me simultaneously nauseous and angry.

She's right, and I don't like it.

A frustrated huff escapes me as I slam the fridge shut and slump against it. This whole situation is shit. Everyone has their reasons for feeling the way they do. Everyone's reasons are valid, in one way or another. There's no bad guy in the situation—just shit timing and a string of unfortunate circumstances.

"*Tudo ficará bem, Nico,*" Ma croons, patting my cheek comfortingly. "You are a good man. Cass knows this. Give it time."

Time.

Give it *time.*

For fuck's sake, the man has been sulking for a month.

Ma doesn't hang around long after dropping that nugget of wisdom. She has to take Sofia to soccer practice, and while my little sister is distraught that me and Amelia aren't coming to watch, she's easily soothed by the promise of ice-cream and a movie later. I get a kiss on each cheek and then they're gone, taking their noise and chaos with them.

The house settles with their absence, the only sound coming from the shower running upstairs and the quiet music coming from the radio. I hum along to a random song as I start on breakfast, quickly filling a mug with fresh coffee when I hear light footsteps creeping downstairs. "You want pancakes, *meu amor?*"

Amelia lingers in the doorway, shifting on her feet. Mussed hair, flushed cheeks, one of my hoodies hanging down to her knees. "Where is everyone?" Something inexplicably sultry lingers in her tone, her gaze jumping around the room checking if we're alone.

"They're out," I answer slowly, turning off the stove and finishing the heaping pancake stack.

Her expression turns downright devious. My brows shoot up as she smiles slowly, long lashes fluttering. "I found something."

"Oh?" I rack my brain for what she could have found that has her prowling towards me, looking like the fucking devil in disguise. Toying

417

with the hem of her—*my*—hoodie, she draws my attention to the fabric skimming her thighs. In one swift movement, she lifts it up and over her head, tossing it aside.

The spatula in my hand drops to the floor with a clatter, my jaw not far behind.

Fuck me.

I swallow hard, my fingers curling around the countertop in an attempt to stop myself from dropping to my knees like a fool.

Fuck me, fuck me, fuck me.

Amelia smoothes a hand down her front, caressing her almost naked skin teasingly. "Do I want to know why you brought *this* to your mother's house?"

Fuck knows. Foolish hope, maybe. God, am I glad I did though.

"Valentine's Day present," is all I manage to stammer out.

Honestly, it's more my present than hers. Her simpering coyly in front of me, covered in strips of lace and green satin, creamy skin and pert rosy nipples visible through the thin material... *Fuck.*

She huffs a breathy laugh, toying with the sheer fabric hugging her hips. "Yeah, I get why you didn't want Cass to see this."

Brazen as anything, she saunters towards me. She jerks in surprise when I halt her movements. "Stay right fucking there," I growl as I sprint past her and upstairs.

As much as I love her current attire, it's not complete.

A handful of seconds rummaging through my bag and I'm thundering back downstairs. Amelia shoots me a 'what the fuck?' look as I stalk her way, twirling a finger in a spinning motion. "Turn around."

She obeys immediately. Sweeping her hair away from her neck, I produce the dainty necklace hidden in my hand—her *real* present. She gasps softly as I clip it around her neck, her fingers reaching up to examine it eagerly, and I try not to let my eyes dip to her lace-covered chest when she spins back around.

A simple gold chain with two charms slides between her fingers. Her thumb brushes a sparkling emerald. "It was my mom's," I tell her softly. Eyes the same color as the pendant shoot to me, wide with surprise, and I silence the protests I know are coming with a kiss.

Ma insisted—literally forced the thing into my hands—the moment she realized something serious was going on between Amelia and I. Dad gave it to her mere months after they met, and it's one of the many things my mother can't bear to look at it without tearing up and clutching her chest but equally, she can't bring herself to throw it away like it's meaningless.

Amelia snorts as she fingers the charm I added, a simple gold letter. "An 'N'? Very possessive of you."

Purposefully, my gaze rakes down her body. "Can you fucking blame me?" I spent *months*—mostly—silently and—sometimes—discreetly fending off horny motherfuckers. Sue me for being a little territorial.

"Where's your 'A?'" Amelia pouts in jest. "Seems unfair."

"I'll tattoo your fucking name on my forehead if you want me to."

Scrunching her nose in playful distaste, she shakes her head. "Please, don't do that."

Capturing her stifled laughter with my lips, the light sound morphs into a soft moan as her tongue tangles with mine. Her greedy hands work quickly, stripping me of my t-shirt, while mine hook under thighs and lift her onto the counter. Lithe legs wrap around my waist, urging me to her, and I groan as her hard nipples graze my chest.

Amelia frantically tugs at my sweats, pulling them and my boxers over my ass and down my thighs. I curse loudly as she grinds her hips against me, the scrap of lace material between us doing nothing to hide how much she wants me already.

"As much as I love this," I finger the strap of her bra, smoothing it down her shoulder and nipping at her bare skin as my other hand dips between her thighs, eliciting a moan out of her. She throws her head back, chest heaving as she pants, when I shove aside her panties and slip a teasing finger inside her, thumb massaging her clit, "I'm gonna love ripping it off so much fucking more."

I'm about to. I'm fisting the material, ready to tear it away and thrust home.

And then, the worst possible thing happens.

A high-pitched scream rings out. We whirl toward the origin, toward the kitchen doorway, where we find a horrified Cass with a hand clamped over his eyes.

Fuck my life.

∼

Amelia falls off the counter.

She drops to the floor with a shriek, cowering behind the island, eyes squeezed shut like if she can't see Cass, then Cass can't see her—and her state of undress.

I instantly move to cover my raging boner, ducking slightly to hide too, and desperately averting my gaze from the girl on her knees dangerously fucking close to my throbbing cock. "*What the fuck?*"

"The door was unlocked!" Cass screeches. Peeking through his fingers cautiously, he spots the discarded hoodie on the floor. With his thumb and forefinger, he picks it up and tosses it our way.

I snatch it from the air and hand it to Amelia. She looks like she's about to burst into flames, either from the embarrassment of being caught or from the anger of being denied an orgasm—both are feasible. In a flash, she covers herself, mutters something under her breath about the roof looking appealing right now, before literally fleeing the kitchen.

Her and Cass don't even look at each other as she scoots past. They do, however, share a revolted shiver.

If I thought there was awkward tension between me and Cass before, that was fucking nothing compared to right now.

He stares intently at the kitchen counter, blinking rapidly. "I am never going to be able to unsee that."

"What're you doing here?" Despite my best efforts, I can't hide the irritation from my voice.

I was *so fucking close* to being buried inside her.

Now, there's a beautiful, horny girl in fucking lingerie hiding in my room, *in my bed*, while I'm stuck talking to her brother.

Cass coughs. "Can you please put your pants on? I'm not having this conversation with your dick out."

Oh, fuck.

"Right," I grumble awkwardly, quickly fixing myself. Dick covered, I round the island, gazing forlornly at the stack of still-warm pancakes.

Sex and pancakes. So close.

I speedily banish any thoughts of sex and the various things I could've done with syrup and whipped cream from my mind before my semi becomes a full hard-on again. "Cass, look-"

"I need to apologize," he interrupts. I frown—not what I expected. "I was a dick to you."

Yeah, you were, I silently agree.

Shifting uncomfortably from one foot to the other, Cass forces himself to look me in the eye. "Using your past, uh, *habits* against you was a dick move. I was being an ass and a hypocrite, and I'm sorry."

"Okay," is my short reply. "I appreciate it."

Cass nods stiffly, shoving his hands in his pockets.

"I'm sorry too," I say slowly. "Not for falling in love with her but for how it all played out."

Another nod, and Cass offers me a small, uncomfortable smile.

A beat of awkward silence passes, the two of us looking everywhere but at each other, before I clear my throat. "So we're good?"

"I'm not saying I'm okay with that," he gestures toward the counter with a gag, "but I believe you when you say you love her. And I trust you with her. Consider this my blessing, or whatever."

Honestly, I could fucking cry. Not for myself, for Amelia—I know Cass' blessing, *or whatever*, means the fucking world to her.

"So," Cass coughs. "Yeah. That's it. I'm gonna go." He turns for the door, another shiver wracking his lanky body. "And I'm gonna try very fucking hard not to think about what's gonna happen when I leave."

Despite the situation, I laugh, dropping my head and coughing loudly to cover it when Cass glares. At least it's a somewhat impish glare, a hint of a smile lingering beneath.

Progress.

57

AMELIA

"What's wrong with you two?" Lynn stares at Cass and me quizzically, assessing our weird behavior.

Neither of us answer. We both keep our gazes firmly trained on our breakfasts, ignoring the half-naked elephant in the room.

I don't think we've looked at each other once since the debacle yesterday. I can't bring myself to, not after he saw me in barely-there lingerie literally on the brink of an orgasm. It took everything in me to even step foot back in this house; I wouldn't have if Lynn hadn't insisted on a family brunch.

Lynn clicks her tongue, unimpressed. "I thought this fighting was done."

"We're not fighting," we grumble simultaneously. Momentarily, I catch his eye from across the kitchen counter before we both look away, matching grimaces twisting our faces.

It's like I can *see* yesterday flash through his brain, the image of me a millisecond away from getting fucked into the counter seared in his brain, just like his horrified face when he caught us is seared in mine.

And I thought a raunchy photo was bad.

Lynn surveys us for a moment longer before sighing, seemingly resigning herself to ignorance. She fixes me with a teasing smirk, and, unfortunately, I can guess what she's going to say before she even opens her mouth. "You have plans today, sweetie? Doing anything fun with Nick?"

A choking sound comes from across the table.

Frowning in confusion, Lynn smacks her youngest son's back as he splutters, tears forming in his eyes. I honestly can't tell if he's crying because of the lack of air in his lungs, or if the mention of me *doing fun things* with Nick has sent him over the edge.

Once he regains his breath, Cass stands abruptly, grumbles a nondescript excuse before scampering out of the room, leaving his half-eaten breakfast behind.

Grooves in her brow deepening, Lynn slips onto the stool he vacated and folds her arms, pinning me with a no-nonsense stare. "Okay, what did I miss?"

Suddenly, I find the dregs of cereal swirling at the bottom of my bowl fascinating.

"*Amelia.*"

Sensing I won't be allowed as easy an escape as Cass, I wince. "Cass walked in on Nick and me yesterday."

"Okay?"

Something akin to a whine rumbles in my throat, and I think that plus the scarlet flush creeping across my skin explains everything clearly enough. I glance up in time to see Lynn's dark eyes widen as realization hits. "Oh," she coughs. "*Oh.*" Her hand flies to her mouth as she holds in a laugh, lips pursing as she tries not to smile.

"It's not funny!" I protest weakly, very much wishing the ground would open up and swallow me whole.

"No, sweetie, of course, it's not," Lynn coos—a big fat lie. "God, no wonder the poor boy looks traumatized."

While she giggles at my expense, I contemplate how hard I would need to slam my head against the counter to remove the memory of yesterday and this conversation. When she adopts a motherly, stern expression, I groan preemptively. "You're being safe?"

"Oh my God." Forehead hitting the counter—too lightly, unfortunately—the cool marble soothes my flushed skin. "I do not need the safe sex talk."

"Who's having sex?" A magnet for perfect-timing and embarrassing situations, James strolls into the room. A wicked smile breaks out as his gaze lands on me. "Ah yes," he drawls, a sing-song quality to his voice, "our little counter-hopper."

A half-eaten slice of toast leaves Cass' plate and sails through the air in a perfect arc toward my eldest brother's annoying face. Chuckling evilly, he snatches it mid-air, winking as he takes a bite. "Hope you cleaned up after yourself."

I'm mere centimeters away from scratching that smug look right off when Lynn quickly catches the back of my t-shirt and yanks me backward. She forces me back in my seat and strides towards James, and it's my turn to smirk when she slaps him upside the head, chastising sternly, "Stop embarrassing her."

"What?" James exclaims innocently, rubbing the back of his head. "Cass said they were making pancakes. Messy job." He snickers as he dodges another attack from Lynn, sauntering towards me.

When he ruffles my hair, I smack his hand away. "Touch me and I'll murder you."

James' gaze drops, fixating on the tops of my thighs where my pajama shorts have risen up to reveal a litter of developing bruises. I wince and squeal as he pokes them and whistles loudly. "Not the only thing being *murdered*, apparently."

"James Thomas Morgan!" Lynn screeches. The dish towel in her hand becomes a weapon, chasing him around the kitchen and whacking him with it as he yelps.

Without hesitation, I take advantage of the chaos and dart out of the room, wood creaking beneath my feet as I sprint upstairs, hoping my mortification stays in the kitchen.

Making a pit stop in my room to change into less revealing pajamas, I force myself to Cass' bedroom, knocking tentatively on his door.

I hear a grunt that I take as permission to enter and push the door open enough to peek my head in. Cass twirls around on his desk chair, head tilted to the ceiling. He waves an inviting hand so I step inside, kicking the door shut behind me. "Why is Mom beating up James?"

"You don't want to know." I plop down on his bed, tucking my legs underneath me. In a nerve-easing move, I find the necklace adorning my throat, sliding the emerald charm between my thumb and forefinger.

Ana almost cried when she saw me wearing it yesterday. Hell, I almost cried when he gave it to me, all cute and nervous as he clasped it around my neck and explained the meaning. The way he manages to switch from downright animalistically lustful to sweet and caring in mere milliseconds will honestly never cease to amaze me.

I glance up to find Cass watching me, his eyes also trained on the necklace. I swear I see a hint of a smile on his face before it disappears and he sits up straight. "What's up, Tiny?"

"About yesterday..." I stammer, only to be interrupted by a raised hand.

"I apologized to him."

"I know. He told me." I wisely decide not to include that we had cele-bratory sex before, in between, and after that revelation. "Thank you."

Cass shrugs, averting his eyes once again. I groan in annoyance. "Come on, Cass. We're adults. Can we be mature about this?" I don't like that there's an awkward energy around us again, so soon after we fixed the last bout of tension.

Cass crinkles his nose, fingers drumming against the arm of his chair. "Keep that attitude when you walk in on me banging someone."

Almost banging, I grumble internally. Interrupted right as we got to the good part.

"I did," I remind him. "Freshman year, Casey Norberg's birthday party." A traumatic night. Not for Casey, she got a hell of a birthday present—but for Cass and me. We both cried—him out of embarrass-ment, me because I saw a part of him no sister should see. Both vomited too, and not entirely because of the alcohol.

It takes Cass a moment to remember the night in question. When he does, he scrubs a hand over his grimace, grunting his acknowledgment. Reluctantly, he tilts his head to smile weakly at me. "At least it wasn't *my* kitchen counter."

I physically feel the blood drain from my face as I choke on air.

A beat passes before Cass guffaws. "Oh my God!" The chair squeaks as he slides further away from me. "In this house or the L.A house?"

I cringe.

"Oh my fucking God! *Amelia!*"

I open my mouth to explain, swiftly closing it because I'm positive it's not an explanation he wants to hear. There happened to be a few times when Nick and I were left alone in the house, usually when the boys had baseball practice, and we'd somehow find ourselves naked and writhing in various rooms, on various surfaces. Mostly, the kitchen counter. Something about the cool marble against hot skin...

Cass continues screeching profanities as he stands and paces the room, alternating between looking at me in horror and shaking his head rapidly.

I can't help it; I start laughing. He's acting like I told him I murdered someone and hid the body under his bed, complete with his prints all over the murder weapon.

His pacing ceases, his incredulous gaze burning into me, and eventually, I hear him expel a breath that could definitely be construed as a laugh.

Before long, the two of us are breathless, clutching our sides, gasping for air.

Cass swipes a hand under his eyes, shaking his head as he gulps down air. "I'm getting rid of those counters."

I adopt a devious grin, unable to help myself. "Might want to bin the sofa while you're at it too."

~

The rest of the week is perfect.

Harmonious, even. No one fights, no one walks in on anyone in promiscuous positions, no long-lost parents appear at the front door.

Everything is normal.

Even the trip home was surprisingly enjoyable. Cass, Nick, and I managed to survive a whole car ride without anyone murdering each other. Everyone looked each other in the eye without cringing. It was all very civil, casual, even felt like *before* at times. They dropped me off a while ago, and both of them made a point out of texting me to let me know they were on their best behavior on the short ride to their house.

The girls aren't back from New York yet. I'm due at the airport to collect them in less than an hour, leaving me with some time alone in silence for once.

Not for long though.

A commotion from the hallway interrupts my unpacking. Someone's shouting up a storm, cursing and stomping loud enough to wake the dead. I ignore it, assuming it's a disgruntled neighbor, maybe someone affiliated with next-door coming down from a high.

But the longer I ignore it, the louder the shouting gets until I swear, it's right outside my door. When shouting turns to the banging of fists, I jolt in fright.

When the voice doing the shouting becomes recognizable, a shiver assaults my spine.

"Open the fucking door, Amelia!"

Holding my breath, I tiptoe out of my room, careful not to make a sound. My hands rest soundlessly against the door, feeling the vibrations his thumping causes, as I peek through the peephole, jerking back when I'm met with the sight I expected. Sure enough, Dylan stands on the other side of the door, red-faced and *furious*.

Self-preservation instincts have me stumbling back, cringing when a floorboard creaks under my foot. The banging stops momentarily before it picks up again, harder this time. "Open up or I swear to fuck I'll break this door down."

I wouldn't put it past him.

With trembling hands, I unlock the door, making sure to keep the security chain in place so it can only open a crack. The chain goes taut as Dylan slams a hand against the door, attempting to shove it the whole way open. I push back with all my body weight, praying to everything and anything that the flimsy security measure doesn't snap. "You need to leave."

He ignores my command, breathing heavily, nostrils flaring. I recoil as his hot breath smacks me in the face, the stench of alcohol and smoke making my eyes water. He holds up a balled fist, brandishing a crumpled piece of paper. "What the fuck is this?"

I know exactly what it is.

He knows exactly what it is.

We both know it means he shouldn't be anywhere near me right now.

"A fucking restraining order, Amelia? Really?"

I almost laugh in his face, catching myself at the last moment and forcing my face to remain stoic. He looks confused, genuinely confused. Like he can't possibly fathom why I wouldn't want him within fifty feet of me.

"You need to leave," I repeat as calmly as I can, trying to close the door properly. Growling, he slams against it again, so hard the wood groans beneath his fist, and tries to elbow his way in. I jump back abruptly as he snakes a hand through the gap and swipes at me.

As hard as I can, I throw myself against the door, managing to catch the tips of his fingers when he's not quick enough to remove them. He retracts his hand, swearing, and I cry out in relief when the door clicks shut and I swiftly lock it.

Panic fills me as I back up, the banging resuming. I reach for my phone, swearing when I remember I left it in my room. I don't move. I'm scared if I take my eyes off the door, it'll cave in and I'll come back out to find him stalking around the living room. He's still swearing, still banging, spitting threat and after threat.

All of a sudden, another yelling voice briefly joins the party before silence descends over the hallway. I strain my ears, trying to determine any sound. When I hear nothing, I creep over to peer through the peephole again.

My brows shoot up in shock when I'm met with the sight of Pitbull—my neighbor, not the rapper, I laugh to myself weakly—slamming Dylan against the wall, his forearm pressed to his throat and a terrifying scowl on his face as he mutters something I can't hear.

Whatever he says must scare Dylan because he slinks away with his tail between his legs, sparing one last glare in my direction before disappearing from sight.

Breath leaves my lungs in a heaving sigh of relief, my head falling forward and colliding with the door. I screech and jolt when someone knocks softly.

"You okay in there?"

Cautiously, I open the door. Pitbull leans against the opposite wall, keeping a healthy distance between us. He looks different than usual, mostly because his hair's grown out a little, the smattering of light brown curls surprisingly me and accentuating the deep blue eyes looking right through me.

"I'm so sorry about that," I whisper, my knuckles turning white as I clutch the door. "Thank you."

"No worries." He dismisses me with a wave of his hand. "Been wanting to do that for a while. The guy's a prick."

"You know him?"

Pitbull nods. "From work. He's one of my uh... *regulars*."

The revelation shocks me a little. In the year I was with Dylan, I never saw him use drugs. God, I really didn't know him at all.

Smiling weakly, I nod my understanding. "Well, thank you anyways..." I trail off, mentally scolding myself for almost calling him Pitbull.

"Atlas," he fills in the blank for me.

"Amelia."

428

He nods in acknowledgement of my greeting as he pushes off the wall. "I'll see you around, Amelia."

A tight knot of panic constricts my lungs as he turns away and starts down the hall. "Wait!" He stops in his tracks, glancing over his shoulder at me, brows raised. "Can you, uh," I pause awkwardly, squeezing the door, "walk me to my car? In case he's hanging around?"

Without a second of hesitation, he hums his agreement and relief floods me. Asking him to give me two seconds, I rush back inside, grabbing my phone and my keys before shoving my feet into shoes.

I briefly consider texting Cass and Nick but I decide against it. It's probably better to tell them in person later. No point getting them freaked out after the fact. I'm okay, he's gone, and I've got a temporary guard-dog.

A pitbull, to be specific.

Chuckling internally at my lame joke, I hurry out the door to my awaiting bodyguard. Atlas walks me to my car, even opens the door for me while his eyes sweep the parking lot. When I'm safely situated inside, he steps back, offering me a small wave and a smile. I mouth another '*thank you*' as I drive away, noting how he diligently waits until I'm out of the parking lot before heading inside.

God, Luna is going to *love* this.

I'm thinking up something nice I can do to thank him when I notice a car behind me, driving erratically and a little too close for comfort.

Paranoia invades my senses.

I take a couple of unnecessary turns, fingers clenching the steering wheel. Every turn I make, the mystery car turns with me. I slow down slightly, my blood running cold as I realize I recognize that car. I've driven that car. The driver's side door and my head are very closely acquainted.

Speeding up again, I take turn after turn, essentially going in a panicked circle. I risk running a red light, the reward worth it when he gets cut off by traffic. The breath I'd been holding rushes out of me in a gasp when he makes a right turn while I continue on straight.

With the danger gone, my fear is quickly replaced by pure fucking irritation. What the fuck was he playing at? Was he going to follow me to the airport and jump me? Rear-end me? *Dumbass.*

In an attempt to relax, I switch on the radio, hoping music will do the trick. A half-laugh, half-sob of disbelief escapes me at the song that fills my car, once again confirming that the universe has it out for me.

She will be loved.

My fingers brush the volume dial when a realization hits me; it doesn't hurt as much. For the first time, the song doesn't draw out the aching pain caused by the hole in my heart. It's there, undeniably, but I don't feel seconds away from collapsing in a broken heap.

I force my hand back on the wheel.

For the first time since Sam died, I listen to it all the way through, tears brimming in my eyes but not falling. Blinking rapidly to clear my vision, I glance aside and for a split second, I swear I see him in the passenger seat, golden hair mussed by the wind, eyes bright and playful, gazing at me with that half-smirk that used to have my heart pounding.

And then the soft crooning sound of singing is drowned out by the crunching sound of metal as my body is thrown sideways and the world goes dark.

58

NICK

SOMETHING'S WRONG.

The house is too quiet. I'm not used to the quiet.

Cass headed out not long after we got home, wanting to get some practice in at the batting cages. We're okay, or as okay as we can be less than a week after he saw me almost balls deep in his sister. On the drive from her place to ours, I got the big brother speech I'd been waiting for and he's probably been waiting to give me. The one I would've gotten if Amelia and I hadn't started out in such a complicated way.

Don't break her heart, don't get her pregnant, etcetera, etcetera.

I assured him that neither would be happening. The former, never. The latter, not any time soon.

Now, I've got a rare moment alone, and I'm not sure I like it. After the week I had, the silence should be a welcome reprieve, but it's the opposite. It feels unnatural, and I weirdly long for Sofia's constant chattering, Mom's inquisitions, Amelia's soft laughter.

Sighing, I decide to use this opportunity to catch up on school work. Exams and deadlines are fast approaching, and I've fallen behind due to being preoccupied with a certain redhead and her sulking brother.

I don't even get an hour of peace before I'm jolted out of the essay-hole I fell into by my phone ringing loudly and persistently. I fish it out of my pocket, gut churning at the caller ID belonging to someone who tends to only call when something's wrong. "Hey, you guys home?"

Kate ignores my greeting completely, cutting me off before I even finish speaking. "Have you seen Amelia?"

Panicked is not an emotion I'm used to hearing from Kate, and it makes me sit up straighter, sends alarm bells ringing in my head. "Isn't she supposed to be with you?"

There's a brief beat of silence before Kate continues, a tremor in her voice, "She didn't show, and she's not answering her phone."

A chill goes up my shine but I shake it off, trying to be rational. "She probably fell asleep or something." A reasonable suggestion—that girl lives for naps. Sleeps like the dead too. I'm always the one shutting off her alarm in the morning.

Shoving away my forgotten essay, I stand and reach for my car keys. "I'll come get you guys."

"No, don't," Kate dismisses me quickly. "We'll get an Uber. Can you go check on her?" A shaky sigh sounds and it's close to the worst noise I've ever heard. "I've got a really bad feeling, Nick."

Fuck.

I agree quickly—I know better than to argue with her, mostly because she's always right. For once though, I fucking pray she isn't.

My hands shake as I race to my truck. I force myself to imagine Amelia's face when she inevitably answers the door in a few minutes, sleepy and confused from a nap, and annoyed that we all descend into a blind panic when she does something as simple as not answer her phone.

Despite my rationalization, I still break every speed limit in a rush to her apartment. Her car's not parked outside, I notice as I sprint upstairs, and I can't tell if that's a good or a bad thing.

No one answers when I knock.

I knock a little harder and still nothing, so I go harder again until I'm pounding on the door and there's no possible way she could sleep through the ruckus.

I jolt when the door at the end of the hall flies open and a furious figure appears. Amelia's neighbor's—the one they call Pitbull—angry gaze lands on me, morphing to confusion for a split second before he folds his arms calmly and smiles sheepishly. "Sorry, man. I thought you were the other guy."

Alarm bells. So many fucking alarm bells. "Other guy?"

"Blonde hair, blue eyes, complete jackass," the guy explains and my heart fucking drops. "Damian or something."

Dylan.

"He was here?" My voice breaks, a little from worry, a little from fear, and a whole lot from pure fucking anger. Not even a beating and a fucking restraining order are enough to get through his thick skull that Amelia doesn't want him.

The guy nods, his expression shifting to annoyance. "Almost broke the damn door down."

One second I'm outside her apartment, the next I'm in my truck. The road ahead of me seems endless as I drive aimlessly, no fucking clue where I'm going, no fucking clue where she is. A hospital? I dismiss the thought quickly; last time Cass and I had to practically drag her there kicking and screaming, that's not the first place she'd go. My house, maybe? That's where she went last time. Unless Dylan fucking kidnapped her or something. Did Dylan ever see her? Did they leave together?

My fist hits the steering wheel, a flurry of shouted expletives flying out of my mouth. Why the fuck didn't I stick around and get the whole story?

The more I drive, the worse that gut feeling gets, the one screaming at me that she's not okay. Something is so fucking wrong, I know it.

I try to stem the panic growing inside me like a weed as I frantically dial Cass' number. I don't give a chance to speak when the call connects, blurting out the same thing Kate asked me as I turn a corner. "Have you seen Amelia?"

I don't hear his reply.

I'm too focused on the chaos playing out before me.

Flashing lights.

Blaring sirens.

An ambulance.

Men in uniform sprinting around an overturned car in the middle of the road.

Her car.

I can't fucking breathe.

"Nick? What the fuck is going on?" Cass' shouts are drowned out by the sound of tires squealing as I abruptly stop the truck, stumbling out the door and sprinting towards the wreck. Her name floats through the air in a scream, and it takes a moment to realize it's me screaming.

Her car is a wreck. A ball of crushed metal. The driver's side is a gaping hole, the door frame warped and in a heap on the ground, surrounded by broken glass and splatters of something dark and rust-colored. I can't see her, I can't see her anywhere, in the car, on the ground, *nowhere.*

An officer catches me around the waist, stopping me before I can get to what used to be a vehicle, before I get to her.

Movement in my peripheral catches my eye, and I turn just in time to see a stretcher being loaded onto an ambulance. A glimpse of red hair and pale skin stained red is all I see before the ambulance doors slam shut and the vehicle drives off.

No.

I turn to shove the officer off me, but my attention lands on something else. There's another car, one with a destroyed hood and a deployed airbag on the driver's side. My eyes flit around the scene until they land on a second ambulance.

A disgustingly familiar man perches on the back, hiding underneath a blanket, looking guilty as fucking sin.

Unharmed.

Not a scratch on him, not a single drop of *his* blood shed.

Pure rage engulfs me as I wipe away the wetness on my cheeks and force myself to walk calmly in his direction.

His eyes land on me and widen dramatically. Bloodshot eyes. *Drunk eyes.* I spot the handcuffs suffocating his wrists and everything snaps into place, everything I already suspected rings true. I snap, lunging for Dylan with a roar. *"What the fuck did you do?"*

My fingers barely brush him before I'm yanked backward, away from him, a man in uniform on either side of me with their hands wrapped around my arms. I struggle against them, yelling at the top of my lungs, promising the one thing in this world he actually deserves, the one thing he's earned. *"I'll fucking kill you."*

He looks terrified and I love it. I thrive off that look in his eyes, the one that tells me he believes me, that he knows if I wasn't being held back I'd be wringing his fucking neck with my bare hands.

Voices urge me to calm down but I ignore them, thrashing against the restricting hands with everything I'm worth. I want to hurt him, I want to hurt him so fucking bad. Do every single sickening thing he did to Amelia but a million times worse. My arms are numb by the time someone carts him away, shoving him in the back of a police car, hidden from my murderous gaze.

As soon as he disappears from sight, the fight leaves me. My legs shake, threatening to give out, so I sink down to rest on my haunches. Just for a second. Just until I get myself together. My chest heaves with deep breaths, the heels of my palms digging into my eyes in an attempt to rip the sight of this fucking mess out of them and stem the hot liquid burning them.

Fucking get it together, Nick.

Sucking in cold air, I straighten up, wiping my hands off my jeans. I feel like I'm working on autopilot as I find someone, anyone, who can tell me what hospital she's going to.

My whole body shakes as I get back into my truck. I'm not sure if it's smart for me to drive, but I know that I fucking need to. I need to get to her.

Cass' voice is still echoing around the interior of the truck, reminding me that he's still on the phone, snapping me back to reality slightly. "Nick, fucking answer me!"

"Cass," he goes silent at the sound of my trembling voice, "there was an accident."

~

The white walls of the waiting room hurt my eyes.

Everything is too clean, too sterile, too lifeless. I rest my elbows on my knees, cradling my head in my hands, massaging the back of my head trying to soothe the ache.

I stop doing that quickly when I feel the ghost of softer, daintier hands doing the same thing.

Straightening up, I stretch my legs out in front of me, groaning internally when my stiff joints pop. I've been sitting on an uncomfortable plastic chair for what feels like hours but must be less than one.

They won't let me see her because I'm not family. Won't tell me anything. She could be lying lifeless on a cold slab of metal in the morgue and I wouldn't fucking know.

I called everyone to pass the time. Her dad, Lynn, Kate, Ma. Every phone call was the same; short, solemn, rife with disbelief. Her dad sobbed, stammered '*please not again.*' He's catching the first flight out—he should be here by tonight. I make a mental reminder to ask someone else to get him from the airport because I don't think I can move.

The automatic emergency room doors squealing open catch my attention. I lift my head as a tall, panicked figure flies through them.

Cass doesn't see me at first. He goes straight for the nurse, the same one who's been shooing me away for however long. They have a fast, frantic conversation, on the brink of an argument, very similar to the conversation I had. The nurse sighs and glares at Cass, who's barely containing himself, before pointing sternly in my direction.

Something flashes in Cass' expression when he finally spots me. With one last snap at the nurse, he stomps my way. The chair beside me creaks as he slumps into it, our shoulders brushing as we breathe a synchronous frustrated breath. "They won't tell me anything because I'm not legally family," he seethes through bared teeth, his fists clenched.

I don't say anything, because there's nothing to say. Nothing I can say to fix this.

"Was it him?"

I nod stiffly.

"Is he alive?"

Another nod, even stiffer this time, my whole body screaming with tension.

Cass scoffs, unimpressed, folding his arms as he turns to face the wall opposite us again.

That's the extent of our conversation.

We sit in silence, alternating between watching the clock and begging nurses for information, being refused every time. A doctor comes out at one point, both of us straightening when we overhear him ask if Amelia Hanlon's family is present and the nurse nods at us. Our hopes are quickly dashed when the doctor only offers a quick glance before striding off again.

When the others arrive, we hear them before we see them. Or more specifically, we hear *her*; Luna storms through the waiting room, yelling loudly at nothing in particular. But there's no force behind her screeches, not like usual. It's a show, a charade, the mask she chooses to wear. She pounces on the nurse, making vicious demands but there's no fire behind them. I wonder if she knows she's clinging to Jackson's wrist where he holds her by the hips, as if she might fall over without the support.

Ben sinks into the chair beside me, his eyes red-rimmed and swollen. A trembling hand slips into mine. "Do you know anything?"

I can only shake my head and stare blankly at the white floor, my view obstructed by Kate crouching in front of me. Bracing her hands on my knees, she dips her head to force me to look at her. Her bottom lip wobbles dangerously, the wetness in her eyes so fucking jarring. "She'll be okay," she whispers unconvincingly. It sounds like she's trying to convince herself as well as me.

For once, Kate does not know something.

I can't find it in me to acknowledge the words meant to provide me comfort. My mind instantly rushes to what the fuck I'm going to do if she isn't, coming up blank because I have no idea.

I have no fucking idea.

Kate sighs and stands, her tired, watery gaze burning into me as she takes the seat across from me, reminding me that as much as I can't imagine my life without Amelia, it's surely only amplified for her, Luna and Cass.

Luna collapses beside her, grasping her hand tightly. Jackson takes her other hand, the three of them linked tightly. My free hand slips into Cass', his grip vice-like as he clutches me. I don't think any of us are particularly religious, but fuck, I swear we all pray to whatever or whoever is listening with every ounce of energy we have.

And then, we wait.

59

AMELIA

Voices.

So many voices thunder around me.

All familiar, all so *loud*. I want to tell them to shut up, to stop arguing, but my mouth won't move.

One is louder than the others, angrier, hiding fear behind a wall of rage. "Why the hell isn't she waking up?"

"I don't know," a calmer voice, one I can't place, replies.

"You said she was okay!"

"I said she was stable," the calm one amends. It says something else but I lose track of the words. They get muddled in my brain, a string of useless letters that I can't decipher.

Someone else is talking too. A serene, lilting tone that makes my heart thud. They're right beside me, so close I can feel their breath, whispering foreign words I can't understand but I recognize the desperation instilled in them, the pleading and the hope-lessness.

"*Querida*," they rasp, sending prickles down my spine because I know that word, I know it so damn well. I yearn to open my eyes, to reply, but my body won't obey. "I need you to wake up now."

I'm trying, I want to yell. *I'm really trying.*

"I need you to tell the bright white light to fuck off, okay?" The voice is trembling, so full of pain that it hurts me because I somehow know that I'm the source of it. I feel pressure against my forehead, hot wet

438

droplets burning my skin. "Please, Amelia. I need you. Please come back to me."

I'm trying.

∿

Everything hurts.

Pain radiates throughout my body, from the top of my head to the tip of my toes. I swear, even my eyelids and my fingernails ache.

With a hundred times more effort than it should take, I peel one eye open, then the other, only to swiftly close both with a mangled whine when bright, offensive light pummels me.

Try again, an inner voice urges.

Another inhuman noise scratches my throat as I force my eyes to re-open, blinking rapidly to clear the groggy film blanketing my senses.

A white-tiled ceiling greets me. A beeping noise rings in my ears like an insufferable alarm. Something heavy sits on my leg, weighing me down, while something cold pinches my hand. I'm in a hospital, that much I know, but everything is terrifyingly unfamiliar, confusing to the point of hysteria, but when my head flops to the side, a wave of comforting calm washes over me.

Passed out in the uncomfortable-looking armchair poised beside my bed, his hand clutching mine, is Cass. Scruffy and exhausted, he looks like he's had a falling out with his bed and his shower. I almost feel bad for waking him but my need to know what the hell is going on wins out.

I try to squeeze his hand but my weak one won't cooperate so I croak his name instead. It's barely audible yet still, he jolts awake. Sleepy disorientation clears the moment his gaze lands on me. "Holy shit," he exclaims, shooting upright. "You're awake."

A choked cough comes out instead of the reply I intended. Instantly, Cass helps me sit up, snatching up a plastic cup from the bedside table. My parched throat screams in relief as I greedily chug blissfully cold water. When I'm done, I slump back onto the bed again, my body spent from even the simplest of movements.

"Where's Nick?" I successfully manage to croak out. I know he was here before; I heard him, I felt him.

"He just left," Cass informs me softly. "Your dad is here too, he stepped out to speak to the doctor."

My dad's here? Why is my dad here? Did I know my dad was here? A million questions run through my mind, each of them met with a black hole of oblivion. "What happened?"

Cass stiffens, frowning slightly and avoiding eye contact. "You don't remember?"

The second the question leaves his lips, it all comes flooding back.

Dylan, Atlas, getting in my car, someone following me. I remember the song, and then the blaring sound of a horn.

And then, nothing.

"Car crash?" I weakly seek clarification. Cass nods solemnly and my throat tightens. "Is the other person hurt?"

In the blink of an eye, Cass' expression turns dark. Devious. Downright scary. "I fucking wish." The venom in his voice confuses me until he continues, "It was Dylan."

Another hazy detail comes back to me, the moment I recognized the car, that I suspected it was him. "Oh."

Fear seizes my body as the sick reality that I am never going to escape him sets in. He's going to follow me around for the rest of my life, a dark foreboding presence never allowing me to be happy or *safe*. Even a restraining order can't keep him away.

When I start writhing in panic, Cass clutches my shoulder to still me. "You don't have to worry about him anymore." I try to argue but he shushes me, continuing with an explanation that freezes me completely, "Amelia, he hit you on purpose. They have witnesses and evidence. That on top of violating a restraining order *and* drunk driving..." He trails off but his point is clear.

I don't have to worry about him anymore.

The permanent knot of terror sitting heavy in my stomach eases but a tiny shred of doubt and disbelief refuses to be banished. "What kind of evidence?"

"There were some texts." Cass sits back in his seat, hands clenched tightly in his lap as he recites the threats that someone I once thought I loved, someone I once thought loved me, made.

That bitch is gonna pay.

If I can't have her, no one can.

I'm gonna make the whore bleed.

I wince at the crude words.

God, I spent a year of my life with an unhinged man.

"And witnesses?"

Cass rattles off a list—a long list. Some pedestrians who saw him speed up and run a red light. The houseful of people who saw him drag me onto the guys' front lawn all those months ago and raise a hand to me. All my friends who saw the aftermath of his rage, heard his threats. The medical staff who treated me, both times. Even my neighbor, Atlas, provided a statement.

My head falls back against the pillow as I let it all sink in. He's gone. For real this time. Or at least, he's on track to being gone. Hopefully, for a long, long time.

And just like that, the dark cloud dissipates, leaving nothing but solace.

And a million questions.

"How long have I been out?"

"A couple of days." Cass swallows hard, scrubbing a hand over his face, an attempt to hide the vulnerability written across it. Dropping his gaze to our joined hands, his admission summons burning tears. "I really thought you weren't gonna wake up."

In unison, we erupt into sobs.

I know we're both remembering the last time we were in a hospital together, the last time we held each other and cried in a hospital bed, the last time we almost lost each other forever. Clutching each other tightly, we silently relive our trauma, old and new.

My chest heaves, jostling my pained ribs, as hot tears aggravate cuts and scrapes I can't see. But when I try to rein them in, one look at Cass' wet cheeks and somber gaze has me crying harder.

"Stop crying," I demand through wails.

A strangled noise escapes him, a cross between an indignant scoff and a sob. "You stop crying!"

"You started it!"

We're sobbing hysterically now, hints of strangled laughter mixed into the awful sounds escaping us. Like two cats dying. Two very loud, slightly unstable cats.

Loud enough to be heard through a closed door, apparently, because it suddenly flies open and a barrage of panicked people pile in. My dad is at the front of the crowd, eyes wildly flitting around the room. His worried expression drops when he spots Cass and I clinging to each other.

Confusion, surprise, and pure joy flicker across his face as he rushes to my side. "You're awake," he mutters, stooping to kiss my forehead. "How long have you been awake?" I don't miss the pointed look he shoots Cass that screams 'you're in trouble.'

Unfazed, Cass swipes beneath his eyes and slumps back in his seat, still grasping my hand. "Not long."

"You should've gotten someone," Dad scolds, brushing tears away from my face while simultaneously scanning my injuries.

"I was about to!"

Dad scoffs and returns his attention to me. "How're you feeling?"

"Sore."

"That's normal," Dad assures me before he starts to check my injuries thoroughly. That is until one of the actual hospital staff still lingering in the doorway coughs pointedly and he's forced to step aside, crossing his arms and all but stomping his foot like a scolded child.

The doctor and the nurses descend on me, asking a million questions, shining lights in my eyes, poking and prodding my tender skin under I'm ready to slap their hands away. I shoot Cass a desperate 'save me' look but he shrugs, too busy tapping away rapidly at his phone.

After what feels like forever, I get the all-clear. Well, almost. They tell me I still have to stay for a couple of nights for observation. Apparently, I hit my head pretty hard and I had some internal bleeding that they're still worried about. Dad kisses my forehead and offers me an apologetic smile before following the doctor out of the room, both of them talking in low voices, leaving me and Cass alone again.

"Great," I grumble, irritated because I'm dying to get out of here. I hate hospitals. Too many bad memories, and now I have one more to add to the pile. I want to shower and sleep in my own bed, preferably with a muscular Brazilian man as a pillow.

"He'll be here soon," Cass promises with a grumble when I ask for the umpteenth time where my boyfriend is. "God, he's going to murder me."

"Why?"

"I made him go home." Cass grimaces through a mouthful of Jello. The Jello one of the nurses brought for *me*. "Told him nothing was going to happen if he left for an hour. You have impeccable timing, you know. The first time he leaves and you happen to wake up."

A small smile stretches my lips for a moment before they flip downward. "Wait, what do you mean the first time he left?"

"Hasn't left your side once, Tiny," he confesses, adding that the nurses took one look at his tear-stained face and relented. "He's a mess. Barely eating or sleeping. I had to tackle him into the shower." Cass nods his head towards the other door in the room, presumably leading to a bathroom.

God, I didn't think it was possible to feel more awful than I already do.

I need to see him, I need to see him so bad, and by the time a commotion erupts in the hallway, when I hear a gruff voice cursing someone out in a foreign tongue, I'm practically vibrating with impatience.

When the door flies open and a ragged, wild-eyed man bursts into the room and freezes at the sight of me, I burst into tears all over again.

In the blink of an eye, he's at my side, a hand gently cupping my cheek as he rakes his eyes over me. Scooting over slightly, I grab his arm and pull him down. Cautiously, he perches on the edge of the hospital bed, never once taking his eyes off me. For a moment, he stares at me intensely, fingers roaming my face like he's checking I'm really here. Eventually, he lets out an uneven breath, and the tension in his body ebbs. "Cass said to come quick," he rasps. "I thought…"

"I'm okay," I assure him, side-eying my brother with a glare.

He simply blinks innocently. "You wanted him here quickly."

Nick ignores him. Gently running his hand through my hair, he cups the back of my head with a featherlight touch, the warmth of his palm soothing my headache. "I was so fucking scared."

"I'm okay," I repeat.

An awkwardly clearing throat draws our attention sideways to Cass. Getting to his feet, he jerks his thumb toward the door. "I'm gonna go call Mom." He and Nick make eye contact, some kind of silent conversation transpiring before they both nod and Cass leaves.

Immediately, Nick's attention returns to me. "Are you in pain?"

"Not really." The nurses hopped me up on painkillers before they left, and Nick being here is the best anodyne of all.

Nick's gaze runs rampant over my face, wincing at every cut and bruise. He runs a thumb over my cheek where a nasty cut sits, presumably the result of broken shards of glass from my car window nicking my face. "I'm so fucking sorry," he whispers. "I shouldn't have aggravated him, this wouldn't have-"

"It's not your fault." The senseless guilt in his voice breaks my heart. "It was the restraining order." My action was the one that sent him over the edge.

Shifting closer, Nick cradles me carefully, lips ghosting my ear. "It's not your fault either."

"I know." And I do.

Finally, I do.

~

Three days pass cooped up in a hospital room until finally, I'm allowed to leave under strict instructions that I get lots of rest and don't indulge in any strenuous activity. I scoffed at that—like I can do anything strenuous with a cast weighing down my leg and my ribs aching like a bitch.

I feel better. Banged up to all hell, but better. There's still an underlying ache everywhere but I don't want to cry or scream every time I move or breathe any more, and I'm getting pretty handy with the crutches. Not that I need them; Nick has developed quite the habit of carrying me around. Yesterday, I made it a meager two steps toward the shower before he scooped me up, letting all the hard work fall on his shoulders.

I love being in his arms, don't get me wrong, but there's only so much staring a girl can take, a six-foot-four hulk of a man carrying a girl bridal-style definitely warrants some gawking.

If I hadn't threatened to beat him with my crutches, he'd have carried me to his truck, probably kept me on his lap while he drove us home.

Part of me wishes he had.

The drive was agonizing. The moment he shut the door behind me, something snapped. My excitement at being free was overwhelmed by anxiety as memories of the last time I was in a car flooded my mind.

When I first woke up, I didn't remember it all. Only the bare minimum, and the rest was filled in by everyone else. It wasn't until I fell asleep that first night that every horrifying moment came flooding back to me. The screaming. The windows shattering and ripping me apart. The awful stench of blood and gasoline mingling in the air. The door collapsing inward and crushing my leg. The airbag deploying and slamming into my chest.

I thought I was going to die. No, I was *convinced* that I was going to die because there was too much blood and not enough pain. I knew I was hurt, I could *see* that I was hurt but I couldn't feel it.

It took Nick hours to soothe me back to sleep after I woke up screaming and thrashing like a wild animal, almost undoing all the hard work the doctors had done stitching me back together.

And as the truck rolls to a stop, signaling our arrival home, I feel wild panic brewing again.

The hand holding mine disappears only to reappear moments later as Nick wrenches the passenger door open and gently tugs me to the edge of the seat.

"Breathe," he whispers, smoothing his hands along my arms. His nose nudges mine as he leans forward, pressing the lightest of kisses against the corner of my mouth before dropping his head to press another on the skin above my pounding heart.

I link my hands around his neck to pull him closer, his simple touch doing a world of good in calming me. Resting my cheek against the top of his head, I smooth my hands down his back, fisting his t-shirt tightly like a freaking baby clutching a security blanket.

It takes longer than I care to admit but eventually, my heart stops racing. The nightmarish memories recede to the darkest corners of my mind. Pulling back, Nick rests his forehead against mine. "Better?"

I nod, craning my neck to press my lips against his, savoring the quick kiss he offers me. Blowing out a deep breath, I twist to grab my crutches, barely grazing the handle before I'm abruptly ripped away from them, scooped up and cradled against a hard chest. My squeal of surprise rings around the parking lot. "Put me down!" I protest futilely. "I can walk!"

"I know you can." Nick smirks down at me, the mischief dancing in his gaze a stark contrast from the concern and fatigue that's been plaguing him lately. "I prefer this."

"What about what I prefer?" Which, despite my complaints, is definitely this.

His smirk grows. "Doesn't matter."

"Brat."

A hearty laugh rumbles in his chest, a sound I haven't heard in days, as he bends to kiss me again. Soft and slow, his lips caress mine, drawing out a smile and a rib-aching giggle when they move from my mouth to the rest of my face, scattering a dozen kisses wherever they can reach.

Somehow, he manages to keep his hold on me while reaching into the backseat for my bag. Shutting the door with his hip, he slings the bag over his shoulder and carries me upstairs, careful not to bump into anything. Despite having his hands full, he manages to jostle my apartment door open, kicking it with his boot-clad foot.

An ear-splittingly loud cacophony of noise welcomes us home.

"She's alive!" Luna screeches dramatically, pinching Nick until he carefully sets me down. A steadying hand settles on the small of my back as Luna throws herself at me, hugging me fiercely yet surprisingly gently by Lu standards. Kate joins our hug, slipping her arm across my shoulders to help hold me up.

Over their shoulders, the guys smile at me widely, repose heavy in the air. Cass has a grip on the collar of Ben's shirt, like he's holding him back from joining. As soon as the girls retreat, my young friend slaps Cass' hand away and races me for me like an eager puppy, reacting like one too when brother and boyfriend simultaneously bark at him to be careful.

My friends' greetings are happy and greedy and completely dramatic considering they saw me during visiting hours this morning.

My hospital room has been a revolving door of visitors, each of them offering their own little slice of entertainment. Nick was a permanent fixture, somehow convincing the nurses to let him stay pretty much 24/7 —it's amazing what an alluring accent and a handsome face can accomplish. Cass was there almost as often as Nick, lounging in the seat beside me as we FaceTimed our mom.

Kate brought calmness, the eye amongst the storm. Luna indulged me with gossip while her slender fingers fixed my matted hair. Ben usually brought his ukulele and got yelled at by the nurses for making too much noise but somehow always charmed them into letting him stay.

Jackson perched quietly at the end of my bed, decorating my cast. It's covered in various signatures and scribbles, but he did proper drawings, real artwork. The incredibly detailed faces of my friends stared up at me, kept me company when they were inevitably forced out. It's kind of pretty, really. I might actually miss it when they saw it off in a couple months.

Nick helps me limp to the sofa and sits me down, resting my casted leg on the coffee table and propping a pillow beneath it. He plops down on one side of me, Cass on the other

"I propose a toast," Luna announces, appearing in front of us, brandishing a bottle of Fireball that she got from God knows where, evoking simultaneous groans from everyone. Her other hand clutches a tower of shot glasses that she spreads out and quickly fills.

I'm about to protest that drinking probably isn't a good idea for me right now, considering the host of painkillers I'm doped up on, but she beats me to it. My glass is filled with plain old water, and she hands it to me with a wink.

"To a helluva shitshow of a year." She raises her glass. Before anyone can knock it back, she holds up her hand to stop us. "To finding love in unexpected places," her gaze flits to Jackson, "and to finding strength in hard ones," she continues quietly, her gaze landing on me as a watery smile stretches her lips, and I wonder if I'm about to see Luna Evans cry for the first time. "I think I speak for everyone when I say I am really fucking glad you are still here, and I love you."

There's a round of agreeable murmurs, tears of my own brimming as each of my friends raise a glass to me, followed by a brief moment of silence. It's broken by Cass clearing his throat. He nudges me gently with his elbow before stretching his glass towards mine. "To Tiny."

Grinning at him through teary eyes, a small laugh escaping me, I clink his glass before knocking back my shot of water, a chuckle escaping me when everyone else in the room winces as cinnamon-flavored whiskey burns their throats.

As the splutters turn into laughter and chatter, I sit back and simply gaze around the room at my friends. My family.

After living so long with a gaping hole in my chest, I am whole. The friends in this room, the man gripping my thigh and the brother with an arm slung across my shoulders filled the gap without even knowing it.

I'm complete.

Battered and bruised but no longer broken.

60

AMELIA

LIGHT SPILLS in from the large window beside me, the warm June sun heating my skin. I tilt my head towards the warmth, basking in it like the plants lining the windowsill while admiring the amazing view this spacious office offers.

I can see the ocean from here, and I swear it's calling to me, begging me to dip a toe in its chilly depths. I probably will, later.

Right now, my time belongs to the professionally dressed woman sitting across from me.

There's a faint smile on the woman's face as she peers at me over her glasses, assessing me clinically like she always does. "You look good, Amelia."

Her words summon a smile of my own. "I feel good."

Gaze flickering to the notepad on her desk, the pen in her hand poised to write. "How would you describe your mood today?"

"Happy," is my simple answer. I learned quickly that straightforward honesty answers are best and easiest.

"You've been sleeping?"

I nod, fidgeting in my seat slightly.

"Any more nightmares?"

"None." My answers evoke a pleased hum from Dr. Resnick, the sound of scribbling filling the air as she jots down notes.

It's been a whole month since my last nightmare. Night terrors, I think they're technically called, the kind where you wake up coated in sweat and whimpering, swearing up and down that what you just experienced was real. Technically, it was real. At one point.

I was a victim of an abusive relationship.

And I was in an accident that almost killed me as a direct result of that relationship.

They got better after Dylan was convicted, when I knew for sure that he wasn't going to show up at my apartment in the middle of the night or attack me in the middle of a work shift.

"Have you made plans for the summer?"

I nod again, the question evoking a flurry of nervous butterflies in my stomach. I'm going back to Carlton for the entire summer. Three whole months in the town I ran from, surrounded by people who know exactly why I ran.

"And how are you feeling about that?"

"Good," I answer unconvincingly, my fingers toying with the hem of my dress. A few seconds of feeling Dr. Resnick's intense stare is all it takes for me to sigh and elaborate further. "Nervous. A little scared. But good." The fact that I'll be surrounded by family helps combat my apprehension. I feel settled with family, with Nick and Cass and Dad and the rest of the Morgans. If they're by my side, I can live with the inevitable staring and whispers that I'm sure are to come, like they've come every other time I've gone back.

"That's understandable." Resnick scribbles some more, pausing briefly before continuing her questioning. "And how is the driving progressing?" she asks carefully, slowly, anticipating my tense reaction.

I stiffen slightly, eyes drifting to my bare legs. A jagged, healing scar catches my attention, where a hunk of metal from my destroyed car lodged itself in my thigh. There's another on my calf, where my tibia snapped and pierced my skin. Permanent reminders of what happened to me, in case my memory ever fails, to accompany the faint one I already had, all on the same leg which makes me feel weirdly unbalanced.

Absentmindedly, I rub my recently-freed limb. I only got the cast off a week ago, and I'm not used to being without it yet. I still find myself favoring my other leg, limping a little, more out of habit than need or pain. I wonder if I'll ever break that habit, or if it's another permanent alteration.

Dr. Resnick says my name softly, reminding me that she asked a question. I meet kind eyes when I look up, patient eyes. I went through two other therapists, useless pushy women who I'm positive spent more time judging me than trying to help me before I found her. Resnick never pushes, only encourages. She... I don't know, she gets it.

"It's... " I struggle for the right words. "I can get in a car without crying, if that's progress."

In the months since the accident, I haven't been able to bring myself to drive. It took me weeks to even be able to be in a car without losing it. Getting behind the wheel is the next goal we're working towards, and it's proving to be harder than anticipated. Harder than banishing the nightmares and overcoming my mountain of guilt, which says a lot.

I find it funny how the accident with Sam never had this effect on me —sure, I didn't particularly like driving after the first accident but it never instilled a deep-rooted fear of driving. Resnick didn't find it funny; she found it to be a wealth of traumatic information. She says it's because I experienced a loss so great, it drowned out the fear, and that the guilt caused by that loss drowned out any concern for my own life.

Why would I fear driving if I didn't fear getting hurt?

"How was the drive here today?"

"It was fine," I shrug. "Nick drove me."

"Ah." The corner of Resnick's mouth quirks upwards. "The handsome man who camps out in my waiting room every week?"

Automatically, I finger the chain looped around my neck, fiddling with the charms as I bite down on a brewing grin. "That's the one."

Every session, every week, he waits patiently for me. Even if he's not the one to drive me here, he's always here to collect me. After the first couple of sessions, I was a mess and he had to practically carry me out; the one-hour appointment often stretched into several hours cowering in Nick's car, trauma-induced tears soaking his shirt as he held me tight to his chest.

Resnick likes him. She says it's good to have a solid support system in place, and he's the figurehead of mine, unsurprisingly.

Though, I don't think what I have could be called a support system. I have people coming out of my ears. I have a village. I have more than I need a lot of the time but I'm grateful all the same because I can't begin to imagine what this would be like if I had no one.

The hour passes quickly. Resnick gives me some new exercises to do to help with my newest biggest fear. She's big on journaling; I've filled almost four in the couple of months I've been seeing her, and I have a feeling I'm about to fill a fifth with all the reasons why I'm terrified to get behind the wheel of a car again.

Dreams, nightmares, every bout of anxiety, everything is recorded on those creamy lined pages. It took me a while, but I get why she does it. It helps to look back, to see how far I've come.

When the hour is up and I leave her office, I barely take a couple of steps before I spot him. Slouched in a chair, flipping through a magazine, looking effortlessly hot and completely oblivious to how the receptionist is drooling over him right now.

I didn't think it was possible, but somehow he's gotten even hotter in the last few months. I think it's the sun, to be honest. I swear to God, it favors him. He's all extra golden and extra bronzed and extra annoyingly perfect.

And all mine.

The love of my fucking life.

His eyes flicker up to meet mine when he senses me approaching. A slow smile spreads across his face as he stands, grabbing for me the second I get within reach and pressing a short, sweet kiss to my lips. I have to resist the urge to smile triumphantly at the receptionist, maybe offer a tissue to wipe up the drool off her computer.

Nick wraps an arm around my waist as we leave the office building, his fingers skimming the tops of my thighs as he toys with the hem of my dress. "Everything okay, *querida?*"

Grinning, I stretch my neck to kiss his shoulder, the closest I can reach without practically having to climb the mountain of a man. "Everything is perfect."

"We're here!" Cass hollers as he shoulders open the front door, his voice ricocheting around the house.

The sound of chairs scraping against the floor greets us as we wander through the hallway, a crowd of smiling faces welcoming us into the kitchen.

"Hi, sweetie." Dad approaches me with open arms, hugging me

tightly. I hug him back before stepping back and gesturing to my cast-free leg, wiggling it triumphantly. The last time he saw me, I was still bandaged up and suffering an intense array of cuts and bruises.

Instantly, he switches from Dad to Dr. Hanlon, prodding and pawing at my leg, interrogating me about my pain level. Rolling my eyes, I kick him away right as I'm swept up in another pair of arms.

"How's my girl?" Lynn murmurs, her voice rife with emotion as she holds me close. Since the accident, we've indulged in numerous lengthy phone calls, way more often than we used to, but they don't nearly match up to seeing her in person.

Her hands sweep lightly over my cheeks, a slight wince overcoming her features. Luckily, the gashes on my face healed a lot better than the ones on my legs. They're barely visible now, but of course, Lynn manages to spot them. A sheen develops in her eyes as she cradles my face. "I'm glad you're home, honey."

The sound of a throat clearing interrupts our reunion. Our attention is drawn to Cass standing beside us, eyes narrowed, a playfully wounded expression on his face. "Your girl is fine. Your boy, however, is feeling neglected."

Lynn rolls her eyes, muttering something about needy men under her breath before giving me one last squeeze and moving to greet her son. Over their shoulders, I spot Nick lurking in the corner with his family, clearly attempting to give us some space.

Sofia catches my eye and her face splits in a grin before she's tearing over to me. The young girl pounces, almost knocking me over as she hugs me. She only loosens her grip when both her brother and her mother chide her gently.

"*Tenha ciudado, minja anjinha.*" Nick grips his sister by the shoulders, a teasing tone to his voice. "*Carga preciosa.*"

"*Peste,*" I fire back my favorite insult.

Ana laughs as she pulls me into a quick but warm hug, kissing each of my cheeks before steering her chattering daughter out of the room.

Mischief glimmers in Nick's eyes as his hands skim up my arms, tugging me to him by the straps of my dress. "Have I mentioned you speaking Portuguese is really fucking hot?"

I bite down on my bottom lip, blinking up at him innocently. "*Uma ou duas vezes.*"

His eyes darken a shade, but whatever he was about to say is drowned out by my squeal as a pair of arms wrap around me from behind and yank me away from Nick. James engulfs me in a bear hug, smacking a big kiss on the top of my head. "For someone who almost died a few months ago, you look fucking great."

"James!" Several people exclaim at once.

My eldest brother grins and circles around to face me, eyes roaming as he gives me a quick once over. Something strangely forlorn flickers across his face at the sight of the new additions gracing my leg, but he quickly covers it up with his signature grin. "Damn, Tiny. Kind of badass." He whistles long and low, gently poking at my thigh. "Almost as bad as what Nicky boy did to you last time."

"Jesus Christ." Lynn and I groan in unison, the former slapping her son upside the head.

Nick's hand lands on my ass, squeezing sneakily as his chest shakes with barely contained laughter. Cass can't decide whether to scowl at James or Nick, so he settles for punching them both. I shove James away, but he doesn't go very far. Instead, he bumps Nick out of the way and slings an arm around my shoulder. "Where's your dad?" I ask him.

"Work. He'll be home soon. Wouldn't dare miss the miraculous return of the Prodigal daughter."

I roll my eyes at his dramatics, poking his stomach.

Catching my hand and peering down at me, a more serious expression overcomes James, his grip on me morphing into something protectively tight as he murmurs, "Glad you're okay, kiddo."

Throat tight, I knock my hip against his. "Careful. Your feelings are showing."

"What can I say, near-death experiences bring out my sentimental side." He pecks my temple. "Love you, Tiny."

I gaze up at James, studying his sincere, protective expression. It's always been Cass and me with the unbreakable sibling bond. My relationship with James was always a lot more playful, a lot more casual, not as close-knit but he was my brother all the same.

The one who settled countless silly quarrels between Cass and me, the one who protected me when Cass wasn't there, the one who comforted both of us when we were lost in grief. I seldom think about what it was like for him to watch his two younger siblings completely disintegrate into shells of themselves, yet be unable to do so himself. He knew and liked Sam too but he always put us first.

Resting my head against him, I wrap my arms around his waist. "Love you too."

~

The walk to the cemetery takes less than half an hour.

I nod politely at the few people scattered around as I weave through the stones sticking up from the ground, the light wind whipping my dress around my legs.

My heart catches in my throat when I find what I'm looking for. A small, sad smile stretches my lips as I rest on my haunches in front of the white marble gravestone with his name etched in beautiful cursive letters.

Sam Davis.
Loving son, brother, and friend.
The song in our hearts.

Setting the bound sunflowers in my hand down, I kiss my fingers and press them to the cool stone. "Hey, Sammy."

I swear a breeze curls around me in greeting as I sit down. Against my will, a seed of guilt blossoms in my chest. This is the first time I've been to his grave; I was too out of it, too lost in grief, in the weeks before we moved away to even consider coming here. "I'm sorry it took me so long to come see you."

I'm not sure what I believe in but I know he's somewhere, watching and listening and probably yelling at me occasionally for being a fool. In my mind's eyes, I picture him sitting beside me. The image of him is so young, and it both blows my mind and hurts like hell that I'm somehow older than him now. Three years older than he ever got to be.

I already want to cry, but I refuse to, not until I say what I came to say. I take a deep breath to steady myself, blinking away the tears.

"There are so many things I want to say to you." My voice is quiet, broken, trembling as I speak but I force myself to continue. "I guess I'll start with I miss you. So much. Cass does too. He doesn't talk about it much but I can tell."

There was a moment this morning, a brief one, when we drove past the old baseball field Sam and Cass used to play on. Both of us paused, overcome by memories for a moment. The pain in Cass' expression was fleeting, but it was there.

"I wish you were so I could thank you. For loving me. I'm sorry I was so mad at you for leaving me. I hope, wherever you are, you know how much I loved you. I'll probably always love you. You were everything to me, and I'm so grateful to have been loved by you, even if it wasn't forever."

I swipe the few stray tears that escape away, replacing them with a weak smile. "It took me a long time but I found someone. I think you'd like him. Cass, my dad and James do, so that says a lot. He loves me and he treats me how I deserve to be treated."

Silent tears are streaming freely now, I couldn't hold them back if I wanted to. Tugging my cardigan tighter around me, I pretend it's a pair of arms comforting me. "I hope you're proud of me, Sam. I'm kind of proud of me, to be honest."

Sucking in a shuddering breath, I rise slowly on shaky legs, brushing blades of grass from my dress. Once again, I kiss my fingers before touching the cold stone, gripping it tightly. "Thank you for saving my life," I whisper. "I'm sorry I was so careless with it for a while."

The stream of tears slows but doesn't stop as I leave the graveyard with a smile on my face and a weight lifted off my chest.

I don't get very far before my eyes land on a tall figure leaning against a parked car. A pair of sunglasses hide his golden eyes, but even from a distance, I swear I can see those dimples.

He's waiting for me patiently, like he always is. Like he always will.

My heart doubles in size, a sob-like laugh escaping me as I realize I'm in the same place as the two men who loved me right.

When I get close enough, I don't hesitate to throw myself at him. I'm quickly engulfed in his grip, his arms acting as my safe haven, as usual. Sliding the sunglasses off his face, I lean up to kiss him softly, craving the comfort. He wipes away my tears, kisses my damp cheeks, whispers an 'I love you.'

The sun shines down on us, reflecting in twinkling gold eyes. Smirking, he murmurs against the corner of my mouth. "Need a ride?"

A laugh leaves me and floats through the air at his oh-so-familiar question, one of the first things he ever said to me. Lacing our hands together, I stand on my tiptoes and kiss him again, grinning against his lips.

"I'd rather walk."

EPILOGUE

AMELIA

Dear Sam,

Hi.

This is weird.

Writing letters to a dead man. Or boy, I guess. Seventeen isn't really a man. Anyways.

Dr. Resnick suggested I do this. Your anniversary was last week and I kind of broke down. Five whole years without you. You've officially been dead longer than we knew each other. It's difficult for me to wrap my head around that. I think that's why it hit me so hard this year. It's so weird for me to remember a time in my life when you weren't in it. It hurts. It kind of feels like I've lost something or like I've run out of time. I don't know. It's hard to explain.

Resnick thought it would be a good idea to do this. As a coping mechanism, I guess. Nick agreed with her but Nick agrees with everything she says. Probably because she's as enamored with him as everyone else is, and most of her advice works in his favor.

He comes with me sometimes. To therapy. When I'm having bad days and don't want to go, he comes and he sits with me and he's there. He's always there.

Anyway, I agree with her too, now that I'm doing it. I think I need it. We all know I'm pretty shit at coping. Like right now; I've barely written anything and I'm crying.

I guess this is my goodbye, kind of. Or goodbyes. I don't know. I don't know how many of these there will be. However many I feel like writing, I guess. I want to talk to you. Not my boyfriend Sam, but my best friend Sam. That's another thing; Resnick says I mourned the love I lost but I never mourned the friend. So that's what I'm doing, I guess. Saying goodbye to my friend. So goodbye. For now.

    Amy.

∾

Dear Sam,

    I watched my brother graduate today. And the love of my life, but Cass is next to me as I write this and if I don't mention him first, this letter might end up having bloodstains on it. He says hi, by the way. He misses you. We both do.

    I'm so fucking proud of him. Of both of them. I swear to God, James and I were the loudest, most embarrassing pair in the crowd. Except for Ben, but that's not surprising. God, you would love Ben. He reminds me so much of you sometimes. Loud and cocky, the epitome of a class clown, but so fucking sweet. A massive dipshit too. But he's our dipshit.

    We find out if Cass is getting drafted next month. Well, not if. He will get drafted. It's just a matter of where. It's gonna be weird not seeing him every day but we'll manage. We always manage.

    I thought of you a lot today. I wondered what you would have looked like up there. Probably like a big, grinning fool trying to trip up Cass. Oh, and your brother came. He sat beside James and me and pretended he didn't know us. We all cried. He met Nick and he agreed that you guys would have liked each other. When you weren't fighting over me, he joked. I punched him.

    The weather forecast said there'd be rain but the sun was shining bright all day. I like to think that was your touch, so thanks.

    Amy.

∾

Hi, Sammy,

    It's been a while. Over a year. Sorry about that. I woke up today feeling like I needed to talk to you, so, hi.

    I graduated three months ago. Nick and I spent the summer in Brazil with his family. It was loud and hectic and the best time of my life. I love him so fucking much. It feels weird, telling you that, but I think you'd understand. I think you'd be happy for me.

We're back in Carlton now. I'm at your grave, actually. I like leaving your letters here. They're always gone when I come back, and I know, realistically, that it was the caretaker cleaning them up or the wind blowing them away but I like to pretend they've disappeared off to wherever you are.

I saw your parents yesterday. First time since you died. They look good, Sam. They look happy. We all went for dinner, my family, Nick's family and yours, and it was nice. We talked about you and no one cried, so I call that a win.

We all miss you, though. We left a chair empty at the table for you.

Amy.

~

Sam,

I'm an aunt.

My best friend had a baby.

God, I feel like such an adult yet so fucking young at the same time.

He is the sweetest little thing. The perfect combination of his parents. So, of course, he's beautiful. Kid's got the lushest hair and these big eyes that I swear to God make my womb ache. He gives me baby fever but not as bad as Nick. Jesus Christ. I swear he's hormonal or having a quarter-life crisis or something.

Anyway. I'm an aunt. And I love it. Auntie Mils.

I swear to God if I end up being Auntie Tiny, I'm gonna scream.

Amy.

~

Sammy,

I had a bad day today.

I almost got into a car crash because, apparently, the third time's the fucking charm. I'm okay. It brought back a whole heap of memories I've been working to forget. I basically shut down, and I haven't done that in a while. I sat in a Target parking lot for an hour because I couldn't calm down. I cried because I miss you. I cried because I miss Cass because he's always somewhere I'm not. I miss Nick too. Him, Jackson and Ben are visiting Cass in New York, a boy's holiday. I don't want to ruin it because I'm incapable of dealing with my emotions. I think I'm gonna call Resnick. Or my mom.

Amy.

~

Sam,

It's been a while. Like, quite a while. Life got busy. I got a real, adult job. I've been visiting Cass while he's trotting all over the country. Nick started his job and has a million high school students mooning over him. Spoiler alert; having a hot as fuck partner who gets drooled over daily never really gets easier. Such a hard life, I know.

Oh, and maybe the ring on my finger weighing me down has hindered my writing capabilities.

Yup. I'm engaged.

I'm gonna be somebody's wife. Well, not somebody's wife. Nick's wife.

Amelia Silva.

I'm taking his last name, no doubt. He offered to take mine—his dad took his mom's name, after all—but Nick Hanlon just isn't as sexy as Nicolas Silva. I would never deprive the world of Nicolas Silva. Besides, I want to be a Silva.

I cannot fucking wait to be a Silva.

Amy.

~

Sam,

I'm a Silva.

We did it. We went to the courthouse, Nick and I and our families. We were going to do the whole big fancy wedding but it didn't feel like us. Neither of us were keen on having a huge audience on the best, most intimate day of our life.

Besides, something else happened that would've significantly hindered my ability to fit in a wedding dress.

Not only am I a Silva but I made a Silva. A perfect little baby girl Silva.

Aurora Cassandra Silva.

Rory.

Cass calls her Cassie, of course, the conceited bastard. She loves it, though. She loves him. I'm almost positive her first word is gonna be Cass, and I don't think Nick nor I are ready for the power trip that's gonna send my brother on.

She is so fucking perfect, Sam. Looks just like her daddy. Figures, doesn't it, that I lug her around for months yet she comes out all Silva. I don't mind though, not really. She's a lucky girl. Is it bad that I'm jealous of how pretty my baby is? Because she is so pretty.

This is probably my last letter. My entire life revolves around a three-month-old now. I wish you could've met her. I still miss you a lot sometimes. I still love you a lot. But it doesn't hurt anymore to think of you. So I think I'm done.

I loved you so much, Sammy. I loved you with my whole heart. And now I love Nick, not with just my heart, but with my entire being. There isn't a part of me that doesn't love that man. I wish you could've experienced love like this because I don't think that's what we had. I don't think I was it for you.

Nick is it for me.

But I do have you to thank because if I hadn't loved you, I don't think I would've been able to love Nick the way I do. And then I wouldn't have Rory. I didn't think it was possible but I love her even more than I love him.

I need to let you go so that little part of me that still belongs to you can belong to them.

Bye, Sam.

~

I lied.

That wasn't my last letter. I have to tell you something.

I have a baby boy now.

We were going to stop after our second, Reese, but I wanted a boy so bad. And I think Nick might've been drowning in estrogen from us three girls. So we tried again, and we got what we wanted because Silvas always get what they want.

Matthias Samuel Silva.

Cass thought it was weird naming him after you but he wanted to name his first kid Cass The Second so he clearly knows jackshit.

Your brother met him the last time we went back to Carlton. He cried and we hugged and then we went to see your mom and she cried too. Matthias was probably so confused, my poor boy. Oh, and Zach has a kid now too. You're an uncle.

Kinda morbid, but I brought Matthias to your grave. I wanted him to meet his namesake. He's so like his dad but I swear to God, Sam, there's a bit of you in there.

I needed to tell you about him. This is my final letter, for real this time. Bye, Sammy.

Amelia.

THANK YOU FOR READING

If you enjoyed the book, please consider leaving a review on Goodreads and the site you bought it from.

Want more?
Sign up to my Patreon for exclusive bonus
chapters!https://www.patreon.com/ejblaiseauthor

ACKNOWLEDGEMENTS

To my own found family for adopting me as their chaotic Internet child. Hannah, Becka, Ki, you are the brightest spots in my life without whom I would cease to function. There are no (non-explicit) words to describe how much your friendship and guidance means to me. Thank you for putting up with my loving bullying and for making me wheeze-laugh at least twice a day.

ABOUT THE AUTHOR

EJ Blaise is an Irish author of all things romance.
When she's not creating unrealistically perfect men, she can be found travelling, reading, and dreaming of running a bookstore café.

Made in United States
Orlando, FL
07 December 2023

40318712R00286